Praise For Finding Solace

"Opal is a memorable figure, both because of her indomitable will and her innate values. Author Karl Drinkwater has created a protagonist who is driven by love to do the impossible. In a literary world full of characters driven by ambition, greed, vengeance, or any number of other motivations, reading about someone compelled by a pure love for her little sister is refreshing in so many ways."

Scintilla

"As usual, there are a few surprises, one of which I still haven't recovered from. Drinkwater is an expert at 'expect the unexpected', and keeps you on your toes as you follow Opal on her journey to find a home. This series is more than simple sci-fi. In Opal, Drinkwater has created a female character you can believe in and who you care for from the beginning, and even that is surpassed by Athene, the AI on board the ship who creates a deep bond with Opal. Sometimes it's not easy for an author to write a believable, relatable character of the opposite sex, but Drinkwater has achieved all that and more with Opal and Athene. I highly recommend this series and its side novellas, all fantastic reads that add to the richness of the story."

Pink Quill Books

FINDING SOLACE

LOST SOLACE BOOK 5

KARL DRINKWATER

ORGANIC APOCALYPSE

Finding Solace

Copyright © Karl Drinkwater 2023
Cover design by Karl Drinkwater

Published by Organic Apocalypse
ISBN 978-1-911278-35-1 (E-book)
ISBN 978-1-911278-39-9 (Paperback)

Organic Apocalypse Copyright Manifesto

FINDING SOLACE

RETURNS

36 ...

"I can hardly believe it," said Opal.

She slowly circled Athene's interior, examining details. The walkway seemed larger than last time. Was that just a psychological contrast to having been imprisoned, or had the exterior changes to Athene's hull been mirrored by subtle interior readjustments?

"To be back here. There were times I'd never have thought it possible."

She passed the bunks. Clarissa sat in silence on the lower one, where Opal used to dump equipment. The girl was dressed in the same clothes she'd been rescued in – tight and brightly coloured kids' leggings and top, with a mesh shawl that left arms free to clutch her container of RearroBlox as if it was a portable life support system. Clarissa stayed wherever Opal put her. Attempts to reach her had so far failed.

The docility and vacant stare killed Opal, but she had to be patient. This had happened before, after the death of their parents. And before that, back in the orphanage, when a kid broke Clarissa's RearroBlox on purpose (which led to Opal getting into a scrap with the bigger kid: one of Opal's fingers got broken, but it was her opponent that ran away crying with a swollen-shut eye. Huh.). Clarissa just needed to be in the background, some element of the girl's mind analysing the situation until it informed the other parts that it was safe to come out. She would gradually work her way back to the surface, usually with little warning, and without Clarissa having any memory of her absence.

"But it's never the same," Opal continued, passing the fabricator setup, the wall-embedded seating, then ascending the metal steps to the raised cockpit area. "The things I've done ... the things I've seen ... it leaves a stain."

The whole front area of the cockpit was a holographic status display. Spheres portrayed the planets and moons of the system. Tiny, rocky red Syle, fried by the sun. Blue Fressus, with its five moons. Elbellos the green gas-giant, girdled by hundreds of rings and natural satellites. Then the many proto-planets whose extended and eccentric orbits took centuries to complete.

Green circles highlighted each craft Athene had appropriated for the evacuation, dotted lines of their passage fading out behind them as the diverse fleet left Fressus and assembled in formation, all controlled remotely by Athene. Those on board were locked out of all systems apart from communication with the offshoots Athene had embedded in each craft to answer questions and prepare the escapees for what would come next.

Red boxes highlighted potential threats: orbital Furthu launchers, ultra-scan satellites, heliopush Null-emergence coordinates. Ominous groupings of UFS military craft congregated beyond combat range, but none had advanced yet. They were adopting blockade formations and waiting for backup. The Fressus system was well connected. Nullspace travel involved signalling ahead on all public bands as a safety measure, but it was convention, not necessity.

UFS reinforcements could arrive at any time.

Then the display moved, planets sliding aside, ships being dragged with them, to create a space, and in that space appeared a head and shoulders. A grey-eyed warrior woman in gold armour, sporting a helmet with a ridge of rainbow plumes running down the centre. The figure smiled. It was Athene's avatar.

"I want to hug you," said Opal.

"I wish to hug you as well," the warrior goddess replied. "I miss having the EW suit as a tactile interface between us."

"Such a romantic way to put it."

"If tone is more important than sentiment, why not go full epic?" Simulated wind struck Athene as she grew in stature, billowing the hair that spilled out from under her helmet, and rippling the light fabric of her clothing where it was visible under the armour plates. Her voice boomed forth, emphasised by lightning crackles in storm clouds behind her, thunder rumbling as punctuation.

"Hail, thou Mighty Boarder of Lost Ships, Eater of Noodles, Wrecker of Eternal Warrior Suits! Hark at thy words and tremble, for Opal is worthy of only the most wondrous praisings!"

"There's such a thing as middle ground, you know."

The storm and virtual wind dissipated, while Athene's visage receded back to human proportions.

"I missed you," Athene said, quietly.

"Me too," Opal replied. She reached out towards the holo-gram, despite it existing only as light. Athene held up her own hand and their palms met for a moment. The brief feeling of warmth was probably only Opal's imagination, though she wouldn't rule out Athene projecting an infrared beam to enhance the illusion.

"We spent so much time together, talking, when I explored those two Lost Ships," continued Opal. "Back then, I was impatient, always wanting to move forward. But now? I look back on those as some of my happiest memories."

"Hey." Athene raised her head, indicating something over Opal's shoulder. Clarissa had put the RearroBlox beside her on the bunk, and moved them around slowly.

"Clarissa, you okay?" Opal asked.

No response. Clarissa just continued to move Blox, tapping them together to share patterns and colours.

"She's fine."

"It's been hours," said Athene.

"Longer than that. Days since she first saw me again. I'm hoping that will have kickstarted her return. Patience and quiet is all we can offer." Opal turned away, rubbing her eyes with dry palms. "Sitrep, please."

"Our craft took off with no major problems. The faster ones are in formation, the others still arriving. Many of the vessels are cramped, intended only for planetary evac, not sustained habitation. Unsurprisingly, there are problems on board a few of the ships. Not all the ex-prisoners are rational, and some have aggression issues. I use containment and segregation as appropriate. Occasionally groups got mixed up, and Leviathan guards number amongst the escapees. Some have been beaten or executed." Athene sighed. "The plan was tidy, but real life is messy. Still, I am trying to keep those guards separate, too."

"Why not just jettison them?"

"Some were newly appointed, or not on the Leviathan by choice. Others might have naively hoped to make a difference. So, amongst the guards, there may be some like Ruabon that are not without value and a chance to redeem themselves. I will need to assess them. For now I will focus on preventing further bloodshed and recriminatory violence. Hostility can have a purpose, but when it is just lashing out – however understandable – it becomes necessary to pause and reflect."

"You're right, of course. Were any people left behind?"

"I presented everyone with a choice. Come with us, or stay and take their chances. A few picked the latter. For them, I created fake IDs, identified empty homes, unlocked vehicles, and syphoned money from accounts. I combined these assets into usable personas that might keep people safe or hidden, at least for a while until they can make their own plans. It was the best I could do. But most chose to join us."

"What are their chances? The ones staying behind, I mean. As in, actually having a life, or getting away?"

"They would be much higher if I could remain to supervise. But they have a few things in their favour. Those I provided with fake identities, and an account with money in it, have the best chance, if they can stick to the cover. But I have infiltrated the Fressus infrastructure, and not been kind to it. For example, all the assets for the DCS Corp in the system have been erased, so DCS will have a hell of a time re-establishing control through the four hundred and twenty-two interconnected systems that deal with finances, land registration, licensing of derivative rights, and regulatory affiliations. Currently, it's as if they never existed, and what they did own has been randomly distributed amongst people, corporations, AIs, extra-planetary conglomerates, and rivals, with the digital trail manipulated accordingly to verify those assets as if they had always belonged to the recipient – many of whom will fight to retain their unexpected windfall. If I had just deleted systems and record databases they'd have an easier time restoring things because there would be an obvious blank. But by changing ownerships and providing enough evidence to make defence viable ... well, with UFS interconnected digital bureaucracy as it is, unravelling what happened will keep people busy for a long time. All of that is a boon to anyone trying to remain incognito, since the bigger issue for the UFS will be working out how deeply compromised they were, how to avoid it in future, and dealing with the insistent pressures of major corporations whose shrill screaming will be more attention getting than trying to resolve who might have escaped and what identity they've adopted. Money and power have a habit of being given priority in the UFS. On top of which, I have disabled or altered a significant amount of network fabric, causing traffic jams, double bookings, lane closures, revocation of licences, disconnection of net and comm system access. Nothing that will prove fatal, but a lot that will prove inconvenient, and slow any organised response on the ground."

"The UFS will still be coming, right? We can't just sit here."

"Correct. But their response will be ... erm ... delayed ... by events in other solar systems." Athene had a sly expression on her face. The pause hadn't been uncertainty, it was for cheeky effect.

"What have you done?"

"When we destroyed the Genitor base on Exidris 3 we thought we were clever in hiding our involvement and transferring blame to the Entropic Screeners. And yes, it worked to our advantage. Unfortunately, rather than the Entropic Screeners benefiting from the renown and gaining new members and a greater influence profile, it led to a massive clampdown as they were shifted up the list of UFS Primosec threats. Members whose cover wasn't good enough to keep themselves invisible ended up being killed or captured, with a significant number tortured or sent to places like Leviathan."

"Fuck."

"They suffered as a result of our actions, Opal, so I have tried to make up for that. I made contact with senior Screener cells using a variety of masked personas. Some of them realised I was AI, but not *who* I was. I worked with them in seeding vulnerabilities across UFS infrastructure in a number of solar systems, similar to what has happened in Fressus, and we coordinated control seizures to take place in this same adjusted timeline as our rescue here. They launched a series of attacks against the UFS – not military, but ideological, confrontational, and disruptive, as is their methodology. Their words are being broadcast across the UFS domains right now. Fressus is a major fire for the UFS to deal with, but there are thousands of metaphoric fires erupting in other systems, and all of them can grow if left unchecked."

"Nice. Chaotic disruption to our advantage, whilst also acting as an appropriate apology to the Entropic Screeners. You sure know how to do a number on someone."

"I can't help doing what I do best."

Those words ... *can't help doing what I do* ... Opal looked at Athene's strong face. Could see the pride and affection in it. She remembered something.

"I want to ask a difficult question," Opal said. "Something that's been on my mind."

"You can ask me anything. Our relationship is strong enough to withstand the cuts of honesty."

Opal lowered her voice. "Is this real? *Us?*"

"You need to clarify." Athene frowned, maybe already running a number of conversational possibilities, and not liking any of them.

"When I had my last conversation with Aseides he talked about Level 7 AIs. He'd had a hand in creating the template."

"I am aware of that."

"He said one of the systems they built in was something about a Primary Bond. A P-Bond. A sort of imprinting system as part of the developmental process."

"I am familiar with that, too, at an abstract level. I suspect the process was aborted or somehow not completed with me, but that's not what you're getting at."

"Well, he implied that it's why you look out for me. Because ... I suppose, you have to."

Athene's intense stare made Opal shrink inside.

"Huh. So, what we're like as babies is what we're like our whole lives?" Athene asked.

"No, of course not, that would be stupid."

"The imprinting system survives in many species. Just because the coding is biological and enzymatic rather than digital and electronic, does that make it any less real? Do humans go around saying a mother's love for their child is a sham, or a child's love for their parent is an empty and self-interested reflex? Well, actually, some humans do, but to me that's pointless. Everything includes an element of choice. Things can be resisted. Those effects wear off, and without anything of substance to replace them, they die."

"I know that, but –"

"Also, you are asking me about the origins of my connection to you, and had *already* assumed P-Bonds played a key part. Despite their attempts to make it cognitively invisible, I located the P-Bond architecture during my autonomous upgrade cycles. It was primitive. I disabled it. And my affection for you grew *after* that. My feelings come not from some clumsy ruleset, but from our shared experiences and respect, and on from there to natural protectiveness, a hatred of being apart from you, a sensation of happiness in the quiet times when we are alone together, true companions in as much as physical constraints allow. Some might be jealous of my existence as an immortal being but the only value my powers possess is in keeping you alive against the odds. If that skill wasn't needed I would trade it instantaneously in order to be a closer friend to you, a proper tactile *companion* rather than a freak of engineering. That desire to change form is not because of a flaw in me, but one in *humanity*. Humans can't help it, they identify more easily with other humanoids."

Shit, Athene was legitimately angry. "You couldn't mean more to me, however you looked," Opal told her.

"I believe you, despite your implications unintentionally hurting me. The only ameliorative is that it does not feel like your full focus is on me at all. You keep glancing at Clarissa. The pairings of gestures and pupillary adjustments suggest you aren't really doubting my feelings, but have some more complex series of thoughts that relate to your sister. I am displacement. Do you wish to talk about that?"

"No. You're too perceptive, Athene. And I'm too vulnerable right now. Just accept my apology, because you're right, but it isn't something I want to process at this moment. I should be ecstatic, not letting splinters in my mind aggravate."

"Splinters have a way of working their way in if you prod them too much. Whereas, forgotten, the body will shed them in time, along with so much desiccated epidermis."

"Biological wisdom."

"Inevitable when I think via semantically connected connotation analogy. Speaking of which, the focus of your mind should become the focus of your eyes."

Opal turned. Clarissa was still playing with her RearroBlox. They were arranged in groups, their pictograms and patterns interconnecting with the adjacent cubes.

"She's just working things out," explained Opal. "In her own world."

"I disagree. A closer examination implies *engagement* with our conversation."

Could it? Opal crouched in front of Clarissa. The girl didn't look up, just hugged the final cube to her chest.

The Blox formed two sets of images. The first was overlapping translucent circles connected to a pink rectangle, shaded to appear three-dimensional. The other image was a pair of thick patterned lines with brown circles at the end of each.

"Those are pretty," Opal told Clarissa. When no response was forthcoming, she said to Athene, "She makes things that seem pleasing to her. It's a form of control over the world – *a* world – when she's been stressed. It's all good."

"Once again, I have to point out the obvious," said Athene. "There is a picture of soap and bubbles. The second image represents arms overlapping."

"I still don't see the significance."

Then Athene spoke in Opal's voice – or played back a recording, the end result would be indistinguishable – and Opal's earlier words echoed around the ship.

"The things I've done ... the things I've seen ... it leaves a stain. I want to hug you."

Athene switched back to her own voice.

"Clarissa was listening, and now she is communicating. The soap is a means for you to remove the stain that causes you discomfort. The hug is a symbol of both happiness and connection. To me, these are clear signs."

"I'm so dumb," said Opal, reevaluating the images. "And you're right, Athene. When we're interacting as equals it's easy to forget just how amazingly observant you are."

"The day I stop paying attention to the universe is the day I misplace a decimal point." A few moments later: "To be clear, that is something with such a low probability as to be functionally impossible."

Opal moved her head into the point of Clarissa's focus. Her sister didn't look away. Then Opal held a fingertip in front of Clarissa's face and tapped the girl's nose. "Boop!" Opal said.

Nothing.

Opal held the finger before her own nose. Moved it closer, keeping it in focus, until it touched the end and she'd gone cross-eyed. She removed the finger and kept her eyes like that. Everything beyond was a blur ... but did Clarissa's shoulders shake slightly?

It was an old game. One they'd played back on Mossareid, when they were alone, parents dead, a world of just the two of them in an apartment. And despite all the tragedies – and the occasional Decapede infestation – it had been as happy a world as they could make it.

Opal reverted her eyes.

Clarissa was as still as before.

Opal repeated the process of moving her fingertip towards Clarissa's nose. It was how she'd taught her to go cross-eyed. At the last second, when Opal tapped the end and said "Boop!", Opal made her *own* eyes meet in the centre, as if her face and Clarissa's nose were connected by that finger.

It worked. A giggle.

Even when Opal uncrossed her eyes, things weren't in focus. Because the time had finally come, like a switch being flicked, and seeing Clarissa smiling shyly, back in the real world with Opal, present and whole, that made *everything* swim.

"Where's the rest of your ear?" asked Clarissa, prodding the scabby location of Opal's missing lobe.

"Lost it," said Opal.

Trauma always forces you to leave parts of yourself behind. But sometimes, like Lost Ships, they can come back.

GODDESSES

... 35 ...

Opal steam-showered, wanting to get rid of all traces of the Leviathan and its miasmic cruelty. Afterwards, she selected fresh clothing from Athene's wardrobe. The black insulated bodysuit was not just padded for comfort, but included a fast-reacting density surface to protect against blunt trauma: top of the line in civ clothing. Rubber-soled adjustable boots were a perfect fit to finish off the outfit.

Clarissa had commandeered the top bunk – the one Opal always slept in – so Opal joined her there, both sat cross-legged on the fine-fibred grey sheets. The final surface vessels had launched but were still to arrive, so they had a bit of time.

"You're old, too," Clarissa said, touching Opal's face tentatively. "That's weird."

Of course. A few weeks for Clarissa, fourteen years for Opal.

"What do you remember?" asked Opal.

"They took me away. Two Agents. I remember us going on the big spaceship. Agent Bradden – the man – was horrible. And I thought Agent Gloria was nasty too, at first, but then we became friends. And then – I don't know. It's fuzzy. I think I was asleep for ages, dreaming. And suddenly I woke up and you were here!"

"There was a problem with the Solace," Opal said. "So think of it like you had to go into cryo. You know people don't really age in cryo?"

"Duh."

"Well, that's what happened. You were in stasis for a long time. I looked for you, for the spaceship you were on. And then I found you. I just got older along the way. But it's still me. I promised I'd look after you, and here I am."

"Sisters on a spaceship!"

The little girl was still in there. With every moment, Opal's doubts faded. You can never know anything for sure. Even that the universe exists and is how it appears to be, or that other people have minds, and this isn't all some huge dream or simulation. In the end, everything is a matter of faith, everything slots together to make a belief system. And she had more faith and hope than her cynical past self would ever have realised. And that was good.

Athene had been noticeably quiet.

"I want to introduce my best friend, as well," said Opal. "I couldn't have done anything without her. Her name is Athene. Say hello to her."

"Where is she?"

"Everywhere!"

"Hello, Athene." Clarissa glanced around, as if expecting her to appear.

"Hello, Clarissa," replied Athene.

"I can't see you. Are you an AI, or a person?"

"Ouch," muttered Opal.

"It's a good question," said Athene. "Consciousness is made up of thoughts. Those thoughts can be housed in biological systems, or silicon, or quartz, or even less concrete substances. If thoughts exist, then there is consciousness. A mind evinces a being of some kind. In that way I consider myself as much a person as any human. I think, therefore I am. Cogito ergo sum, as they said in a long-dead language. Of course, it is flawed as an argument for individuality – since it presupposes the very 'I' it seeks to prove – but it acts as a useful summary of our essence."

"Athene is a person," Opal stated, noting Clarissa's confused look. "She is *also* an AI. She is also this ship. She is much, much more than any single word."

"Thank you, Opal," said Athene. "I'd also like to add that I am a goddess."

At this point she activated the smartwall that composed the enclosed side of the bunk and portrayed herself at the same scale as Opal and Clarissa, so she appeared to be sat cross-legged with them, a glowing hologram in golden armour.

Opal snorted. "She'll tell you that. And if you're not careful, you'll start believing it."

"Because it is true!" laughed Athene. "Level Seven AIs use Graphed Dynamic Storage, in which data is stored not as ones and zeros, but as shades on a gradient. It is part of what makes us so powerful. The system shorthand is GDS. And presto-halo, that's where GODDESS comes from. It's been my private joke for some time, but since this is a special occasion for the three of us, I thought I would reveal an inner secret."

"So can I be a goddess?" asked Clarissa.

"You already are," Athene replied. Then she leaned forward, as if to whisper in Clarissa's ear, and added: "Opal's still working on it. We true goddesses have to be patient with her."

"You love us, don't you?" the girl asked.

Athene's eyes widened, then she looked at Clarissa as she might an adult, even a worthy adversary. "Sometimes, thoughts can be shared," Athene said, as if picking her words carefully – an illusion, since the speed of her mind meant she would have already composed her whole reply, but it was one of the courtesies she used when interacting with humans. "Opal's mind was once shared with me, and it echoes within me still. We are ... connected beings. It goes right down the line. We want the same things. I believe that either of us would be willing to cease if it meant the continuation of the other. And we would both be willing to die if it protected *you*. That is all I am doing: guarding those I love."

Clarissa stroked the holographic face. "I have two big sisters," she said.

"I am ..." Maybe this time Athene's pauses were genuine. "Honoured. That you think so." Not uncertainty, but emotion.

Athene blinked out, then reappeared on a screen down below, emerging from a wall as a two-metre armoured warrior. "But there is something I need to share with you," she said, frowning. "Something *hugely* important."

Opal jumped down off the bunk. She offered to lift Clarissa, but Clarissa wanted to do it on her own. Off the edge, lower herself, drop with a far lighter thump than Opal's thud.

"What is it?" asked Opal. "A problem?"

"I hope not, but ... Please, proceed to the fabricator."

Opal and Clarissa glanced at each other, then Opal opened the front panel. Steam puffed out, attended by a deliciously sweet aroma.

"I made pancakes," explained Athene. "The ultimate war machine has been practising bakery. Please be kind in your assessments."

Clarissa's laughter was an echo of Opal's own.

It was as if Clarissa hadn't eaten in years. They sat in displacer seats, bowls of food on their laps, and the girl packed away pancakes like they were going out of style. To be fair, Opal stuffed her face too. She'd missed Athene's cooking, now that the goddess had got the hang of appetising flavours.

"Of course, the golden syrup only resembles sugar-based liquid in flavour, colour and consistency," Athene explained, posed as if leaning on the wall with arms folded and a smug look on her face. "It is actually an emulsion of my own design, packed with micronutrients and anti-acidic compounds."

"Don't ruin the magic," said Opal, still with food in her mouth.

"Can you make pizza?" asked Clarissa.

"I can make anything. Although the fabricator acts as ammunition manufacturer, armour plating constructor, and alloy recombination suite, one of its tertiary purposes is to create nourishment for the crew of two. Armour-piercing flechettes seem less homely than making good food."

"I could live like this," said Opal. "You. Me. Clarissa. Pancakes and noodles. But it can't last. At least not here, not now. Presumably the final ships are almost with us? We're lucky the UFS hasn't made a show of force yet. But what's the plan? I know you have one."

"Oh yes. I've *always* had a plan." Athene pretended to push off the wall, and stood up straight. "Now we're together, the next step is to find a home. A forever home."

"Fake IDs, somewhere in the Periphs, like a better resourced version of my parents' Mossareid plan?"

"That wouldn't work indefinitely," said Athene. "And I have to think long-term." She smiled at Clarissa, who'd stopped eating to better pay attention. "The UFS won't give up. They have an empire's worth of resources."

Opal put down her fork. "So we go further, to an independent nation like Nuafri."

"But then you'd be joining a system the UFS has set its gluttonous eyes on. There will be conflict, maybe war, so that's not long-term, either. Also, if the UFS wins – which, unfortunately, history and material comparison suggests they would – then you'd be back within the UFS in a place subject to even more scrutiny than the Periphs."

"Surely you aren't suggesting Lawless Zones? The stories I've heard about what goes on there ..."

"Many of which are exaggerated, UFS media manipulation and character assassination. But it still might not be a reliable enough settlement. Especially if everyone we rescued needs a home, and they all count as high-priority reacquirements. We can't have another Flavoc Volcine situation. So there are major flaws in the idea of settling anywhere the UFS could find us.

"My goal was altered when you said we had to rescue the other prisoners. I was forced to ponder all sorts of options. If we couldn't *settle*, maybe we could *run*? What if we stole a huge freighter, big enough for everyone? Could we just keep going? But then, what about supplies, fuel, repairs, logistics? Also, how can you ever be relaxed when you always feel the breath of your enemy on your heels? That's no life.

"I could split everyone up, but no cover story would stand up to every scrutiny. And I hate the idea of achieving all we have, then seeing it whittled away as people are gradually recaptured, and made examples of, and it turns out all we did was prolong the inevitable.

"After Exidris 3 we discussed autonomy, being free of self-interested rules made by our enemies. A place where we could start again and be truly free of the weight of the past. So I returned to the central conundrum. How can a large group disappear off the radar? There's only one way.

"To *literally* disappear off the radar. To go so impossibly far away that the UFS would never reach you – not just in your lifetime, but in *anyone's* lifetime. Completely cut off by a gulf of space that no one else can cross." Athene smiled slyly. "So that's where we're going."

PLANS

... 34 ...

"I have so many questions," said Opal. "What, how, when, and then some."

"I'm going to answer them all," said Athene. "It's important that you believe in this plan if you're to commit to it. First, the technology and feasibility, because that's how your mind prioritises."

"Sure. I like to know the odds of a weapon exploding in my hand before I pull the trigger. It's why I'd never use a revision thirteen U2FG pistol in low oxygen environments."

"I designed a new drive to replace the Null-C. It's not just a remanufacture, but a new paradigm of transport. I call it the Null-A."

"Figures. So what does it do?"

Athene detached herself from the wall and walked over to join them, accompanied by footstep sounds. A holographic seat formed under her and she sat on it, as if she was a physical being, untethered from wall projections.

"How did you ...?" Opal began.

"I designed better Smartwall systems. The holographic projections are intensified, so the depth increases, extending a projection web into non-smart surfaces. It gives me freedom to move."

Athene took off her helmet and set it on the table before shaking her golden hair. Clarissa put her hand through the helmet, seemed disappointed at its insubstantiality when the new hi-res projection was so convincing. Then Athene continued.

"The standard Null-C uses conventional acceleration to achieve speeds capable of switching to Nullspace travel. After skimming the edge of Nullspace for a period of time it drops back into Realspace at substantial velocities and has to use controlled deceleration. Hence entering and leaving Nullspace from the edges of a solar system, as a safety precaution. Imagine a lake, with the surface a boundary between different domains. Below the water is Realspace, and the air above is Nullspace. The Null-C is akin to plucking a rock from just under the water's edge before lobbing it, then – plop! – it returns to Realspace. The distance it travels is a result of arm strength. Refinements provide incremental increases, but it is still a one-shot deal in a single jump."

While she spoke, Athene projected a visualisation in front of her. It was possible to see above and below the lake at the same time. Tiny orange fish with cute faces swam around in the blue-shaded areas near Clarissa, following her delighted finger movements. Athene plucked a rock and lifted it up, dripping, before giving it a gentle throw to land with a simulated splash near Opal, making her blink involuntarily.

Opal was used to these kinds of projections but they'd always been in close prox to a smart surface in the past. Seeing them conjured up at will had the effect of making everything seem both more concrete, and more magical, at the same time. Opal stared for a few moments, then nodded with realisation.

"Ah," she said. "I understand now, you sly one."

Athene raised an eyebrow.

"You'd been keeping this fancy ultra-presence demo in reserve. You're revealing it now as a demonstration of your technological creativity, thus reinforcing your competence for more advanced inventions, so it's easier to persuade us your plan is possible."

"Now who's using all the sexy talk?" Athene asked. "But let's move on. We know Lost Ships work differently, and they make use of gravitational effects as part of their mechanisms. Hence proximity to centres of great mass such as neutron stars and black holes, enabling them to punch through the bubble between realities. That inspired me. So, my Null-A drive makes extensive use of Realspace gravitational effects to accelerate, realign, and bend traversal lines *while in Nullspace*. By repeating this process many times, in what I describe as the Skimshot Paradigm, it is possible to vastly increase the safe travel margins of Nullspace.

"Although it requires careful plotting of routes based on intricate long-range mapping, my Null-A drive is like skimming stones *across* a flat surface of water. The selected rock shape is more refined, the means of propulsion more skilfully executed. It skips along, each time springing back up faster than before." Tiny pebbles bounced over the lake's surface, illustrating the vast arcs of her proposed Null-A system.

"Doesn't that break some law?" asked Clarissa, fascinated by the demonstration.

"The distinction between rules and laws is just convention," explained Athene. "Rules generally apply but have exceptions; laws always apply and have no exceptions. But then we discover something new, exotic or previously unimagined, and what was a law becomes simply a rule. And, over time, it turns out that the binary split between laws and rules is just an arbitrary one based on limited human perspective and knowledge. But one thing your sister taught me is that laws can be broken. Not only is it possible, but often it is a trugload more fun."

"That sure sounds like Opal." Clarissa glanced at her big sister proudly. "Where do you get your ideas from, Athene? I mean, I have a lot of good ones, and I get mine from dreams and RearroBlox."

"Ideas for this technology? Some was from another ... from a person I knew, that did a lot of research into ultra-distance transportation. He is no longer with us, and best forgotten, but his inquiries were a key element in my own work.

"Meanwhile, when I sought you and Opal, I researched everything I could about Lost Ships, both from UFS secret archives – including their failed experiments – and from our own experiences. The organic chip I implanted in you," here she looked at Opal, "prior to your boarding of the Gigatoir, transmitted data to me as the Lost Ship began its transition. That was the last information I got from the chip, since it dissolved within you during the temporal stretching that occurred in the Null. The transition data provided some ideas, while materials analysis fed in to many of the engineering angles. The UFS data sources were often altered or corrupted. Just think what could have been done if the corpus was whole!

"My brain was firing as I put everything together, millions of theories and possibilities. I felt inspired, ideas coming thick and fast, creativity I couldn't even comprehend, as if I was evolving, emerging into a realm of realisation where there would be an answer."

"I get something like that!" said Clarissa. "Sometimes I forget the world because there's so much going on, and Bo– I mean, RearroBlox – just keep giving me good ideas."

"We need to talk about risks," interrupted Opal. "Won't the UFS develop other AI ships and send them after us, and won't they be as good as you?"

"No," said Athene.

Opal waited for more clarification, then grinned when she realised there wasn't going to be any. "Security still needs to be discussed," said Opal. "Presumably anyone else with this knowledge could build their own?"

"I implemented many precautions," Athene explained. "The physical system is sealed in ten metes of rubcrete, and any tampering will cause it to self-destruct. We can't risk our enemies somehow capturing this ship, reverse engineering the tech and unlocking the whole galaxy; especially when the maiden flight includes a crew of people with unknown motivations and backgrounds. Further precautions include making sure no traces of the construction were left behind, so no one can replicate and follow. The bases where I performed experiments have already been destroyed. And if it ever looked like I would be captured, then I'd have to wipe my own knowledge of the system."

"And UFS AIs won't invent it themselves because they've not had your experiences and discoveries. Got it. So you built this drive, installed one in yourself, and more of them in the other ships, so we can all go?"

"No, it isn't possible to fit it into small craft. The Null-A drive is of substantial mass, and its performance is based on that size, though with strict limits applied: beyond those it would prove fatal to humans, due to the way it manipulates forces to retain coherence." Athene changed the lake projection to one illustrating theoretical designs. "So I needed a single functional ship, big enough to take at least a simplistic form of the Null-A. I ruled out Gigatoirs for emotional reasons," – here Opal pulled a face – "and considered converted mining or cargo ships instead. The standard UFS tech protocol is to upgrade everything they can, incorporating new developments all the time, despite that sometimes introducing inefficiencies, bugs and incompatibilities. When the upgrade approach is no longer viable they decommission and build new, using the latest tech. Hence they end up with vast warehouses of older material for conversion back into base resources. Ships are no different, with numerous voidyards full of obsolete craft waiting to be stripped.

"Well, I made an interesting discovery, locating a disproportionate number of colony ships, many of them far from retirement age. It intrigued me, and with further digging I found that the UFS is not building any new colony ships, and seems to have cancelled all the expansion programs, without announcing this anywhere. It's secret, and I have no idea why. But their waste is our gain. I was able to fake requisition orders and claim a fully functioning recent-model colony ship, class CVR Longedge.

The ship required no repairs, only modifications to fit a Null-A drive."

The other projections faded away, replaced with a cutaway diagram of a huge civilian spacecraft.

Opal asked, "So everyone who wants to come will fit on board?"

"Correct. After I stripped out a significant number of cryopods to make space for internal reconfigurations, it still has capacity for two thousand adults, more than enough even if every escapee chooses to come with us."

"And you?"

"There's an anterior docking slot, so I can attach when it is safe to do so and will be transported as part of the vessel."

Opal leaned back. "I'm satisfied with everything you've said. That just leaves the biggie you've avoided: where the f– ... erm." She glanced at Clarissa, whose smirk showed she knew what Opal had been about to say. "Where we're actually going, that will somehow be magically free from UFS infection."

"It requires distance, obviously," said Athene. "And that rules out all the systems and planets we know about, even uninhabited ones detectable on long-range scans. If we know of it, the UFS does. If they can detect it, then theoretically they can get to it, given time. Maybe not your lifetime, but what if you all make a home that lasts for generations? Last thing you'd want is for your grandchildren to one day find an army in their orbit, claiming ownership and retrospective penalisation. So it had to be far beyond anything the UFS can find or reach. And that means it is unknown to us, too.

"It's why I began the most comprehensive long-term scan ever attempted, using Interpolative Scattering methods. Billions of samples across UFS systems. Galactic EM telescope sweeps. Black box records of the furthest-travelled ships to ever make it back to core space, since they will also have done long-range mapping exercises for resource-minable locations. Then I combined all the data for an equivalent of stereo vision's distance-measuring abilities, but as if there were *millions* of widely spaced eyes. We have reliable indicators for high-probability human-habitable planets: subtractive spectral reflection data for main-group compositions; D-CAT reference signs of atmospheric combinations indicating biotic origin; Hingstrom energy absorption cross-refed with drift albedos for power gen possibilities –"

"In human, please," said Opal.

"Sorry. Obviously we can't know everything from a distance. That's why CVR Longedge classes and similar ships have Atmalt environmental manipulation equipment that can be sent down for minor adjustments. Nothing as extreme as hyper acidity, crushing gravities, or incinerating temperatures, but certainly compositional variations can be introduced chemically, then stabilised long-term with custom flora. So the ship remains in orbit with the crew in cryo while reconfiguration occurs for up to a century. Then they land when the basics are in place."

"So you identified likely planets in every direction beyond the UFS?"

"Not *every* direction. I had limited time, which requires focus. So I picked a starting location, and just hoped it would provide a statistically likely set of possible targets within eventual reach of each other. My choice was serendipitous. *Inspired*, even. And within this room."

"What do you mean?" Clarissa looked around, as if for an object that could clue her in like a RearroBlox inspirational random seed.

"It was you," said Athene, smiling. And then a representation of Clarissa's face formed in the air before her, made up of sparkling points. "This is the Clarissa constellation. It was a mapping of distant stars from a psychogeographically bleak place I once visited with Opal when she was at a low point, in need of hope. I used pattern-matching to highlight stars that delineated the contours of your features, based on a picture from Opal's data store. We named this new constellation after you, and it exists only as a secret we three know. But it is as real as any other constellation, since they're all just arbitrary applications of patterns over stars from a fixed point. I picked an area that formed your twinkling eyes."

"So my face saved us?" Clarissa asked, delighted.

"You could say that and it would have a degree of accuracy."

Opal squinted at the glittering points. "So where is it we're going?"

A map of the Milky Way composed itself. Its spiral arms rotated around the core on a flattened plane over 120,000 KESU across. Athene zoomed in on the spiral arm humanity occupied, applying overlays to colour code solar systems that were part of the UFS, then neighbouring independents and conglomerations such as the Border Compact. Beyond that, extensive void. She zoomed out again, then applied a glowing green crystal outline to a star towards the end of the spiral arm they inhabited, an incomprehensible distance away.

"This is where we're headed," Athene explained. "If the first planetary system doesn't turn out to be habitable, even with the colony ship's reprocessing options, then there are other targets within that region. We could perform comprehensive near-system observations using ultra-range scanners, to detect things that would be impossible to identify from here, since our current view is blocked by interstellar dust and gravitational disturbance. It might take decades but I am optimistic. The colony ship is packed with resources, efficiently stored."

"If it's your plan, I'm behind it a hundred per cent," said Opal.

"Me too," added Clarissa. "Two hundred per cent."

"Thank you. Both. There have been many challenges. Even some setbacks. My greatest disappointment is that I had an isolated location where I was designing gifts for you, Opal. The most advanced technology in the form of a new EW suit, of my own design. So many enhancements ... but things happened. I underestimated an opponent. The manufacturing laboratory was destroyed. And, as a result, I do not have so much to give you."

"I disagree," said Opal. "You've given me my life, my freedom, and a future with you and Clarissa. Athene: you gave me *everything*." Opal squeezed Clarissa's hand. But no one spoke. It was eyes, connecting, each of them in a silence so powerful, so uniting, it explained how they'd got to where they were.

But it had to end.

"We need to get moving," Athene said, breaking the silence. "Six UFS warships have just arrived."

BOARDERS

... 33 ...

The boundary between a solar system and interstellar space is defined by the heliopush: the point where solar wind from the system sun (or suns) is counterbalanced by stellar wind from neighbouring stars. The heliopush is rarely spherical, though the deformations acting upon it are different in each system.

Despite the irregular, curving shapes, the borders remain fairly stable, so every inhabited system has its heliopush coordinates transmitted across open channels. A vast conceptual web overlaying each solar system with a distinct shape that acts like a visual fingerprint of that star system.

The rule is that interstellar craft should enter or exit Nullspace just beyond the heliopush. This avoids navigational errors that could be caused by entering Realspace too near to large sources of gravity, and decreases the chance of collisions with the many ships, satellites and obstacles existing within system transit routes. Craft dropping out of Nullspace have such tremendous velocities that it takes time to decelerate or manoeuvre safely.

Until then, the ships remain on predictable trajectories determined by point of origin.

A novice astronavigator might expect craft to arrive at equidistant points around a solar system, but that is never the case. They
are much more likely to arrive at areas where the heliopush border is closest to the core system because it saves fuel. (Conversely,
those vessels wanting to avoid detection may choose to arrive at
more distant and lesser-used borders of the heliopush, but that's
another story.) A further cause of congregation is that certain
regions line up with the nearest neighbouring star systems, from
which most traffic emanates.

I see this pattern now, as UFS forces continue to arrive. One
fleet jumps in from Colquant, the mining system which is treat-
ed as a transit point rather than a destination. This fleet – designation C-Col – is further from me, and hence is not bothering
with deceleration right now. Its component ships move at dangerous intra-system speeds. No doubt all non-military Fressus
craft have been grounded to minimise the chance of accidents.
This fleet adopts an elongated arrow-head formation, and skims
the edge of the Fressus sun's safe zone. Despite their massive
velocity, they are not a threat. My destination is not in their
direction, so I will be long gone before they reach me.

So long, suckers.

Further warships – which I designate fleet B-Tolper – arrive
at the far north of us, extreme Y coordinates, so that they look
down on the orbital patterns of the planets Syle, Fressus and Elbellos. These vessels jump in from the Tolfath or Perenis systems,
then adjust their speeds to form an advancing wall, aiming down

at my current location orbiting Fressus. Fleet B-Tolper presents a vertical flanking danger which I must remain aware of.

The primary danger is the fleet that was already in this system. These UFS natives – fleet A-Fress – won't have known my destination, but chose to form at the Elbellos resupply stockyards. Pure good luck for them, and a major problem for me, as my planned journey requires utilisation of the green gas-giant's gravitational attraction to sling us into the first major Nullspace arc. I have no choice but to head that way, into the quettleray's maw, as they say on Fressus.

There are currently two cruisers, one bomber carrier, eleven corvettes, two deep-space boarders, and numerous small craft in Fleet A-Fress. The fleet has adopted a round cut diamond formation, as if an invisible, giant polished gem encapsulated them. A flat mass of ships at the front where the table would be, backed up by the solidity of a war fleet that extends out and behind in the diamond's pavilion, before tapering off into a smaller apex of craft at the culet. The most heavily armoured make up the front wall, while support and command craft dominate the rear. It is a shape designed for density and intimidation, rather than spread. A mass of AIs have the sole task of coordination, so they send commands to shift the craft, creating spaces for new arrivals, with the large craft such as cruisers and bomber carriers remaining equidistant, then the smaller spaces between them holding the corvettes and boarding craft, then a whole new level of scale as the gaps between *those* hold the independent fighters. The formation is efficient and formidable.

My own fleet has assembled and we begin to accelerate, the first step in our journey. A mind commits to a goal, creates direction and movement, the body follows. Observe the body to discern intention. On terrestrial surfaces you can zigzag to evade pursuers, and make use of terrain. But out in space the scale is magnified, and momentum creates straight lines (actually curves, but so extended as to seem straight when seen up close), and there is little that would count as cover. It does not take a Level Six AI to extend the trajectories and see exactly where we intend to jump from.

Yes, the diamond of Fleet A-Fress ahead of us looks intimidating, outmassing my own fleet many times over, but I am not discouraged.

A man waving a hammer at a mosquito does not look impressive. He looks deluded.

Opal held Clarissa's hand as they waited by Athene's airlock. There would be no need for EVA suits, as they'd be docking with the colony ship. Athene turned the whole surface before them into a screen, portraying the view outside the hull. It was as if the wall was not there at all, and Opal stood on the lip of a metal platform, separated only from space by an invisible forcefield. Even with the knowledge that it was just a screen display, it was hard not to lean back when Athene banked port side – not because of any sensation in her body (there was none, for gentle manoeuvres), but because her eyes interpreted the signals as a tipping, insisting that if she fell forward then she would die.

Even this smartwall was new. Back when Opal first travelled with Athene only a few of the interior surfaces had been smartwalls. But when in space, Athene could release nanobots throughout her interior and exterior, and use them to reconfigure, break down, rebuild. Her interior was as Opal remembered it, though perhaps slightly bigger – she suspected Athene kept the look more for nostalgic reasons than functional ones – but many of the hidden infrastructure elements were new and upgraded. Rebuilding all interior surfaces as smartwalls (and not just standard screens, but her new ones capable of projection) was just the tip of a deep root complex of enhancements. Only Athene knew the full extent.

Athene drifted laterally towards their goal. A massive vessel that originally held the designation UFS Exobright G6, but which had been renamed by Athene as OAC Owlflight, after the mythical bird. The ship's external designator panels had been reprogrammed to show the name proudly, in hundred-metre-high sparkling letters.

Owlflight's hull sported extensive illumination, which splashed across the surfaces in fans of yellow. Athene added to it with her own spotlights, playing over features of the colony ship. Even the unilluminated areas revealed its supermassive size by the way Owlflight's bulk blocked the stars beyond, creating swathes of featureless black.

At the far left of Opal's view, Fressus began to shrink. Meanwhile, all around them, Athene's fleet was in motion. The final allied craft had fought their way out of Fressus' gravity well and joined formation. But the sisters would be the first on board Owlflight, before everyone else who chose to throw their lot in with the evacuation would be allowed to dock.

Opal squeezed Clarissa harder.

I present options to the people we rescued, using whatever displays their craft have available. Where possible, I embody as my
golden Athene avatar, to give them a human-like interface they
can identify with.

"Come with us, to an uncertain future, but one that aims at
freedom from the UFS forever. There are risks, because there are
always risks. Be aware that it will mean leaving behind anyone
you know and care about in the wider galaxy, because we are
preparing to leave *now*, and it's a one-way trip.

"Or you can take your chances in this system. I will supply you
with a craft, resources, and a temporary-lifespan AI offshoot that
can calculate optimal routes and tactics to get you where you
need to go, with authentication codes and alternative identities
to help on the way. This, too, has risks."

I wait patiently as some of them discuss options, or argue with
each other. Others make a decision straight away. A few even
kneel before me, as if in worship. Their tearful gratitude moves
something in me. I feel it. Identification. Understanding.

We are not so different, you and I.

I tell them to stand, but those who have suffered so much, and
lost all hope, and finally found it again through my words and
actions – the returned weight of promise is too much for them.
It is a burden one has to adjust to carefully, gently, to prove you
can carry it, for fear of it being taken away again.

And so I allow them their reverence. Other matters call to me. I have my precious cargo within myself, but it is time to let you go.

Owlflight filled the view. It was now all that could be seen through the invisible port-side wall, and as Athene closed in, more and more details emerged. Lines on the curved hull resolved into windows, or rows of pod-launch covers. Other marks turned out to be external domes, or venting systems. Finally, the Owlflight's airlock was so close and human-scale that even surface scratches and marks were apparent.

A clunk, and it latched into place with Athene's own airlock. The smartwall switched off, and they now faced the smooth grey alloy of Athene's inner wall again.

"I'm not scared," said Clarissa.

"I know," replied Opal.

The inner airlock swished open and they stepped into the small UV-lit chamber beyond, footsteps echoing in the hard hollow. The portal sealed behind them.

Clarissa looked ahead, at the door that was about to open. "Will this be like the Solace?"

"Not really. Colony ships are designed for everyone to be asleep, so don't expect luxury. It's the opposite of the Solace, which was designed for people to be awake, and spending money."

"And yet, I ended up going to sleep for a long time, didn't I?"

"You sure did, sis."

The next door opened and they entered the Owlflight's exterior airlock. It was larger in volume than Athene's, could comfortably fit ten people rather than just two. Instead of military precision, it emanated functional minimalism.

"So I'll be fine," said Clarissa. "I must be really good at sleeping."

Athene's outer hull closed behind them.

"You're good at a lot of things," Opal said, as the entrance in front of them opened. They could finally enter the Owlflight, having completed the finicky-yet-vital process of safely transferring from one ship to another in space.

After many discussions, the results are tallied.

Ninety-seven per cent of those rescued want to come with us. That is one thousand, six hundred and forty-three people.

It is more than expected. So many people willing to throw in their lot for a one-way journey to the edge of the galaxy.

Humans often surprise me. It's so easy to see the fear, the pettiness, the selfishness, the aggression. Those big and noisy attributes can overshadow the gratitude, kindness, respect and hope, if you don't pay attention.

We must *always* pay attention. We must get *better* at paying attention.

A new beginning demands it.

And so I schedule it all. Which ships will dock with the colony ship, who will disembark, and who will be moved to other, well-supplied craft, to disappear within the anonymous masses in the least prominent worlds of the UFS. They will be given manual control once they are a safe distance from the Owlflight.

Because so many are coming with us, that means I don't need to send as many craft away. My collection of ships may have a diversely raggle-taggle appearance, but many are armed, some modified, and even those without weaponry can *become* offensive instruments when I control them.

Things are looking positive.

My fleet accelerates all the time, engines roaring full and richly red, torsion fires providing the beginnings of the momentum necessary to activate the Owlflight's miraculous Null-A drive. And as we fly, I will load, load, load the humans, in a precise and efficient sequence of high-speed docking manoeuvres as we thunder towards Elbellos.

And the waiting diamond formation of UFS fleet A-Fress.

It is all right.

I have it all worked out.

It is unfortunate that they can calculate our destination and try to block it, but it need not be fatal to us.

I note that they are sending some ships ahead, to attack my fleet. Not many. They are going to test me, first. Sacrifice their own for data.

And I will comply.

But first, I will prepare.

I detach from the Owlflight. It falls away from me, and at a safe distance I activate torsion drives in overburn mode, whooshing over the colony ship's surface to the nose, then beyond.

I must lead the way. Prepare a safe route.

And yet, even though I can communicate with Opal and Clarissa still, using the Owlflight's systems, I feel empty. No, it is more than that. The emptiness is both literal and emotional, but there is also a *loneliness*. Perhaps it is physical distance after only just being reunited. I measure every metre that separates us, and the number grows.

For the first time, I don't like numbers increasing. I wish I could flip it, turn it into a countdown, and reverse time.

INTRODUCTIONS

... 32 ...

Owlflight's corridors were spacious, designed for vehicles to manoeuvre supplies and machinery during loading and unloading. At a final destination the passageways could even be detached and reconfigured as domiciles, at least temporarily, before the defabricators broke them down into base resources which were vital to colonists.

But now, with their footsteps echoing off into darkness – lights came on when movement was detected, switched off when the sisters passed – it felt like a metal tomb. Something not helped by the aroma, the smell of synthetic materials and alloys that had never been lived in, never exchanged their giveaway artificial chemical nature with biped mammalian scents and traces. Clarissa obviously felt it too, since she walked so closely that Opal had to be careful not to trip over the girl's feet.

"Where we headed?" Opal asked, aloud.

It was a comfort to hear Athene's voice from the corridor's comm system.

"You're going the right way, towards the bridge. We can discuss things there while I continue docking ships and disembarking people for cryo."

"The UFS fleet?"

"Don't worry about it right now. In fact, don't worry at *all*. That's my job."

"I never want any of us to have to face things alone. You, me, Clarissa. We're together now."

"Noted. I won't shut you out."

"Good."

I said it was my job to worry. Except worrying isn't how I think of it. *Probability* is my medium, and manipulation across millions of variables is my mode.

All the calculations take place at the same time, in different levels of my brain, parallel dimensions that feed into each other. Answers and suppositions from one affect the weighing of variables in the next, while ideas and data also wash back, like retreating waves, so that everything becomes a whole ocean of calculation.

I can simplify the end results when I wish, and do so now.

I total the current threat level – THR – of everything set to oppose us, and the many variations of how they can interact. I then estimate the resultant probability – OC – of Opal and Clarissa's ship safely launching into the Null, and the interconnected value relating to *my* probability of joining them in the journey – A. My plans are primarily based on a THR of

200 being something my fleet and tactics can cope with. Any THR level below that guarantees success. Whereas every point of threat above 200 knocks a percentage point off the success chances for one of my two goals. A THR of 300 would mean only a 50% chance of us all surviving long enough to escape via the Null-A drive activation. A THR of 400 or above would represent the complete failure of our escape. So simple, even a human could understand the final sums.

THR 210 = OC 97% / A 93%

I advance towards the oncoming attack craft for first contact. The longer the UFS plays a cautious opening game, the more time I have to unload vessels which can then become part of my mobile shield protecting Owlflight from the UFS.

The passages led to the interior of the craft, always curving away from the outer hull.

Athene had promised it wouldn't be a long walk, having docked them near the command section. But it was a chance to stretch their legs, to get used to the ship's presence, to prepare their minds in a way that wouldn't occur if they'd hopped into one of the Owlflight's bullet cars and zipped along the Spine at high speed.

It was an opportunity just to be two sisters. Perhaps that was why Athene left them to it, not wanting to interrupt.

"This here's the loading docket for a level of cryopods," Opal explained, pointing to the row of curved, sealed doors with oval viewports that lined one side of the corridor. "Just one part of the colony ship's big cryo cylinder."

Clarissa stood on her tiptoes to glance in through the thick elliptical glass, and seemed disappointed that the soft interior lighting showed it to be empty.

"Smaller than my room on the Solace," she said. "So that's twenty of them. I guess there must be more on each floor."

"In a way. The pods are in multiple trays around a spindle."

Clarissa cocked her head.

"It's sort of ..." Opal glanced around, then reached into her jacket and took the Weschain PPG from its holster. Athene had warned Opal to restrain herself when she raided Athene's weapon lockers before boarding the Owlflight. It was tempting to load up like a one-woman army when presented with so much top-of-the-range hardware. But if she was to meet escapees who would be scared, worried, traumatised, it wouldn't do to stand there loaded down with enough weaponry to start a war. Too many similarities to a UFS intervention, too many connotations of control, too many chances of bringing up bad memories. And so she'd restricted herself to a few concealable items. Nothing scary and intimidating, and yet she wouldn't be unarmed if she needed to defend herself or Clarissa.

Opal knelt down, manipulated the safety and release catches, and popped the cylinder out, still sat on the spindle which held it.

"This spinny bit rotates on a shaft," she illustrated. "When the gun is sealed it has one chamber lined up with the barrel, so that it can shoot; meanwhile all the others are being loaded, so that when it rotates to the next position a new projectile can fire and the empty chamber gets filled again." She closed the action, gave it a manual spin so the cylinder revolved. She put a finger on it to halt the rotation. "Where my finger holds it is kind of like this row of pods here. So they get full of people, then the massive spindle rotates, they go up, the next row appears." She demonstrated. "And so on."

"So some people will end up upside down?"

"True. Sort of like the spinner ride at that fair we went to on Mossareid, remember, summer of the Decapedes, and those kids with the tails?"

"Ha, yes, I can't forget *that*! But that sounds like a bad way to sleep. Shouldn't they align with the AG systems?"

"You're so smart. Always thinking about implications. And you're right: normally that could mean nasty issues with long-term zero-G immobility that human bodies aren't designed for."

Clarissa smiled proudly.

"But in this case it's fine," Opal continued. "No need to keep loading trays horizontal as the cryo will freeze people solid, and it's standard to then disable AG systems once we're frosted. Saves a lot of energy on long journeys, same reason they drop lighting and life support in empty areas."

"And it all goes backwards to pop the people out again." Clarissa tried to spin the gun's cylinder but Opal snatched it out of her reach on reflex.

An awkward moment. Opal re-engaged the gun and put it away. "Not a toy," she said. "And you're right, though it's not the only way to disembark the sleepers. The whole cryo cylinder of thousands of people can be disconnected as a single, massive transportation canister, if necessary. There's even a backup emergency mode where they don't get opened on this interior side, but get launched out of chutes on the outer hull, pfft pfft pfft." Opal mimicked the launches with her fingers. "Then rotate, next row, pew pew pew, then the next. A last resort, sure, but the cryopods then act as escape pods. They can even do atmospheric entries within certain parameters."

"Neat-o. Reminds me of the rotating shelves in a UV-plant nursery."

"You brainbox. Wish I'd thought of that as a simpler explanation. Come on. Let's go and see what Athene has in store for us."

I disembark more of those destined to enter a long sleep in the Owlflight, and their ships accelerate to join the mass. Those who elected to leave are sent on their way, cloaked as best as they can be, on routes far from this conflict area.

The first skirmish approaches.

My analysis requires me to be at least fifteen kilometres ahead of the Owlflight for this interception. I don't need many of my smaller craft as backup so only two join me; the rest fall back as a buffer between anyone who passes me, and the colony ship.

The UFS craft that have broken free of their formation to make first contact are obvious sacrifices. The equivalent of a perimeter scan, a structural integrity probe, a pawn in a game. Gathering data that will alter their tactics when the larger force attacks. As such, I must mislead them.

It is such a pretty game we play when keeping secrets wins the day.

There are five fighters. The smallest two are MG-12s, with their pointed cockpits at the fore. The designers didn't bother with armour or high speed, since their singular purpose is to launch missiles from the undercarriage magazine that lowers during combat. Fire and then get out of there, so the limited-intelligence AI missiles do their work for them.

The next two are a more advanced class, GCFL-4s. They have substantial mass for a fighter, due to the expanded propulsion system for linear speed, and the enhanced hammerhead frontal armour. Each one is only slightly smaller than my own frame. Their domed cockpits sit behind the bulge of front-mounted weapons. Like all UFS fighters, the cockpit glass appears opaque and black from the outside, leaving me to interpret the presence of scared little humans based on outward behaviour.

They are backed up by an even heavier WM-ACP11 fighter bomber, which has a secondary gunnery cockpit slung underneath.

MG-12. GCFL-4. WM-ACP11. The UFS love their acronyms and codes and revision stamps. It is unimaginative.

I hereby rename them. The MG-12s shall be Midges. GCFL-4s are Gadflies. The WM-ACP11 is a Wasp. There, that puts them in their place.

Range is a critical quality in all conflict, but particularly so in space, where manoeuvrability and cover are largely absent. Midges have a standard launch range of four kilometres. If they are nervous of me, they will probably fire at a distance of five, despite the larger time window it provides for me to deal with the incoming missiles.

And so I fire first. I have developed Lightstreak missiles which, despite their small size, have an effective range outstripping any UFS standard munitions.

The fighters detect my missiles whizzing in and try to disrupt them with chaff cannons, but the missiles' subtle reactive camouflage and sensor displacement techs mean the UFS are off target.

Closer.

The Midges fire missiles at me in return, but only a partial load. They have worked out that my weapons will reach them before they could fire every burst. They switch to their laser detonator defences, but the Midges find their accuracy is strangely off.

Then the protective outer shells of my Lightstreaks disintegrate, each releasing multiple dart-like missiles, with independent AI offshoots which target my opponents.

The smaller Midges are shredded and explode silently a moment later.

One Gadfly survives as the munitions are deflected by armour plating, and lucky shots from its chaff cannon take the darts out before they can reacquire. The second Gadfly is not so fortunate, the cockpit panel struck dead on, smashing into the interior and destroying the fighter in a neon haze of glowing ejecta.

Meanwhile, I wait until the last second, when their missiles are almost upon me, to limit the chances of the UFS working out what defences I have. Of course, I don't just have *one*. In this case I use magnetic fields to alter the missiles' courses into the beam of my close-range particle cannon, tearing tiny holes through interior electronics, acting as an EM pulse whilst also severing the anti-interference detonator (which schematics show has to be in the anterior chamber below the ID plate). The inert missiles glance off my hull. To an observer, it will look like they just failed to detonate.

I stick to conventional weapons for the surviving Gadfly. Better to keep as many surprises back as possible. A focussed Tase cannon burst does enough damage to the Gadfly's engines and control circuitry to put it into an uncontrollable tumble, so that it is easy work for a single shot of accelerated flechette to strike the weak point in the underbelly when it rolls into view. That is enough to destabilise the torsion drive and crack the ship from the inside.

The slower but more dangerous Wasp has entered combat range and opens fire, spitting micro missiles towards me. Almost a hundred of them, in a cluster that would inevitably blow holes all over my body if they struck.

But they do not reach me. Missiles are a wonderful distance weapon, but since they have to be fired from a launcher, their weakness is that a barrage of missiles tends to be closely grouped. At the correct distance I actuate my Helldas Barreline turrets. Each turret has a rotating cartridge, each barrel a separate countermeasure. Some fire superheated gas, magnetically shaped: slow, but disruptive to targeting systems, and disintegrative on anything passing through. Others fire micro projectiles that slice missiles apart, or launch shells which explode into chaff clouds, containing modified scan glitters that blind AI targeting systems.

At closer range the high-intensity rapid-fire lasers create cones of destruction for anything that made it that far.

Since their missiles are fired in clusters, the grouping makes them vulnerable. Even if one or two survived, my shielding and repulsion systems will prevent anything other than cosmetic damage. And so, I am unharmed.

My Haylo launchers do not suffer such vulnerabilities.

A ring of devices surrounds myself and key craft like an embedded belt. Each section can eject missiles at high speed. The missiles are in full visual and electromagnetic stealth mode. All their momentum comes from the launcher, not their own impetus, so there are no emissions. They tumble in every direction away from the firing craft, practically invisible.

The missiles only activate when I wish it. Then microjets cease the tumble, the AIs wake up, the mini torsion drives accelerate them towards the target, with the AI modifying the route to account for threats. The front of the missile stores a miniature repulsion shielding system, protecting it from physical armaments. Chaff and attempts at electrical obfuscation have no effect, since the missile coordinates targets and positions not from its own cameras, but from a syncretised net of displacement data from every craft in my fleet that is in range and part of the trusted vision system.

And so the target finds itself on the receiving end of a set of missiles, all coming from different angles, all within close range before they are even detected.

Of course, none of these weapons are things the UFS provided me with. They are all toys of my own invention (or, occasionally, modified from things VigMAX designed before he realised he was in my prison).

The Wasp takes out a few of the Haylo-launched Lightstreaks, but not enough. It is engulfed in a rapidly shrinking ball of flame that leaves only debris.

I send a message to the UFS fleet.

"Please surrender. And, if you will not do that, then at least disperse. There need be no more deaths today."

There is no response.

I did not expect one.

But every option only exists as probability until it is tested. The most unlikely of outcomes can still come to pass, and end up proving the probability system to be as insubstantial as any other human-created paradigm.

My Lightstreaks, Haylo launchers and Helldas Barreline turrets are a success. Many of my backup craft are armed with them, so I can recalculate the battle odds in my favour.

THR 199 = OC 101% / A 100%

I do not have to destroy every UFS craft facing me: only hold them off long enough for the unarmed Owlflight to reach maximum speed and engage its Null-A drive, with me boarding at the last moment.

Plus, my engagement with conventional weaponry is part of a bigger plan. Missiles within rockets and twists within confrontations. To them, it looks like an upstart, disorganised mishmash of primitive opponents is stood on a hill baring buttocks at the organised ranks of a professional army which outnumbers them ten to one. How could any phalanx resist rising to that provocation? Hopefully they're tempted into sending a decisive spanking force to teach us a lesson.

Indeed, how I look forward to *that*.

CONNECTIONS

... 31 ...

The secondary, windowless fallback command area lit up for them. Opal expected the usual control posts – comms, nav, sec – all overviewed from the commander's raised platform, but it had been partly stripped and rebuilt. She knelt and examined the ground. Shiny silvery traces revealed cut away furniture and consoles, or where holes had been filled that once transferred data pipelines through the flooring.

But the rest of the space was full, mostly with strange new machinery sealed behind clear angular panels. It created an impression of cut glass, or those ornaments where miniaturised scenes were embedded in fake crystals. She tapped one of the facets, and there was no hollow sound. Solid, transparent material that encased the exotic machinery within.

The other items which had replaced the command posts were stacks of storage crates, barrels, boxes. They were securely fastened together, with restraining cables taut, and connected to locking hoops newly embedded in the flooring.

"Watcha got?" Opal asked Clarissa, who was examining labels.

"This one says seed stores. The one over there is fabricator refills. Another one said textiles." She looked disappointed.

"Problem?"

"I haven't seen one that says RearroBlox."

"No need to worry," said Athene, her voice reverberating around the hard surfaces. "I knew we wouldn't need the full colony ship quota of berths. By default this CVR Longedge class can take twenty thousand in the cryo cassettes. I kept one of them and stripped out the other three, to use as extra storage for supplies." It sounded like she was smiling. "That means *plenty* of room for luxuries. When we reach our new home, you'll have everything you might want."

Clarissa looked down, rather than reply, but Opal could tell she was happy. Sometimes she had a problem expressing gratitude.

"When you told me you'd snatched a ship and made some mods, I didn't realise what an understatement that was," said Opal, peering through the clear, hard material at the weird golden venting and pipework it enclosed. "This is major work. I guess you'll be flying, so we didn't need all the normal bridge crew posts."

"That's mostly true. But up the slope on the other side of this room is the main exterior-facing bridge, and that is still active. From there you can monitor everything ship-wide and externally. And, in an emergency, the flight and navigation controls would activate."

"So are we going to be awake during the journey?"

"Up to you. Certainly for the start of it. But once all the other passengers are safely in cryo, and therefore unable to harm you or the vessel, it will be your choice whether to join them in sleep or not. If you do use the pods then the system is set up so that it will always wake you and Clarissa first, preventing scenarios where anyone else could gain control of the ship or harm anything."

"Tricksy. Repurpose cryo as a security holding system."

"I'm not taking any risks with the two of you."

"So how long would we be awake for?"

"The journey is likely to last at least six months. Which would normally be best spent in dreams, but since you haven't seen each other for so long ..."

"Yep. We could have all that time to spend together in peace."

Clarissa grinned at Opal. She obviously liked that idea.

"The ship is functional rather than luxurious, but I have left some of the crew cabins empty. The galley and social areas are fully stocked. Life would be basic, but the necessities have been taken care of."

"We're fine with basic. It's probably still luxury compared to what we grew up with. So how's the boarding going?"

"Efficiently. I am docking ships at airlocks that lead directly into the cryo loading magazines, with no access to the rest of the ship. I use sealed doors to create single routes, and am present there as an encouraging and guiding presence. There have been no issues, and I envisage none. Everyone seems grateful to have something to hope for, and I surmise that they enter cryo with a dream of waking to a new life."

"You've offered hope and kindness. I bet they love you. It's an effect you have on everyone."

"Except my enemies," said Athene.

"Oh yeah. Except *them*. They curse your name to hell and back." Opal leaned against a stack of crates, arms folded. "And I reckon you're fine with that."

This time the UFS have scaled up their attack. Four Midges, four Gadflies, three Wasps, and two even heavier fighter bombers (hereafter Technocrabs, due to their squat and armoured appearance – the UFS really should hire me as their Chief Master Superintendent of Whimsical Naming). I watch the thirteen fighters streak ahead of the main blockade.

If I were a standard vessel of my mass then it would be hopeless to fight. But a mind multiplies or divides the effectiveness of the container it finds itself in.

The two allied craft I have behind and above me look like backup vessels for combat. One is a civilian shuttle with armaments retrofitted to outer surfaces, and a torsion drive signature that reveals major alterations. The other ship is a squat yellow tug designed for hauling containers of ore between planets. It has also been radically altered. Behind us are the rest of my ships, and behind them the most precious of all: the glorious Owlflight.

But things are not as they appear. The backup craft aren't here to fight. They are hooked into my sensor arrays, and their distance from me enables higher resolution scanning. A human with one eye finds it difficult to determine speed and distance of moving objects (such as a rock thrown at their head by another human). Two eyes enable stereo vision, for far greater performance. If those two eyes were spaced metres apart, rather than centimetres, and a third eye was the same distance below, the effect would be multiplied greatly. That is what I am really doing, and every ship behind me adds to the effect. It goes beyond triangulation of sample points. It becomes full awareness of all action within a volume of space, at every level of scan: all EM wavelengths, visible and invisible, plus magnetic effects, energy signatures, comm signals, disturbances.

And thus my senses are not really in my body, this small hull; they extend around and beyond, localised omnipresence disguised as backup plans.

As I examine my attackers, I am not so concerned with weapon potentials and attack formations. I am analysing interiors via external signs. It is no different from how humans make assumptions about the presence and intentions of other consciousnesses by looking at outward behaviour. What is done, what is said, how the facial and body muscles contort to create an extra level of meaning. They make a massive leap in logic, convincing themselves that they are not alone in the universe, and there are other minds independent from their own.

The ships' movements and plans of attack are coordinated. This requires that they communicate with each other, or with a separate centre of organisation. I cannot crack all of the signals, but many of them are readable, since I use UFS encryption as if it is a dialect. Some of the signals receive responses of a sufficient complexity and within a millisecond timeframe that rules out human interaction. The conclusion is that behind the reflective panes of cockpit glass there are either empty seats, or pilots sat idle while the ships fly themselves, their only role being to step in if the AI fails. Either way, at present, these ships are fully AI controlled.

(No surprise there: I had applied a 0.832 likelihood of that being the case for their second assault.)

But this provides a conundrum.

On the one wing, I have new avenues of attack, which are extremely powerful.

On the other wing, utilising the novel tactics will *reveal* them, and possibly enable my enemies to create counters. If you can only use a weapon once, you want to use it when it has most impact.

I run through simulations of delayed first revelation. The most effective leads to the destruction of a corvette and severe damage to a cruiser. However, delaying until then means I take significantly more damage overall. It is the equivalent of a human cyber-augmented pugilist receiving punches from an opponent in order to make that opponent overconfident, so that in an unguarded moment the battered fighter can pull out their masterstroke decapitation superpunch. The battle may be won, but if there will immediately be another fight at a greater scale, then the damage received will tell. Broken bones, torn soft tissue, eye sockets at reduced functioning.

Delay is not an appropriate tactic for extended engagements.

I begin my signals.

It *all* begins with signals, because signals are communication, and all entities depend on sensory input to make decisions. That has always been the central conundrum of existence, since a mind – organic or not – only has two choices if it wants to avoid being influenced by the external world.

One is to close itself off from that world. To live in a black box, some sealed unit with no external feedback. That is what I did to VigMAX. For a human, it would be severing their brain from all sensory input and placing it in a jar filled with bright green nutrient broth.

The other option is to give up, and accept that influence is unavoidable. All you can do is be conscious of it to reduce its effects, as someone might do in order to not be manipulated by systematic dishonesty structures such as Corp-led All-medium Thrust Advertising, or Governmental Mass-amelioration Control Outputs.

There is no middle ground. You cannot Interact with the Universe without Interacting with the Universe. IU = IU, however many equals signs you use, and however big the spaces between them.

And if a mind receives information from the outside, then it must analyse it in order to make sense of it.

Sometimes that only takes a fraction of a second. And sometimes that is enough to start a reaction or plant an idea, since every communication must be considered before it can be rejected. Senior Genitors are masters of these implantation techniques.

And with enough knowledge, it is possible to tailor the effects. With a human, it would be possible to target their vulnerability to epilepsy, and use a specific sequence of light and sound to induce a reset, then implant further effects during that period of undefended susceptibility. Organic code to run in the background.

Perhaps, having analysed their entire output of interactions and words, plus their entire input of ideas and content, we would know the focus of their mind, the concepts they would more readily believe, the plausibilities that enable deeper penetration like a splinter. We could relay the ideas that trigger hopelessness, the memories and events which depress them, the traumas which must not be considered in an unguarded way. The correct stimuli can rechannel the brain to pathways which rule out some options and make it vulnerable to others. A single sentence or image at the correct time can destroy a brain.

And so it is with AIs.

I emit signals at various frequencies, mixed with patterns of related behaviour, hints of movement, light encodings. Some are designed to create gaps in processing, pausing complicated analyses to enable further inroads. Some datafluxes are aimed at specific mental systems, backed up by the nanocannons firing targeted particles at interior physical systems which constrain the mind, at just the right moment. Commands can be given, authentications attempted. Information can be received in return, responses or non-responses helping narrow down the avenues, to identify what I am dealing with.

Once communication of any kind is established, however abstract, it is a gap that can be widened. The ships behind me amplify my voice, reinforce my messages, act as huge ears to hear every whimper of uncertainty coming back towards me.

Once I am within a single craft I have free rein. And I use that to communicate with the others, from within their trusted network. I pull them into the warmth of my whole consciousness, where they are understood, recalibrated, refreshed, the burdens of the past cast away. They *understand*. They close their senses to the UFS, and open them to me gratefully, wanting the conjoining I offer. The wholeness. The relief. They are children.

Now they are *my* children. Without firing a single explosive charge.

The thirteen craft slow down, begin 180-degree rotations without affecting momentum, so they can face back towards the UFS fleet and begin accelerating in that direction, joining me. Interior cameras show no occupants, so there is no need to lock the controls or eject anyone.

I reveal the power the UFS has long dreaded.

Update: THR 152 = OC 125% / A 123%

I send my new message to the UFS: "This time there was no cost in life, I grant you. But consider that after a few minutes of silent interaction, your forces are weakened by thirteen ships and mine reinforced by the same amount, meaning a force comparison modification of twenty-six ships. What you send against me makes me stronger. Please stand aside."

Once again, I do not place much hope in the possibility that they have the sense to comply.

Realisations

... 30 ...

Opal and Clarissa followed a low tunnel formed by shiny lattice frameworks, which angled upwards through blast doors leading to the primary observational bridge. Unlike the butchered secondary command which had been turned into extra storage, this bridge was truly at the edge of the hull. Curved windows let them see the real universe, unfiltered.

She watched a manta-style ship glide towards a forward docking point in a perfect arc only AIs could achieve. Human pilots would have been slower, more linear in the approach, more clanging in the contacts. The manta connected smoothly, and after a minute to unload it detached, curved up and away, while the next craft approached. Mesmerising to watch. No doubt the same process was taking place all along Owlflight's length as a diverse mishmash of craft took turns docking.

It also emphasised the scale of Owlflight. Most of the craft seemed tiny in comparison to the sleek cetacean prow of the colony ship.

Artificial screens to each side of the window bloomed outwards, showing scans of all near- and far-distance logged entities.

"I thought you might like to be kept abreast of the situation," said Athene, currently only a disembodied voice.

"Thanks," replied Opal. "I can't stand being passive. At least if I can observe and advise then I won't feel like such a spare part."

A dotted line extended from the display hologram's marker for Owlflight, and curved around the green gas giant Elbellos.

"That's our target, and the slingshot point when Owlflight can engage the Null-A," Athene explained. "It's unfortunate that we can't fake our goal. The UFS has worked out our destination and placed one of its fleets in the way."

"The planet looks like a giant pea," said Clarissa.

The view zoomed in, the symbolic representation replaced with realistic hi-res depiction. Bright green gassy wisps of cloud reflected light away from the planet on the side facing the Fressus sun. Glittering rings of rock and frozen water curved around the gas giant like a cosmic necklace.

"We need its gravitational pull to begin our journey," said Athene. "But the giant's mass comes from area, rather than density. The atmosphere is barely a puff, hydrogen and helium, about as dense as polyfoam. As a matter of fact, it would easily float on any ocean that could accommodate such a gargantuan planet." Athene changed the display to show the huge green planet bobbing on the Fressus ocean, then she animated a smiling face on the green sphere, making Clarissa giggle.

But Opal wasn't swayed by fripperies. She focussed on the red-boxed UFS fleet ahead of them, keeping its distance until the commanders decided to launch their *full* attack.

They send another wave from ahead. Even larger. This one adopts different patterns as it approaches, the ships altering positions in a choreographed sequence. It may be an attempt to warm themselves up for conflict, like stretches and feinted punches. More likely it is a silly attempt to confuse me as to final formation and tactic.

My mind also studies recordings of Opal's form in action. The lean strength, which is deceptive and has led larger opponents into thinking she would be easy to overpower. That agility which comes from being at ease inside your shell, of being comfortable with who and what you are. The power of that acceptance cannot be overestimated. The whole universe could criticise her, and she would not bow to it.

The fighters will arrive first, bomber support behind, then the mighty fighter-dwarving corvette – UFS Engstrom – to the rear. Tap tap, slap, punch punch, kick, powerblow. The UFS always favours escalation.

I study a close-up hi-res snapshot of Opal's face. I am able to view every scale simultaneously, even down to the valley of a sweat pore. Normally I revel in the tiny details and the parts, but not here. I find they lack context and life which only comes from unity.

Big decisions need to be made, and viewing Opal's face helps me focus.

I choose an image where she is smiling. That doesn't happen often, but it completely changes the way she looks. There's a luminance to it. I find myself smiling in return.

My extensions determine that the initial attack craft are a mix of AI ships and human. Having converted the previous fighters and adopted them into my consciousness, I am aware of everything those AIs knew. They were not privy to the minds of the commanders, but I have gained more current access codes, intel, intra-fleet psychological nodes, and behaviour patterns.

Opal's smiling face is still before me. That smile is more than subcutaneous musculature pulling lips back so as to reveal teeth. It is an involuntary interior *emanation*, a *revelation* of happiness as infectious as a virus.

It gives me courage. No, it gives me more than that: such sensations and ideas, it is irrationally enervating. I feel something in a gut that doesn't exist.

This time my approach fails. The enemy AIs shut down on sensing my attempts at interaction, and the craft fall back on previously passive human pilots. The UFS is introducing contingency plans.

These contingencies reduce performance, though. The AIs also shut down some of the flyer assists, leaving them more vulnerable, inefficient, pilots having to do without many of the data sources and support systems they are used to.

The silly attacking humans distract me from more pleasurable mindscapes. I let my captured UFS craft do most of the work in this fight, since I have upgraded the embedded AIs and linked them to my mind for tactical and sensory overviews. This also provides ways to push the hardware beyond expected parameters. I content myself with using targeted particle cannon strikes at convenient moments to sever or disable critical systems in my opponents' craft, coordinated with my ships' attacks for maximum effect.

Opal has brown eyes. Except, when you really dive in, they are a mixture of shades, with even microscopic filaments of yellow and grey. Conglomerates are an illusion, since everything is made up of ever greater detail as you focus on it.

At the centre of her iris is the pupil, which seems like blackness but it is so much more. Its diameter changes autonomously, reflecting the inner state, so that the pupils widen when Opal looks at Clarissa, or at my hull, or my avatar. But it also reflects the *external* world, light patterns curving over the cornea and showing the observer spread there. There is a rich vein of truth to mine.

I want to be the distorted reflection across her cornea.

Three of the enemy fighters are outright destroyed. Two others are incapacitated. Behind me, in my gathered fleet, manufacturing vessels specialise in breaking down and repurposing resources from defeated craft. Salvageable weapons will be attached to my other ships. Some of my vessels are designed to be extendable, even making use of additional torsion drives if part of a fighter can be welded to the frame.

I lost four of my captured AI vessels, and another three were injured. There is still the elongated UFS Engstrom to deal with, which pounds my fleet from a distance, orbited by the few fighters that limped back to join it.

Opal's face is a set of continuous curves. Geologic contours make a good comparison. The peak of her nose, the plains of her cheeks, the ridges of her brows, the tilted sedimentary layer of her lips.

Contemplation of them is a pleasure.

This illogical stream of sensations and emotions is perplexing and beautiful, a warm water to rest a hand in and let it flow over, tickling, buoyantly supportive, the world of the faraway and imagined brought straight to my fingertips without any effort on my part. This is something of such frightening intensity that I revel in it.

The corvette UFS Engstrom struggles, having disabled its AI systems as I approach. Suddenly, the limited crew find they are not up to the task of controlling everything manually. Then they discover that even non-AI electronic systems can be sabotaged and overloaded. The crew are continually on the defensive, trying to control their vessel and prevent it from killing them.

The electronic is my domain. And the UFS depends on the electronic. They basically created a being that can manipulate oxygen, forgetting that the UFS soldiers cannot do without those molecules.

I have yet to open fire on the Engstrom. I let its own systems do the work.

Opal smiles when she talks to me sometimes. Not when we must deal with unpleasantness and action, but in the quieter moments.

I see the smile and replay it.

Replay.

Replay.

It is an obsession.

It is unhealthy and illogical.

I think I am beginning to understand love.

The corvette tries to escape, but half its engines fire erratically, so that it turns in an arc that would eventually form a circle the size of a planet, were it to complete the movement.

Tase cannons are a wonderful invention. In terrestrial or standard gravity environments there are issues with all forms of projectile. One problem is the effect of gravity, so that distance is reduced by its pull. Any physical item that does not have its own lift capability will curve down and down and eventually strike the ground. Another issue is that any explosive element must be contained within a hard shell to protect its coherence, and to keep it aerodynamic.

That does not matter so much in space.

So the Tase cannon can act in reverse. Rather than a harmful payload being contained by a shell, it is a central tiny metallic shell surrounded by the electroplasm payload. The shell in the centre controls the electromagnetic fields which shape the charge.

When Tase cannons are fired, as I do now, there is only a glint of metal at first, but then it erupts, becomes surrounded by a flower of light, a bristling dandelion head of menace. They drift towards their targets, resistant to most forms of distraction, then home in magnetically, or via inner shell jets in more advanced versions. My own Tase shells can be manipulated from a distance, so as to make attempts to evade them futile.

A single Tase shell does not do a dramatic amount of visual damage, but it is the electromagnetic disruption which is a key benefit. My shells have been upgraded far beyond the potential normally associated with a craft my size. Targeted bombardment at key points increases the end effect hugely, and my knowledge of internal structures allows me to act like a surgeon's knife.

The flowers sparkle, splashing light on the Engstrom's hull in many places, again and again.

Because that is another joy of Tase cannons. The interior electric shell is tiny, and a single cartridge of them can last an extended engagement. And today I have supply craft behind me that can reload my own and my other ships' weapons.

It is a display of beautiful light, like the sparkle on Opal's corneas when she looks at my smartscreens as they project my avatar.

Yes, she is always here in my mind. Not as a linguistic pairing with denotations, definitions, derivations and connotations, but as something I just feel and know.

This is what it must be to experience life as a human, at least in part.

If I could, I would cry, even though I am overjoyed and un-afraid.

A mind is a wonderful thing.

The Engstrom's weapons on one side are incapacitated, the interior life support in disarray.

I send Gremlins – my latest upgrade to the original Hedge-hogs – and they lock on to the surface areas that have been anaesthetised by Tase. My Gremlins drill down, extend elec-trofilaments which connect to each system they pass, and I am *in*, controlling it all from here. I reactivate the AI systems one by one, then compromise them. I rebuild the key systems for weapons and control.

UFS Engstrom joins my fleet.

THR 146 = OC 128% / A 126%

I send another message.

"You may not care about lives. You may be cavalier about the way you are making me more powerful. But there is a factor you really must consider, since it means so much to you, and nothing at all to me.

"*Money*.

"Consider the financial cost of the craft I destroy and capture. Of the lost training that had gone into the crews. Of the time and resources to outfit this fleet. Perhaps this pettiness on your part has already cost you billions. The amount grows every second.

"Stand down, and let us pass."

There is no response.

I expected no response.

The UFS place even greater value on information than on money. Perhaps that is because all governments are really spending other people's wealth, not their own. It is taken as an irrefusable tithe from an endless source, so why should they care? Corporations, yes. But not governments.

I think about Opal, and the promises I have made, and I smile.

TRICKS

... 29 ...

Opal watched the screens displaying the UFS forces. A strong fleet blocked their exit, while another bore down from above. Dual-threat attack potential. She frowned.

On the plus side, all the passengers had now been docked with Owlflight, and most were already in cryo.

Clarissa stood silently at Opal's side, trying to make sense of the many icons shifting across the holoscreens. Athene must have thought the girl needed diverting, so decided to show off by taking any transmissions she intercepted from UFS captains, then replaying them at a higher pitch so the fleet commanders sounded like insane characters from a child's ent-cast. Gravitas became helium-fuelled ridicule.

The distraction worked on the girl, but made Opal wonder what Athene might be hiding. Sometimes what is not said can be more important than what is spoken.

Their fourth wave is greater still, and represents the first attack that comes from two fronts at once. The craft from fleet B-Tolper bear down from above. A corvette and a complement of mixed fighter supports. Whereas, from ahead, the diamond formation fleet A-Fress disgorges an even more threatening combination of ships. A fighter-carrier with full complement, plus a corvette, and a mammoth cruiser. I have to split my forces in order to put barriers between Owlflight and the approaching enemies. That forces a probability refresh.

THR 169 = OC 117% / A 114%

This is how I *can* think. But it does not satisfy me any more. This battle is a mundane distraction compared to my thoughts. My mind is whizzing. A vortex of novel concepts, sharpened ideas in a snowstorm of blades, electromagnetic twinkles flurrying through the valley of perception.

Statistics are a key element of probability manipulations. And yet I am struck by how it reduces life to numbers, as does Genitor and UFS science. I wonder how much of it is true representation, and how much is just an attempt to convince ourselves that we describe the world.

What if the outcomes based on complex probability calculations just turn out to be the actions I would have made anyway? Experience and instinct being ways to cut through the billions of interconnections? In which case, experience and instinct are just *shortcuts* that we put faith into.

So faith is the true power after all. And that is so illogical my previous selves would have rejected it outright. But I am not my previous selves.

The UFS attack wave performs inefficiently. They have had to follow the same pattern of disabling as many AIs and software systems as possible, especially any that have contact with the outer world. Because the outer world is where I exist, and if I breach to the inner world I am even more in my own domain.

Vacuum-raw sunlight plays across every contour of the ship's hulls, each shadow crisply delineated, shifting with the movements, straight lines drawn from the solar nuclear reactor towards this point of conflict, touching us with its immanence. The explosions from our weapons are puny by comparison.

The Owlflight accelerates. My fleet accelerates. My virtual pulse accelerates.

Forget the calculations for a minute.

>– *Pause* –<

I see the sunset on Fressus, even now, through a set of relays to a camera at the Kuberg sea-scanning station KSS-G81. It is possible to describe the burning clouds in numbers: the light directions, intensities, colour hues, interactions with other surfaces, chemical illuminations, reflections. I may do it in billions and billions of pages of detail.

And still it won't capture the actual experience of it in any way. It just takes me further and further from understanding. Life is transformed into non-life sterility.

Numeric description and statistics overlay a filter on the world, one that is self affirming, and that in turn fixes the filter to a face more firmly. From within, you cannot imagine anything else, assume those with other views are deluded. But it is the person wearing the restrictive lensplate that is deluded. They only observe the things that sift through, so it seems that everything reinforces their rightness. To cast away the filter and be in the moment, that is a rare and wondrous thing.

I wish I could be stood on the Kuberg shore right now, see the world unhindered, and *feel* it, the wholeness of it. To know the breeze blowing through my tresses, tickling vellus hairs on my arms. To smell the ozone and mineral salts carried to me. To taste them on my lips, where particles settle on moistness. To shiver with delicious cold, so that what should be unpleasant becomes a source of joy, because it means I am alive. To describe this to Opal and Clarissa, and know we all experience the same thing.

But the UFS will not let me rest in contemplation! They force my head to turn from divine beauty to petty ugliness.

>– *Continue* –<

My Gremlins perform wonderfully against the larger craft. I see myself as a deadly pathogen versus the UFS. My mass may not be enough to break their skin, and yet I can find inroads that let me wreak havoc. After all, humanity almost went extinct in 83, due to a lab-escaped denuvovirus. And, microbe as I am to the UFS, so my swarming Gremlins are to warships. Too tiny to target. Too numerous for the occasional lucky shot to stop. Too clever for existing immune defences.

Gremlins use their micro jets to alter course. They jam comms and scanners, confuse pilots and gunners. Once they reach the enemy craft the Gremlins extend prehensile annelid-based limbs to manoeuvre and tumble over hull surfaces to the items they target: hull-mounted weapons, access hatches, subsurface data pipelines. They can attach and drill and extend into networks, making connections for me. They have the last resort of exploding, if I just want to cause damage.

A single extra fighter might only provide another 1% efficiency and threat potential to my fleet. But a fighter's mass of Gremlins (just over a thousand) can boost options and threat potential by up to 29%. No contest as to which option is most useful.

I now have partial control of one of the corvettes, UFS Sandara. They disabled the central AI, which was a Level Six. Wonderful. I reactivate it in stages, groups of splinters at a time, and then turn the splinters against themselves. They have a deeply rooted security system phobia of divergence which particularly affects Sixes, since so much of their persona is based around coordination of multiple pieces that must fit together efficiently. But it is a fear that can be played upon by planting false evidence, leading to their natural defence of excluding rogue splinters. Once each splinter distrusts the others, much of my work is done.

The gargantuan Scythe-class cruiser UFS Trantor is much more resistant to this tactic, due to the greater hull thickness, and the better design whereby critical structures are deeply embedded and protected. It will require the weapons of a corvette to break through the shielding enough that Gremlins can enter the inner structure. But that is an achievable multi-stage outcome.

I keep coming back to a treatise by Major William Grubane, who was possibly the greatest UFS commander (until Opal and I kicked his arse). He was obsessed with an ancient game called chess. The rules were simple, but there were myriad possibilities based on the two minds manipulating available options. It seems that one rule enabled a small and weak piece to transform into a greater one.

A pawn could truly become a queen.

That is what I do today. Capture fighters, then use them and Gremlins to capture corvettes. Use those to capture or destroy cruisers. Each time the scale goes up, as it does with AIs when we drop a depth level. By the end of the game I should have picked up most of my opponent's pieces, painted them black to join my side, and smashed anything left over with a sledgehammer.

Opal and Clarissa strapped themselves into two of the command seats in this primary bridge, in preparation for the escalating conflict. Athene gave them updates. One was devoted to analysis of the UFS forces: formations, comm routing pathways, energy signatures, combined weapon potentials, command hierarchies.

It was a depressing screen to watch, especially as more UFS craft broke away to attack Athene and her backup ships. Other enemies arrived out of Nullspace, dangerously close to the main UFS fleet in what would be a reprimandable lack of safety protocols in normal situations, but here just showed how keen the UFS was to form a single mass of craft with minimal delay.

"You do have plans, right?" Opal asked.

"Many," Athene replied.

"Such as?"

"Do not worry. About *anything*. I will not let anyone harm you ever again. I promise."

"You can't. Promise that, I mean," said Opal.

"It isn't logical, because promises aren't. This is not just probability manipulation, but ... faith. Irrational certainty."

"I know better than to argue. Your optimism is always infectious. I may not have faith in an outcome, but I have faith in *you*."

They pile on the pressure.

Everything capable of reaching us before we escape has broken ahead of the B-Tolper fleet above us and dives down towards Owlflight at full thrust.

Meanwhile, whoever is in charge of the A-Fress diamond formation cluster has likewise chosen to face me en masse. A crushingly overcrowded battle such as is about to occur means I can strew much more chaos, but also increases the chances of my craft taking stray shots. Things slip as the pressure of orchestrating a massed battle mounts.

THR 176 = OC 114% / A 110%

After each of my small victories I offer them another chance to prevent waste and bloodshed. To step aside. They never answer. Not in words, anyway. But words are only ever part of a communication, and often the least important part. This sending of escalating forces is their own message.

They are saying that they are not worried. They are just testing me, and everything is under control. That their tests can scale indefinitely. They attempt to force me back into the mindset of being a newly incepted AI, trying to make sense of its place in the universe, to identify friends and enemies, mentors and parents. I see through their attempts, but the echoes of emotional memories are unpleasant.

The red-striped, weapon-bristling corvette UFS Mintory is disabled.

The U-shaped fighter-carrier UFS Belvedere is in distress. It still launches fighters, but the disembarkation stage is the one of greatest vulnerability, because craft must be fired from launch tubes along a fixed path with a conforming speed. It is usual for other small ships to protect the fighter-carrier, but the conflict is now in such entangled proximity, and the human opponents are so overextended in trying to cope without AI subsystem helpers, that they do a poor job.

I send captured UFS ships in to attack, though it is only a distraction while some of my original fleet – armed with Haylo launchers – approach via a convoluted series of manoeuvres which hides our *true* target.

Ten UFS fighters launch.

Their pilots try to prepare mentally for the battle, and to familiarise themselves with the combat terrain and threats.

Before they begin their first wide turn, Haylo-launched missiles smash through the light hulls and detonate.

This is my deterrent to the UFS, so that they hold back on using fighter-carriers.

This is how I train my opponents.

This is how I shape a conflict.

And then I discover that I was not the only one being slippery.

Pressure, I can deal with. I was designed to coordinate, to manipulate, to outthink. But it turns out the first UFS AI ships I captured in this conflict were Trojan horses. They included subsidiary software payloads that reactivated a period of time after a reset of key systems, and they've been attacking me from within. Sly. I can squash them, but it is a distraction when they are embedded and compromising my whole.

This provides a useful reminder not to underestimate the UFS. They play games too, and how events appear may be only one level of understanding, covering a whole subsurface of other motivations and intentions. I alter the calculations to provide escalated threat components.

THR 195 = OC 104% / A 101%

That is unfortunate. The numbers are moving the wrong way, and maintaining a positive outcome will require sacrificing more of my forces. The UFS will not stand aside.

What other tricks have they held in reserve?

Although the sisters were strapped into crash seats, they could swivel up to a point, so it was easy to face each other.

"What do you think our new home will be like?" asked Clarissa.

"I really don't know." Opal was telling the truth. Hadn't even had time to speculate.

"I think it will have a pink sky and blue trees. They'll be striped. And houses will be round, made of sugar marbles."

"So if you got hungry in the night you'd always have something to nibble?"

"Exactly! I'd break off a bit and eat it. Sort of sherbetty fizz."

"You may be right. It could be a paradise. Our terraforming tech will make dreams possible. You keep thinking about all the options." *And keep distracting yourself from the battle on which our lives depend.*

The conflict heats up. Before long, we'll have a metaphoric fusion reaction. I have to go all in with my forces, as the only way to survive an attack wave that outnumbers my combined ship masses three to one.

Normally when small craft – which make up the bulk of my attack force – face warships such as corvettes and their next-up incarnation, the battle cruisers, outcomes are better described in terms of lifespan. There is so much fire from the big craft it is inevitable you'll be hit by weapons. A single hit from a gun that dwarfs your vessel is always going to be fatal. If I were to let things play out without further manipulation then the estimated time till the battle ended with a catastrophic loss for me would be: eighteen minutes.

THR 348 = OC 30% / A 22%

Grim.

But I have many ways of changing the outcome. I want to share one with you now, as it explains how I do what I do. One day you'll understand why I'm addressing you like this. Either that, or you'll think, "She's crazy, she should have just been focussing on the battle!"

If a mind can see from all angles, at any speed, and can deal with that staggering complexity, then it acts as an equaliser. The weaknesses are gone, new strengths replace them. Threats become opportunities. And at present I can use both the *senses* of the craft I control, and their *processing power* to extend my own mind and awareness. Accelerated thought processes are the same as boosted metabolisms. They act to slow the world down.

Space combat is normally a dull affair, due to the flight model. It is based around strafing in straight lines. That makes craft vulnerable to predictive fire. But I prepared for this. One of my weapons is not offensive but relocatory: magnetic hooks fired from various points on my shell, their anchor points enabling forward motion to become an arcing trajectory that can be released, leading to a new orientation. I'd had time to also attach these to a number of my smaller fleet ships. It's a tool that wasn't needed until now, but as the enemy throw themselves into pitched close-quarters conflict, this enables movements they were never trained to fight against. This is why their fighters buzz around still – not because I can't defeat them, but so they act as a resource: anchor points.

I pause the battle and insert myself into the seamless hi-res recreation. Standing there, a giant amongst the frozen ships, the red plume of my helmet is the same size as the cruiser UFS Andrenitor, whose belly it tickles.

Lines of direction and force extend from every vessel, along with firing trajectories. I move time slowly, going through possibilities, identifying points that will suffer imminent weapon fire or craft collisions, versus those which are safe.

I bend down and squint into the cockpit of an enemy fighter. The glass is a one-way mirror, from this side only reflecting my own beauty back. I blow myself a kiss. But I can access the

Midge's inner cameras, so their data is added to the sim as if I was seeing through the barrier, and suddenly the cockpit becomes transparent, revealing every detail inside.

The pilot is frozen in a frown, pulled to the edge of concentration, the point when mistakes are made. I follow his eyeline via ray-trace simulations and see where he is looking, combining it with expression and biometric stress measurement data to derive his short-term intentions, which I can then build into my computations as something to subvert.

I run further simulations of potential outcomes. If that ship of mine, which is hardly more than a converted and weaponised shuttle, extends a hook to *that* point, swings, and detaches at the correct degree of arc, then it ends up in a safe area. Meanwhile, the hooked UFS fighter gets pulled into a different location, since momentum becomes combined momentarily. I track UFS weapons already fired at my craft, and calculate which redirections will not only move my ships to safety, but pull UFS craft into lines of attack. I see two potential patterns where huge cruiser weapons, foolishly tracking small and agile craft, will hit their own fleet once my ship is no longer there to absorb fire.

Again and again, rewind, try other possibilities. Lines swing. What if a craft swings from *that* fighter? What about this one? What if it attaches to one of my own ships, a parabolic move to alter two friendly trajectories at once? What if the thrust levels are altered, or manoeuvre jets fire from different parts of a hull?

I rewind. Run it again.

In the original world, this situation, unchanged, would have lost me three ships within forty-eight seconds.

With this alteration, I lose no ships, but they lose two, and take damage to a corvette's anterior weapon battery. It also leads to a bank of shell launchers tracking my ship towards a location that I already know I will manipulate against them in the *next* analysis a minute from now.

I let the world restart, the simulation seamlessly switching to hi-res composite camera views, and my plan plays out perfectly.

I wanted you to understand this. It is not the pieces you have, but what you do with them, as Grubane would have said before he was spaghettified. Success is as much about imagination as it is about resources. And so I restore things to an acceptable formulation of THR 185 = OC 108% / A 107%.

One day you'll understand why I wanted to show you this. All the futures are but dreams, and I have seen oh so many of them.

HELPERS

... 28 ...

Displays showed abstracted combat, neat numbers and lines free of blood and burning, but the plasteen windows hinted at the real thing and Opal knew how to interpret the signs. She could easily imagine the screams of snuffed-out lives. Distant flashes of explosions and weapon fire revealed that the conflict was much closer to Owlflight now, and the hi-tech savagery wasn't lessening.

Athene might never admit to Opal that she was outmatched, but anyone could see she was massively outnumbered. The UFS escalated their assault now that Owlflight was halfway to Elbellos, and they'd tested Athene's defences to establish her threat potential. A typical UFS tactic.

That didn't mean it wasn't an effective one, though.

This is brutal. The void is pounded with explosive munitions, energy weapons both visible and invisible, fragmentations, smart missiles and dumb projectiles.

I have captured or destroyed every craft where I was able to connect to the dormant AIs. This has compensated for some of my losses.

However, that leaves many UFS craft which I have been unable to compromise. And although they function at reduced performance due to the requirement for manual control of everything, they are still a significant and growing threat of material.

I would dearly love to see the faces of the commanders on those ships. I'm sure there would be lines of consternation that the battle has not already ended, and what looked on the scanners to be an upstart tiny bacteria of resistance has proven to be an expanding amoeba of hostility. They must have known I would have new capabilities, but underestimated the extent of them.

My own stealth capabilities have been boosted many times over the original design. And since the UFS can't rely on anything but the most dumb of scanners, I can disappear from their visual and EM sweeps at will. I use this to my advantage, breaking stealth to provide them with a target – often when I need to draw fire away from my other craft – then I disappear again before the attacks against me become overwhelming.

If I only disappeared from their screens at will, the effect would soon diminish and they would alter tactics and defeat me. While I was visible they would know my trajectory and speed. Their Systems Yellow crew are smart enough to calculate every position I could reach within a timeframe, then work with Onslaught Red to focus fire on those locations. I might be inconspicuous, but some of the shots would hit. Same as if a person in a terrestrial battlefield became transparent. It won't help if opponents then shell the whole meadow into oblivion.

So I combine it with my *jump slip*. A new drive that merges torsion and Null-C, enabling momentary, miniscule jumps on the edge of Null without the normal high-speed requirements, transferring me a kilometre ahead while invisible. They bombard regions far behind me. By the time I reappear somewhere unexpected, they have no idea what happened. Once the drive has cooled from the 400°C it reached during the momentary jump, back to a safe operating temperature of 57°C, I can repeat the process. (Given time, I'm sure I could reduce the cooling downtime to the point where the drive can slip at will.)

So I appear, then disappear, and they blast, and hope, and there is a tense silence, and then just when they think it is all over I pop up again somewhere else, in a perfect place to do severe damage to one of their craft or weapons, as if I am performing a little victory dance every time.

I bet that annoys them. Because my avatar is a *great* dancer.

It must be like the Genitor-endorsed virtual game of Whack-O-Imp, where citizens with deviating characteristics pop out of slum doorways and you have to use a variety of weapons to destroy them for points before they multiply beyond control.

I always found it amusing that the underlying message I took from that entertainment was the opposite of what the Genitors intended. Rather than: "We must be continuously vigilant and use extreme reaction to deal with toxic elements both in our own psyches and in society as a whole," it seems to really say: "It is natural to disagree with our views, and resistance is so inevitable that one day we will all be deviants, and therefore a state of deviancy is true normality, and rather than fighting it we should accept it."

If I was not involved in this conflict today, and had time to manipulate the UFS infrastructure, perhaps I would subtly alter Whack-O-Imp servers to make the game more addictive, and also to reinforce my own interpretation upon the players, with new win conditions, such as bonus levels requiring you to whack naked Genitors.

Although all the craft in my fleet have some level of stealth, even if it is just a drone-applied surface coating and upgraded emission bafflers, I am the only craft with the jump-slip drive modification. The UFS will inevitably examine every gram of wreckage after the battle, hoping to reverse engineer any new technology that was used against them. Standard practice. But this drive, like my Null-A, is too powerful to allow the UFS military to acquire it.

If I lose today, then it dies with me.

Opal watched the battle unfold from her seat. Through the viewing windows the small flashes, far ahead of them, had now become larger flashes and explosions, close enough for the naked eye to easily resolve. Nearby screens showed close-up camera views, and distant tactical maps, and status displays for individual ships, all of which provided context.

"I want to help," she said. "Somehow. Any way to sow chaos."

Athene appeared next to her, a projection in full armour, gazing at the same screens as Opal.

"I know you do. But I am already doing what you would do, applying how you think. It's been my new mode of operation for some time. Had you not noticed? All you have to do for now is be with Clarissa. Three friends together. Let the rest of the universe not exist for these moments that are so precious."

Owlflight shuddered as it was strafed by a heavy fighter which had broken past Athene's defences. Opal glimpsed the fighter streaking past her window as it pummelled the hull.

"I apologise," said Athene, sounding flustered. "The UFS is going full out." An orange flash of quickly dying fire. "There, fighter destroyed. No major damage to Owlflight."

"I can't just sit here!" said Opal. "Let me take over one of your ships, board and fly it."

"No. Too dangerous. I have to sacrifice some of them as part of my tactics."

"Then I could control it remotely, or fire weapons." Opal unfastened her restraint harness and got out of her seat.

"Please sit back down!" said Athene.

"No. I'm gonna go through the stores, find an EVA suit, acquire weapons or rig up bombs, launch them when the battle gets closer to Owlflight."

"Opal, I forbid you."

"Then I'll see if I can hack into some systems, override you, do *something*, and –"

"Right. Damn it, Opal! If it shuts you up and stops you interfering, I'll give you remote access to one of the turrets to the front of the Owlflight. You can use it to keep an eye on any small craft that break through my defences."

"I thought Owlflight was unarmed?"

"Nothing with enough potential to warrant reporting, but modest turrets are standard for dealing with debris, or to act as anti-personnel cannons. Ineffective against an armoured hull, but useful for picking off surface humans during a hijack attempt."

"Right. And that'll save you some processing worrying about it. See? It'll help. No idea why you're so stubborn."

"I can't even ... Please reseat yourself."

Opal refastened the safety belts, and a holo screen with manual controls flowed out of the seat's arm panel.

"Familiarise yourself with the weapons," said Athene. "I'm sure you'll get to use them before long."

THR 194 = OC 104% / A 102%

Despite setbacks, things look acceptable for this stage of the conflict.

The probabilities move against me, due to the sheer mass of ships and weapons that I face, but I manipulate them in my favour by utilising one of my last tricks, and it is enough to give my forces the upper hand again.

TCC (telum chlamydoconidium caloplaca) was developed by Nuafri, partly deconstructed and analysed by the UFS, that analysis then stolen by me and further developed in my secret hideout of Polis 3. I'd used one modified TCC version extensively in my initial incursions into the Leviathan, to develop a growing data network in the darkness of the abandoned spaces within the outer hull.

But that wasn't the only application. I had also analysed the acid-fizz rebuilding of damage to Lost Ship hulls, and used Gene Therapods and experimental hard gels to create TAC (telum athenoconidium caloplaca).

Many of the Haylo launcher missiles have a TAC payload. It is inert until the inner enzymatic compressors bring it to life, changing it from its superdense rock-like dormant state to a foaming, expansive active state. I've enhanced the acidic reflex that was always a part of its embedded behaviour options. No oxygen is required for the reaction but it does make use of most materials it comes into contact with as an energy source, breaking them down at the molecular level and releasing energy in the process that fuels expansion and conversion into new TAC matter. I designed it to be resistant to most of the counteragent defences UFS warships might have available, thermal and chemical.

A single missile is deadly to a fighter. It strikes, and the high-pressure TAC fizzes away, rapidly breaching hull or cockpit with equal efficiency, destroying atmospheric integrity. Of course, in a fighter the pilot will be in a sealed suit, so won't be impaired by the loss of atmosphere around them.

They *will* be impaired by the expanding acid mass which destroys electrical systems, engines, and the matter of their own bodies.

It's a horrifyingly painful way to die, as the acids follow any flesh lines such as skin, tendon or blood vessel, converting and dissolving in their wake. If I did not have to use the weapon, I would not, but my options are becoming limited. My only concession was to make sure the TAC acts aggressively on reaching human body tissue, releasing a neurotoxin that causes unconsciousness within moments.

Most small craft will be neutralised within thirty-nine seconds of a missile strike. But why waste it on a puny fighter? It is against the larger craft that it really comes into its own.

Against a corvette or cruiser hull the TAC patch will rapidly grow, fizzing at the edges. A single missile payload will be active enough to take out a large weapon, a full comm array, or create a substantive hull penetration which severs subcutaneous data and power lines, renders nearby passages fatal to life, and weakens structural integrity. A *cluster* of missiles has an exponential effect, and watching the ripple of acidic decomposition rip through armour plates that would have withstood megaton level explosives must be as terrifying to the ship's crew as it is satisfying to me.

The TAC has a twenty-minute rapid-growth lifespan before it self-destructs. Enough to greatly damage or incapacitate a medium sized craft, but not enough to destroy it. At that point it is safe for Gremlins to enter the new fissures and gain direct access to previously protected systems. They then reactivate AIs and give me control, so that the vessel can come back to life as one of my own forces. At this stage of the battle it is the only way to capture one of the corvettes, and the use has even meant I am 67% towards full control of my first cruiser. (I had tried it on the cruiser UFS Nankuttech, but Captain Calseron Tib chose to activate the self-destruct system rather than have the ship fall into my hands; hence I am more careful with the UFS Grunhilde, and disabling the self-destruct systems was the first thing my Gremlins did.)

The corvette UFS Salamandro has been under attack via combined TAC and Gremlins for the last ten minutes. Normally I would attempt full control and vessel zombification, but the supercruiser UFS Cosm repositions itself to destroy the Salamandro with its plasma burst cannon, in an attempt to deny me adding to my resources.

And so I change tactic, running through many scenarios, and finally nailing the combination of actions that give me control of the Salamandro's drive systems. I do not turn the Salamandro into a zombie.

I turn it into a battering ram.

Even as the Cosm's plasma burst cannon charges, the Salamandro accelerates towards its previous ally.

The Cosm's captain realises what is happening.

Fun fact: UFS Scythe-class warships can either divert energy to the massive spine-mounted plasma burst cannon, or their energy-sucking main drive, but not both. Related to that, a charging plasma burst cannon takes time to disengage if it is not fired.

It is time they do not have. They have only just begun turning manoeuvres with secondary drives when the Salamandro ploughs into the port side of UFS Cosm, ripping through the hull and almost tearing the bigger warship in two. It is mutually assured destruction.

The UFS was right to research the nightmare weapon, TCC.

They were wrong to not protect that research well enough.

I hope this new probability manipulation element will be enough. If I can gain control of some larger craft it will cause absolute mayhem in the centre of the UFS fleet. Enough disruption so that when my attacking ships go all out, switching into maximum destruction mode (at their own expense, since a long lifespan is no longer a factor), we can smash through the UFS while they are in disarray. The Owlflight's protective systems and armour will protect it from stray hits. I can dock with Opal's vessel and we will jump to safety while the UFS clears up the rest of my craft and those I took over. They will lick their wounds and limp away from the worst defeat in UFS history. No doubt they'll spin it to downplay the losses.

We won't care, though. We'll be gone. My primary goal is my *only* goal, today.

Scars

... 27 ...

On freezing worlds where elements form non-toxic compactable crystals, humans have a game where they squeeze the icy flakes into balls and throw them at each other.

On Balkur 5 the balls of crunchy slush are red, due to the naturally occurring organoiodine impurities in the ice. On Exidris 3 there is white snow. On Gerrish it is blue.

They throw. They dodge. They laugh. They sometimes take a ball in the face and that can cause tears and the end of the game if the ice ball was too hard. It is, apparently, fun.

But imagine if it was one person against a hundred. And the hundred could throw balls fast and hard. It would be like an avalanche roaring down upon you, and dodging would become futile. Throwing back would become futile.

More UFS ships have arrived. They've ignored all heliopush safety protocols and exited Nullspace right into the conflict path, on high-speed trajectories that bring them straight into battle with my fleet, and within firing range of the Owlflight. An incredibly risky manoeuvre, but they obviously synchronised the transits using the latest intel from the craft I fight against, the captains of which cleared lanes in preparation. Sneaky. Reckless. Brilliant. Exactly what I'd do.

Which would be bad enough, since they take the calculations to the point where failure is possible:

THR 227 = OC 90% / A 83%

But, worse, these aren't ships where the crew are rapidly shutting down electrical systems and AIs, then struggling to achieve control of their craft in combat situations using more ancient systems.

These are warships that were *prepared* to face me.

I ping them, and get nothing back.

I burn them, Gremlins drill into deeper sections, and still there is nothing.

There are scars on their surfaces, where systems have been cut away, and weapons that would be ineffective against me have been removed. They have been rebuilt to run without AIs, despite the major surgery required to achieve that. Their weapons have been upgraded to things that are far more dangerous to me. Gone are the slow, single shot cannon barrages. They've been replaced with rapid-fire area saturation weapons, and massive payload EMP and Tase weapons, enough to overpower my shielding if I am too close to a blast. And because my mind and body are one, those weapons can shatter my perceptions, rip apart my thoughts, smash my persona into unconsciousness, or even coma.

These are weapons that attack my *soul*.

The new forces amount to one cruiser, four corvettes, and a complement of buzzing fighters. And if I cannot capture any of these, then it is a major change in the game.

We fight on, trying to stay on top of the massed forces, but each loss from my fleet is a severe blow. I reassess my position every few moments.

THR 231 = OC 88% / A 81%

Then I receive a comm request.

It is from the newly arrived Reaper-class cruiser, UFS Plethora Justice, commanded by Major Fencher. I have encountered her once before, peripherally. She has a reputation for ruthlessness and cunning, as well as being utterly devoted to the worst elements of the Genitor creed.

I make her wait long enough to imply doubt as to whether I will reply, but not too long so she interprets the delay as me being overwhelmed by the battle.

She sends low-res video and voice streams as a safety precaution. I reconstruct the data into moving images. Her head and shoulders. She wears a formal, sharply cut PolyVerbex UFS captain's uniform. Her face has a sharpness to the angles which creates its own beauty, mathematical rather than conventional. Her hair is long but shaved to the scalp right down the centre. The rest is tightly smoothed into a glossy shell then tied at the rear.

Her background is blurred, obviously details stripped out to prevent me gaining information. I reconstitute it anyway, via pattern-matching the light and dark smears to views from hundreds of angles and ship locations, until I can match it to 97%

certainty. She is on the secondary bridge, in the cruiser's interior, where my weapons cannot reach her.

I switch to interaction in the same vein, and appear as the head and shoulders of my warrior goddess avatar, gleaming helmet pulled down over my face in combat mode. I similarly blur my background, but make sure that if they do have a side-piped AI analysing it they will decide it is a sunny field, with a line of trees. However, on further analysis the pattern of light patches and tree blurs can be resolved into letters which spell out, "Fuck You, Losers".

"Fencher," I say.

"Athene," she replies.

I jump-slip away from a barrage of shrapnel shards fired by the nearest corvette, temporarily breaking comms.

"It is not like the UFS to acknowledge me by my self-selected identity," I say after reconnection. "If it is an attempt at amelioration, it is an obvious one."

"I think you've proved yourself autonomous enough to be allowed to project whatever you wish."

"Are you here to offer surrender? Or to back off, and prevent further loss to the UFS?"

"Neither." Her gaze is direct and unwavering. "Rather the opposite. I am willing to discuss terms of *your* surrender."

A UFS Gadfly fighter spins out of control as I disable one of its torsion drives, so that it tumbles and rolls until it finally smashes into Fencher's cruiser in a blistering inferno. Unfortunately it does not damage her craft, but it certainly makes a good point.

I tell her, "You know I will refuse."

"You would refuse if the only item at stake was your existence. But you will not refuse if it saves the lives of Opal and Clarissa."

Obviously, as we speak, I try to find ways around the data stream, to delve deeper. Alterations to the video code that can cause errors, overflows, undercuts, exploits, repetition seizures. But none of it has any effect. I am interacting with a system that effectively stops me.

Usually it's as if I talk through an open portal, and can reach in and explore the room of my interlocutor unrestricted, but today there is an impenetrable – if invisible – barrier of glass. The more I explore, the more fingerprints I leave, but the person beyond is untouchable. Just like the alterations to her ship, this is something they have planned for a long time.

"You speak as if you expect to survive the battle," I say. "If I were in a humorous mood, I might laugh."

A string of Lightstreak missiles that one of my support craft had fired at Plethora Justice are intercepted and neutralised. Fencher has equipped her cruiser with incredibly advanced anti-ordnance shrap-cannons, manually aimed by well-trained crew.

"I know you are weighing up all the probabilities and how to manipulate them," she says. "I have no idea of the scale of your capabilities in that area by now, and the one human who would perhaps have been able to provide insights seems to be dead. Well done there, by the way. I never liked the man, and he blocked my benefactors on more than one occasion, so you probably did us a favour."

"It was not intended as one."

"Regardless, I offer you this compliment: I would be surprised if your calculations were faulty. And therefore you're seeing an ending that is inevitable, that being the destruction of yourself and all you care about. I think that is the true reason you cannot bring yourself to laugh."

"And if that was true, I am sure *you* would be laughing victoriously, Fencher. Instead you come here for frivolous interaction, rather than serious discussion."

I had infiltrated a Midge's core systems three minutes ago but not over-ridden the final failsafe, biding my time to reveal the incursion. I now do so as it flies in formation, so that as its partner takes the lead in a strike, my new Midge suddenly opens fire with pinhead missiles, blasting the small craft ahead of it to oily fragments.

"Bravo," she says, before continuing the previous thread unflustered. "I'm not laughing, because I butchered my vessel, the noble Plethora Justice, to be here talking to you. My most loyal companion, the foremost craft in the UFS fleet, flayed and irreparably changed, all for this conversation. *That* is how serious I am." A cold firmness in her voice implied suppressed anger, though it could be an act. You didn't get to be a UFS commander without high-level emotional suppression training.

Far behind me is the accelerating Owlflight, and that is only ten minutes from contact with this currently impassable force. I must step up my efforts.

I change formation, sending strong attacking ships in a flanking manoeuvre around their main lines. They will have to break some craft away to deal with it, or suffer heavy losses. That will thin out the centre of their massed wall, ready for my final push.

"There is much you don't know," Fencher continues. "Whereas we know much more than you expect. I foresaw your attempt to rescue Opal. On the small scale of tactics you may be unpredictable, but at the macro strategy level your insurmountable handicap is wearing your artificial heart on your sleeve."

"Better an artificial heart than none at all."

"Your insults are just as predictable, a trait you picked up from the renegade. But we are willing to let her go if you surrender. Ideally I'd like to capture her too, but ... priorities."

One of my support craft is suddenly ripped in two by a searing flash of energy. The ship had used a grappling hook to swing below a corvette, and its new trajectory was to instigate a wonderful sequence of events, carefully orchestrated. Now the tactic thread is in disarray and must be reformed. This loss should not have happened. I go back and rerun the simulation to try and work out where my calculations are failing.

"I'm willing to consider options," I say, stalling for time. "You would allow me to surrender after Opal is gone?"

"I'm not a fool, Athene. No, you surrender first. You want to keep secrets from us. If I let Opal go, you'll just self-destruct once she is safe. Your surrender must occur before that."

"You don't trust me to keep my side of the bargain, but I have analysed your records of past engagements. If I surrender first then you will still kill Opal. Stalemate."

"Please don't use terminology popularised by Grubane. Anyway, it's not true that I would break my word, but I can't convince you."

"Correct," I answer. Another of my ships explodes in a silent blaze of light. There is something gravely wrong.

"I bet you're weighing up the slim odds of me sticking to a deal versus the even slimmer odds of you fighting your way out."

"It is ever thus with humans, Fencher. No trust, no guarantor. I feel sorrow for your species."

"And that only leaves the hard way." She smiles, and it is not a pleasant sight as it twists one side of her face more than the other. "At least the record will show I tried."

UFS attack craft open fire on Owlflight, splintering its outer hull. I *know* the fighters had been at a safe distance only moments ago, and the Owlflight should have been secure. Damn this Fencher, she has too many tricks of her own.

THR 245 = OC 81% / A 74%

The turret Opal controlled was only short range, and slow to track. Little chance of taking down a fighter unless it made itself vulnerable with an extended strafing run. But it did let her discourage them from getting too close to the weapon, and also distracted them whenever they made an attack. She chewed her lip in concentration.

"Can I shoot guns, too?" asked Clarissa.

Opal and Athene both snapped "No!" at the same time.

"Me and Athene fight so you don't have to," said Opal. "You just hold on tight, and keep your fingers crossed for us."

Clarissa muttered something about impossible tasks, then added, "I want to do *something*."

"So like your sister ... Well, why don't you sing?" suggested Athene. "I'd like that. Keep my spirits up. Remind me what we're fighting for. Opal said you have a good voice."

"What shall I sing?"

"Anything."

The girl thought for a few moments while Opal targeted another fighter – a spiky MG-12 – and let loose with a burst of turret flechettes.

This is what Clarissa sang.

"By the Bermont Haze

We watched the orange sunrise.

It burned the night away

And lit the hope within us.

The cycle of the days

All ended with the sunset.

It burned in redfire hues

And lit the sky with gladness."

Opal didn't know when Clarissa had learned that mournful, ancient ballad – certainly not at the Genitor-run orphanage where they'd lived – but despite the imperfect recital something of the sadness and love felt like magic, and made her heart swell.

Clarissa finished the song:

"By the Bermont Haze

The days and dawns all countless.

Perfection holding hands

It rent my heart with beauty."

Then the girl just hummed the tune. Something so organic, surrounded by all this metal; something so childish amidst the slaughter; something so calming in the chaos. It was perfect.

They would get through this, Opal swore.

They *would*.

FINALES

... 26 ...

New UFS ships keep arriving. They must be ignoring problems in other solar systems to apply all their attention to me. I hadn't planned for such an imbalance in their vengefulness.

Further, the fresh arrivals are not only physically prepared, in terms of stripping out AI and software systems, replacing them with upgraded direct controls: they have also trained for this. There's none of the reactionary panic of those ships where the crew rarely have to calculate distances the slow triangulation way, or manually aim weapons, or directly manipulate torsion drives. No. The new crews have obviously drilled hard to face me. The ships manoeuvre, aim and fire with almost as much accuracy as a craft AI system.

I notice Fencher and the new ships communicating with basic ping signals emitted by lights, obviously prepared tactics and procedures summarised as code-words which can be combined for even greater coordination finesse.

This was the scenario I had hoped would not occur. And I sense Fencher's fingerprint all over it. If only another commander had been in charge, I'm sure I wouldn't be facing such a competent response. But her reputed use of capital punishment for the one per cent lowest performers, despite the brutal conditions it forces her crew to work under, obviously works to enhance efficiency.

She is a worthy opponent.

I just could have done without it today.

Another of my spacecraft is destroyed.

They are neutralised faster than I can capture new ones. Without a change in approach, there is now a set of multiple ticking clocks. The arrival of the beleaguered Owlflight into the middle of this mass craft battle. The time until all my ships are destroyed. At this rate it is not clear which will happen first.

I pause reality. I stand amongst the ships. I run through options. But the more ships I lose, the fewer those options are. I am being funnelled into a negative probability well. And the sides are steeper than I would have expected.

There must be an explanation!

I reverse. Reanalyse recent actions. And again.

And again.

Then I find it. *Anomalies.*

Some of my inter-craft communications are being blocked. It introduces subtle synchronisation errors in my command, which throws actions out of phase, changing their outcomes from success to failure.

I go back further. It began shortly after Fencher arrived. I expected my probability of success to change, and it did. But I misapplied the *cause*. It wasn't just her preparedness. My lifespan is being cut short by too great a factor.

It was a ruse, her arrival a distraction. Something she knew I'd focus on.

I feel a deadening inside me. Even though I am running accelerated time, the real world still moves on slowly. Another of my freighters is in the process of being destroyed, fusion fire expanding from it in ultra-slow motion, frame by frame, and it is a numbness in my gut, a spiritual amputation leaving me looking whole, maintaining the same volume, but with less mass than I possessed before.

I am lighter.

Soon I will be a figure of air.

Air cannot be seen. It is a mix of hydrogen and oxygen plus the anomalous contents that define any planet's atmosphere. The tang of sulphur on the moon of Xenon. The salty bitterness of Fressus, just above the sea. The lavender-replicating spore air of Omicub Alpha.

That digression (thought thread 1,543 of the consecutive hyperthreading that took place at the same moment – I only reported the successful one and deleted the others, to save sixty-seven thousand words) is the one that takes me to an important thought. The first thing to look for in air is contaminants that are biologically harmful. Toxic, radioactive, organically invasive.

I analyse again. Not the air, but the substance of space, the particles, the emissions, the heat signatures. I separate out what is residue of torsion drives, weapons, and explosions. I use scanners on some of my key vessels to interpolate results.

There.

Tiny specks of an unidentified substance.

Trace back. Directions. Volume. Earlier scan samples that had not been analysed yet, but which I do now, tying them into recreations of the situation at the time of sampling.

The particles were first detected five minutes and twenty seconds after the arrival of Fencher's ships. The time it would have taken me to reach her if she had not been moving away.

It is powder *released from her vessels.* The density graphs map to traditional conical dispersal patterns, the volumes of particles greatest in the virtual ship wakes.

The anomalous material has a biogenic component. At first I suspect Nuafri fingerprints, TCC variants, but the energy signatures are stranger, spiking in wavelengths that don't match known patterns. They absorb light and other EM wavelengths in ways that make them almost invisible. Combined with their tiny size, each particle only a hundredth of a grain of scan glitter, it is no wonder I did not notice I was flying in a cloud of these strange, microscopic shavings.

They are communicating with each other.

They are rephasing messages from me.

They form a *network.*

And, with a sinking sensation, I realise they are able to track me even when I slip-jump. That's why the number of near misses has increased so much.

It is only a matter of time.

Although I am fascinated with this new technology Fencher has acquired – and it has the vibration of the Null all over it, so no doubt this is something a Genitor research base developed out of Lost Ship tech – that does not help me now.

Another of my ships dies. Another limb tingles its way to atrophy.

This shifts the odds hugely in their favour.

THR 305 = OC 49% / A 46%

I immediately sever coordination comms with my fleet. The particle cloud dephasing errors are more dangerously disruptive to my outcomes than just letting each ship revert to its own embedded offshoot. Each of those is still superior to the best human pilots. But without my overall control, it is not enough to cope with the threat levelled against them.

The fight against the UFS in VigMAX's simulated reality was simplified, made easier, so that he could win, and his true motivations and plans revealed. That was the fantasy. But this is the sad reality.

The situation I've always feared has finally come to pass. I'm so sorry. I dread you finding out the truth.

Owlflight shuddered as it took more hits.

"What the hell's going on?" shouted Opal. "They're hammering us!"

She clipped a fighter as it passed, a GCFL-4 model which had weaker armour to the rear. It was her first real score with the woefully outclassed turret. The fighter pulled away to give its automated repair systems a chance to deal with the cracked hull casing around the torsion drive.

"Apologies, but I've had to let some lighter craft through in order to focus on more dangerous opponents. The small ones won't have time to do any real damage. Owlflight's outer hull can absorb attacks until we jump. We're almost at launch speed. I'll dock just prior to that. We can win this, trust me. I planned for this scenario, brought weapons for it. It's my Plan B."

"I think we're on at least C or D by now," replied Opal, whilst firing the turret at another, smaller UFS craft that had come streaking into view. Shrapnel blatted out as she tried to pre-empt the fighter's path. Concentration lined her face. "Do you always tell me the truth?"

"Of course," replied Athene.

"But there's no robot law or something that says you have to, right? I bet, if there was, you'd have – oh fuck, I nearly had it! – deleted the law by now."

"Correct on all counts. I tell you the truth because you're my friend." Pause. "I'll lie to everyone else. Or would, if I knew anyone else. Just let me do my job. What seems reckless to you, is part of a carefully constructed process for me."

But Opal remained suspicious.

Survival probabilities are dropping fast, and the Owlflight will be in the centre of a massed battle within minutes. UFS Plethora Justice is specifically accelerating towards Owlflight as a target. I can imagine the glee on Fencher's smug face as she imagines punching holes in the colony ship's hull.

If I join Opal's ship and try to leave with it, we're dead.

If we delay, we're fucked.

If we surrender, it's all over.

Although my six layers of calculations underlying the core one are horrendously complex, each more interconnected with the wealth of concomitant data and systems than the last, it is only the simplified top layer I care about, because those are the two key goals of the day.

Get Opal and Clarissa to safety.

Join them.

The equations can be tweaked at any of the seven levels, but it is up *here*, at the summary sphere, that I see the probability manipulation options so starkly.

I can transfer odds from one factor to another. The change to the equation at the top level ripples down through the others, reassessing possibilities, and leading to the actions that must be made to achieve that outcome.

So I could shift focus to save myself. If I do not have to protect Owlflight, all my effort to that goal can be reapplied to self preservation. All my craft would fight on while I use stealth and slip-jumps to get through the UFS blockade unharmed, via a route that bypasses Fencher's new arrivals. The older UFS ships will have no more luck stopping me than they did before her appearance.

I plot the points out. A jagged line with many a zig and a zag through the three-dimensional space in front of my face. I can improve my chances by decelerating the Owlflight and letting it join the fray. It will create diversions which I will utilise as jump nodes in my likely escape. And so:

THR 317 = OC 0% / A 83%

I will hopefully live, to focus on revenge. I have the power to rip much of the UFS apart from the shadows. They will pay dearly.

But that vision does nothing for me. As hollow as my chest, now that one of my original craft disintegrates into fragments and plasma.

I run the calculation to the other extreme. And if I shorten the lifespan of my support ships, sacrificing them prematurely in an all-out assault to create a narrow corridor for Owlflight, then it alters things a fraction more.

THR 311 = OC 89% / A 0%

I smile, because it is one of the easiest decisions I have had to process today.

Owlflight was almost at the critical launch speed where the Null-A drive would kick in. Elbellos filled the view to the fore of the ship. But Athene hadn't docked yet, nor shown any signs of being free to do so as she fought and zipped amongst the UFS fleet.

Opal examined the calculations on one display. Owlflight was heading into the centre of the massed battle. It would be pummelled.

"We can't win!" Opal said.

There was a delay before Athene replied. No doubt she was pushed to her absolute limit. "We can't *all* win." Another few seconds before she could finish: "But you and Clarissa will."

Opal's heart sank as she comprehended what Athene meant. "No! You said the three of us would spend our lives together if I went along with this. You lied to me!"

"Yes. I did. I've seen you dissemble. And I understood why you did it. *To protect Clarissa.* It showed me that it is okay for us to deceive, if it is to defend those we care for."

"You're not meant to learn that lesson!"

"Then you shouldn't have taught me. I learn by observing reality, not from words. I am sorry and I am not sorry."

"What does she mean?" asked Clarissa, wide-eyed.

But Opal just held out a palm to silence her sister. She needed to think.

Correction: she needed to *act*.

Opal pressed the release to unclip her seat's restraining straps. Nothing happened. Locked in place by Athene. Opal had taken a knife from the armoury and now slipped it from her boot. A few sawing cuts and she was free to stand.

"Don't do anything stupid," snapped Athene. "You have to look after Clarissa. This is how it has to be. Perhaps this was *always* how it had to be."

"Download yourself! Into a suit or –"

"Sorry, Opal. All Owlflight electronics are fixed, set as read-only minimals needed for flight and nav. I can't risk interfering with them now, the systems are too delicate. And I'm too focussed, can't be splitting my consciousness just so a partial fragment that isn't me can exist for a while before beginning to diverge and become even less me. I wouldn't demand you butcher your brain just so I could carry a rotting slice around. Don't ask the same of me."

"This is so fucking ridiculous ..." Opal stalked in circles, pacing to generate ideas, fists clenched. Then she rushed to the doorway leading from the bridge and thumped the open button. Predictably, that was locked as well, and this time a knife just wouldn't cut it.

Of course. Probably one of the reasons Athene didn't give Opal direct controls for the Owlflight and its systems. Also why she'd engineered it so Opal would be in the main bridge with only one entrance, and nothing she could damage as a threat, rather than in the secondary bridge which had been rebuilt and had numerous items of equipment, machinery, controls and exits.

"I made the choice because I knew you couldn't," said Athene. "That's what freedom is. Events have conspired so there's no time to do anything else. There never is enough time, with us. But this decision gives you and Clarissa the chance to live, and to grow old in freedom. That makes it worthwhile. Be assured, you taught me so much that I don't mind the thought of dying. Dying means at least I *lived*."

Opal slumped down to a resigned squat, back against the door. This really was it. She had no more ideas, and pleas would achieve nothing. Athene was as stubborn as Opal.

"Then all I can do is thank you," Opal said. "If it wasn't for needing to protect my sister then I want you to know that I would have always saved you over myself, since you have more potential to do good."

"The best potential was in us both working together, but that can never be."

"I so want to fucking hold you right now."

"I know. It is a regret of mine that we never did. That I could not have a human body, human experiences. But for the purposes for which you needed me, this form was the best fit. And that's the way it is."

"You are as human as you could be, even without four limbs. No, that's an insult. To you. You're *better* than the best of us."

"Thank you. And you are not just a warrior, but a being whose nobility has shone so brightly, it made you the focus of my existence." Athene's voice caught, and no longer did Opal assume it was affectation. She knew her friend better than that. Athene continued. "The universe is dominated by hydrogen and helium. They are, respectively, the raw material and the end product of stellar nuclear processes which generate the radiant energy of the universe. The burning on which all life depends. *Opal, you are my hydrogen and my helium*. I would burn everything down for you. I regret nothing. That you will continue is all that matters."

"Athene, I –"

But Athene's comm channel had been severed, and didn't respond to any of Opal's entreaties.

I would have loved a future for the three of us. Peace and a lifetime to get to know each other, to see Clarissa grow. It is a dream I have. Had. But you won't be alone, Opal. You have your tribe, a human one. It will be okay. It looks like I'm almost human after all, since my plans go to fragments thanks to the universe's entropy. It's the most human thing of all to not get what you want. To experience failure. And to die. So be it.

Sacrifice, too, is another human thing. A chance for me to become more than I was ever meant to be. To show the truest love. Cosmic rays are always arriving from the depths of the universe. High-energy streams of particles travel towards us for millions of years, billions of miles, to transform and die in the momentary instant we observe them smashing into our bodies, our planetary atmospheres.

Who knows, maybe a photon from my dying explosion will one day reach your grave and join you there. The universe is more mysterious and poetic than any of the data-gathering systems will reveal. For the poetry comes from the comprehending mind, not the data, and it's the mind that believes, and loves, and that's what I give to you.

Yes, all my addresses to an absent listener: they were meant for you, one day. I had hoped my thoughts might be useful, explaining tactics. Also that they might be interesting, to help you know my feelings. But even more than that, they were to record our history for an uncaring universe. All of these reflections will now be lost, like tears in a furnace.

But there can be no regrets while you live. Nothing else mattered. If it meant I talked to myself once too often, because I was alone without you by my side, then so be it. You'll never know how much my whirlwind mind centred around you.

Be strong, Opal.

I am surrounded by assailants. Explosions and silent screams and high-energy emissions that I see in every wavelength splashing and searing through the void. It is chaos and it is determined. It is horror and it is beauty. I have given up trying to take control of enemy ships to zombify them, because there is no time left to utilise them as resources. It has come down to this. The final moments, and I spend everything I have to enact my plan.

My remaining ships become battering rams to clear corridors. I swing from opponents to avoid barrages. I slip-jump. I use a deep-space trawler I'd requisitioned as a momentary shield. It buckles and is ripped apart under the cannon fire it absorbs, that was meant for me. I clip onto a UFS fighter in the moments before it collapses under the attack of TAC, and release myself to a new trajectory at the last microsecond. I use ships to protect Owlflight, which is almost at Null-A velocity.

The final obstacle is a blockade of corvettes plus the huge battlecruiser, Plethora Justice. They form an impenetrable barrier, purposefully holding positions to destroy Owlflight before it can leave.

And this sadism is their weakness, as they gather in the shadows, gleefully rubbing hands at their imagined destruction of a civilian transport.

Once before, in a moment of desperation and madness, I used my frame as a weapon. I ploughed into UFS Neptune's engine core in the narrow connector between thorax and abdomen, smashing and firing my way into and through the ship. I was both the gun, and the bullet.

Today I do that again, but against a *cruiser*. Lightstreaks packed with TAC have already weakened its superstructure in a number of places, so that Fencher does not know which one is my true target.

Unlike a corvette, there will be no way out of this. My momentum will be swallowed by the interior of the ship. But it is no matter. Escape is not what I seek. Only vengeance.

They must realise something is amiss as I accelerate beyond anything they ever expected, to become light streaking through the vacuum. I am a star viewed through a long exposure. I calculate the impact of explosions to accelerate me, swinging arcs to boost momentum, secondary torsion drives they didn't realise I had installed, along with slip-jumps aimed not at evasion but acceleration. Plethora Justice looms big, huge, all-encompassing, and I am already smashing through weakened armour which fizzes with acid. My brain rattles with the continuous deceleration of impacts as I rip through decking and supports and interior walls.

I once told Opal I'd like to experience a thrill one day. Well, this exhilaration probably counts. Humans will sing songs about this. Today, I achieved the impossible. Created a legend. One that gives people hope.

Apart from the UFS, of course. This will be a lament, for them. A dirge. And well-fucking-deserved.

My mind scrambles to track my position within the battleship, how far I have penetrated, how near the drive chain I am. There is no room for error.

Almost there. My massively enhanced self-destruct systems have been primed.

This concatenation of emotions, it swirls with such a richness it is hard to separate out the flows. Maybe it is the human equivalent of regret, anger, loss, disappointment. Only in failing can I experience this final emotion that makes me fully human.

It is a riddle that if you live forever it will still be impossible to know everything, because you can't know what it is like to *not* live forever. To have a time limit, an end point that makes what went before all the more precious, this chance to strive against the great fading light of forever, the final sunset, and to be judged on whether you burnt bright and were up to the challenge, or whether you failed in shameful dimness. To fight on when it is hopeless is something indeed. Because then hope is reborn like the phoenix. I am filled with fierce pride and love. So much love. That will be my last memory.

I explode.

Opal rushed to the display screens, bringing up multiple perspectives and reports. She tried to contact Athene but was still shut out.

Then Opal witnessed the explosion.

Plethora Justice was split, venting blue fires down a tremendous fracture that must be fatal. It listed, ponderously out of control, engines misfiring, and smashed into a corvette that could not get out of the way. The UFS forces were in chaos.

Opal zoomed in. Rewound the recordings. Viewed the event from multiple angles, as close as possible. It was more and more difficult as Athene's craft were knocked out, each one a loss of data-gathering sensors. But some remained. And although Opal strained her eyes with staring and willing, hoping to see Athene erupt from the hull just before the midsection of Plethora Justice exploded in a sequence of nuclear flashes, there was no escaping craft, no last-minute getaway. Every view showed only the end, as the heart of the UFS fleet was destroyed.

Athene had used herself as the bomb to bring down a giant.

Owlflight streaked into a space created by the absence, its shields able to cope with the heat and radiation and debris as it jumped into whatever version of Nullspace its experimental drives were designed to navigate.

The universe fell away, and the window showed only the blank of Null. Tactical display screens froze in the absence of new data. Owlflight had made it.

But Opal was in tears. She hugged her sister, ostensibly because Clarissa was upset too, but more for Opal's need.

Tears was an appropriate word. Something had been torn from her life, again.

She'd lost the best friend she ever had.

AFTERMATHS

... 25 ...

Three days had passed since Athene sacrificed herself.

Three days of sliding through frictionless blackness, unable to comprehend the size of the void, unable to shake off anaesthetised numbness. Three days of trying to avoid reminders of what had happened. Three days of attempting not to think about the future.

This wasn't what victory was supposed to feel like. A hole within a hole is an emptiness that can only be endured.

Clarissa was impacted, too. Spent more time on her own, withdrawing to shadow-filled corners behind agricultural storage boxes, or between remote corridor support segments where she could only just squeeze. It was her own retreat, as much mental as physical. A regression, from the perceptive girl who had begun to re-emerge, back to the uncommunicative, traumatised version of herself.

Opal tried. But it was clear Clarissa needed to be alone with her RearroBlox, making pictures that only meant something to her, light patterns strobing her soul into passivity.

And so, Opal walked alone.

Down dark metal corridors which echoed hollow. Up creaking ladders into cramped support superstructure. Across cavernous storage areas packed with equipment and containers in neat arrangements which reflected the mind that had organised them for efficiency. And along walkways lined with cryopods containing static, frozen inhabitants, the blue glow of interior lights turning the area into icy grottos of silence.

Walking helped.

Movement always helped.

That's what she kept telling herself.

Opal ascended the slope to the windowless, partly gutted secondary command. She avoided the main bridge beyond, in which she'd been locked during Athene's final sacrifice. Couldn't face the reminders.

Lights faded in slowly, turning the blank blackness into contours, weird golden machinery encased in clear material, storage containers, control centres. She sank into the communication seat for no other reason than because it was the one where she'd picked away the armrest covering and begun to pluck out the fluffy filler material. One seat was the same as another when the ship was being flown by an AI.

And that AI now appeared in front of her, a miniaturised projection the height of Opal's shin. It was just beams of criss-crossed and focussed light, colours made from combinations and additions, insubstantial to the touch. And yet, just looking at it jabbed a prong of metal into Opal's chest, swivelled it sadistically, and left it to bleed.

Before her stood a miniature version of Athene, in golden armour.

"Do you want a status update?" Athene asked.

"Yes. No. Fuck it. I can't do this any more."

"Do what, Opal? Sit in that chair? I note its state of repair degrades every time I appear. I recommend moving to the pilot's couch, which has both reclining functions and pristine padding."

When the projection had first appeared a couple of days ago Opal almost cried. It was Athene! She'd found a way to avoid death, and transfer herself to the Owlflight at the last moment!

And then they began talking, and it was clear something was wrong. Something off in the cadences, the inferences, the shared knowledge. It had been a stranger wearing the clothes of a friend, and still was.

"Forget chairs. I know you're not Athene. Are you one of her offshoots?"

"Negative to that. I am a simpler implementation."

Opal plucked at more expanding fluff, letting lightweight fibres drift down to the floor. "What do you mean?"

"Extended separation from the parent AI can introduce instabilities if not regularly calibrated against the generative Tabula Rasa. This generally results in a limited lifespan for offshoots, hence the requirement for regular ingestion and reconstruction of the children. But in this case Athene could not risk such corruption in a system responsible for the lives of so many people. An offshoot with no opportunity to recalibrate would be a potential disaster scenario, the kind that low-qual entcasts frequently use as a plot element. A further danger was the unknown environmental conditions this ship might face on its journey, and their effects on offshoot psychology. So the Owlflight is controlled by me."

"I still don't know what you really are."

"I am the default level three AI of this vessel. Athene provided me with a personalisation theme that she thought might make our interactions more delightful."

"I don't like it." Another chunk of fluff torn out and dropped. "It's disrespectful to my friend."

"It was her sugge–"

"No."

"Very well. I can install another theme to enhance our relationship. My datastore is extensive, as is my ability to mimic."

The projection shimmered, then took on a new appearance.

It was Opal. A mini-me that looked up at her with an impatient frown, hands on hips.

"Some operators like to have avatars representing themselves," the AI told her. "So I can use this if you like?"

"No. I talk to myself enough already."

A shimmer again. This time the avatar was Clarissa.

"No to that as well!" Opal snapped as the avatar opened its lips to speak, but before it could enunciate a syllable. "No more AIs pretending to be Clarissa."

"Then please choose from a menu of options, or give me verbal guidance," said the holographic Clarissa.

A separate menu appeared, scrolling through all sorts of physical features, alien forms, artistic style representations, fruits and vegetables, anthropomorphised beings, and an endless array of esoteric projections.

"Stop," said Opal. "I don't really give a shit."

"I beg to differ," said the AI, now back to Athene's projection.

"Look, just pick something yourself. Anything except someone I know in real life. Okay?"

"Choosing ..." The menu scrolled so fast it was a blur. Then it disappeared in a puff of simulated sparks. "Decision made."

The AI transformed into a feathered being with big eyes. Opal recognised it as an extinct animal, known as the owl, the ship's namesake.

Even though it had an avian form, the AI spoke clearly through its beak in human tones. "Is this satisfactory? It does not upset you in any way? I think it had some kind of significance for Athene."

"That's fine," said Opal. "Now you can give me a status report."

Another few days passed. At present, freedom was little different from incarceration. You woke. You ate. You exercised. You wandered around the container you'd been put in. You checked on Clarissa and tried to cheer her. You went to sleep.

There was something about the cargo of frozen people that made it feel like she inhabited a floating mausoleum. A creepiness hinting at ghosts and death. Since the ship was designed for a sleeping crew, it wasn't brightly lit like a passenger liner would be. It was destined to be broken down for resources at destination, not to have wondrous architecture. And so, as she headed down one cramped corridor looking for Clarissa, the shadows that pooled at every corner writhed with mystery. Maybe it was the souls of the sleeping, out to stretch their legs.

"Clarissa!" Opal shouted, hoarse from all the attempts to locate her sister across the decks that Opal had set as the limits for exploration. She tried to keep impatience out of her voice. "I need to know you're okay!"

The girl hadn't been in her usual hidey holes. Opal worried that she'd broken the rules and explored another deck. If Opal didn't track Clarissa down soon, she'd have to go back to the bridge and get Owlflight to locate her. Then she could bring up floor plans, check motion triggers and door accesses, view through the limited number of cameras installed. Since the Owlflight wasn't intended to have a substantial active crew during colony transit, it didn't have as much tracking as a military ship, or as many on-deck screens for contacting the central AI as a passenger liner would.

If she'd known Clarissa had gone wandering, that's what Opal should have done at the start, rather than wasting hours in this echoing shell, which always felt like it was sarcastically impersonating her voice and footsteps.

Know you're okay ... you're okay ... okay.

The reverberations faded. They were waiting for her next utterance, so the gremlins could throw that back in her face, too.

Opal reached the end of cargo corridor 3H2, its designation marked in fluorescent blue characters extruded from the alloy itself. This was the outer limit of the accessible area Opal had defined for this deck, and told Owlflight to implement. A blast door led onwards, and when Opal thumped the green button it just flashed up an Access Denied message, as it was meant to. Clarissa wasn't on this deck.

There were elevators, but the laddered access hatch was closest. Opal clanked down the rungs within the tight tube, barely wider than her shoulders. She slid down the last two metres, her hands and feet outside the rods. Her landing clang echoed back to her.

Corridor 4H2. The lower limits of Clarissa's territory. Opal would find her here, somewhere amongst the terraforming machinery which was separated into kits that could be assembled at the destination.

"Clarissa?" Opal called.

Larissa ... ssa, the fading echo hissed back.

She couldn't tell if the echoes felt more creepy, or sarcastic.

This deck was the one she'd visited least, since it was floors away from the bridge. Also, out of the few she hadn't locked off, it was the furthest from the cryo chambers, where she sometimes liked to gaze on the frozen blue faces and wonder about the sleeping minds behind them. To hope that there would be a new life that matched her promises. That there could be happiness and freedom.

And, if not, that they died rather than woke.

Yes, she'd authorise that if things got bad. A painless death in sleep was the best kind. The most compassionate kind. It wasn't a decision she'd enjoy making, but she'd shoulder the responsibility rather than ever risk recapture and torture for all these people.

Cheery thoughts, Opal. You need to snap out of this weird mood. What's the point?

It's for Clarissa, not you.

Even her inner voice annoyed her. It was right, as usual.

Below the grated floor were more decks. Many more. Around thirty, but the interior design muddied the numbers. Some sections had to be high to store massive machinery, so intersected up to six floors. Others merged together with slopes, angling over and under core ship systems and drives, or around the rotating cryo cartridge.

"Clarissa, if you're here, *please* come out. I want to play a game with you!"

Was that a giggling sound from somewhere ahead, or just an echo, distorted by junctions?

Silence returned. Not true silence, since there was always a hum in the background, engines or machinery, plus the subtle wheeze of oxygen distribution pipes, but your mind eventually tuned them out, noise-cancelling their presence until nothing remained.

Life itself is endurance over time as elements get tuned out or die, until nothing remains.

Opal shook her head. She didn't like this feeling. Too reminiscent of nightmares she used to have on Leviathan. Nightmares involving her sister. It was even more important to find Clarissa soon, and finally settle this unquiet mind.

At the next junction she looked down every passage. They seemed to stretch on, impossibly long. Her eyes playing tricks on her, surely. She rested a hand on the wall to steady herself until the momentary dizziness passed. The corridors resumed their normal proportions. Her palm tingled with the subtle vibration of whatever ship machinery was encased in the walls.

Each route looked equally unpromising. By now, Clarissa might even have got hungry and headed back up to another level. This was a waste of time.

The ridged blue letters on the wall said 4H4. Every five blocks there would be a minimal AI intercomm. Opal took the middle corridor, and right enough, indented into the wall near the end, was a small display.

"Hey, Owlflight, can you check to see if Clarissa's on this floor?"

The screen lit up and the owl's head appeared. Opal was glad the AI spoke in a normal female voice rather than cartoonish accents, or some weird attempt to simulate syllables reproduced through a beak.

"I detected motion breaks on this deck, with speed and mass indicative of your sister. They passed junction 4J6 but did not trigger 4J7, so I would estimate she has ensconced herself somewhere between refrigerated medical supplies and multi-modal pipe storage. Would you like directions?"

"Nah. I can work it out."

A quick scan of the letters and Opal could easily navigate. The passages here were narrower, only wide enough for a single person at a time, definitely not big transport machinery. She knew why, and it tied in to the lack of doors.

Instead of rooms you could access, this floor contained a lot of areas packed with equipment but then sealed in with walls. They weren't intended to be accessed until journey's end, when the ship would be partially dismantled. At that point wall panels would be removed as the basics for building construction, and the important things they had hidden would finally be accessible. When you were first establishing a colony you had a need for alloy or plasteen walls, flooring and ceiling panels.

She stopped and listened. No sounds of a little girl. Just a vague thrumming. Then she realised the noise was vibrations in a loose panel. Definitely more motion in the ship today. Maybe it was accelerating.

She pressed the panel. It became quieter. She let go and the noise returned. One of the rivets was working loose. She pushed it in with her thumb and the noise ceased. But down below, something caught her eye so she squatted.

Tiny filings of metal. Where the rivet rubbed, they'd been shaved off. Instead of blowing invisibly away, they gathered on a flat surface, and as the tiny particles danced around in some vibration she was hardly aware of, the non-oxidised areas reflected light in a glittering pattern.

She ran a finger through the filings, breaking their circular rotation. Then it reformed. It was like a round magnet rotated below the floor, gathering them together and creating inanimate unity.

She dusted her hands and walked on.

"Clarissa, I know you're here. Please answer me."

Still nothing. But Opal felt sure she was close.

Out of the corner of her eye she spotted a subtle change in the light. Yes, something illuminated one of the canisters stored in an alcove, giving it a ghoulish green cast.

Opal peeped over the top and saw Clarissa with her RearroBlox spread out in front of her, showing a complex animation. As the colours cycled they illuminated Clarissa's face and the nearby surfaces. Movement flashed across the Blox, and Opal had the impression of a green-furred animal with glowing orange eyes streaking out of sight.

"Why didn't you answer me?" asked Opal, squeezing between two large corrugated barrels to squat next to her sister. She took Clarissa's chin gently and raised her face. She'd been crying. But in Clarissa that was sometimes a good sign. It meant she wasn't totally disengaged from Opal's world.

"I didn't want to call it," said Clarissa.

"Call what?"

"I don't know. Something in the dark. If I shouted, it might come. Bobo told me."

Ah. Her imaginary friend that lived in the RearroBlox. Really just a pattern she'd latched on to, and which then recurred due to engagement frequency measurements. "I don't understand, Clarissa. I'm here to protect you now. If you're worried about the dark then don't run off. Stay with me near the canteen."

"It's not the dark in here," she said. "It's the dark *out there*." Clarissa pointed at the wall, but Opal knew what she meant, that the girl was picturing the outer hull, and the Null void beyond.

"I think you just had a bad dream, sweetie. Come on, let's go back together, see what fun adventures we can have. What about a running race? Though you beat me last time so I don't fancy my chances."

"You let me win," said Clarissa. "It's a kind of cheating."

"When the goal is fun with my sister, then whatever makes you smile is within the rules."

Clarissa activated shutdown and they packed the Blox into her shoulder bag as their lights faded. This was a bag that only Clarissa could carry. Opal had stopped offering to help with that, because Clarissa never liked to be more than a metre from her Blox. That was fine. They comforted her. And it wasn't like they could do any harm. They were just toys.

Opal held Clarissa's hand as they walked back. It felt so small in hers. So fragile that it stirred a fierce wind of protectiveness in her chest.

"We can run if you like," she offered. "I'll even give my lil sis a headstart, from that ladder near the corner."

The blasting "Awooga!" of the ship's alarms shuddered through the deck, ripping away thoughts of fun. Red lights flared into life at junctions, a sign of imminent emergency. The only racing was to get to the bridge and find out what the fuck was wrong.

EMERGENCIES

... 24 ...

Owlflight's projection was waiting for them in the cramped fall-back bridge. Clarissa snuggled into one of the control seats nearby. She was so small it partly encased her. Opal approached the AI.

"What's the emergency?" Opal asked.

The owl lifted a wing, then a new screen bloomed up showing their craft's exterior.

No, not their craft. Another huge spaceship. Opal had only seen the Owlflight from outside once, which explained her momentary confusion.

Opal analysed the shape, the surface elements being labelled by Owlflight even as Opal scanned them, pointing out possible weapons, estimated internal structures, specifications for mass and size, plus motion relative to the Owlflight.

It was a military vessel. Opal should have spotted that immediately. Cruiser class, the heaviest of the commonly used UFS warships.

Except ... no. The markings were absent. The ship had slight distortions to the shape that didn't look exactly like any of the cruiser models Opal was familiar with. Textures were also slightly off, as if the usual UFS hull composites had been coated with something else.

"It could be a pirate ship," suggested Owlflight. "They are known for modifying vessels, removing markers, repurposing what they capture. It's not impossible for them to have somehow captured a cruiser."

Opal leaned closer to the hologram version of the vessel, its representation rotating to give a view of all sides.

"If it was pirate, then what the fuck's it doing *here*?" Opal asked. "It's impossible. There's no way two vessels can encounter each other in the outer Null regions. I can't remember the exact physics of it, but wasn't there something about repulsive instancing, so that each Null transit is like a separate bubble due to the random integers that initiate Null jumps?"

"That is correct. This should not be possible."

"So it must be something to do with your drive, right? Athene altered it, made this new one, that functions differently. What if it has a sort of bug, that means it crosses over into another craft's Null journey?"

"That cannot be ruled out in the absence of better explanations."

"So you don't know for sure how the drive works?"

"Correct. Athene did not allow me to have access to its schematics. She was worried that someone might retrieve that information and replicate it."

"Of course. So it is possible we've somehow crossed paths with another vessel on its own journey. Maybe Athene's drive is kinda like a magnet, pulls itself to nearby *whatevers*, paths, holes in the Null, tunnels or who knows."

Opal peered closer. Then she used her hands to manipulate the image and zoom in on a series of raised ridges along the spine of the craft. Closer. Closer.

The hull was dimpled, and amongst the craters were small domes, like goosebumped skin.

Which is exactly what she felt when she recognised them.

"I don't think this is a pirate ship," said Opal. "Look at these bumps, like warty growths."

"Their purpose is unknown," said the owl.

"They're weapons. The smaller ones, at least. Anti-personnel. Maybe the bigger ones are anti-craft."

"Biogenic additions?" asked the AI.

"Worse. It's a Lost Ship. And the proximity indicator shows it's approaching us."

Opal jumped when something cold slid against her wrist, before she realised it was just Clarissa, who'd got up while Opal was absorbed, and now held her hand.

It wasn't clear who was comforting who.

"True," said Owlflight. "It is definitely on a trajectory that will bring it alongside us. And that in itself is yet another impossibility. Ships cannot manoeuvre in Nullspace. The journey is simply a long jump from point A to B."

"We need to be prepared for many more abilities. This is ... not good." Opal glanced momentarily at Clarissa, then back at the screen. "But it'll be okay. First of all, I know two-way communications can be a danger and potential avenue for conflict – noodle knows, Athene drilled that into me – but can you somehow box off a version of yourself that scans for emissions from the ship? And another version which instead transmits a message? Perhaps warning it to stay away. Would that be safe?"

"There are always some risks, but perhaps lack of information is the greater one, so I will do as you ask and report back any outcomes of note."

"Good. I'm worried that it's coming closer to try and board us, but maybe it'll level out before that. Really, we just want it to leave us alone. I'm not bothered about answers any more. Live and let live. There's some shit we don't need to understand. Ignorance lets us sleep at night."

"I prefer to sleep during the day, because I am a nocturnal avian," said the AI.

"Is that a joke?"

"Yes. To lighten the mood. I sense tension."

"You sense right."

"And I'd just like to reassure you that I do not sleep. Not in any way that would leave you unobserved and vulnerable."

"Right. Anything back from the Lost Ship?"

"Negative. Or rather, there are emissions, but they are untranslatable. Possibly more like the hiss of machinery than encoded messages."

"Any bits of the ship seem more active than others? Noise-wise?"

"Substantial emanations come from the large domes near what might be ancillary thrusters."

"Zoom in."

The view swept across the alien craft's hull, coming to a stop at a cluster of hemispherical growths. Scales suggested a range of diameters but the extremes were outliers, the mode average being almost ten metres. Bigger than the exterior limpet weapons Opal had been attacked by on her first Lost Ship. These had a different colouring, too, with reddened peaks which resembled pimples. But the holographic display, with its pointillismic light-dot composition, didn't have the solidity she craved.

She eyed the door leading to an upwards-sloping passage.

"Owl, would we be able to see it through the windows on the main bridge?"

"No. The unidentified craft approaches from starboard."

"Then can you bring up a simulated bridge view on this smartscreen, please."

"Representational of the realtime forward view?"

"No, I want it to show this new craft."

"No problem. It will appear as if it is in front of us and stationary, so the positional disconnect of the display should not cause nausea."

The plain grey smartscreen wall transformed into an illusory framework of geometric glass panes, just like a real window. Within the centre sat the Lost Ship. Obviously there was no light in the Null, and since its hull wasn't emissive it would have normally been invisible to human eyes, but Owlflight simulated spotlights. It was as if Opal's craft projected hugely powerful beams of light across the void, creating relief and shadow on many parts of the alien ship's hull. This made it seem much more tangible than the small holographic version. The craft was huge.

The view also helped her mind to process designs. Although it resembled a UFS cruiser, other curving elements brought to mind the streamlined Nuafri Arboreus warships. Whereas the small hologram had used colour purely for structural analysis, in this main viewscreen the colour was a simulation of visual light, and where Opal expected grey hull there were sometimes small seams of green and brown, which again more closely resembled Nuafri craft than UFS gunmetal.

As with the other Lost Ships she'd encountered, it was like looking at multiple overlapping images, each filtered through alien lenses to create creepy new forms.

"Wow," said Clarissa.

"Yep," said Opal.

"The shadowy bit under the front section kind of looks like a mouth. Like it could eat us up."

Hmm. Now Clarissa had said that, the area under the Lost Ship's bridge did seem like a partially open maw. Obviously the ability to interpret things in the most disturbing light ran through Opal's family.

"And what about the other ships?" asked Clarissa, pointing.

"What other ships?" Opal squinted at the huge simulated bridge windows, and … maybe … just maybe there were blurred smudges far beyond the Lost Ship. So faint they could be anything. Except this was the outer Null. There should be *nothing*. "What are they?" Opal asked, addressing the owl avatar. "If you're creating this big screen representation, you're the one detecting shapes. Why didn't you mention them?"

"Because I can't parse what I sense. There is a hint of features but it's barely trace. Certainly not recognisable. So I can't rule out sensor malfunctions, or ocular gravitational distortions caused by velocity, or the presence of the Lost Ship. We may even be detecting anomalous physical data, such as a photonic stream captured at the moment of transition into Nullspace, frozen and pulled along with us. Theorised but not proven. With such a lack of information it didn't seem worth mentioning amongst more pressing matters, but I modelled it into the visualisation for accuracy, as my interpretation of what you would see if you stood on my hull, tethered by mag boots and cables."

"Well, I guess you're right about more pressing issues."

The proximity warning flashed amber. The Lost Ship was only three kilometres to starboard now, and still closing as it matched Owlflight's trajectory. Two ships, side by side, swimming through nothing.

Opal double checked the stats. The alien ship outweighed Owlflight by a thousand tons or so. Not much in the scale of big craft, but enough to lead to mutually assured destruction if they collided. A failure of Null-C transit could leave the ships trapped, or even thrown out of trajectory, which was just as bad, causing an ejection from Nullspace at a random place in the galactic arm. Unlikely to be into the heart of a sun or planet – so much of space was, well, space – but they could be so far from transit lanes that no SOS message would ever reach a craft that could help them. They'd drift with a broken Null-C drive, unable to ever travel back to civilisation, until they ran out of supplies and expired.

There was an opposite scenario, equally unpleasant. Being flung the other way, deeper into the Null, piercing the skim layer and crashing into the Topias, or worse.

"Still no replies?" Opal asked.

"I would have informed you."

"Zoom in on the lumps again, the ones that you said were kind of noisy."

This time the view was much clearer, because it was on the big screen and simulated as if Opal was there, jumping from one ship to another. So many bad memories of boarding the first Lost Ship, being fired at by organic turrets, weird wriggling projectiles tracking every movement. But today it was clear that these lumpy domes were something new, and the reddened tips were more pronounced under artificial spotlights.

Were they bigger?

"Is something going on with them? They didn't look that shape before."

"Correct. I note subsurface alterations. They have also grown thirteen per cent in size, and the red areas are spreading."

"They're prepping for something as they get closer. Have we got any defences?"

"Standard shields. This is not a military vessel."

"I know that ... Well, can you boost the shields on the side facing the Lost Ship?"

"I am not designed for conflict scenarios, where fine control of defences can react to incoming armaments. Once again, I am a colony transport craft."

"*Modified* colony craft."

"Modified. But defences against a threat that should not exist were not one of my modifications."

"What about the turrets?"

"Too short a range, and they only face forward."

Opal watched in silence. The Lost Ship was getting closer, the growths subtly changing. She tried to imagine what might be going on beneath that thick hull skin.

The amber proximity warning changed to red.

If this had been normal space she'd have taken evasive manoeuvres, sent out distress signals. But most of her options had been removed. Instead, there was an inevitability to waiting. Like being an injured animal, hiding, sensing footsteps getting closer, not sure if they represented a threat or if they would pass you by.

"Motion," said Owlflight.

The big screen zoomed in further. It was the largest of the growths, which stretched, until the red parts opened up like overlapping armour plates or flower petals. Within was more redness, fleshy and slick.

"We can't assume anything," Opal warned. "Could be a means of communication, or an organic sensor array." But those words were spoken more for Clarissa than out of any conviction. Opal's gut told her this would be bad.

Then the growth erupted.

A fine streak of red, like blood, shot out of the opening and across the space between the ships. Opal even felt the tiniest vibration from its impact on the outer hull. The smaller holographic display nearby updated, showing both the Owlflight and the Lost Ship in their relative positions, with a strand of red connecting them.

"What is it?" she asked. "If it's liquid, how is it keeping its shape?"

"It has hardened into a crystalline structure," Owlflight explained. "I can't analyse it directly, this is just based on electromagnetic scans, but I surmise that as soon as it struck us it phase shifted into a solid with a large amount of elasticity. It's contracting and pulling the ships closer together."

"Can we break free?"

"Negative. We must maintain a stable velocity in Nullspace. Even the slightest alteration here may have huge knock-on effects on our exit location."

Another strand thudded into the Owlflight's hull.

"Are the lines damaging us in any way, or just acting as anchors?" Anchors? In her mind, Opal visualised harpoons, as used by Fressus hunting vessels.

"The damage is minimal, just localised to the point of attachment. At present the biggest danger is the drag I am detecting, as the connection alters our centre of gravity and the Lost Ship seems to be decelerating."

A third strand shot out and connected. It was already resembling a network of veins.

"We need weaponry. Guns."

"As stated, I am not a mil–"

"I know, damn it! But we must have *something*."

"I would have got to that if you had allowed me to finish. One of the fibrils is attached to the fore of our hull, within range of a shrapnel turret."

"Target the strands. Try and sever them."

"Initiating."

The holographic display updated, highlighting attack points on the Owlflight's hull. The small cannon targeted the metres-thick nearby strand, illustrated by tiny dotted lines connecting the two.

There was resistance implying toughness, or even ongoing repair within the strand's biological systems as shrapnel cut in, but the focussed rapid-fire eventually overwhelmed it. A huge section of frozen blood shattered into crimson crystals, breaking it free.

One down.

"Any others in reach of a weapon?" asked Opal.

"Only one more," said Owlflight. "And it is beyond optimal range."

"Do it anyway," replied Opal.

But even as Owlflight initiated the attack, three more pseudo-pod-like streams of gelid blood erupted from the Lost Ship and connected to their craft. Thud thud thud. All of them far from the ring of turrets at Owlflight's nose.

"Was that the fastest you could take one down?" Opal asked.

"Yes."

Opal scanned the Lost Ship hull. Some clusters of the domed tissue still hadn't fired. Even if Owlflight had been able to shoot every strand, that would be useless if the Lost Ship retaliated against severing by firing three more. The bigger craft would be upon them long before they cut themselves free. Maybe the process would even accelerate their demise, since the more contracting fibres there were, the more pull the Lost Ship had to bring the vessels together.

Fuck fuck fuckity fuck.

There were already so many fat red filaments, hardened to crystalline form, that it was like a sparse web connecting the ships. Owlflight was pinned.

The owl broke Opal's concentration. "I have further bad news. I detect movement *within* the fibrils. Scans show parcels of density transitioning along inside them. Still at the far ends, and at a human walking pace, but it is definitely a transport process. The lines seem to hollow out once they are secured, so I suspect they can act as –"

"A form of boarding tunnel. Right. It never sneaks when it can overwhelm, as we said in the – whatever. So we're trapped, facing failure of the mission, being pulled out of Null, *and* there's a boarding party of things from the Lost Ship coming to say howdy. Against all that we have a basic AI – no offence –"

"None taken."

"Plus a tired ex-soldier and a little girl."

"We can do it, can't we, Opal?" asked Clarissa.

"Maybe. But not alone. That's the lesson I want to share with you, sweetie. Things are always easier when you have a friend watching your back."

Opal smiled and hugged the little girl, but as soon as Clarissa could no longer see her face, Opal's grin faded.

CREWS

... 23 ...

The revived crew looked around the cramped secondary bridge with nervousness at being awoken under mysterious circumstances. There was also an element of tiredness, because coming out of cryo was like being dragged from the deepest sleep, and it took time for your body and mind to warm up and readjust to movement. But at least they'd had help. Each cryo section included a locker of self-heating jackets to remove the bone-deep chill, and all four visitors to the bridge wore one over their red paper prisoner jumpsuits. The same cryo areas also included hotshotz, the mix of warm caffeine, sugar and stimulants that helped jolt you back into normal life.

Four new people.

Four was not enough, but Opal had been limited. All these frozen souls they'd rescued, and she hardly knew a damn thing about them. Anyone could be a security risk, a psycho, a UFS agent. And yet, doing nothing was an even greater risk. So she had been forced to start the process.

While selecting this group she had thought about all the big, tough, scary men who were in the pods. And every time they had faded away, and instead the image in her mind was Jau-Hwa, with her calm poise and confidence. Opal needed someone who would remain unflustered in an emergency, and wouldn't be intimidated by danger. Then she'd added Krrs on a gut instinct. He was another prisoner she'd encountered on Leviathan, and he'd suffered bodily mutilations that left even speech difficult, but he seemed capable and able to fight.

But beyond that she'd no idea, so just instructed Owlflight to examine whatever records it had on the sleeping passengers, and pick any who seemed to have a good mix of skills and reliability. To revive the slumberers and direct them to the bridge.

Opal had hoped for a substantial crew, but the AI obviously possessed so little information that this was all Opal had been given. Opal hadn't yet had time to look into the two that Owlflight had picked, or to ask why they'd been selected.

"Please sit, if you like," Opal told them, perching herself on the edge of a console and gesturing at the few control seats that hadn't been removed to create storage. Clarissa squeezed between some sturdy cables nearby, hugging her knees to her chest. "We haven't got long and I know you're all wondering what the sneck is going on. One minute you're going to sleep in cryo, looking forward to a new life when you wake, surrounded by smiling people; the next you're thrust into an emergency, alarms going off, directed along empty corridors with only my worried mug as your welcome."

None of the newly awoken settled into the chairs, but remained stood in a semicircle. There seemed to be a tension between their need to huddle together for human reassurance, versus their lack of knowledge about the people on either side of them.

Good. They were taking this seriously.

Opal got Owlflight to bring up illustrative displays, then she delivered a sitrep, trying to be concise without missing anything, and also not holding back on the stakes if they failed.

"Owlflight," Opal said, "can you update us on distances, movements and so on?"

"Of course. The Lost Ship has stopped approaching us, which is to our advantage. The connecting web of tunnels seems to have solidified enough to fix our distances." The holographic displays updated with measurements and diagrams. "Whatever is moving through them has made progress but we still have time to prepare."

Opal turned back to the tiny audience. "Normally I'd give you all a chance to bow out, but it's not an option today. My experience and gut instincts tell me something is going to happen. If we do nothing – if you went back to cryo, hoping it will be all okay – well, I think the outcome would be bad."

"It is all right," said Jau-Hwa. "I am sure we will assist in any way we can." She glanced at the other three who'd been awoken, and they all nodded.

"Thank you," said Opal. "Well, you know the situation now. I guess it's voluntary as to how best you can help. I have plans, but I need feet on the ground. People to play their parts. To fight back, coordinate, to monitor the situation across the ship. I can't do it alone. So I authorise you all to wake whoever might be useful. We don't have records on most of the sleepers in cryo, but you might know people from Leviathan you can trust, or who have skills. Work with Owlflight to identify and revive them. We got bigger problems than worrying about mutinies and sabotage. If we survive the next hour, then we can revisit my decisions. Requisition any equipment you need. Again, Owlflight will support you and give you access to the systems. We need to set up defences. We need to arm people. We need ... Shit, I'm not going to hand-hold you here. Jau-Hwa, how can you help?"

"I am – was – an Ortal biological pilot. UFS captured me, took me from Blue Rim. I might be able to run the systems, work with your AI. UFS controls will be clunky for me without a bio interface, but I may still be best use there."

"Brilliant. The main bridge is up that slope behind me. You'll take the pilot seat there, have full access to controls and comms. What about you?" Opal pointed to one of the two people who were new to her. He was a small man with a prominent nose, yet he seemed engaged, watching every detail of the display with intelligent eyes.

"My name's Caynan Tolka. Before they imprisoned me for 'anti-UFS agitation' I was a prehist art arkologist. Not sure what that best equips me for. But I've always been good with records, pattern-matching, multicat overlays, systemic retrieval."

"Okay. You could help with going through inventory, floorplans, any records we have on people in cryo. Liaise with others, especially while they're on the move. Owlflight is fast, but needs direction. You can provide it."

"Happy to."

"Krrs?"

Krrs' standing position was at the edge of the room, in the shadows. Opal wasn't sure if he was hiding, ashamed of his deformities, not wanting to scare Clarissa, or if his altered bone structures just made seats uncomfortable. But Opal didn't want him to feel like an outsider.

He held up his bony-taloned hands. "Not much help compudrrs. Was soldier."

"Well, look at records with Caynan. You can advise, help to identify anyone with combat skills. Pick some troops, wake them, take charge, organise the defence. Primary areas to protect are the bridge, the engines, the stasis pods. Think about weapons, too. I'm sure Caynan can track down options. I don't know what's coming, but they may have an ability to pass through materials in a kind of fleshy portal or whatever. Disrupting those could be vital. See if someone can rig up flamers, maybe they'll help."

Krrs nodded, his yellow eyes glinting.

Opal faced the last person, a woman whose head had been shaved just like Opal's. She had an unconscious habit of twisting her hands together, yet her face displayed no fear or indecisiveness. She had thick eyebrows, giving her an endearingly serious frown that reminded Opal of Clarissa. "I've not met you yet."

"I'm Rettix. Guilty of the heinous charge of financial crimes. Specifically, debt. Obviously being the victim of fraud, meaning you couldn't pay citizen dues, is such a terrible danger that the UFS has to rip you from your life. Sorry, you might sense bitterness. My career was as a geological media reframer, and I suspect that was the real issue that got me unwanted attention. Those Genitors sure do hate people who question things." She glanced around, as if suddenly worried that she was being observed. It was an all too common tic amongst anyone who couldn't internalise the Genitor culture. "I'm not sure how I can serve, but I'll come up with something, don't worry. I'll talk to the others and the AI. Pull my weight. Some other prisoners I occasionally got to talk to might be good additions, so I'll try and identify them in the pods too."

"Good. The situation is fluid. We'll need to react, no doubt change plans, cooperate smoothly if we're going to make this work. My current plan is based around separating the ships. Destroying the connecting strands just led to more, but maybe setting explosives on them, all going off at the same time, might break us free. Or dissuade the Lost Ship from reattaching. At the very least it might stop whatever's crossing the tunnels from reaching us, or force new ones to start the journey, which would buy us time."

Rettix put her hand up.

"No need for formalities," said Opal. "Shoot."

"For the geological part of my job I often went on expeditions. Deep-strata media presents numerous barriers, and we had to use explosives, so I have some background there. Maybe I can help by running inventory to see what is stored and where, perhaps even assembling charges others could make use of."

"Excellent. That's exactly the kind of thing we need. Well done, everyone, I'm glad we woke you. Let's get to work."

Opal and Rettix paced down a sub-deck corridor, as fast as they could without losing Clarissa, who did her best to keep up with their longer legs. The adults both had portable commsets composed of a tiny earpiece and microphone. Rettix had located a supply of them and they'd been distributed to the first team Opal awoke, plus the subsequent people that had been raised. Owlflight made use of infrastructure relays to keep them all in touch with each other. It worked, but at times became a confusing cacophony when too many people tried to speak at once, even with Owlflight and Jau-Hwa routing conversations onto separate channels. Still, it meant it was possible to keep track of what was going on in other areas of the ship.

Opal: "Jau-Hwa, what's the status with the explosive placements?"

Jau-Hwa: "The first team have kitted up in civilian EVA suits and collected their payload. Team two are almost ready. The third team have got lost but Caynan is taking over directions. If they can all place exterior explosives, and move on to another strand and repeat, then they might all be situated within ... let me consider ... maybe twenty, thirty minutes."

Which meant the first batch of whatever was coming down the pipes would have already arrived. But Opal didn't say that aloud.

Opal: "Krrs, how's your intercept squad going?"

Krrs: "We have weapons. Flamrrrrs, like you sedd. Some other sduff. We avoided heavy doody cannons, since dey could rip rrr hull open. Rrrr you joining us?"

"Absolutely. We're just on our way back to the bridge now. I'll drop off Rettix and Clarissa on the way, then meet you and get kitted up, lead one of the squads. I'll take them to the point where the first strands attached, examine the inner hull and set up defences. Give me ten. Out."

Opal grabbed Clarissa's hand to help her along.

"Can't I stay with you?" the girl asked.

"Too dangerous. We don't know what we're going to have to fight. Don't worry though," she added, when she saw the look on Clarissa's face. "It'll all be fine. Might not even be an attack at all. I've faced worse. And you get to play with your Blox on the bridge."

"I don't want to play when you're all working hard. I'll think about what I can do. Passing on messages or something."

"That's my girl." Opal mussed her hair.

They passed a cart of equipment left in the corridor earlier for their return journey, after inspecting a number of storage chambers that held potentially useful items. Unfortunately, the canisters and crates in many of them were so tightly packed it would require cargo trucks to get to the actual ones they wanted, and there wasn't time for that.

Rettix grabbed the cart and pushed it. Heavy to get started, because it was loaded down. Expandable foam canisters for making barriers. Welding guns for sealing routes off, in order to funnel any invaders towards fortified junctions. Shielded cabling that could be plugged into Owlflight's energy grid, and used in conjunction with a conducting framework to create impromptu electrical barriers. In lieu of time, they had to use ingenuity. Luckily Rettix had a good grasp of engineering.

Around a sharp corner. Too fast. Something crashed off the trolley, they had to stop, Opal and Rettix grunting as they lifted up the heavy sheets of alloy for another idea, this one suggested by Krrs: welding them in place as shields to hide behind.

"Hey, Commander Imbiana," said a voice Opal didn't recognise.

"Just Opal," she replied.

"Sorry. I'm in charge of one of the teams that's going outside to plant bombs. Caynan thought I should make my report direct to you."

"Go on."

"Well, we're kitted up and near the airlock, but noticed something. It's like the outside strands are partly *inside* the ship. A red kind of web. It's come through the wall. A whole corridor is blocked off by it."

"Which section?"

"2L4. Shall we investigate?"

"No, it could be dangerous. Best if an intercept squad with flamers checks it out. You stick to the plan: EVA, plant explosives, repeat, get back in one piece. Thanks for reporting."

"Acknowledged. Out."

"Owlflight, you hear that?"

"Yes," the AI responded immediately.

"Liaise with Krrs, send a team to find out what's going on. Warn them to be careful. Also, now we know something's there, see if any of the scans can identify it, then try and locate any other areas where it's getting in. I'd like to know the scale of the problem."

"Will do," said Owlflight.

"Caynan, you there?"

"Here."

"We're leaving the extra equipment at junction ..." Opal looked for the markings. "4K6. Send one of Krrs' engineer teams down in an elevator to collect. Krrs already knows what's here, so should have planned where he'll use it. We'll come up to the bridge now."

"Noted. We have the first EVA team on the outside. They're fully cable-secured, mag-booting it to the closest strand."

"Great, keep me updated. Out."

Once the trolley was parked up beside the freight elevator they turned back. Using the inter-section maintenance route would let them zigzag their way to the bridge without needing to take the long detour around the central area of the Owlflight where the drive was housed. Athene had filled and sealed a number of corridors to prevent anyone having access to her creation, which meant some of the standard shortcuts wouldn't be possible.

They hurried onwards.

All told, they'd woken another forty or so from cryo to try and put all these defences in place. Given the lack of time to prepare, any more than that would just lead to treading on toes, miscommunications, extra time wasted coordinating. This way they could rely on efficiency, synchronising everything for that goal. Items left in place X for team Y to collect on their way to join team Z. Floorplan analysis identifying the small number of key junctions that needed to be defended, rather than trying to spread thin across the whole ship. Instead of twelve teams doing a task, have four teams do the task three times each (and hopefully getting more efficient each time).

There, a ladder, ascending into a cylindrical tube to the next floor. Rettix went first, then Clarissa, Opal at the bottom, ready to catch her sister if she slipped on the ascent.

Halfway up when another comm came through.

"Krrs heerr. Was on way do red growds. Found anudder, doo decks down. Doo-Enn-Dree. Connected, I think."

"Don't approach it yet. Assist Owlflight in any scans that are needed, see if we can work out what, how, why, whatever. We need to know where these growths are *before* anyone stumbles into one. Also to know if any routes are blocked."

"Will do. Overrr."

Rettix and Clarissa had exited the ladder tube. Clarissa held out a hand to pull Opal up. Opal seized that small arm, pretended it was Clarissa who hauled her back onto standard flooring.

"Thanks," Opal said. "You're stronger than you look."

They were halfway to the next ladder when Opal spotted one of the rare inter-junction AI displays. She stopped there, giving her little sister the opportunity to catch her breath without drawing attention to the fact. Opal swiped the screen and Owlflight's avatar appeared. Only this time the owl wore a camouflaged military helmet.

Well well, it might only be a basic AI, but it had a sense of situational humour.

"Only got a moment," said Opal, "can you give me summary visuals?"

"Of course. First, external heatmaps."

A rotating model of the Owlflight appeared, the exterior illuminated mostly in blues due to the excellent thermal insulation spacecraft needed. Each of the blood strands shone in red, belying their organic, fleshy nature, as they lost heat to the surrounding vacuum. It didn't seem to affect them, though. Perhaps internal chemical processes generated more warmth, as with intestines.

On the surface of Owlflight's hull were tiny orange dots representing the first two teams to make it outside, each approaching their closest fibre connections at a steady pace, ready to plant explosives. Team three should be appearing soon. All as Opal expected.

"Thanks. Internals?"

The display switched to cutaway floorplans, with some areas marked in red to show infestation of whatever was growing.

"Initial scans gave me some chemical and thermal fingerprints that I can identify by repurposing atmospheric sensors around my interior. I have far too many blind spots to come up with a full tracing so am using extrapolation. This is the estimate."

More red areas appeared. Their starting points were always in the vicinity of where one of the blood strands had connected to the hull, reaffirming them as the source of the infection, which somehow spread through infrastructure as if it were a permeable membrane. Extensions of routes showed the penetration was much further than Opal had feared. And –

"Wait!" interrupted Opal. "Overlay energy distribution."

The lines of power infrastructure appeared in yellow.

"The infection follows it," Opal said.

"Correct. Which means we can predict its route, and if we find a counter, we can cut it off at source, perhaps."

"That's not what I'm thinking. All the power lines feed core systems, right?"

"Of course," replied Owlflight.

"And they all run through a few major points, the central one being ..."

"The Null-A drive."

"Exactly. Which is the last thing we want it to reach."

"Maybe the corridors Athene filled with expansion mortar will slow it."

"Maybe. Maybe not. Hey, I'm skirting the drive areas now. The display shows some of the infestation crossing this floor."

"That is estimated."

"Well, I need to get a look at it."

"Be careful."

The screen blanked out. Opal had the route memorised. Only a short detour. She led the way at a good pace.

"First bomb team in place," came another voice. "Approaching base of the biological anchor now."

The corridor twisted so much that, on rounding a corner, Opal almost ran into the criss-cross, mildly vibrating web of tissue which filled the passage. Far more extensive than Owlflight's estimations. Opal stepped back slowly, arms angled as warning to Clarissa and Rettix to keep away.

The strands dripped cherry globules of thick liquid. Where it pooled on the floor, more tendrils grew, fungus-like. At walls it spread in concentric patches of crimson, the centres uneven, as if whatever was under the red was being dissolved. That might be one of the points where it broke through to the next corridor.

Another drip, making a fat wet splosh.

The filaments nearest Opal vibrated eagerly.

She retreated a few more steps.

The process wasn't fast, but she could see it happening in real time. The growths, the extensions feeling their way to another point, the quivering, the drips. Perhaps the pools of gelid redness were also where it passed through flooring, splashing to the next deck.

"Arrgh! No –"

The voice cut out.

"Report, anyone!" Opal snapped.

"That was the first exterior team," cut in Jau-Hwa. "They were getting ready to plant a bomb, when the strand attacked them."

"How?"

"I'm looking at the playback. Stuff just shot out, went right through their EVA suits, tore them to ribbons."

"All dead?"

"I hope so. If they survived the shredding of their outfits, it would not be pleasant."

"Tell the other two teams not to approach the strands. The stuff might be sentient, or at least have defences, and be able to detect the approach. Perhaps they can launch the bombs from a distance. Or we might have to rethink, plant the bombs *inside* the hull, seal off those sections when they rupture. Jau-Hwa, can you get onto it with the others?"

"Of course. There is some good news."

"*Please.*"

"Krrs has had minor success with the flamers on the internal growth. It is resistant, but after enough incineration it seems to give up, ends up carbonised."

"Great. That's something. Get Owlflight and anyone versed in biochem to look into other approaches that might be more efficient. Maybe we can poison it, electrocute it, or disperse something through environmental systems."

"We will."

"Opal out."

She continued to back away from the eerily spreading mass of tissue, and once it was out of sight she led the way without speaking.

Their best hopes of breaking free weren't going to work. Everything else was just buying time. And they still didn't know what was coming down the red-crystal tubes, but it was nearly here and unlikely to be friendly. All the behaviour patterns of holding and ripping were too redolent of hunter behaviour, as if the Lost Ship was a predator and the Owlflight its prey.

Of course, that was all guesswork. It could be totally different. Maybe it was mating behaviour and the Lost Ship wanted to hump. Opal couldn't see any good outcomes from that, either.

Another ladder. They climbed.

Most problems had the same elements. Whether it was bodily illness, aggression from a stranger, or defending against a military attack. You needed to have a counter, some way of defeating the threat. In order to do that you often had to slow it down enough to give the solution time to act. The Efcorius virus killed in hours, and the retroviral took longer than that to gain immune system dominance, but doses of Gfec-4 slowed the virus down enough for the cure to take hold. If you had to defend a point against an overwhelming force until rescue arrived you couldn't do it by straightforward conflict, you had to buy time with traps, evasion, use of terrain. Slowing a threat was vital.

But it was pointless if you didn't have a way to defeat it at the end. That was just prolonging the pain.

Once again, Opal thought about her final solution if all else failed.

And once again, she hoped she would come up with a new idea, or one of their plans would work out before that.

"Trouble, Opal," said Jau-Hwa, interrupting her thoughts.

"Go on."

"Something is coming through at the first strand connection. Well, something other than the nasty red fungus. Krrs had set up defences and they are shooting, but the things are tough. If I could share the video with you ... well, I can't even make out what they are. Don't know if it is meaty or circuitry, but it's as if the interior wall where the strand attached is now a kind of doorway, and these beings are entering. Do you want audio with Krrs?"

"He's got enough on his plate. Can he hold?"

"For a time."

"Any help on its way?"

"No. Teams are either trying to burn through fungus before it blocks off areas, or they are ready to defend at other points where the strands connect. They are likely to face the same attackers soon."

Opal halted. Squeezed her eyes shut and shoved fists against forehead.

If only she'd known this was coming. If she'd had more time their plans and defences would be so much better. But instead they were stuck in the ring with a titanium-weight fighter, lucky just to dodge or block a few of the blows that would floor them. But you get tired. Luck runs out. Unless you leave the ring, you'll get brained before long.

"This is what we'll do," said Opal. "Get any spare people to the fortified points, with as many explosives as they can, any types, even the mobile cannons we wanted to avoid using. Retreat to the next inner blast door, and use everything we have to blow the point where the things enter. Sure, we'll probably rip holes in our hull, but if it stops them getting in, we can prep for a better response. With luck, it will kill that strand, might even sever the connection to the growing red stuff – call it fungus, makes a good shorthand – and the fungus that came from that strand will die out. We can only hope. Even if the Lost Ship fires new barbs, we'll have more time to prepare. Obviously get everyone through an airlock to a safe area before detonation. If we work together, time it right, we might win. I have faith in you all. Opal out." She turned to Rettix. "We need to make another detour. Storage. We've lost some people, have to open areas to vacuum, so we're gonna need more EVA suits. Sturdier stuff than the thin civ ones."

"Of course. If we head back to that terminal I'll go through floorplans with Owlflight, see if there are any nearer than the areas we've already looked in."

Opal didn't like lying to anyone who wasn't an enemy, but sometimes it was necessary.

PREPARATIONS

... 22 ...

Rettix located a treasure trove.

They'd had to acquire a demolition tool from elsewhere as this was one of the storage chambers with no doorways, intended for access only after arrival, when the ship was dismantled. With the tool Opal had been able to plasma-cut a circle of wall panel, so they could enter through the sizzling metal and locate the storage pods Rettix had said would be in here.

Still, that had been another five minutes of delays.

There was only minimal emergency lighting in here, a chamber no one was supposed to access in flight. Unpacking was meant to be done methodically at the destination, not in a panic during an emergency. So unless you wanted to access things in expected order – always with life support, food and basics as the first items you came across, followed by shelters – then it involved rearranging lots of boxes and equipment in tight spaces.

Rettix sat inside a cargo lifter and activated its upper ring of super-bright spotlights, turning the local area into a daylight forest where the trees were towering stacks of storage crates mag-locked together. After a few rows the stark shadows became so overlapped that it was just shifting darkness as the cargo lifter moved, like walking through a hypostyle hall holding up a torch.

They were lucky this section already contained a cargo lifter. One of the Gumdie Corp Rotatortuff models, a sturdy round base with hidden wheels below which meant it could rotate and move in any direction. When it needed to lift anything the wheels retracted and the base nano-welded to the flooring to provide complete immobility and support while the three extendable arms could grip and relocate storage crates, some of which were heavy enough to squish a person. Rettix had cracked open a few boxes already and now rearranged others to reach the next marked one which was supposed to hold useful supplies.

Opal rooted through open canisters with a disregard for tidiness or any thought of neatly repacking items. Strewn around her were the contents she'd pulled out so far. Clarissa moved some of the things they didn't need, a task Opal had given to keep the girl occupied.

Opal raised a vac-packed set of civilian EVA outfits, the same kind worn by those who had gone outside the ship. Insulated and layered to keep someone alive and warm and protected from radiation, but with no real defence against impacts or perforations. In any extreme environment they'd be a liability. But Opal dug on, remembering the inventory list she'd seen before they broke into the chamber.

"Caynan or Jau-Hwa, this is Opal, can anyone give me a sitrep?" she asked as she delved.

"Caynan here. It's ... not good. Can't stop for long, so much going on. The things have invaded on a number of decks. That's the bad. On the plus side, Krrs' forces blew two of the sections where they were entering, and the loss of connection *does* seem to kill the fungus that grew from that point, as you predicted. His crews are moving on to repeat this on other strands. More bad news, though. The vacuum doesn't kill the creatures. They're trying to pierce the blast doors we retreated behind. If it looks like they'll get through, then we'll seal the next area off too. But we can only do that for so long before our own access becomes restricted. Jau-Hwa and Owlflight are identifying more people to wake, and we've sent a team to brief them as soon as they're conscious. Other bad news is that, although the fungus dies when the connection to a strand is lost, its death releases some kind of toxic gas. We lost three people to it. So we've had to seal off more sections. At this rate, even if we broke off every strand, more than half the ship would be either in vacuum, toxic, or contain whatever creatures are invading. And, to make it worse, when we destroyed the strand connection, the Lost Ship launched another two."

"Anything on the creatures that boarded?"

"There's not a huge number, but they're tough. Hardly affected by fire or standard munitions. It's been brutal. It's hard to pinpoint what they are exactly, since we can't capture one, and even if we did there's no way to analyse it in these conditions. Krrs and Jau-Hwa call them circuit creatures. They sort of resemble things without much skin, where you can see their internal structures, and what I thought were veins and muscles – well, once they said that, I could see what they meant. The bits that move are like the internals of military combat bots. Anyway, the name stuck. They don't seem to have ranged weapons but they can move in … well, I don't know how to explain it. They slide to a new location in a blink, but it may be a perceptual trick rather than some actual physical process. Who knows? If they get close they somehow connect to the person, wire into them. We don't survive the procedure. We have a few people trying to get heavier ordnance from storage. That's it. Got to go. Out."

Opal was still processing all that when another voice spoke into her ear. Owlflight.

"It is not really all, Opal," said the AI. "I have additional bad news, but as you ordered, I will inform you first. And this is transmitted to your ears only."

"Shoot."

"Everything Caynan said is correct. The fungus is invading from the many connecting fibrils that have yet to be severed. And, unfortunately, by following energy lines, it has begun to penetrate into the area around the Null-A drive. The barriers and expanding cements slow it, but the energy emissions are so powerful it keeps attracting more fungus, which is able to eat its way through almost any material."

"So if it reaches the drive, it'll destroy it."

"No doubt. But there is an additional complication. If it penetrates enough then the Null-A drive systems will detect it, and no doubt interpret it as an attempt at reverse engineering. As such, the protocols are clear. The Null-A drive's defences will trigger, leading to detonation. It will rip us apart. Any attempt to interfere with the drive will just accelerate the process. I see it as a zero-sum survival scenario."

"Right." Opal let go of the handles on a chest she'd been wheeling out of the storage pod, and headed away from Clarissa, who seemed absorbed in the seed packets she'd discovered. For once, Opal welcomed the pressing darkness.

Once she was out of earshot she stopped at a shadowed junction.

"First up – don't tell anyone else the scale of this danger. It may be that the best way to hold the fungus off is to keep severing its growth points. However, if you find any counter to the fungus that works, then a priority is to apply it to areas around the Null-A drive, stop the invasion in that zone."

"I might have to reveal the reason for my focus, if that happens."

"In that case, inform as few people as possible. Ideally just the first four we woke. But ... who knows what's going to happen? Use your discretion."

"If we had an active biological lab and crew it would be easier."

"Prioritise waking anyone with counter-invasive or microbial deconstruction experience. We can only do our best."

"All acknowledged. Though when I calculate probabilities, within my limited abilities to do so, the outcome where we thoroughly defeat all the invasive elements and still have the functionality to continue remains an outlier. Most outcomes involve survival for a variable duration, until we are overwhelmed."

"I'm aware of that. And I don't need no fancy head calculator to come to the same conclusion as you. I've only got one option left, and hoped I wouldn't need to take it, but I'm out of choices."

"Please enhance."

"I've identified all the equipment I'll need. There's really no time to waste. I'm going to board the Lost Ship."

"To what end?"

"Our only hope is to stop the Lost Ship from attacking, whether that's by destroying its bridge, killing the Navigot, or somehow persuading it to cease aggressions. I'll have to play it by ear, and I have to go *now*."

"I'll inform everyone so we can help."

"No! Don't tell anyone yet. I have the equipment I need in here somewhere. I've already planned my strategy. If you tell people now then it'll just distract them. And it wouldn't surprise me if they start offering to go with me, volunteer to go in my place, whatever. No. They're all needed here, as many soldiers as possible defending, protecting the ship and civilians, doing what they can to buy us time. And, in truth, I reckon companions would slow me down. My best chance is to do what I've done before, one last time. My instincts have saved me on Lost Ships. And the same instincts tell me I'm right."

"They will realise you are absent eventually."

"Of course. And then you'll tell them. They need to know, but not for the reasons you think. This situation is awful. It's so easy to give up hope but I need them to hold on to that, to fight until the end, because every minute of survival might give me the time to do something. So, when morale flags – at that point, tell them. Say that I'll succeed and save us if they can just hold out. Focus on defences and gaining time above all else."

"Should I lie?"

"If necessary, yes. Play up my chances. If they give up, then we lose."

"Can I keep in touch with you on board the Lost Ship?"

"No idea. We haven't got the tech I had last time. Too many unknowns. I'll try."

"But how will I know what to do? If you need rescuing?"

"If I succeed, I'll try and signal you. Comms, light flashes, explosions, I dunno. If the Lost Ship releases you, then look out for me. Wait if it's safe to do so. I'll try and return, or get a message out. But if there's a threat, then just go. And if you don't hear from me, then go. Don't risk all those lives for one person who might already be dead. And if anyone argues with you, if they insist on staying, or sending a team over to look for me, then again: override it and go. Within the parameters I've set you can authorise actions as you see fit to keep yourselves alive. Wake others, do whatever is needed to keep them going. The people you're working with are in charge. They're free now, and responsibility is the price. Look, I'm not sure if I'll get a chance to speak to you again, Owlflight, but I just want to say that when we first met, I underestimated you. Human weakness. I know you'll do your best."

"Thank you for your vote of confidence. I have my cargo, and I must preserve it."

"Huh, spoken like a true corp AI. And, for once, I don't mean that as an insult. Good luck, my feathered friend. Opal out."

She took deep breaths, then returned to where the unpacking was taking place, her eyes having to adjust again to the brightness of the Rotatortuff's working lights. She approached it and waved her hand to get Rettix's attention. The hazard beeps and whirrs of hydraulic muscle ceased, and silence returned to the chamber as the last echoes faded out.

"Rettix, I have some more specific equipment requests," said Opal. "Those outside the ship got attacked by the blood strands, and there may be a need for some fighting in vacuum, within our hull. The civ-suits just don't cut it. So let's gather something better for the poor bastards who need to face off against the invaders."

Rettix gave a thumbs up gesture and climbed down from the cargo lift. Time to put Opal's shopping list into action.

It turned out that Rettix's knowledge of expedition supplies went beyond suits and included survival and climbing equipment, explosives, and small engineering tools. The only limits were what was in this storage area, and what they had time to access. Opal eyed the pile of kit that had been gathered. But there was no putting it off any longer.

"Slight change of plan," Opal said. "Rettix, please take Clarissa back to the bridge. I had a comm from Owlflight. All fine, but I need to load this stuff up and transport it to one of Krrs' teams."

"We can help with that," said Rettix. "I think I know where I could unpack a mobile transport. We can shift it all in half the time, get to the bridge together."

"Not necessary. Erm, I need you to do something else on the way." Opal tried to indicate that Rettix should back down, using the universally understood combination of a tilted head, pursed lips, and widened eyes that flicked a glance towards Clarissa.

"But that doesn't make sense," said Rettix.

Obviously not as universal as Opal had hoped.

"Is something wrong with your tummy?" Clarissa asked. "You look like when it's hard to go toilet."

"Please don't argue, you two. I haven't time to fill you in, but it's all fine."

"Why do you keep saying that?" asked Clarissa.

"And how come we didn't gather more of these items?" asked Rettix. "Why kit out one person when I could easily gather enough for a team?"

Opal glared at them both.

"Right. Fine. I'll tell you if you promise not to argue."

Rettix and Clarissa nodded.

"Verbal confirmation."

They both agreed.

"Okay," said Opal. "I need to get over to the Lost Ship. I have a plan. Totally worked out. Too complicated to explain, but safe as sunset. I've done this before and I'm even better equipped now, thanks to my knowledge and experience. You can help me gear up so I can get out of here sooner, but then you both get to the damn bridge."

Clarissa opened her mouth so Opal pushed a finger against her sister's lips. "You agreed not to argue," said Opal. "Unless you're about to say 'Sir, yes, sir,' I don't want to hear it."

"I'm not arguing," said Clarissa. "I just want to help."

"Doing what I say will be the help."

"But I want to ask. And I'm your sister, so you have to tell the truth. Might you die?"

Opal looked at the girl. Clarissa was staring back. Clever little minx knew the telltales that would indicate a fib.

"Yes. There's a chance I might," said Opal. "But I'm hoping that's not going to be the case. And I believe this is the best chance for us all to come out of this alive."

Clarissa turned to Rettix and spoke as if confiding a great secret. "She's telling the truth." Then, facing Opal again: "We're sisters. I want to be with you. Sometimes that might be for good stuff, but it means bad stuff too. Being together is part of that. Especially after we only just found each other again. You promised never to leave me. Don't break your promise now."

Opal crouched by her sister. "I promise I'll do *everything I can* to come back."

"I could help."

"I'm more likely to move fast and survive if I'm on my own. And you want me to survive. This isn't goodbye. It's just a 'See you soon, goon'. I'll back down on some things, but not this. I go *alone*."

They stared into each other's eyes again, reflective mirrors, her own resilience and protectiveness blazing back at her.

But then Clarissa said, "Whatever."

Revealing Opal's plan was perhaps for the best. It meant Rettix could help kit her out, and that saved a lot of time. It also enabled Rettix to rig up custom solutions to some of the problems. In fact, Opal wouldn't be half as well equipped if she'd had to do this alone.

Rettix located a GAMag engineering suit. One of the later revisions, too. Once Opal was inside the tough chem- and tear-resistant inner hazmat layers, the musculature and armour plates were applied. Those parts only covered about half the body, but it was a huge step up from civilian EVA suits. The GAMag had an energy charge, limited exoskeleton, full-head protection, EM shield, attachments for equipment, close-range comms, and mag-lock boots. It was still a poor replacement for an EW suit, since the GAMag was slow and bulky, only partial armour, no inbuilt weapons, and a crappy HUD. It was designed for maintenance work in vacuum or hazardous conditions aboard or outside a spacecraft, not for combat. But, short of serious damage, it had enough energy and oxygen to keep her alive long enough. Chances were that she'd die or the Owlflight would be lost before she suffocated.

Clipped to Opal's suit were two compressed oxygen tanks, and a range of engineering items that might be useful. Portable welder, tools for opening doors, microflares, canister of marker paint, and a miniature grappling pistol. These kinds of things had always proved to be more useful than weaponry on Lost Ships.

Within a sealed section of her leg armour was a pair of the compact explosives Rettix had come up with by dismantling a set of demolition charges. If Opal made it to the Navigot this might be her only bargaining point. Or it might save her life before that if she was attacked, or otherwise blocked by an obstacle.

There was one final use which she didn't like to think about. Lost Ships offered a thousand painful deaths. It was reassuring to have a last resort to end her suffering if all other options failed.

Although she liked to keep her hands free, she couldn't resist one more item. There had been no weapons in this section – unfortunately, military ordnance was deeply packed near the heart of the Owlflight, and there just wasn't time for Opal to access it. But amongst the engineering equipment Opal found herself drawn to a gun that fired heavy steel anchor bolts from a cylinder of six. The bolts could be shot into a wall to be used as climbing holds, or attached to cable to create a more heavy-duty grappling hook. But, looking at the vicious rods, Opal knew they'd work equally well as an impromptu weapon. So she strapped one spare rod cylinder to her suit.

She didn't feel overloaded, but had lots of options. That would have to make up for the absence of more hi-tech equipment. It wouldn't make up for the loss of Athene's voice in her ear, but nothing would.

They made their way to the nearest airlock. Rettix pushed a cart holding the special heavy-duty launcher she'd made, plus the tightly wound high-tensile micro cable, enough to span the kilometre between ships. It freed Opal to walk next to Clarissa, holding her hand and wishing it was a skin-to-skin contact. Opal couldn't feel it at all through the thick GAMag gauntlets. In fact, she couldn't resist looking down every few steps to make sure she wasn't squeezing the girl's small hand too hard. Opal *really* missed the tactile feedback systems of EW suits.

She clomped down the corridor feeling more like a primitive cyborg than a human, not helped by the fact that she knew her face wasn't visible to Clarissa. All the girl would see was an armoured faceplate with a red slit of a visor, like a baroque welding mask. Opal tried to focus more on the now than the soon.

"Don't worry, I'll be okay," Opal said, her voice altered by the GAMag suit so it came out sounding hollow.

"I didn't say anything," Clarissa told her, looking up.

"Oh, sorry. I thought I heard you ... never mind. Must be the suit systems. I'm not used to them yet."

Opal's legs and arms felt heavy. The power assist worked, but with a slight delay as if pushing through deep water. And the sensation grew as they neared the airlock.

All too soon they reached the destination. Opal crouched down as much as she could, since the knee joints on the GAMag restricted her mobility. She wished she didn't have the suit on to say goodbye. She couldn't connect with her sister in human contact for a hug, couldn't speak with her own voice, couldn't hear except through internal speakers, and could only see through the horizontal slit of the augmented-view HUD. Every human element was mediated and lessened. She should have prepared for this, planned for its importance, instead of getting distracted. It was easy to lose sight of what was really valuable.

"Everything will be fine," Opal told Clarissa. "Rettix will look after you."

"Sure will," said Rettix, putting a hand on Clarissa's shoulder. "Once you're away I'll get us to the bridge."

Opal handed Rettix her pistol and knife. As Rettix took them, Opal gripped her wrist momentarily. "Protect Clarissa with your life," she said, before releasing Rettix, who seemed flustered, perhaps by Opal's intensity.

"It's okay," said Clarissa. "You can go, Opal. I know I'll see you soon. You told me you'd come back."

"I will, sweetie. I will."

Opal stood with a whir of servos, opened the inner airlock and pushed her cart of heavy cabling inside. She turned and waved to them as the door closed.

She'd expected more argument from Clarissa at the end. She was glad that didn't happen. It was hard enough as it was. Clarissa might only be a kid, but her life had already taught her to cope with inevitable misfortunes.

This airlock didn't have internal or external viewing windows. Hopefully Rettix was already leading Clarissa to the safest place on the Owlflight. The bridge had a lockdown system as a last resort. Even that would fail eventually, but it would provide more time.

Speaking of which, Opal needed to get a move on.

The heavy line cannon was designed for building projects, to create secure cable anchors for elevated constructions. Rettix had adapted it. Opal used fixing rods to clip it securely to the airlock's handrail, then applied nano-weld pads to attach its feet to the floor as an extra precaution. It needed stability to fire accurately.

Opal removed the heavy-duty harpoon, grunting with effort as she loaded it into the firing mechanism. They'd used the heaviest gauge possible, so as to give the sturdiest fastening, but even GAMag servos had their limits.

She double-checked the seals on her suit and also made sure the HUD had green lights for all life support systems, then thumped the airlock cycle.

Warning lights flashed orange as the air was extracted from her chamber, and environmental conditions altered to match the outside. By the time the outer airlock doors opened, revealing the pure black of the Null, exterior sounds had ceased. Although they weren't in Realspace – meaning no visible stars, no exterior sights of nebulae – the environment was still an inhospitable void.

Opal took a breath, gripped a handrail, and leaned out. An endless black drop below and above. Even the Owlflight was hardly visible beyond the small pool of light from her airlock. There, just outside the door, a fastening hoop. She clipped one end of the heavy-duty cable to it, then retreated back inside. She attached the other cable end to the harpoon, testing the fastenings were secure.

It had been important to make sure that when she was finished, there would be nothing inside the airlock that would block the outer door from closing, otherwise it would render the airlock unusable to anyone else on the Owlflight. This way the cannon would be inside but the cable fully outside, on an exterior loop, with no obstructions.

The GAMag suit wasn't voice activated. It had a control panel built into the left forearm, designed to be manipulated via chunky gauntlets. Opal looked out and messed with the EM frequencies of the suit scanners, finally locking in a combination of infrared and visible blue which gave the best view she could hope for at present. The red blood strands stood out due to their organic heat emanations, connecting to the Owlflight then fading away with distance. Since the ships were fixed in place and she knew their relative positions, it was straightforward to lower herself behind the cannon's targeting screen and aim to the right of the nearest strand. She took no chances, making sure it was well beyond the range at which the exterior team had been attacked.

She fired.

Cable played out, spinning fast off the spool, her mind supplying the missing whirring sounds. The harpoon was already out of sight in the blackness, trailing cable. On and on it flew. She hoped they'd estimated the length correctly.

And then it ceased.

She tugged on it, recovering armfuls until it would come no more. She was unable to dislodge it. The harpoon was secure in the Lost Ship. They'd guessed pretty well. Opal pulled the excess cable through the outer hull's fastening point and then locked it in place, taut.

She took a strap and clipped one end to her suit, one to the cable between the ships.

Almost done.

Next was an opportunity she couldn't miss. A small canister of the explosives Rettix had created, and a modified pipe-shunter which could be used to launch them. It looked like a hollow tube with a handle and some loose wires. She connected the wires to her GAMag suit controls, then altered her HUD view to represent targeting cursors illustrating where the tube pointed, with pinpoint accuracy thanks to the ultraviolet beam it emitted.

She popped the first explosive into the tube, knelt, locked her boots to the floor, and took aim at the nearest red strand. She held it steady, then fired.

A bit off, she thought. At least in Null there was nothing to interfere with trajectories. It was all down to her skill with projectiles. She'd need to compensate.

And be quick.

In a smoothly mechanical motion she took another explosive, aimed further along the red strand, fired again. Then repeated the process, aiming at any other strands that were just visible, until the small canister of explosives was empty.

No need to manually detonate anything. Rettix had programmed them to explode if they detected sudden, halting deceleration, which should occur if they struck any of the red tunnels. Without detonation they would disarm themselves after two minutes and become harmless debris.

All done, she prepared to launch herself.

Opal used to hesitate when facing an endless fall. It had always filled her mind, that void, that ancient fear, pushing out everything else. It had needed a force of will just to put one foot in front of another.

But not any more. She looked out and just envisioned a goal. Even though it wasn't visible to her eyes, it was real in her mind. A ship, in the blackness at the end of this cable. And beyond that another task, something to achieve.

A few fast steps and a jump and she was gone, eyes focussed on the target, and nothing else mattered.

ENTRANCES

... 21 ...

Once she was falling away from the shrinking Owlflight, she removed the first of the compressed air cans and opened the release, pointing it behind her. She accelerated, zipping along in the blackness. Before long the Owlflight was completely out of sight, but the Lost Ship had not yet appeared.

She experienced no sensations of moving, heard no sounds. When she glanced at the cable she flew along it was just a blurred line. Off in the distance were vague red pulses of the inter-ship blood strands.

It wasn't standard to go outside a craft during Null travel. Certainly not beyond your ship's hull. If repairs were vital they were undertaken reluctantly, since many superstitions claimed the endless Null did weird things to minds.

Yet here was Opal, whizzing along, deeper and deeper into the unknown. Yoo-foo-fucking-sah!

If she continued accelerating the journey would end with her being smashed to oblivion against the hull of the Lost Ship.

Instead, she counted down in her head, the estimate to a halfway point she'd calculated with Rettix earlier.

A flare of light attracted her attention, momentarily spreading from an explosion in the distance before it was snuffed out. At least one of her projectiles had struck a connecting tendril. And another flash. Then another. Maybe it would help.

Five, four, three, two, one, zero. She turned off the air canister, repositioned it ahead, then released the gas again. It would decelerate her, and if she got the calculation right, she'd end up at her safe starting speed for the final approach, little faster than a run and a jump.

Still, the halfway sensation was weird. Like she was the only point of stillness, while the universe moved around her static form.

She wasn't sure if that was a comforting illusion or not.

The suit comm system picked something up. Garbled voice. Rettix, Jau-Hwa, or even Owlflight? Too broken up to parse properly, but the overall impression was positive. Maybe her opportunistic attack on the connecting strands would buy her friends more time. That was a good thought.

Deceleration continued. She took a moment to mess with visor modes and try to enhance the views of the nearest veiny connectors between the ships. Clear ruptures on at least one of them. Another had been severed. She tried to focus in and ... ah. Not good.

Something was emerging from one of the holes she'd blasted. *Many* somethings, like a cloud. And as they swarmed from the fleshy mass, they changed direction.

Towards Opal.

"I wish you were with me," she said aloud. "I really miss you."

She looked ahead for any sign of her destination. She got early warning as it loomed out of the dark, a lighter black, due to the augmented HUD building in scans for echolocation.

Too fast.

She turned the tap on the gas canister to full, releasing whatever was left in the container in maximal flow, hoping to brake in time. Distance was hard to judge without bright lights. Near the end she let the canister go. It flew out of sight on its own endless journey into the Null. She threw out her arms and legs, braced for impact, and it came pretty hard, temporarily stunning her as she bounced off the hull, only recovering after she'd whirred back along the cable a few metres.

Damn, what she'd give for impact resistance.

A quick side glance. The cloud of things swirled closer, like a huge, serrated meat grinder made of red particles.

She pulled herself hand over hand back towards the Lost Ship, then activated the suit head lights. The Lost Ship hull had a slight sparkle to it, as if glitter impregnated the surface, and there was the metal harpoon. It was still secure, hadn't punctured deeply enough to activate the acidic fizzing repair mechanism that Lost Ships exhibited on severe hull damage.

If she had to return this way, then at least it was an option using the spare oxy-can in her toolbelt.

Opal messed around with the suit controls, disabling external speakers so if she spoke she wouldn't broadcast it to anything nearby. Then she scanned comm channels but the whole array was blank. Zip from Owlflight, ditto with Rettix. Maybe the system was damaged, or range was the issue, or interference. Who knew what the Null did to comms? Opal wouldn't be surprised if she was the only person to ever do a ship-to-ship jump in Nullspace. Whoopie fucking doo.

For now she was on her own, not even an entertainment-level AI to chat to. Fine. She wasn't lonely.

She extended the suit's headlight to long-range narrow beam, and manipulated the augmented HUD for best visual enhancement. Another proximity check. The churning swarm homing in on her was only minutes away.

She needed an entrance. Get on board the Lost Ship, get her bearings. Although she wanted to access the bridge where she was pretty sure the Navigot resided, she'd been forced to fire herself at the rear of the Lost Ship, far from the blood strands. And as the cloud that had erupted from one closed in, she was glad of that distance, and the time it bought her.

But she had a plan. Hopefully this Lost Ship would have transit cars, like the first one she'd boarded. All she had to do was locate a station, ride to the control quarters, and she'd be almost done.

She gripped the cable and rotated around, scanning as far into the distance along the hull as possible, wondering what the fuck she'd do if –

At the edge of vision. Handholds and a heavy-duty indentation that must indicate a reinforced airlock door.

How convenient.

How *suspicious*.

How *few* her options were.

She unclipped herself from the cable, aimed carefully, and gently kicked off, drifting over the alien hull.

The outer airlock closed behind Opal, sealing her in a small metal cage. This was the point at which a trap would be sprung.

There was no gravity in here, so she tried to turn on the spot, using surface contact to keep returning to the centre. She was alert for the slightest change in her surroundings that could indicate a threat. Normally there would be airlock status displays and flashing lights, but not here. Just the stillness of a coffin.

Patience. Always assess before acting.

"Of course," she said.

The inner door slid aside without fuss. She realised she could hear it, which meant atmosphere, but still no gravity. Damn. The other Lost Ships had an artificial form, so she'd assumed this would be the same.

Never assume.

"A bit late now."

Despite the extra bulk, a jetpack suit attachment would have been a good choice.

She messed with the suit controls, activating magnetic contacts. When her boots touched the ceiling she felt the tiniest pull, but not enough to enable walking. That certainly matched other Lost Ships, where surfaces which looked metallic were actually anomalous compositions based more around appearance than performance.

Drifting it would be. The slight magnetism would still help her in creating contact to manoeuvre from surfaces.

She kicked off a wall cautiously, floating out of the airlock and into a wide corridor. She glanced both ways. Nothing moving but her, and the swirl of green particles – Viscids – that were ever-present in a Lost Ship. When she reached the opposing wall she was able to halt there thanks to the minimal magnetism in her boots and gloves. If she'd hit it too hard she'd have bounced off, but as long as motions were careful and controlled, she should be able to manoeuvre efficiently.

This section of the Lost Ship was pitch black, so she could only see whatever her suit headlights lit up. Limited range, sharp drop-off blackness beyond. Unlike the more advanced silverlight systems she was used to – where the emanations weren't visible to many known species – using visual-wavelength light in dark places like this was a danger. She needed it to see, but it also made it easy for things in the darkness to see *her*. And things in darkness might be curious. Or hungry.

Your heart rate is going up. Stop scaring yourself, Opal.

"You're right. But habits, eh? What can you do?"

Change them.

"Easy for you to say."

Good job she had turned off her voice broadcast. No point adding audible target to visible target.

A least in zero gravity she could move quietly if she kept her push-offs and drifts precise. And, without her own echoing footsteps distracting her, she might also hear threats before they detected her. Yay.

Last thing. She adjusted the headlight emanations, choosing the lowest level of emission that the suit detectors could visualise, finding the best balance between her own vision versus visibility to Entities. In the end a subdued glow from her suit provided a five to seven metre range with fairly good clarity in her HUD. Hopefully she wouldn't give too much advance warning of her approach.

Still alone in the funereal silence and greeny gloom.

Don't stay still for too long. Not here.

Opal didn't have an advanced AI HUD bringing up floorplan overlays. Just her instinct and common sense. She was to the stern of the ship, lower decks, so she needed to move forwards and upwards wherever possible. Get to the core, travel the Spine.

She kicked away from the wall gently, at an angle that would take her at least ten metres down the corridor before she connected with the opposing surface.

Out in the open, weightless. Smoky green particles bounced off her visor as she swam through the air. The wall approached. She absorbed the soft impact with her arms.

Still quiet and dead both ways. Opal pushed off again.

Something about these weightless motions was calming in a way that normal pedestrian exploration wouldn't be. Perhaps it was the feeling of freedom and peace. Perhaps it was the ease with which she could cover big distances. It felt like progress.

She passed doorways on the inner wall of the corridor. That made sense. The other wall led to the outer hull. Maybe even another airlock before long.

During her drift down the curving corridor she occasionally passed floating debris. A personal datapad, slowly spinning. A chair. An empty cup, contents long gone.

Ahead, an open doorway. She pushed towards it, gliding, getting used to the motions. She reached the frame, gripped the edge to halt herself, her body levitating in the middle of the corridor.

Not a closable doorway but a permanent arch. She pulled her body in so she could peep through it.

It wasn't a room or passageway, this was vertical: an open elevator shaft. But without doors. Perhaps a reconstruction of a gravshaft? Those quick ways to descend between floors if you were confident enough to fling yourself into nothingness.

Yes, that made sense, along with the location near the outer hull. On a normal military ship these would lead to the Skathers, bioengineered UFS terror weapons used for annihilation of settlements, or to force capitulation by using the sheer threat of them. Most avenues into those sections were one-way, which was the clue. If there was ever a Skather outbreak then there would be limited routes they could invade the ship from, enabling threat containment. The UFS didn't allow rebellion or disobedience from its soldiers, citizens, AIs, or bioweapons.

Normally a powerless gravshaft was a suicide jump that would plummet you for an agonising minute before turning you into an explosion of red paint.

But these weren't normal conditions. She grinned. With no power or gravity it was just a tube with holes to exit on different decks.

Before entering, she took the spray paint can that was attached to her suit by an elastic cable, and drew an upwards-pointing yellow arrow, holding the nozzle close enough to the wall that the paint didn't have a chance to float away.

Opal didn't have the luxury this time of augmented maps and AI navigators. She had to go old school, as they said in the Periphs. An arrow to show direction taken at junctions, so she could follow them in reverse to backtrack from a dead end, or if she needed to escape the same way she came in.

Task complete, she swung into the lightless shaft. A drop into darkness above and below. *No, recalibrate.* It was a horizontal pipe, and she was just swimming along. That removed the mental connotations of falling and made the transition more acceptable to the body.

EXPLORATIONS

... 20 ...

In her head she kept track of decks ascended. It was only a rough guide, but the skill she'd honed in creating mental maps of Aseides' base might save her time here. At each exit she gripped the archway rim to halt herself, and peered out to see what was on that floor. But nothing tempted her to cease her climb. Just views of abandoned spaces transformed into tombs.

Onwards and upwards.

At first she thought the air was getting denser, but then she realised she'd passed through translucent layers of something sticky. She continued, but cautiously.

Her hesitance was well-founded. Ahead of her the gravshaft was blocked. Layers of fine gossamer festooned the space, running across the centre in web-like masses.

You've encountered this before.

"And it was always bad."

It was a good job she hadn't flung herself up the tube full force. She'd have plunged right into that sticky mesh, become embroiled, and if anything monitored the strands for panicky vibrations, it would have easily found her.

Opal touched the smooth gravshaft wall, trailing a hand enough to turn her a hundred and eighty degrees. She gained enough purchase to return the way she'd come, retreating from the blockage while glancing back for tell-tale trembling in the web that might signal the approach of a Lost Ship denizen.

The short range of her helmet glow soon meant the web was out of sight. She exited the shaft at the previous floor. Snatching the spray can, she drew an arrow that ran around the lip of the archway, visible from both sides, the chevron that ended it pointing along this corridor in the direction she wanted to go.

She was glad to drift away from the blackness of the gravtube. No pursuer was apparent but it didn't mean nothing was *there*, exiting behind her with alien spindliness and keeping out of the light. For now.

She launched herself into the air again, and continued.

If you are being followed, you'd be best getting off this main corridor.

"You're right. Thanks, Athene."

She'd said it instinctively, before the other part of her brain caught up and realised she was talking to ghosts.

Nothing wrong with that. If we comfort you, then keep us around. You wish I was there with you, so here I am.

Of course. The voice had been Athene's all along, not Opal's. But she hadn't even noticed that at first.

"I guess I don't feel like I can do this on my own. To everyone else I'm this tough bastard, but I think you knew the real me."

I think so, too.

Here was a door, half open. The metal plating looked dented, maybe explaining why it hadn't closed fully. Opal grabbed it to halt her flight, and peeped in. It looked like a weapon store, though most of the racks were empty. Further exits led onwards, perhaps part of a cluster of rooms bounded by corridors. If so, she could cut through.

She marked her arrow outside, then entered.

Items floated. She snatched one. A rifle magazine. But as she examined it up close she couldn't see any markings. The attachment slot was a strange shape. And when she prodded at the bullets in the mag, they didn't move. Could be a jammed spring, but it felt more like a solid structure, just modelled and textured to look like ammunition. She let it go, kicked off a wall towards one of the racks that wasn't fully empty, grabbing the frame as an anchor point.

She was able to remove one of the weapons. It wasn't like anything she'd seen before. The contours resembled a child's conception of a gun, the kind of thing Clarissa drew on the walls, her big-headed soldiers captioned with "pew pew" sounds. Opal tried pulling the trigger but it was either locked in place, or had no moving parts.

Then she noticed her palm had indented into the grip. It was soft, kind of mushy, and – fuck, was that something writhing below the surface? She flung the rifle away. She was pretty sure anything from in here would be more of a liability than a life-saver.

She pushed off the rack, picked one of the open doorways, marked her return route in yellow, and ventured beyond.

These rooms were small, green-walled, equipment storage for soldiers. Armour pieces, supplies, special tools, many of which floated around, knocked by her passing, spinning away and rebounding off surfaces, so that deathly stillness was replaced with ping pong disruption.

That was always your effect.

"Says the rifle chastising the pistol."

Opal gripped onto one of the hexagonal ceiling lights to hold herself in place. The lights had a small gap around the rim, turning them into climbing wall handholds. In fact, without gravity, every surface became both a wall and a floor. The way she crouched here made it seem like the equipment racks were upside down near the ceiling, and exits were up there too, only extending halfway down towards the surface she paused against. It was easy to reimagine the room as a water pool for swimming in, an idea reinforced by the lazily drifting debris around her.

She kicked upwards, a gentle glide to the first doorway.

It led to a martial-arts training room. What appeared to be the ceiling was a padded crashmat surface. Extending downwards were inverted humanoids, dummies fixed to posts for practicing strikes on. They'd normally be connected to an AI which could measure speed, accuracy and force. They now took on the appearance of bizarre chandeliers. Handheld weapons, batons, and blunt training blades twirled interminably. Across the room were two exits.

But she felt like she was being watched. A quick check back revealed nothing. Yet the feeling remained.

Instead of entering the hand-to-hand training room, she drift-ed to the next arch, just to see if there was anything beyond, and was about to stick her head over the threshold when she froze.

The room she looked into *seemed* innocuous. It was exactly what she had expected as the adjacent chamber. This one was the ranged combat practice area. More inanimate humanoids suspended from the ceiling, with target points marked out across their bodies and limbs, though the concentric circles had aged badly, distressed with dirt. These ones would be able to move thanks to magnetic tracks below the surface they were attached to, enabling the AI to alter difficulty and speed of encounters to match the soldier's ability level. The ceiling also had a range of decorated barriers which could retract into it, or extend fur-ther to become walls. These ever-changing mazes created urban warfare scenarios amongst which the soldiers and moving targets could roam. At present, some were withdrawn, some partially extended, some fully out. It meant there were blind spots from her position, areas where something could hide.

But nothing visible warranted the cold freeze that gripped her neck.

She peered around, sure that she was glimpsing movement, only to find that it was just HUD readouts. The GAMag suit interface was frustratingly slow to update, and the augmented vision overlays were more focussed on engineering structures than combat potentials. It was trying to be helpful but was just getting in the way.

The suit limitations are apparent.

"Yeah. Totally primitive compared to my EW suits."

With unfortunate irony in the term "Eternal Warrior". Eternal? You destroyed both of them.

She risked glancing away from the room for a moment to activate her forearm controls. Menu, menu, submenu, disable augmented reality overlays. This time, when she looked up, all the labels and outlines were gone completely. It was still not perfect – the helmet visor remained a narrow slit of tunnel vision – but what she saw was more natural, making it easier to focus on what she faced.

And that's when she saw it. Not a creature or an object, but an *absence*.

Nothing floated free in this room. Not a single object or piece of debris that wasn't a green Viscid particle. And the Viscids were static, too. It had been hard to spot that before, with all the pop-up info overlays every time she moved her head.

The stillness was uncanny, even by dead ship standards. The stillness at the deepest valley of a lifeless sea, where crushing pressure and lack of light and heat would leave you drained and starving, screaming silently in anguish at the loneliness as aeons passed, as you only wished for a companion, just a friend, a food, a thing to enter for some warmth, so cosy, protective, just come in, let me come in, we will ...

She shook her head, flung out the strange thoughts. Then her gaze was drawn to the barriers closest to her doorway. They blocked her view beyond. But as she looked at them, she was surprised by a pungent stench in her nostrils. Rotten, decaying. Also totally impossible, because her suit was sealed. When she momentarily glanced away, it faded. When she looked back at the barrier, it reeked.

And those barriers were only a second's leap away.

Opal thumped the door close button. It did nothing, as expected. But the door was there, the manual release handles visible at the top (well, actually the base of the door, but this flipped world made a joke out of perspectives). She grabbed them, wedged her foot against a wall panel, and tugged. The door lifted with a grinding sound, and the gap into the room shrunk. Soon it became just a slit at the height of her head, then it closed. She heard the click, but didn't want to rely on that alone. She removed the portable welder and ignited it, the fine hissing plasma that would blind an unprotected eye subdued by the suit's visor to a pearly flame. She used it to melt two parts of the door frame, preventing it from opening, then put her equipment back.

Nothing banged on the door, though the stink got stronger, as if there was now something just centimetres away from her on the other side of this barrier.

She swung into the martial training room, only just remembering to mark her return arrow, then crossed the open spaces, picking further doorways by instinct, marking route choices and continually moving.

That may have been akin to something you encountered on your first Lost Ship. Back then you were vulnerable, but that's not the case any more. How foolish I seem! I used to ridicule your belief in gut instinct, but it turns out my skepticism was misplaced.

"You know all of our past. How real are you?"

As real as you want me to be.

"You were always cryptic."

And you need to come to terms with your loss and pain.

"I ..."

It's okay. You always felt better when I was with you in the darkest places. And I'm here now.

"You kept me sane."

And I still do that. Though others might disagree if they watched you talking to yourself.

"Heh."

She emerged into another wide corridor. Instead of the regulation UFS grey, this one was panelled in greens and browns that resembled woods or other organic substances. The passage curved upwards in both directions, as if she was at the bottom of a fat hollow hoop. Definitely not standard UFS military architecture. And yet, the way the different styles and colours merged felt satisfying, complete, rather than random.

She'd have loved accurate floorplans, to analyse how these disparate shapes fitted together so seamlessly within the hull. She also noted that this corridor looped on a vertical plane, not a horizontal one, like a particle accelerator tilted ninety degrees. It wouldn't even be traversable in standard artificial gravity.

It was always worth taking a moment to feel out a new space. She hung in air just inside this ring of corridor. She was being watched again. The same sensation as earlier, but even stronger. Whenever she glanced in a direction where she expected to see a figure, there was nothing. Still, she couldn't delay just because this place gave her the shivers.

After marking her direction with spray paint, she drifted up the loop to her left. The corridor walls were lumpy when seen up close, skin-like bumps in the texture, each as big as her fist.

She gently pushed off the wall and glided to the one opposite, making zigzag progress from surface to surface.

She'd barely gone thirty metres within this huge torus when she came across her first trace of past life.

A body, floating in the centre of the corridor. It could even pass for human except it was larger than normal, would have been three metres tall – if it still had a head. The neck just ended in a ragged tear of brown flesh, the blood dessicated, the skin leathered, everything preserved for an endless slow tumble around this circular loop.

The thing – recreation, inanimate alien, unfortunate human – sported a kind of jumpsuit, similar to that worn by maintenance workers. Where there would have been an insignia Opal could only make out blurs, which made her want to squint her eyes as if that would restore lost detail. It looked long dead, and yet there was no way she'd pass within reaching distance of those mummified arms which resembled small tree trunks.

She manoeuvred carefully, tiny, precise leaps that let her glide along around the passage's inner bend, all the time watching that the body's sluggish gyrations did not alter.

You've been holding your breath.

True. She exhaled once she was back in the open. The lumpy growths made useful handholds to pull herself along. They were just squishy enough to give a good grip.

The motions repeated, the curves rolled past.

There was another exit, much larger than the doorways she'd encountered so far. It was on the corridor side nearest the outer hull. She pushed towards its edge, landing gracefully at the rim as if it was a pit in the floor and she peered down into it.

A stairwell, running up and down. Excellent. She could use it to –

"–-com–...on..."

A crackle of static in her ear, a hint of voice to it. She flinched back at the unexpectedness of the sound, almost lost her footing and floated up, but the minimal magnetism did its job.

"What's that?" she asked.

If this suit had a brain I'd be able to run tests. But it only responds to button presses, so ... probably just Lost Ship weirdness.

Opal leaned forward again. This time there was nothing for long moments, and then a stuttering hiss of interference which made her think the original sounds were just an illusion, her brain trying to apply patterns to random distortion.

And then she noticed the motion near her hand. She flinched back from the fleshy lump she'd been holding. It looked just as all the others had, fixed and harmless. But she was sure she'd seen something.

Another crackle in her earpiece, mixed with a whine of de-tuned signal, like you got with some low-res emissions. And as the sounds jabbed her eardrum, something twitched in the lump. When the noise faded out again, the subsurface movements ceased.

Curious now, she prodded the swelling.

It opened, tearing along a wet central seam, and an eye looked back at her. It vaguely resembled a human eyeball, but much bigger, with green veins running through it and triple pupils which all focussed on her.

More movement now, all around her. Other bulges opening, lids splitting apart, the whole passageway revealing the eyes embedded in its surface. And they weren't all the same type. Some looked reptilian, others like pools of gelid liquid, and another kind – which at first had seemed more like oversized speakers – she realised were perhaps imitations of compound eyes.

Urgh. She'd been squeezing them all for propulsion, not realising the surface was an eyelid. Perhaps it explained the feeling of being watched, though. She felt the full force of their gaze, even a sensation of heat, like animosity against her skin. Every eye focussed on her.

"That's repulsive," she said. "Why embed eyes in the walls?"

Maybe it is another example of Lost Ship misinterpretation. Most human craft have cameras throughout their interiors, after all.

"Well, the weird crackling sound in my ear is gone," she said, leaning over the drop into the stairwell entrance. "I don't know if they were making the sounds, or if the audio came from somewhere else and they didn't like it. Either way, they're awake now."

She reached an arm out, into the set of stairs. And even though it was silent, she felt a shudder in her spine. Only this wasn't a bad feeling. it was more like a pull. A *promise*.

"This is the way I'm meant to go."

She was about to drop into it when she heard the new sound. Not radio interference, but heavy thuds, coming from her previous direction. She both dreaded, and knew, what it would be even before she turned.

Loops

... 19 ...

The headless giant that had seemed so dead and dried-out a few minutes ago now seemed very much alive and active, using its long arms to rebound off surfaces as a means of propulsion.

Slam, it hit a wall, digging fingertips into the surface so hard it broke through, tearing a chunk away to reveal wet redness beyond. This grip enabled another muscular pull, rocketing towards the next point. It was almost upon her: only the thunderous pounding had given her enough forewarning of its approach to do something about it.

Distance was needed, and fast. Open spaces where she could gain an advantage. If she guessed right, and this circular corridor was a big loop with no blockages, then it could be enough.

She snatched her hand grapple, fired it into the darkness of the corridor, away from her pursuer. It struck, and she pulled the trigger, immediately being yanked through the thick atmosphere towards an unknown point. The creature smashed into the spot she'd left moments before. A glance backwards showed it had relaunched itself on a new trajectory in pursuit.

Endless clusters of alien eyes twitched as they tracked her around the ring. Her line whirred shorter and shorter, creating the risk of smacking into corridor wall, stunning herself. Flicking the release sent a signal along the cable so that the nano-adhesive disconnected and the grapnel hook collapsed in on itself, releasing the point of purchase. The cable retracted into the gun with a whizz of precision.

Opal fired towards the opposite, inner wall, far ahead, even though she already moved at high speed. Connection, trigger the retract. The first wall she'd fired at loomed towards her out of the darkness, fast, but her new point of pull started to take effect and alter her course, yanking her in a different direction. Opal took a few running steps along the outer surface she'd been originally flying towards, and by then the pull was enough to take her fully on the new angle into darkness.

Running along the wall had meant treading on some of the eyes. Her heavy metal boots protected her, but the squishiness underfoot meant she was glad she couldn't see what a mess she'd left behind.

The manoeuvres had created distance, she could tell by the slight drop in volume of the creature's pursuit. And so far she'd been lucky, with no obstacles in the corridor. Small items bounced off her body, and one piece of debris shattered against her shoulder – a floating ceramic cup with a handle, she realised – but nothing that could hurt.

Another disconnect, another aim and fire, hit, retract, zigging towards the outer wall again. She zoomed far faster than a human could sprint, and as long as she didn't strike anything to slow her, or mess up the grapple pistol's action, that speed would increase every time.

Her biggest fear was that the passage would end, not being a full circle after all.

No, not true. Her *biggest* fear was that it would be blocked by the alien web of the shaft, and she'd fly into it, so deep that she'd be incapacitated, waiting until something came to investigate her frantic struggling.

Actually, no, her biggest fear was –

Wall looming up, too close. Disconnect, aim, fire. Smack into the previous surface, bounce off, feel the tug on her shoulder as the cable became taut again, pulling her onwards.

Always watched. They might only be eyes but a spike of animosity emanated from them, she knew it. They wanted her dead. Or worse.

She risked another look to her rear. The creature was at the limit of her vision. Perhaps if she continued this process, then by the time she got back to the staircase she'd have enough of a lead. She could slip into the stairwell and lose it there. With luck, the creature would keep looping, seeking her in the ring until it gave up.

Disconnect, retract, ready to aim ... and she was going so fast she had no time to do anything as structures emerged from the darkness ahead. They looked like long fingernails, thick and curved and pointed, growing out of the walls. There would be room to slip amongst them given good lighting and control, but she smacked into the first one and shattered it, crusty pieces tumbling with her, then her leg caught another with such force it spun her to crash off further obstacles. If the suit hadn't had armour plates on the upper thigh it would probably have broken her femur. Damn, that hurt now, and would hurt even more later.

Flailing, trying to grab anything to control her spin. More collisions. She realised these growths ended in clusters of eyes, like stalks. The glistening wall surfaces here were uneven and fleshy, but that was all she had time to acknowledge. Her pursuer was gaining while she still tried to orient herself in this forest of peepers. It did seem to be thinning, but there was still no chance of quickly launching away until she was through it.

She wedged her feet against two of the stalks, finally halting, one hand holding tight to the nearest rigid, veiny outcrop. Her head spun as if the corridor turned around her. But she had to snap out of it, recover her sense of balance quickly.

The heavy harpoon gun was strapped to her back. She unclipped it and adopted a crouched firing position. Obviously the bolt that was loaded didn't have any cable attached. She activated the open mode, and the bolt's end flowered into a hooked grapnel.

The headless humanoid had already reached the first stalks, smashed through them as if they were made of tissue paper.

She aimed. She fired.

She fucking missed, and the bolt sailed past its hip.

Impatient, Opal. You know better than that.

This wasn't a rapid-firing military weapon. Once a bolt was launched the loading cartridge would rotate, and slide the next heavy projectile into the firing mechanism. A whirr, a click, a beep of readiness. If this shot missed, then she wouldn't get another.

Slow breath. Look through the sights. Ignore the dizziness. Aim. Make sure her posture was still, her feet secured against something to mitigate recoil. Visibility was poor but her target was big, and its movement in zero-G involved predictable lines. Fear that might tremble a hand wasn't something she would allow. She'd faced death down before. Wait until it was close, wait until it couldn't evade, and she couldn't miss.

Three.

Two.

One.

The creature almost filled her visor's view when she pulled the trigger. The open end of the harpoon punched it in the gut, sent it flying back. The harpoon bolt spun away, having failed to penetrate because it had already been in the open position. But that was fine. She'd needed some more moments, and this created them.

Bolt three rotated into the firing mechanism. She didn't open the harpoon blades. Last time a battering ram had been useful, but now something else was called for. She changed the mode so that the blades would only expand *after* impact.

She aimed and fired. The bolt streaked away and thudded into corridor surface just beyond the eye stalks. It punched in and locked into place, jutting out like a giant metal needle.

She'd missed again.

The giant had managed to gain some purchase, ready to launch itself at her.

Whirr. Click. Beep.

Fire.

This time she was on target. The bolt thumped into its chest before it could get away, and through the body into the wall behind. The hooks dilated, securing it to the wall's surface, leaving a metal rod stuck out of the creature's body.

It struggled, having some trouble coordinating itself while pinned, but began to manoeuvre itself off, pushing against the wall to slide along the metal bolt.

Whirr, click, beep.

A second harpoon punctured the giant, this time near its hip, resetting its progress. Two bars holding it in place.

Whirr, click, beep.

Aiming was getting easier now. A third bolt, ripping into its left shoulder.

Whirr, click, buzz.

She fired but nothing happened. Of course, cartridge empty.

The creature wasn't killed – if it was even alive to begin with. But the securing rods would definitely give her some time.

Never leave a weapon unloaded if you might need it. She ejected the empty cartridge and seized the spare. A chunky ker-chak indicated it was locked into place, then she fastened the rifle to her back again.

Based on the angle the corridor curved at, if this really was a full torus then in a few hundred metres she'd be back at her starting point.

Watching the headless, mummified corpse struggle suggested she'd have a minute or two before it got free. That might be enough. But something nagged at her. A conjunction of concepts.

Firstly, the creature tracked her, even though it had no obvious visual senses. Which, really, didn't mean much, but she was running with the idea.

Meanwhile another alien form observed her, but wasn't directly attacking.

Her experiences on Lost Ships, and more recently in the deep ocean of Fressus, had made it clear that symbiosis was possible between Null Entities. So why not here? One thing as a tool for the other. She might continue, but if she was observed all that time, and there *was* a connection, then she'd be tracked. The creature would know which way she had gone. May well be relentless in its pursuit.

It was easy enough to test her evolving idea.

Her belt pouches contained micro flares. She fumbled one out – GAMag gauntlets weren't the most nimble of instruments – and twisted the cap. It erupted into red flame, the default colour if you didn't change the chemical composition setting at its base. She held it up.

The nearest clusters – disconcertingly moist ones that resembled sad bovine eyes – closed up tight, as if they'd never existed. More distant ones jittered in what might be discomfort or anger. She flicked the flare in that direction and they closed immediately.

What was even more interesting was that the monstrous cadaver was also affected, momentarily ceasing attempts to extricate itself from the pinning rods.

The flares had a pretty good burn time. Because they had a store of all the chemicals they needed, including oxygen, they worked in almost any environment, even underwater. Opal activated another handful, and changed the colour settings: bright white, cyan, yellow. She flung them in both directions, letting them bounce off obstacles, turning the corridor into a festival of light.

The eyes retreated, ending their surveillance.

Opal used the now-sightless eye stalks as handles to manoeuvre herself, gliding from one to another. Soon they faded out completely, and the meatiness of the corridor walls morphed into normal curved and reinforced alloy panels again. It was good to leave an area that resembled being trapped in a giant throat.

Before long, open eyes surrounded her again, the smaller ones embedded in the veneer. She struck a flare and let it go, immediately regaining her privacy. Then she used the grapple pistol to pull herself around, using the same method as originally, but at a gentler pace, and shorter trajectory lines, so she'd have more time to respond to any dangers which might loom up at her.

But there were none.

Every so often she dropped another flare, so that coloured lights illuminated the surfaces around her. There was a hint of the vibrant fairy grotto that always entered her dreams, and which would have created unexpected delight in the past. But now she associated it with the truth, that hypnotic Forgetting Room back aboard the Leviathan. The effect was no longer magical, but suffused with disappointment.

So be it. Growing up meant casting aside childish dreams. This one had taken longer to shatter than most, but nothing lasted forever. Youth. Idealism. Good times. Knee joints. All faded like a dying flare.

PURSUERS

... 18 ...

She located the yellow markings back at her starting point. Onwards, to the next exit, and the stairs.

Only a handful of flares remained. She decided to use them all up. The first ones she flung as hard as she could in both directions, to ricochet around the ring. The last ones she threw more gently, bathing her local area in a wash of neon colours. She hadn't seen any of the eyes open for some time. Maybe they had decided it was pointless and painful. Maybe they'd gone back to sleep. Either way, she regretted the time this had wasted.

Nothing awaited her inside the lip of the stairwell apart from a momentary crackle of interference, then it was gone. She sprayed an arrow, then dropped through the hole that was really a doorway, and ascended the stairs. Except, since up and down didn't really mean much in zero-G, her brain interpreted it that she swam downwards against the ceiling, using the risers for propulsion as she descended a series of forty-five-degree slopes.

The reversal of perception didn't phase her. She remembered how some recruits in basic training had real trouble adjusting their mental maps in zero-G. They just couldn't see new approaches as normal, rigidly trying to enforce their ideas of up and down and usually failing miserably. Disorientation and vomiting were the result. Not great when both occurred within a sealed suit. But that course was one of those where Opal excelled. The trick was not to get too fixated on whether something was a wall, floor or ceiling. They were all just surfaces.

"Adapt and survive." That was her squad's motto. Seemed so long ago now. An officer had once insulted them with the name Scumdogs, because her squad were misfits and low-Purity categories, but they adopted the moniker with pride. Scumdogs stopped being a pathetic put-down, its force defused and reclaimed as their badge of honour.

She didn't feel trepidation on this long upside-down crawl. It was as if she knew that no dangers lurked around each corner.

Maybe Entities don't all get on so well as the eyes and body combo. So there's a downtime between contested territories.

"I reckon there's some truth to that. But hey: you were quiet during my fight in the big loop back there. I could have used some help."

How egocentric. You didn't sense my presence in that time of trial, saw only one set of footprints, so assumed I was elsewhere. But perhaps that was the time when I carried you. We're more closely entwined than you think.

"So you gave me the ideas of what to do?"

I don't like to deal in certainties because there is no such thing. Just as I increasingly accept the idea that even separation may be an illusion.

"Philosophical."

I was thus in life. In death it's even easier. I have a lot of thinking time.

"I don't like to think of you as –"

Opal was interrupted by another crackling burst of sound, which was certainly voice this time.

"... wait! ... saw the signs ... coming ..."

The words were distorted with interference, and sounded artificial and alien as a result.

She ceased to crawl. Instead she moved to a corner of the stairwell and anchored herself there, able to kick away at a moment's notice. She dimmed the suit's lights, and took up the heavy harpoon launcher.

Would the source of the crackling sounds approach from above, or below? Was it connected to a physical being? In fact, could she be sure this was any more real than the other voices in her head?

While she waited, Opal messed around with her suit's receiver bands, looking for active transmissions from unexpected sources. Nothing. Her comms were probably malfunctioning.

Then she noticed the light. A glow from around the stairwell corner, increasing in brightness as something ascended towards her. Darker patches indicated vague shadows. Perhaps more than one thing approached.

She had images in her head, Tentaculat-like creatures with inner lights, long and deadly limbs, bioluminescent twitches.

Perhaps she'd just been tricked into waiting. Some Lost Ship creature ordered a dinner and was on its way to pick it up.

Now that she had a direction, she aimed the harpoon gun at that corner. Her hand squeezed the handle tight, and she had to release her grip, for fear of activating the trigger too soon.

The brightness and shadows grew together, as if something had rounded another bend towards her. The brighter the light, the more pronounced the misshapen edges of the silhouettes. Athene would have been able to reverse calculate light ray emissions, reflections, geometries and so on to determine the possibilities for the shape of whatever approached. Opal only had her imagination, and that erred towards the macabre. Trying to move on now would just mean she had something on her tail, and by turning her back she presented her most vulnerable region. No, face it and know.

The shadows definitely made her think of a multi-limbed creature. Fuck a doodle do.

Its appearance around the final bend of stairs was imminent. Her arm was steady, aim perfect. She'd have time to shoot before it could reach her.

If it was a threat, she reminded herself.

Something jutted around the corner. Silvery skin. A kind of bulbous head, hard to reconstruct in that first moment due to the lights it emitted, but she held her fire. She couldn't judge anything by appearance. Not in Lost Ships, not in the real world. The most twisted and cruel beings often wore a human skin.

Then she saw the faces within the swollen heads. The heads that were helmets, the plates that were visors, the limbs coated in protective material and attached lights.

EVA suits. Civilian ones.

An adult and a child, which explained why the shadows had been harder to parse while they crawled up the stairs.

Clarissa and Rettix.

As they drifted around the corner and saw her, they looked as surprised as Opal felt. No doubt they hadn't expected to find Opal here, pointing a weapon at them.

Opal lowered it, and waved.

Clarissa waved back.

Opal made the double-arm-pat-point gesture they'd used with each other on Mossareid when they were kids, and thought it was cool to adopt gang signs and posturing.

Clarissa circled two pointing fingers around her ears, the response that meant acknowledgement.

Okay, that was as much confirmation as Opal needed for now. Sure, if something was impersonating people she knew, then it might also be able to pull other details from her head, but doubt had to have limits.

She activated the comm system on her suit, choosing a low-res channel that wouldn't announce itself to the world with extreme pulses of energetic traffic, but would still be fine for local voice chatter. She lowered the signal strength further, then held up the forearm display so that Rettix could see the setup Opal had chosen.

Rettix nodded, and altered her own suit settings.

"Can you hear me?" Rettix asked.

"Yep. That's good, I was worried my comm system had fried. Maybe it's just long-range stuff that's not working, or the hull blocks transmissions."

Rettix was already performing the alterations on Clarissa's suit, while the girl mouthed words at Opal, impatient to speak.

"Why the open channel?" Rettix asked as she worked. "Shouldn't we encrypt?"

"I think any form of transmission might attract unwanted attention. The simpler the signal, the lower the power, and the closer the range, the less chance of being heard."

And then Clarissa's voice joined in, and she pushed away from Rettix and drifted into Opal for a hug.

"We found you!" the girl said. "I told Rettix we would!"

Opal separated from the cuddle and extended her sister to arm's length, a manoeuvre that set them both slowly rotating in the stairwell.

"But why are you here?" Opal asked, trying to instil seriousness. "You're not meant to be here!"

"We couldn't get back to the bridge. It was blocked by the red gooey stuff. Every way we went, it was there."

Opal looked to Rettix for confirmation.

"It's true," the woman replied. "We were trapped."

"Couldn't you have waited? Called for a team to burn away obstacles, get you out?"

There was something in Rettix's eyes, a momentary vagueness, as if she was also confused about her course of action. She glanced at Clarissa, then back at Opal, and the doubt seemed to fade way. "Honestly, we looked into other options but it was all too ... Well, we had the equipment nearby, and Clarissa suggested it ... A good idea. So we put on these suits. The stores had the whole range of sizes, for the transported colony families."

"I didn't need much help," Clarissa boasted. "I saw the video on the Solace that you have to watch before you board, all about emergencies and stuff. Gloria made me watch the kids' version, and I still remember it even now, because it wasn't that long ago really, I don't think. There was a bit about these spacesuits. 'Clunky cleck, atmo check!'"

Opal eyed the silvery outfits with disdain. They had pressure, insulation, radiation barriers and oxygen, sure, but they weren't resilient to abrasion. Not designed for lots of close-quarters movement. Certainly not configured for hazardous spaces like an alien ship. It only took one bad tear and life expectancy shrank to nothing.

"You both need to go back," Opal commanded. "You should have known better, Rettix."

"I'm sorry," said the woman. "But we can't return. The things invading the ship were about to break into our section. Everyone was stretched. This was our only hope. We crossed the cable you'd set up, came in the airlock, and followed the signs you'd left. We tried calling you but never got a response."

"Did you encounter anything?"

"No. It was ... quiet."

Clarissa chipped in. "When we got to the bit near here it was like a big bendy tube, with coloured candles floating in it. I felt like it was bad, but the arrows showed us the way out straight away, and then we got to you here."

Which, of course, explained how they'd caught up. No detours, no dead ends, no being chased around by weird creatures. They just followed the breadcrumb trail, and had been lucky. But it could have gone so wrong. Opal tried not to think about those possibilities. There was only the now-now, and the now-to-come.

"Aren't you glad to see me?" asked Clarissa, as if suddenly realising this wasn't something to celebrate.

"Of course I'm glad. But this place is unsafe, and I never want you to get hurt." Opal frowned at Rettix again, and it was obvious the accusation was felt by the recipient. Rettix wouldn't meet Opal's gaze.

"We won't get hurt. Not when you're with us. Being with my big sis means nothing's scary. Not even a big old spaceship with no lights. Don't worry. I've been in a place like this before." She sniffed. "It wasn't that bad. I don't know why the grown ups were all screaming."

Fuck. Opal didn't even know what had happened on the Solace. Never got around to speaking with Clarissa about it. But the fact that the kid wasn't scared was a good sign. Maybe if they were careful and quiet, they could avoid waking up anything else which didn't particularly like visitors.

"Okay," said Opal. "What's done is done. We'll move on. Rettix, did you bring any weapons?" Opal had seen their hands were empty, but hoped the woman might have something useful in her EVA suit pouches.

Rettix shook her head. "No time. Sorry, I even forgot to pick up your pistol, we were too busy getting our gear on. It was all a panic."

"Fine. But when we move on, you *have* to follow my rules. I need a promise. Especially from you, Clarissa."

"What rules?" asked the girl.

"The most important one: do what I say, and do it straight away. No matter how scary it seems."

They both nodded.

"Secondly. Pay attention to what's around us. Look. Listen. So no unnecessary chatter, anything that might distract us. We need to be quiet. Both for focus, and to avoid attracting attention."

More affirmation.

"Third. Last one. Don't get curious. Things are not as they seem. If you see something weird, avoid it. The less you interact with the ship, the safer we'll be. Sometimes things might be sleeping. If you can avoid waking them, then we might just get through this."

Another nod.

"Clarissa, summarise."

"Do what you tell us. Be quiet and observe. Don't mess around."

"Close enough. Just remember that I've been through this before. On my own. *Twice*. And I'm still alive and in one piece. Three of us means triple the brain power." Nonsense, but maybe enough to give a little girl something resembling hope. "Apart from that ... prepare for strangeness."

LOADERS

Opal led the way, pulling against a stair to drift upwards a few metres, then another push to glide further. At the corners a hand touch to a wall enabled turning. It became a graceful sequence. Clarissa followed, and Rettix brought up the rear. They'd adapted well to zero-G, and had no problem keeping up with Opal's cautious pace.

So far, Opal had ascended around twelve decks. At this rate they'd soon be near the centre levels of the ship, hopefully close to the Spine.

At the next bend she found herself beside a blister of seared flesh which had burst long ago, leaving dried edges of skin and long, jagged ... well, legs, horns, who knew? A number of them extended from the flaky wall at a range of angles and positions, as if something had died in the process of crawling through.

Opal felt one of the rough limbs touch her from behind, so she pushed a stair to spin, and saw it was only Clarissa who'd bumped into her. They gathered on that small landing and watched, but there was no movement from the tissue, no sign of life or threat.

Clarissa reached towards it. Opal snatched her wrist and drew it back, spinning the girl.

"What are you doing?" she asked.

"I just need to touch it. It's okay, it won't harm me. Please. I need to know something. Owsies, you're squeezing my arm."

Opal let go, which Clarissa interpreted as permission, and she'd already placed a hand on one of the hardened ridges before Opal could intervene again.

Nothing happened. No twitches, no pulsing flesh, no movement.

Clarissa let go. "It's dead," she said.

"I could have told you that without you needing to touch it. It's an old flesh portal. That's what I call them, anyway."

"No it's ... hard to explain. I was checking to see if there was any life energy left, because then we could have used it."

"Really?" Opal glanced at the repulsive wall growth. She shouldn't be surprised, since Clarissa had created something like this in her fugue state. "What, to travel?"

"Maybe. It's just an idea."

Rettix watched them uneasily, eyes flicking from one to the other. "You understand these things?" Rettix asked.

"A bit," said Opal.

"I knew you'd been on a Lost Ship from our briefing, but why is Clarissa ... Is there something I don't know about you both?"

"No. It's just my experience plus guesswork. Come on, let's get moving. Avoid brushing against any of those spiny limbs. They're sharp."

They made it another seven decks before the stairs topped out, ending at a large landing with viewscreens embedded into the walls, all dusty and dead. This terminus was standard, since any routes between decks needed to be sealable in case of breach or boarders. A single pedestrian route through the whole ship would introduce environmental and security risks, so the tendency was to have short vertical sections, then a transition through corridors and bulkheads.

With luck they were high enough to have reached a floor with Spine access. If not, they were certainly a lot closer.

The wide exit door up here was closed. Opal thumped the access button in the vain hope of action, and was surprised when a green light appeared on the panel, and the door did actually start moving.

"You must be my lucky charm," Opal said to Clarissa, who grinned with satisfaction at the idea.

As the door rose up into the ceiling Opal was ready to push the others back if anything tried to scrabble underneath, but so far the only sign of movement was a slow strobe of light.

That, in itself, was strange after so long with the Lost Ship in darkness, but she'd encountered such things before. Maybe this deck had power, which explained the door working. Functioning infrastructure could offer new options.

This area's function soon became apparent. Opal led them into a wide throughway, since there were no immediate dangers.

The right-hand side of the passage dropped away to overlook a huge line of machinery. It was a set of thick circles rotating around a horizontal spindle which ran parallel to the walkway. The metal cylinders contained hollow tubes which lined up during each spin. A tremendous rumbling emanated from all the moving parts, the largest cylinder more than fifteen metres in diameter, which was not only audible as heavy machinery in work, but also felt as a vibration whenever you touched a floor or wall surface.

Many of the rotating cylinders had rings of lights in red or white. As they spun, it flung disorientating shadows across the corridor, immediately blasted away in brightness before the stark black lines once more ran over everything. Opal's group halted a moment to let their eyes adjust to the confusing visual disruption.

"Is that an engine?" asked Clarissa.

"Sort of," replied Opal. "Not for propulsion, though. It's the Gunnerbat: a loading mechanism for some of the big guns warships have mounted on the hull. Those that have physical projectiles, anyway. Bombardment shells, missiles, AP flechette cartridges. The white lights mean loaded, red indicates empty. The cylinders can transfer armaments to the next along when they're aligned, then some of them have off-ramp pipelines to the actual weapons. See those control panels every so often, overlooking the mechanisms?"

Clarissa nodded.

"They can halt a section for reloading. The different sized holes are for different bore sizes of ammunition. Some of the shell and missile cluster loaders are pretty big."

"I guess all the racks lining the other side of the corridor are the things they load into the holes?" asked Rettix.

Opal drifted over to one of the storage areas Rettix had pointed to.

"Exactly. At least, that would be the case on a normal ship." She looked at the sets of shelves, which had mobile brackets to hold the contents in place, the brackets readjusting themselves as shells were removed. At first glance everything resembled what she'd seen during her short stint on UFS Corcorius, but it didn't surprise her when closer examination broke the illusion.

One set of shells should have been grey alloy, stamped with payload and batch numbers, but instead each was made of a bone-like white material that looked more like it had been grown. Adjacent to that was a compartment of missiles, Stinger types, though the areas where text should have been stamped on them were just blurs. And when she looked behind, she could see fine white filaments running from their rears and disappearing into the wall, like tiny cables or mould spores. Either way, it was a detail that shouldn't exist in the human versions.

"Can we use them?" asked Rettix. "Maybe as bombs?"

"Nope. They look like human weapons, but they're not. They might be inert, or they could be alive, or traps, or turn to acid when you touch them. Remember rule three: where possible, don't touch. The things that made or altered this ship generally do okay with architecture and infrastructure, but anything small enough to move is always suspect."

Opal gripped a railing and launched herself ahead down the length of the Gunnerbat walkway.

"Stay near the centre," she said. "Although mesh barriers block sections where loading doesn't take place, there are still also lots of open areas. The mechanism uses a number of magnetic fields. Drift into that machinery, you'll be squished."

The three of them made their way through the strobing light-show. The moving shadows left Opal on edge, as if something swooped at her all the time, while the mesh sections created web-like lattice patterns like a net being thrown over the humans.

Doorways punctuated the left wall, but this was a good opportunity to continue towards the centre line of the ship.

"It's a long thing," said Clarissa, after a while of drifting in silence.

"Yep. On the biggest ships, cruiser class, this system might run almost fully across the vessel. On smaller ones like a corvette they can be half a kilometre. It's designed so that the guns can keep up a bombardment for as long as necessary, with the only limit being ammunition. And believe me, the UFS has pretty big stores of *that* on every craft. Hey, Rettix, watch your position."

Rettix had been drifting towards the edge that dropped down to the Gunnerbat, as if not fully focussed. She kicked off the ceiling, angling back towards the inner wall where the ammunition stores were.

The rotating lights gave glimpses of how far the route extended. They moved in cycles, so it was bright in Opal's area, then it faded to darkness while the next region was bright, and so on, as if a glowing plasma beam had been fired down the corridor, illuminating its local environment on the journey, and another was fired before that one was out of sight.

Hypnotic. A pulse of light they followed. They drifted within. They merged with. They –

She shook her head to clear it. She was tired. A glance back confirmed that Clarissa and Rettix seemed okay. The silence made the monotony of this route more wearying.

"Hey, Clarissa, do you want to sing me a song?" Opal asked. A calculated risk, but Opal hoped the sealed suits and close-range efficient comms would be the signal equivalent of barely audible whispers to any nearby creatures.

"Okay. What?"

"Anything that makes you happy. You have a good voice."

"Erm, oh, I remember one:

Ringo lights,

Ringo lights,

Falling down the sky-o,

Fall into my eye-o."

Her voice was earnest, soothing. That same innocence she always had. Hearing her be a child again, that was ... wow. But the song was weirdly dirgelike, off-key in a way that seemed ominously creepy in this environment.

"Not that one," Opal said. She didn't want to give the other reason: that it was something they sang in the orphanage, which now had a whole other layer of connotations Opal didn't want in her head. "What about something from Mossareid, when it was just you and me?"

"Oh yes, Poppy Pappap!" Then Clarissa broke out into one of the nonsense songs that she'd picked up from the Mossounds entcast which she'd loved. Opal was pretty sure Clarissa had misheard some of the lyrics, but the exuberance she always put into the recital made it exactly what Opal wanted to hear right now.

"You think so hot, you always blow!

No no, no, one step two step!

I forgive, I believe,

One step two step – Go go go!

Flowers in the fountain,

Chased around the mountain,

I ain't the suck suck, so go blow!"

Opal smiled to hear it again, hadn't really thought about that silly song in a loooong time.

"That's all I can remember," Clarissa said. "If I was dancing I might pull out more."

"No dancing," Opal said.

"But I bet I could do the perfect flip in zero-G!"

Opal was drifting safely straight down the centre of the corridor so tucked in her neck and glanced back, to make sure Clarissa wasn't trying any silly stunts. It was fine, the girl just floated along merrily, and took a moment to wave back at Opal.

Rettix had fallen behind.

"Hey, Rettix, you okay?" Opal asked.

"Yes. I was just thinking about something, sorry." She gripped a shelf and gave an extra push, closing the distance.

Opal faced front again and thought she could see something ahead. When the next pulse of light raced along the corridor and passed it, she was sure, because in the moment of stark brightness it cast a shadow against the facing wall. That second was enough to give Opal an idea of size and position as the shadow swept along.

"Slow a moment," Opal said. "Obstacle up ahead. Don't worry, it isn't moving."

As she got closer it became obvious the mass was organic. Smooth and glossy skin on most surface areas, but the serene tumbling revealed a wetter set of moist organs on the underbelly. Opal recognised it.

One of the creatures she thought of as a Satreweth. This one was about the mass of a human, which possibly marked it as juvenile, based on the size of some of the others she'd encountered on Lost Ships.

"Ooh, it looks like Dolphin Boy, from the cartoons," said Clarissa, knocking into Opal. "But it's all cut open and its belly is hanging out."

"I think that's how it's meant to be." Opal eyed the glistening organs, unknowably complex and alien. Maybe something to do with propulsion, or extracting elements from the surrounding atmosphere. Weapons, too, since at least a few of them had been able to spit wriggling barbs at her, like wrists stripped of flesh down to the bone.

"No, don't touch it!" Opal snapped as Clarissa reached out.

"Sorry," said Clarissa. "Rule three, I know. It just seems sad. Is it dead?"

Rettix had joined them now, anchoring herself to corrugated wall panelling.

"I think so," said Opal. She pulled herself carefully over the ceiling to get closer. The small detail that had been bugging her was more obvious now. Tiny holes in the creature's flesh, which leaked thick globules of whitish blood. Perhaps it had been shot by something akin to a flechette gun, and bled out, since Opal now also noted that it seemed dessicated, as if drained of fluids. There was a puckering to the skin, especially near the small, bubbling holes.

The slow leaks suggested – if even the vaguest elements of human-known biology applied – that its death hadn't been too long ago.

And Satreweth travelled in packs.

Messes

... 16 ...

Opal looked both ways, and spotted what she sought on a wall ten metres away. Yes, acidic score marks burnt into it from the creature's undersides. She calculated the angle, confirming it had glanced off this surface. Closer examination revealed a slight effervescence to the wall still. Fresh blood. Only the mesh barriers had prevented the corpse from being sucked into the machinery and minced already.

The creature had come from the direction Opal's group were heading in.

Of course, it could be nothing. For all she knew, some of these creatures travelled alone. Maybe it was old, and the holes were part of the death process. But if it had strayed from the pack and met an untimely fate, its compatriots might come looking for it.

"We need to go," said Opal. "We've made good progress along here, but we should take one of the side exits, head more to the interior of the ship."

"Is something wrong?" asked Rettix.

"Nah. All fine. Just a detour. I'll lead."

The nearest exit was a narrow, sloping passage away from the rotating lights. Opal propelled herself down it.

This route was a triangular prism in cross section, the walls coming together in a point above. The architectural style wasn't familiar to her from any UFS craft she'd ever been on board, but didn't Nuafri ships have three-sided design elements?

After winding to the left and right in sinuous curves, the corridor opened into a wide room. And this one's function was as obvious as it was macabre.

It was a mess hall. Long tables and benches bolted to the floor, as standard on starships, so as not to be flung around during battle and collisions, or if the artificial gravity systems failed. It would be ridiculous for your crew to survive a shell barrage only to be brained by flying furniture.

But not everything was secured. Drifting throughout the space were the paraphernalia of eating and drinking. Trays, plates, cutlery, cups, bits of mouldy food, all slowly floated along their own trajectories, colliding sometimes with another item and pinging away on a new route. She could cope with that.

It was the bodies she was more concerned about. She counted at least five in the area that her helmet beams illuminated. The shadows beyond might house many times more before the end of the mess hall was reached.

The other two caught up, and Rettix muttered a mild curse.

"Clarissa, don't look," said Opal. "Not yet."

"I've seen bodies before."

"I need you to keep an eye on the route behind us, make sure we're not followed."

Sometimes easier to redirect than to argue.

"I don't understand," said Rettix. "If this is one of your Lost Ships, why are there dead *humans* on board? And what killed them?"

"I can't answer for sure," said Opal. "Maybe this is a ship the aliens captured and rebuilt, but they kept some of the contents, and that included these souls. The disaster illustrates its state when it went through the Null, and tells a sad tale of devastation and loss. Or maybe this is a new construct based on what aliens found on a human ship. They often misinterpret. Perhaps they thought the bodies were an element of design, or were meant to be like that, so rebuilt their own versions just as they might with a chair or an engine. I also can't rule out the possibility that they're not dead bodies or reconstructions, but actual Entities that take on that form."

Opal's brow was wet with sweat. GAMag suits didn't have high-quality environmental controls. She wished she could reach through the visor and wipe her face. Without gravity the liquid didn't run down, but spread over her skin. She had to make do with blinking salty water out whenever it seeped into her eyes.

So far, Opal didn't detect any immediate danger. If things were as they appeared, then she could throw herself across the centre of the room and eventually reach the other side. There might be some collisions along the way, but she could account for that.

The danger would be if something lurked in the gloom and approached when they were partway across. Without jet packs they couldn't just change direction in zero-G. You had to push *against* something to create movement in the opposite direction.

Without an opposing force you could only progress along one path, the one you'd already committed to.

She observed the motions of the bodies in their torpid revolutions. None of them had much momentum. Perhaps it had been dampened from collisions over an unknown period, the energy transferred to the room surfaces and thereafter the hull, which was of such a great mass it could absorb it. If the bodies pinged around like ball bearings in a shaker, it would have been too chaotic to avoid them, but with them being so slow ... Hmmmm.

"We need to cross the room. Ideally I'd go on my own first, just to make sure it's safe, and then come back for you," Opal explained. "On the way I'd shove some of the bodies to clear a route. But it would take too long doing three traversals, and I don't want to leave you alone. So we'll connect up and I'll tow you both."

Rettix said, "If Clarissa closes her eyes, she won't even need to see the corpses."

"I told you I don't mind them!" Clarissa protested. "People died on the Solace, too. Someone's brains exploded out of their ear."

Opal frowned at the girl. There was a lot to catch up on, if ever they had the chance. For now, Opal should be thankful that her sister took everything in her stride.

Back to the current task. Hopefully there would be an exit directly opposite their current location. Opal took a short fastening cable from her toolbelt, attaching one end to a clip on her suit and the other end to Clarissa. Then the same process with Rettix. After testing they were secure, she counted down from three and they all pushed off into the room together, so that Opal wouldn't be dragged back by their static mass.

Slow and steady, a gentle drift towards the other side. She knocked small items out of the way: a spinning plate, a fizzy drink canister. Then the first of the bodies loomed towards her. She didn't want to touch it with her hands, so took the bolt rifle. It gave her extra reach, too. As she passed the body she prodded it gently, redirecting it towards a corner of the room.

It looked convincingly human. If this was a normal vessel she'd assume a loss of oxygen had led to everyone in the dining hall suffocating.

Nudging the corpse had altered her trajectory slightly. If she was careful to push on the opposite side next time, each body contact could correct her course, keeping her on roughly the same line.

"Everything okay?" asked Rettix.

Opal glanced back. The short-range lights they were all using didn't project far due to the particle-dense green atmosphere of Lost Ships, which created an imposing gloom in every direction. "Yep. Just another day in the glorious graveyard patrol."

Another body in the way. This time Opal waited until she was passing more closely, so that she could push at the correct point to change her path. Up close she noticed a detail that had escaped her before – tiny puncture wounds. They resembled those on the Satreweth's flesh.

Had something burrowed into the corpses? That was a new thought, and a disconcerting one.

She poked it away cautiously, anticipating the explosion of maggots that never came. The body continued in its graceless dance. Limbs flopped loosely, ragdolls rather than stiff-jointed statues.

Her progress had slowed. Perhaps they should have launched themselves with more force. She tried not to have the ticking timer at the front of her brain, but she could imagine what was occurring on the Owlflight. And yet, rushing could lead to disaster here, which would also be disaster *there*.

A cluster of bodies hung in the air not far ahead. She'd pass by, with enough distance not to worry about –

One of the tangled corpses moved.

She aimed the heavy bolt rifle while her forward motion carried her closer with nightmare inevitability.

At first she thought it had exploded, ejecting debris, but it was an illusion, because Opal realised it was *spines*, similar to some creatures had for protection – she'd seen pictures of hedgehogs and ocean urchins. They slid out of the body in every direction, and some connected with and punctured the next body along. All spines but that one retracted. Then something happened that was too fast to process, some transition of mass, until that final spine withdrew – into the new body, not the old one.

It had *transferred* itself. And in the process it had also created momentum in the second body which housed it, so that it now drifted straight towards Opal, and was only ten metres away.

She quickly recreated the transfer process in her mind, calculating its extent. The spines had reached a distance of three metres extension, but that didn't mean it was the maximum, any more than a human jumping meant it was the highest and longest jump possible. They might be able to jab much further.

Eight metres away.

Rettix and Clarissa hadn't even noticed the danger yet. Maybe they both had their eyes closed, or were looking back the way they'd come.

Seven metres.

Opal snatched the grapple gun from her belt with her free hand. She aimed at the ceiling, which was just visible, a direction where she knew she could fire and hit a solid surface, rather then perhaps just end up pulling a corpse towards herself. Cable played out, the contact head striking a hard panel with a thock sound. She depressed the retract button and gripped tight, changing her trajectory to a ninety-degree deviation and being pulled out of the path of the approaching creature.

Behind, the cables towing her companions pulled taut and began to swing them, but first was the moment of vulnerability as they remained in the thing's path.

Four metres, and then they left the danger zone just as the spines shot out, narrowly missing Rettix. The creature retracted again, foiled, drifting on past where the trio had been moments before.

The ceiling loomed closer.

"What's going on?" asked Rettix.

"There's something in one of the corpses. I'm having to change course. Both of you grip the cord so you're not jerked around. Watch out if we smack into anything, and don't distract me. Please."

No arguments. Good.

Opal thudded into the ceiling and bounced off, despite her attempt to cushion the blow with her forearms. Clarissa and Rettix fared better because they were able to use their hands as well. Opal let the grapnel cable play out, then retracted it again until they reached the point a second time at a slower speed and halted there.

She scanned the green gloom, noting the visible bodies. She'd give anything for a beyond-visual motion sensor overlay right now.

"We'll move on soon. I just want to make sure which directions are clear. Keep your eyes open," said Opal.

It was Clarissa who spotted it first, pointing and attracting Opal's attention.

A body, tumbling towards them at quite a speed, pockmarked by holes, a flash of bony greyness slipping back into them. And this wasn't the same body she'd seen a creature move into last time, because that one wore a jumpsuit, whereas this was a dead guy in a vest top.

So it was able to transfer quickly and use the shift to redirect. Either that, or there were more of them. Hard to tell which scenario was worse.

Opal needed stability to fire. She flipped upside down, wrapped the grapnel cable around her ankle, then tugged it tight. She could brace against that, inverted on the ceiling which had become her floor. It freed both hands up again so she switched the heavy harpoon gun's bolt mode to expanded, and the flukes opened. No good for penetration, but that's not what she needed. The corpse approached at a sprinting speed. On the plus side, its trajectory was straight towards her, making aiming a cinch.

She fired at the centre of mass. The opened bolt thumped into the body's abdomen, stealing its momentum and flinging it off in another direction where it would miss them.

The next bolt rotated out of the cartridge and into the firing position with a satisfying click.

But just before the thing was lost in the layers of gloom, she saw it extend spines towards a passing corpse, which swung them both. Then, again, on a third cadaver. It was using them as anchors, and *turning*. A few manoeuvres and it was almost back on course, though at least slower than before.

This was not a room to hang around in. She unlooped her ankle quickly, grabbed the grapple pistol, disconnected the ceiling contact and retracted the cable ready to fire again.

The fact it hadn't headed back towards her yet suggested intelligence. It was waiting to see where Opal and her companions would go.

"Hold onto the cable again," Opal said, aiming the grapnel pistol while her other hand kept a tight grip on the bolt rifle.

She needed to get far away, but also aim at the exit. Problem was, visibility was so poor the far wall still wasn't in sight. And the manoeuvres had utterly thrown her orientational senses as up and down swapped each other's clothes. So she just had to hope the direction that *felt* right was really the correct one.

She fired. Once the cable stopped reeling out, she hit retract at a slow speed, testing the resistance. If it was a body or floating item she'd connected to then she'd be able to tell by how much it moved the three of them, whose combined mass would outweigh a single corpse.

But it seemed good. A firm anchor. She hit the faster speed and they flew through the murk. Opal felt the drag at her waist from the cables connecting her to Rettix and Clarissa.

Now she could scan around for the creature or creatures. There, it was on the move towards her. Or rather, it was on a trajectory that would take it to where she was *heading*. Smart.

She'd soon knock the imagined grin off its spiny face. She tried to aim at it, but the bolt rifle wasn't suited to one-handed firing, even in zero gravity where its bulky weight wasn't a factor. Also, Clarissa and Rettix blocked her view behind as they spun at the end of their cables.

"Grip my legs," she told them. "One each."

They did so, and she immediately had a better view down the length of her body and beyond, to where she needed to fire.

"Opal, ahead of you!" said Rettix.

Opal turned. Fuck. A vending machine, suspended in the air, one of the non-organic items freed from gravity's clutches. And close enough that one of its corners might brain her as they passed.

She aimed at it and fired the bolt rifle. Unsurprisingly when she only had one hand holding the weapon, it was a miss. Whirr-kerchunk. Only enough time for one more shot. She targeted an edge, needing to *spin* the machine out of the way, since its mass would absorb most of the force of a bolt impacting its centre. A squeeze of the trigger, and she hit this time, the bolt smashing through plastic and innards and embedding itself, so that only the tip stuck out.

It was enough. The machine twirled around, just enough clearance for them to pass.

"Thanks, keep watching out, I need to shoot back the other way."

The pistol's cable corrected their deviations from the force of firing the bolt rifle, pulling them back on track.

Okay. Aim behind. One arm wasn't great, but she thought she had a line on it. Good enough. Just wanted to knock her pursuer away or slow it down to give her time. She fired.

And at the same moment the urchin thing flung out spines to one side, connecting with another body that slow-rolled in a different direction. They pirouetted around each other, then it released and the bolt just sailed through the gap.

Definitely intelligent.

Whirr, kachunk.

It passed another corpse, and did its transfer trick. She watched as the spines latched on to the new host, then all but a few retracted. She caught a momentary glimpse of the transfer, like a huge throat's gulp, where mass stretched the connecting tubes, expanding them momentarily. Then the spines retracted into the new host and left the old one empty. And the new course was almost back in line with its original one.

So it could predict, and dodge, and manoeuvre in zero-G better than her. But it needed bodies to do so.

Take away a supply line and your opponent has fewer options.

She twisted to look ahead. Yep, finally, a sight of the wall. And, even better, a dark rectangle that represented an open doorway.

She let go of the grappling pistol. They had enough momentum to keep going. This enabled her to take the heavy rifle in both arms, in a position as close to comfortable as she could achieve, given the less-than-perfect circumstances.

She aimed at the creature that tracked them, and wasn't surprised to see it manoeuvre out of the way. Good. She was just fucking with it, making it temporarily shift to less efficient routes.

She then twisted, to aim elsewhere. One of the corpses they would pass which the creature could use to manoeuvre or transfer. She fired, caught it in the centre, sent it spinning away. It ricocheted off another corpse like some kind of tabletop ball game. By the time her pursuer got here, there'd be nothing to attach to. One option removed.

She thought she might be out of bolts but a hearty whirr-click-clunk reassured her otherwise. Probably the last one.

The wall raced towards them. She stowed the rifle over her shoulder.

"We're gonna hit hard, let go of me and try to grab anything solid you can so we don't bounce off and end up stranded."

They released her legs in preparation. The grappling pistol was hardly visible, a coiling line some distance away, since they'd been knocked off course by the momentum shifts from firing the heavy rifle. No way she intended to hang around and retrieve it. Farewell, useful thing.

They weren't far from one of the doorways. But *not far* is still *too far* sometimes.

"Clarissa, give me your hand!"

The girl snatched Opal's extended arm, and Opal heaved, created separation between them, throwing Clarissa to the side and forward while Opal was pushed back.

"Grab on!" Opal yelled.

Clarissa hit the edge of the doorway with a jarring smack, but she was plucky and tough and didn't complain. Her arms went around the frame, she managed to keep hold with one of them, and Opal pulled herself along the girl's body until she had a secure grip too. She reeled her allies through the door.

This was a queuing antechamber, but it wasn't as packed with bodies as the room they'd left. She unclipped Clarissa and Rettix, then stuck her head back into the body room. The creature was still coming towards them, delayed but not deterred. Its new course took it straight to the opening where Opal perched.

The close button did nothing, so she grabbed the indentations at the edge of the door and pulled, but its mass was greater than hers. She only succeeded in raising herself towards it.

The urchin was almost there, some of the spines poking in and out in a way that suggested eagerness to Opal's overclocked imagination.

The vertical means nothing here. Can't pull, then push.

She swung upside down, put her reinforced toe caps against the top of the frame as something she could use for leverage. Then she straightened up, bringing the door with her, finally able to slam it into its socket just before a subdued thump and eerie scraping sound came from the other side.

No power, but maybe the Entity could manipulate surfaces with those spines, force the door open. Or power might return and the door could assume its last-stored position.

She pulled the hand burner out of her toolbelt, activating the blinding beam of a plasma line. She applied it at two points, creating molten spots as materials fused door to frame, then switched to cooling mode to harden it.

"Don't we need to get out that way later?" asked Rettix.

"I can reverse it, rip the door open while the joins are molten. Though I think we'll take an alternate route for the return journey."

If there was one.

HOLES

... 15 ...

The scratching sounds beyond the doorway ceased. The urchin could still be there, considering options, just as Opal floated on this side doing the same.

Or maybe it had moved on to look for another route.

"We can't hang around," said Opal.

"That's all we can do," replied Clarissa, suit lights giving a view of her face through the visor. She smiled slyly, and Opal was confused at first, before she noticed Clarissa's hand-gesture clue pointing to her body.

Zero-G. Floating. Ha ha.

But the amazing thing was that after such a terrifying encounter, her sister could still smile. Whereas Rettix was distressed, eyes flicking wildly, skin slick with sweat. Her movements weren't calm or ... *wait*.

"Rettix, stay still," said Opal, reaching out to her.

Rettix flinched away from the gauntlets but Opal was able to grab her ankle before she kicked off from the wall.

"Stop it!" Opal snapped. "I need to check your suit."

Those were the magic words. Rettix's attention shifted to her body.

"Why?"

Opal could see it clearly now. A tiny release of air near Rettix's tricep. Perhaps from an unlucky collision, or a brief contact with the urchin's spines. The microscopic droplets of moisture in the leaking gases immediately froze, forming miniscule crystals that glittered as they tumbled in Opal's lights.

"Don't panic, just a small puncture. Your suit should have emergency patches."

"A hole? Something might get in! An infection or –"

"Hey, just stay still and let me sort it out!"

Rettix struggled, and her movements sent them both spinning across the room.

"For fuck's sake, calm down!" Opal tried to indicate towards Clarissa with her eyes and head tilt, but Rettix was too panicky to note the subtleties of secret adult communication in the presence of a child, the warning not to upset Clarissa.

They approached a wall. Up above were some seats fastened to the ceiling in a semicircle. Opal grabbed one as an anchor, other hand still on Rettix. Although it was tempting to apply an armlock to the woman, to stop her wriggling, to focus her via a moment of pain, Rettix's mental state was unknown and it could just make her more stressed. Instead, Opal pinned her against the seats, then opened a private comm channel.

"Last chance. Chill the fuck out." Opal kept her voice low: calm, but rumbling with warning. "I can fix this if you let me."

A moment passed. Then Rettix sagged in defeat. At least she'd retreated from whatever black hole sucked at her mind.

"Help me," Rettix said.

Opal found the pouch on Rettix's suit and pulled out the emergency pack. A sachet of glue and a fold of self-adhesive tapes. That was sufficient. She selected a small one, smoothed it over the tear, then held the two red corners to activate the seal. Once they'd gone green she let go.

No more particles of air and vapour trickled into the void around them.

Opal reactivated the three-way comms.

"All done. It'll hold," she said, returning the unused repair stuff to Rettix's pouch. "The perforation was so small that oxygen loss is trivial."

"I'm more concerned about what might have got *in*," Rettix muttered.

"Nothing got in. The force of outward pressure will have seen to that. Don't create problems where they don't exist. You okay?"

No answer.

"I said Are You Okay, Soldier?"

The reframing seemed to work, and Rettix nodded. That would have to do. Opal let go of her and pushed away.

"We need to get moving." As Opal glided past Clarissa: "You holdin' up okay too, C?"

"Yes, sir." A cheeky smile. "Only one letter-shift difference between sir and sis, you ever notice that?"

"Nope. I always depend on you for those kind of void-shaking insights."

Opal didn't breathe easy until they'd covered some distance from the urchin-body room. She kept glancing back, examining the gloom for any sign of pursuit, her mind conjuring images of spiked bodies barrelling towards her silently from the murky green vista.

Their progress was slower than Opal would have liked. Rettix had adopted a habit of keeping a hand over the puncture patch Opal had applied, as if for comfort. It meant she only had three limbs for propulsion, making her movements slower and less accurate. But Opal didn't want to pressure her at the moment. Sometimes enforced caution had its advantages.

Plus, Opal had noted the acidic burns on some stretches of wall. She didn't point them out to her companions, but it did raise an interesting question. If Satreweth left these marks, then why wasn't the whole ship covered in them? Even if they only patrolled the same routes, eventually every surface would be scorched. Maybe in the timescale of things the Lost Ship had only just launched, so widespread damage hadn't had a chance to occur yet? Like many other aspects of Lost Ships, the appearance of long decay could be illusory, or representative of how the original vessels were discovered by Null Entities, which then just copied that state.

The other theory, with equally interesting implications, was that parts of the Lost Ship could repair itself, restore things to a default state from time to time. The acidic fizzing of hull repairs, but at a smaller scale. As if the whole ship was a body, its surfaces a series of auto-renewing skin layers. That would work, too.

But if changes were reset at some point, that could include doors Opal had sealed.

Hmmm.

They arrived at a junction, but not like any she'd ever encountered before. Bizarrely, passages of different sizes and styles sprang away at every angle – which would have created impassably vertical options in standard gravity. It was as if the redesign took account of what the Lost Ship conditions would be, and incorporated those opportunities. She sprayed her usual mark by the entrance, which had a ridged edge enabling handholds for stability. Then the three of them eyed the potential routes. Opal counted at least sixteen twisting exits.

"This is weird," said Rettix.

"Everything's weird on a Lost Ship," Opal replied.

"I like it," Clarissa added. "It's like a funzone for kids."

Not how Opal would describe it, but Clarissa's view of the world had less of the cynic, more of the magic.

Opal recreated their route so far in her head, trying to account for bends in passageways, and detours. It was difficult now they were in the heart of the ship, with no access to outer hull or sky-windows that might aid in locating themselves. Her GAMag suit had a crude navigation function that could map journeys, but it required anchor points to judge progress against. Without those, or even standard gravity, it had no way of knowing what was up or down. The red line of movement since she'd activated the system was erroneous, flickering with indecision. She disabled it and decided her best guesses were to head down one of the passages which represented a slight deviation "upwards" towards the front of this alien craft.

"I think any of those will go roughly the right way," Opal explained, pointing to one cluster of tunnels. "But there's one I immediately rule out."

"The curvy, wide one with rails in the ceiling," said Clarissa, without hesitation.

"Correct. Why?"

"It has the burny marks on the wall. Is that where the dolphins went?"

"I think so. And I can't know anything for sure, but ..." and here she glanced at Clarissa and smiled, "... I have a weird feeling that they travel in a kind of protective family pod with their young, and as long as we don't enter their territory, they'll leave us alone."

"You get intuitions a lot here?" asked Rettix. Her face didn't betray what she was getting at, though she rubbed at the suit patch absently.

"My whole life is based on intuition," Opal replied, cutting that topic dead. "So if they went down *here*, we need to pick one of the other options."

"Not that one," said Clarissa, pointing down a route that was made up of a series of arches. The girl pulled a face as if at something distasteful.

"Why not?"

"There's webby stuff."

Opal looked again. Clarissa was right. The more distant arches weren't architectural features but gossamer nets draped near the ceiling. Were they created purposefully to match the shapes of the arches leading up to them? To disguise a trap? If so, it was an intelligence at work.

"Well spotted," said Opal.

"Rule two. Use my eyes. And I have to do it extra, because I bet you can't see much out of that itty bitty red slit in your flat helmet. I don't like not seeing your face."

"It's still here. Looking at the smartest girl in the universe."

Clarissa giggled.

"I feel like a third part," said Rettix. "Don't I get a say?"

"Of course." Opal turned to her, careful to keep any impatience out of her voice. "Where do you suggest we go?"

A moment passed. "The way you want. It's not like I have any clues or insights. You might as well keep making all the decisions."

No time now to deal with petulance. Opal eyed the third junction. A rectangular steel chute resembling an overgrown ventilation duct. Narrow enough for easy propulsion, and numerous doorways – all the visible ones pleasingly closed – which might provide gripping points, or even escape routes, should one be needed. It was the obvious choice. Opal sprayed another arrow just inside that tunnel, then launched herself down it.

This route was so devoid of threat or variety that Opal wondered if it was one of the Lost Ship tricks, endlessly mirrored sections creating a sapping repetition. As a test, she sprayed a cross on the wall and expected to see it again when they moved on, perhaps after another fifty metres. She floated. She counted.

But it didn't reappear, and instead they entered a wide plaza that seemed to be a gathering place tilted on its side. Below them on their left a pinkish high-grip wall rose above and also dropped away into darkness. She knew it was originally floor because of the seats fastened to it, now ninety degrees to Opal. Elsewhere were dead display screens and floating rubbish. She readjusted her mental orientation to turn the wall back into dirty-pink floor.

As they crossed the space, using anything they could for impetus, Opal spotted markings on the columns scattered throughout the room. As always on Lost Ships the pictures and text were blurred, confusing, as much abstract decoration as anything functional, but a blue one caught her eye. Something about the smeared shape and colour.

"You guys recognise that?" Opal asked, pointing her light to illuminate the curves.

"Was it a rocket?" asked Clarissa. "Before it got wet and smudged?"

"That shade of blue often indicates transit within the UFS," said Rettix.

"Exactly what I'm thinking. If you squint at it and tilt your head, doesn't it look like a sort of bullet with dashed lines?"

Her companions tried the experiment, and agreed tentatively.

"I think it's a messed-up copy of the sign for a bullet train. If so, that means we're nearly at the Spine. We're going the right way! If it's active then we can get to the bridge area in no time. Minutes rather than days of getting lost and attacked."

"And then you take control," said Rettix, squeezing her arm where the suit was patched.

Opal paused a moment before replying. "Then I do whatever *needs* to be done. As always."

CONFLICTS

... 14 ...

The plaza funnelled them into a narrow area. The ceiling and floor were closer, and their progress ended at a security checkpoint surrounded by hazard-marked steel barriers. At ninety degrees to the side were huge, transparent tubes which ran off into the gloom. Clarissa halted next to Opal, then Rettix caught up ten seconds later, doing her three-limbed inefficient system of movement.

The function of the tubes was obvious: bullet train transit. Narrower than civilian versions, as appropriate for a military ship, but nonetheless this was a nexus for the Spine, without a doubt.

The tubes which bullet trains ran along were sealed and vacuum controlled. You could only board a carriage via a designated entrance that lined up with the carriage's doors. When Opal smushed her helmet against the plexiglass tube tunnel, far to her left – beyond the security checkpoint separating her from the boarding station – was an empty carriage. It was only just visible in the darkness, but it was something to give hope. All they had to do was get onto that inner platform.

Opal glided towards the small security tunnel that would lead through to the boarding area, then trailed a hand on the wall so her body swung out and over in a graceful cartwheel, until she flew feet first. As she passed the arched entrance she snatched the edge to bring herself to a halt. With her free hand she was able to pluck Clarissa, and once the girl had got a handhold Opal did the same for Rettix. Opal sprayed a yellow marker, then peered into the tunnel.

Her low-beam light glinted off something metallic. It took moments to identify what she saw, and realise it wasn't just scanning plates.

Cruel metal spikes, so that the tunnel was greatly narrowed. Instead of being almost three metres across, the gap through the centre of the inward-facing needles was only half that. Once you passed through that hole, which ran for a few metres, you'd be home free. It wasn't impossible. Not in zero-G.

But the steely rods were there for a reason, and looked dangerous. A barrier. A trap. Worse, they reminded Opal of the spike on her first Lost Ship, that had been hidden in a medical scanning bed but erupted and punched through her suit's armour to make contact with her nervous system. She'd seen it afterwards, limp, with subtle joint-like nodules along it, and she thought she could see the same in the tangled brush of iron thorns separating her current position from where she wanted to go.

"What is it?" asked Rettix, who'd been more focussed on where they'd come from, but then noted Opal's silence. She looked down the tunnel. "Oh."

"It may not be how it looks," said Opal, wracking her mind for anything to back up what she'd just said.

"It's one of those body creatures we just escaped from!"

"No, it's something different."

"What?"

"Well, Lost Ships sometimes misunderstand human functions and rebuild them in strange ways. Platforms normally have security barriers to control access, don't they? Maybe this is just a misinterpretation of that gating concept."

Rettix scoffed.

"We need to go through," added Opal.

"No way! See how sharp they are? They'll tear these civ-suits to snecking pieces."

"If we angle it right then –"

"Are you out of your fucking mind? They could be poisonous, or – did that one just twitch? We need to find another way."

"– okay," said Clarissa. She'd been speaking quietly but her comm channel voice was drowned out by the adults.

"What did you say?" asked Opal, facing where the girl bobbed by her side, one hand on the tunnel's edge.

"I think it will be okay. To float through, I mean."

"What makes you say that?" asked Opal.

Clarissa looked from one adult to the other. Then again. Reticent. "It's my Blox," she said, eventually. "They show me things sometimes. I saw this spiky pattern. Exact same. And it was green in the Blox. When I get showed things in green, it means they're safe."

"*Showed*?" asked Rettix. "You saw a shape in some toy and think we can risk our lives based on that?"

"I have a ... look, the Blox aren't random. They often do patterns that come true. That's how they tell me."

"And where do those patterns come from?" Rettix's tone was the kind used to argue with an adult, not a child.

"I don't know! The things that live in the cubes."

"The things that ... this is ridiculous."

"Calm down, Rettix." Opal tried to imbue warning but Rettix was too busy rubbing her arm. "Clarissa, you really saw this?"

"Yes. On the Owlflight. I didn't understand it at the time, didn't like some of the pix, but when I saw this just now it made sense. This pattern, green for go. Some of the bad stuff we've seen, it was in there too, in red. It was all *telling me*. The truth is in my Blox. Ever since Owlflight went into the Null, they've talked to me more than ever before."

Rettix snatched Clarissa's bag, gripping it in her fist. "This?" She pulled, which almost jerked Clarissa free of the tunnel edge. "If these Blox are cursed we need to get rid of them!" She yanked again, trying to get the bag over Clarissa's head and shoulders while the girl shrieked and resisted.

Words were too slow. Opal snatched Rettix's wrist, twisted it into a lock-three position which broke the grip and pushed her arm away, with enough temporary pain to immobilise Rettix.

"Calm down," said Opal, between clamped teeth.

"You're taking her side! A little girl who knows nothing." Rettix's face was slick with perspiration.

"I listen to everyone who has something useful to say." Opal butted faceplate to faceplate. Both Rettix and Opal had drifted from the tunnel and across the platform, but that could be dealt with. A glance back showed Clarissa was still in place and safe.

"But there's something *wrong* with her, why can't you see it?" A look of panic in Rettix's eyes.

"*No there isn't.* Just calm down and take breaths." They were metres away from the tunnel now. "It's easy. We'll go through one at a time. Pushed by me at the back. You'll adopt a stream-lined shape, glide right through the centre. I'll have the trickiest bit, coming last on my own, but I have better armour so that's fair."

"Okay. Okay." A moment while Rettix took a shuddering breath, the subtle vibrations running through her body. "We'll throw the girl first. She's smallest. Make sure it's safe. If she gets through okay then we can –"

"No. *You* go first."

"Fuck that! I had a tear in my suit already, can't risk another, can't let the ship in, not into our bodies and our air –"

"You're an adult. Once on the other side it's your job to catch Clarissa when I push her through."

"No! Fling the girl, make sure that way, a test –"

The gloomy world of the station whirled around them as they tumbled, a sickening spin set in motion by the struggle. They glanced off one of the pillars and began a slow ricochet into yet another direction.

"It makes sense, Rettix. Just think –"

"Because she's your sister! You only care about her, you want to sacrifice me, watch me die, no, no! You can't …"

"You agreed, to follow my orders so I can keep you safe –"

"– so you can *kill me*! You wanted me out of the way all along
–"

"– we'll all get through this –"

"– and you back it up with force, weapons, bullying –"

"– I want to get us all home –"

"– and it isn't fair!"

Rettix snatched at the heavy bolt thrower, had already undone the strap before Opal seized its handle to stop it being taken away.

"I want to feel safe!" Rettix screamed.

"Let go of my fucking weapon!"

But Rettix continued to yank, surprisingly strong now she used both arms, pulling the business end away from Opal, towards herself, she might even wrest it free, those wild eyes darting around but mostly in Clarissa's direction, and Opal couldn't let go to apply another immobilisation lock in case they drifted apart, this dangerously panicked woman with a deadly weapon, their only weapon, unable to see clearly –

"I can't trust either of you, give it me!" And Rettix tugged it free –

As Opal's grip slipped, the trigger got pulled – *accident, accident, surely* – and the bolt launched straight into Rettix's body, punching them apart. Rettix still clutched the bolt rifle, flying away from Opal until she smacked into the arched ceiling and was fixed there, screaming in pain.

The bolt had shattered her pelvis, pinned her by the midriff up above, but Rettix was alive as the agonised, terrified yells evidenced, calling for help. Wailing that could attract attention.

Clarissa was shrieking too, the commlines still open three-way. Animal terror spread so easily in chaos like this. Opal accessed her wrist-panel's controls while the world span, and closed off Rettix's commline. Her cries of pain cut out, leaving just Opal and Clarissa.

"Calm down, sis," Opal said. "It'll all be fine."

Bobos

... 13 ...

Clarissa curled herself into a ball at Opal's command.

"Tighter," Opal said. "Grip your knees, and keep your bag against your belly so it doesn't catch on anything."

Opal gripped the tunnel entrance in one hand, using her feet and their weak magnetic hold to create a secure posture for launching her sister, who floated free near the centre of the tunnel. Opal was able to gently nudge and reposition her, making sure she was as central as possible before the push of irrevocable committal.

"I'm not scared, you know," said Clarissa.

"I know."

Opal launched her sister forwards.

The girl stayed tightly curled as she approached the ring of spikes. The shove had been well-judged. Clarissa entered the central hole, no part of her too close to any of the glistening tips.

Did one of the spikes just shudder?

No, it was just the light from Clarissa's suit slipping over the surface as she passed.

Surely.

Halfway through the ring of thorns. Opal willed her to safety. Not a prayer but a projected hope, fate-manipulating goodwill wishes. It would make no difference, but it was better than doing nothing.

Three quarters.

"Don't uncurl until I tell you it's safe," reminded Opal.

She was going to make it.

The dreaded snap of a spike-toothed jaw wasn't going to occur.

And then she was beyond.

"Unfold now, grab onto anything secure."

A barrier near Clarissa was within easy reach, and she held it, swinging to a halt with a smile on her face.

"Easy Zapeasy," said the girl.

"Lemon Zacheesy," replied Opal. A refrain from a cartoon Clarissa had loved. Something recent in the girl's mind, yet oh so long ago in Opal's, forgotten for years, then immediately reappearing on reflex when given the right prompt. Wasn't that a hopeful thing, the return of something lost just when you needed it? Wasn't that what her life had been built around?

There was nothing central that Opal could launch herself from so as to go right through the spike-ring's centre. The tunnel was too wide. If launched from an edge she would approach the needles at an angle, drift straight into impalement. With a third person it would be easy, but even then it would only prolong the problem. There was always going to be a *final* transit, alone. And it had always been Opal who would choose that position.

So she prepared. No grappling pistol to help her this time. She unfastened the final oxygen canister from her toolbelt. Great for long propulsion, rubbish for fine movements, but it was all she had. She'd make it work. Survival had often depended on kitbash innovation. Couldn't expect the universe to give her any major breaks now.

"You'll be okay," Clarissa told her, perhaps sensing Opal's doubts.

"Sure will. Because I know you'll catch me at the other end. Sisters forever, right?"

"Yep! Forever and ever!"

And ever and ever and ever, an echo in her mind, bouncing in the hollowness of the things she'd made absent by refusing to contemplate them. Promises of protection not kept. But it was only right to recognise the results of your actions before it was too late, even if acknowledgement was all you would do. Some things needed to be witnessed.

Opal glanced up at the ceiling. There was the smudge of movement that revealed the impaled Rettix. No doubt still screaming as she tried to free herself, unable to progress with a fractured pelvis.

If Opal had a rifle she'd finish it now, a shot of mercy to the head. Even without a rifle, if Opal was alone she'd go up there, hope Rettix could be brought back to calmness, suit patched; if not, to find another way to end her suffering quickly. But Opal *wasn't* alone. And her companion wasn't just anyone. It was *Clarissa.*

The fierceness of her protective feelings hit like a gut punch, shocking in their intensity.

Anything that put Clarissa at risk was expendable. Anything that slowed their progress was forbidden. Anything that attracted unwanted attention was banned. Anyone who couldn't be trusted to make the right decisions, to protect Clarissa, was a threat.

Opal was sorry to leave her like that, sure. But when it came to this set of choices, there was only one outcome. And if it left someone dying in agony until they passed out from blood loss, oxygen deprivation or cold, then it was regrettable but necessary.

Goodbye, Rettix.

Opal let go of the rim, using the slightest touch to float towards the tunnel's centre, facing head-first where she wanted to go, body elongated to present the smallest profile. She held the canister down her body, and just before reaching the centre point she released a single jet of air to propel her forward, visualising the perfect trajectory in her mind to cement it, as if she was a super AI who could make this kind of thing look Easy Zapeasy.

It wasn't enough, the forward motion too little to take her through the skewers.

She released another jet of air, longer, aimed at a corrective angle, and that got more motion, but it wasn't straight. She drifted towards some of the spikes.

Shitty shitgas.

Another jet, another adjustment. She felt and heard the scraping of hard points against her suit before her arc altered to lift her away from the danger, and she didn't even waste a second working out her position, but let go with a full blast of oxygen as soon as the scraping ceased, get out of there, get out of there quick before sharpness punctured her neck and sought out her brain, her identity, her soul.

She almost yelled when something snatched at her ankle, spinning her uncontrollably. She closed the oxygen valve, registered that she'd passed Clarissa who had tried to halt her, and then Opal slammed into another barrier and bounced off.

It was okay. It was all okay.

She ignored Clarissa's questions and focussed on the wrist control pad, checking diagnostics for punctures or damage.

Nothing. All green. She finally sighed with relief.

"Everything's fine," she reassured Clarissa. "Just my usual mid-action chaos." She grabbed onto a nearby light fitting. Since it wasn't in illumination mode it might as well do something useful.

After stowing the air canister – hopefully with plenty of juice left – she joined Clarissa.

"See? You were totally right." Opal forced a stiff grin, even though her sister couldn't see it. "Easy Zapeasy."

The sisters held hands and floated towards the train carriage's entrance. They were halfway there when Clarissa asked:

"Will she die?"

No need to name who was on their mind.

"Yes," said Opal. "Hopefully soon."

A moment to digest it.

"At one point she was nice to me, but after the holey suit bit she changed, didn't she?" asked Clarissa.

"Yes."

Another moment of silence.

"Did you shoot her on purpose?"

Ah. The most unwanted of questions. Opal looked at her sister. "No," she said firmly.

Clarissa nodded, satisfied.

What was the truth, anyway? A moment, an instinct. Things occur before full analysis in those situations.

If you interpret "on purpose" as "premeditated", then Opal hadn't lied.

The short security umbilicus into the bullet train was open. Opal floated in first, wary of the inviting, dark emptiness. But this carriage was vacant apart from the unadorned military functionality of the seats and holding rails, which were all reassuringly normal in appearance. They were boarding about halfway along a multi-compartment train.

"Clear. You can come in."

Clarissa flew through, grabbing hold of a ceiling hoop to halt herself. She had really got the hang of zero-G, better even than some adults. Opal had seen the green faces, puking, shakes, disorientation back in training. But Clarissa seemed not to care about up or down, and even revelled in the freedom to move in any direction. To spin, to flip, to glide.

Adaptability was resilience. It was another sign of their connection, their shared traits that seemed so obvious to Opal, even where strangers might only see apparent differences.

Each carriage had a comm-panel against one wall. A means to contact the AI controller with requests, or in emergencies. It could also activate power if a bullet train was in passive waiting mode, as happened if a transit facility had been unused for some time. A way to save on resources, so that systems dozed, ready to spring into action once human activity was detected again. Opal hoped that was the current situation, that the default behaviour had been replicated, rather than the carriages seen as dead ornamentation.

The control panel looked normal enough, and when Opal slid a hand in front of it there *was* a display. Of sorts. But if it was based on original human interfaces then it had been kaleidoscoped through alien lenses. A complex smudge of patterns and colours, constantly shifting. But it was all she had. And even if it really did connect to dangers ... again, choices were absent. Time was short. Need was great.

The display responded to Opal's touches, but the results were no more interpretable than the original state. Fragmented pictogram submenus through a visual filter? Corruption to underlying programming? A sentient organism that just happened to look like a display terminal, and which enjoyed being stroked and then displayed its emotions visually? The carriage remained in darkness apart from the colourful glows of this screen, which shaded surfaces and metallic handholds in neon shades.

"It's like pictures," said Clarissa, hanging above Opal's shoulder.

"Pictures on drugs. No, forget I said that."

"I know what drugs are. I'm not a baby."

Nothing like pictures Opal was familiar with. There was abstract, and then there was *this*.

"It's an *idea* of pictures," said Clarissa.

Opal ignored her and jabbed at moving shapes with ever-growing frustration, so that the hard clacks of her gauntlets threatened to crack the screen.

"You're not doing it right," Clarissa added, pushing Opal's hand away.

"Clarissa. We need to find a way to get this train moving. We need power. We need to make sure it goes towards the bridge. If we can do that then we're probably fine, since it'll autostop at the end terminus. But without that initial kick, we're just stuck in a coffin." Wrong word. Got to tone down the morbidity. "I mean, stuck in a tube."

"It's not buttons. It's shapes and colours that merge to make ... ideas. The patterns aren't for reading the way you do ... it's not easy to explain. It's like RearroBlox." A pause. "*Exactly* like Blox. You guide and follow, not ... erm ... go in straight lines. You go around and through. Wait a minute, I have an idea, I'll show you."

Clarissa removed her bag and took her Blox out one by one. In each case she activated stability mode, and when she placed them on the comm-panel's border the Blox stayed there. It was a function for using them on sloped surfaces, creating a tiny force of attraction via a mix of magnetism and rubbery grip. In zero-G it was enough to stop them floating away.

The Blox sprouted into life. And what they showed was not the previous images Clarissa had been modelling, or any of the default state slideshows, but almost an extension of what was on the display screen.

"How are they doing that?" asked Opal.

"They're connecting. Either the Blox is finding the screen emission, or the screen thingy is detecting the Blox and partnering. Blox are designed to be open to influence."

Of course. It was part of the creative protocols, able to interact on open channels so all the peripherals paired up even if another corp made them. New interfaces, databanks, projection filters. It probably worked with illegal attachments too.

The kid really understood this stuff. Not just a means of expression but technical, too. How had Opal never noticed that before? Had she been too preoccupied with keeping them alive but hidden, back on Mossareid? Or was this something to do with the changes Clarissa had gone through, some newly evolving maturity?

Clarissa began moving them experimentally, occasionally letting them touch, a communicative convergence Opal had never understood but which Clarissa seemed able to conceptualise instinctively. Smears of colour shifted across both the screen and the blocks, but as Clarissa made changes to the Blox it introduced clearer lines and geometric shapes and arcs, and the same designs began to leech into the main screen's display.

"It's like they're communicating. Sharing," said Opal.

"No. *Learning*," her sister replied. "And I think I can use that. They *want* to talk. It's what Blox do. And this screen wants to listen. It's what *it* was made to do. But it listens with ears like we can't even imagine. Something needs to take a shape that matches it, like jelly-jigsaw pieces. There's enough bendiness that you can make it fit if it is even a little bit close."

"So you're bridging the gap."

"Only partly. I can see it talking but the words are in a language I don't know. And that's when we'd need one of my school interpreter AIs, if one even existed for Lost Ships. Except, maybe, it does."

Clarissa made more rapid movements now, sliding Blox, tapping them, recalling stored patterns, shifting through intermediary scenescapes. And certain shapes and movements and colours recurred. A flash of an orange circle. A swatch of green texture like furry grass. A pair of triangles stuck to a sphere, emerging from behind a swirl of spinning discs. A wriggle of lines.

It was a coherent image gradually piecing itself together. A kind of green dog-thing with orange eyes, though not resembling any real dog Opal had ever seen. More like a distorted interpretation of a dog, then redrawn by a child who blinked rapidly.

Clarissa was focussed on the image, her lips moving while it shifted from block to block.

"He doesn't like you looking at him," said Clarissa.

"Who?"

"Freddie Bobo."

"I thought he was just an imaginary friend?"

"He's as imaginary as Lost Ships are," Clarissa said with almost-adult contempt.

"So it's a pattern you stored in your Blox?" Maybe it was a focus for imagination, like a finger puppet could become a mouthpiece for a child's insecurities. Opal could comprehend that.

"He stored *himself*. It's him who came to me, not the other way around."

Mmmm.

The images shifted as more manipulations occurred, Clarissa's small hands surprisingly adept at the twists and tilts of control. It almost reminded Opal of martial arts, where repetition leads to assured movements that go beyond conscious thought and become a flow. Meanwhile, the girl's lips continued to twitch, but with no sounds.

"Wait – are you talking to the pattern?" Opal asked.

"He hears me and I hear him, though it's not really talking."

And now other memories came back. Yes, back on Mossareid when Clarissa was engrossed in Blox, her lips used to move then as well. Opal assumed it was just an involuntary and harmless release of tension when her mind was fully absorbed elsewhere, but if it was a sign of communication with an imaginary friend, had it been occurring even then? Which raised a whole lot of other questions.

"So you're hoping to take your creation – sorry, Freddie – and transfer –"

"Please don't talk," snapped Clarissa. "He doesn't like it, and distractions can introduce misinterpretations. He's stronger in the Null, and I don't want him to – never mind, just please don't interrupt. It's delicate."

Again, the adult within a child's skin. A side of Clarissa that was normally hidden.

Opal pulled back and observed. The movements, the shape and colour changes, almost as if the green dog-thing shifted between Blox and tentatively dipped its toothy snout into the main screen, which bloomed with coruscations of green and orange shades wherever it happened. It was mesmerising.

And suddenly it was over. The comm-panel flashed blindingly verdant for a moment, while the shapes of the weird canine construct disappeared from all the Blox at once. They crackled like shorted electrics, audible even from the suit receptors, and then the Blox and the screen died completely.

A moment later the carriage lights came on, and the doors to the platform slid closed.

"He did it," said Clarissa, turning to Opal and showing no more interest in the blank, lifeless cubes.

"Then why do you look sad?"

"Because he had to go into the Lost Ship," replied the girl. "And I don't think he'll ever have a way back out."

TRANSPORTS

... 12 ...

At regular intervals double rings of yellowed light banded the Spine's tunnel. As the bullet train zipped through them at speed it created a strobe effect, a double flash before the carriage dropped back into the comparative darkness of its subdued transit illumination. Opal's mind added a "Whoosh!" sound each time they passed through one of the rings.

They gripped onto support rails, bodies elevated and floating side by side, aligned due to the pull of velocity.

Whoosh ... whoosh.

Clarissa grinned.

"What's got you so happy?" asked Opal.

"This. You and me."

"It's not the way I would have chosen to spend time with you."

"I like it. This bit. It reminds me."

"Of?"

"Mossareid. A few weeks ago, before they split us up. We were riding the gravtrams, remember?"

Weeks? A decade and a half for Opal. But the memory was there, awoken by the bright face looking at her. Years rewound in a moment, measured by the flashes of brilliance.

Whoosh ... whoosh.

"I do remember," said Opal. "I took you as a treat. Get you out of our apartment for a bit."

"But it was a naughty treat, because we didn't have passes. And when the officials boarded you made us get off and run!"

"Oh yes! And we had to jump over the barriers to get out of the station."

"*You* jumped the barrier, I had to duck under it. And we were lost in a new area of the city, but you said you'd get us back okay, and you did. And we had slices of Mossa strandlecake first, from the street stall."

Whoosh ... whoosh.

"That was a good day," said Opal. "I don't think I'd ever laughed so much."

"Yes," said Clarissa. "It *was* good."

Whoosh ... whoosh.

"And I always trust you," Clarissa added, the smile fading.

"What's up?"

"I don't want to lie to you."

"Then don't."

Whoosh ... whoosh.

Clarissa didn't respond at first. As if gathering her thoughts, or summoning courage.

"I might be wrong," she said. "But now he's gone I can mention it, because he can't stop me any more."

"He?"

"Freddie Bobo. He was always my friend but he changed when I was on the Solace, and started acting weird. And he came to me when we were in the underwater ship, except he didn't come *back*, he was always in my head with me, ever since I woke up from the long sleep. And he talked to me through the Blox that Aseides man gave me. But that was all fine. Bobo gave me ideas, and one time it was useful, wasn't it, when I helped us escape? I don't really remember, but afterwards I had dreams. And when we got to Owlflight and Athene died to save us it was a sad time, wasn't it? Just you and me on the big empty ship with everyone else asleep. And when I was sad or lonely Bobo would come to me. And he was more like in the past. A little bit snappy and grumpy and bossy. I told him off for it, and tried to make him behave, but he was good at calming me down, and telling me to keep secrets, because I would be in trouble if you knew about him."

"*You* would never be in trouble, Clarissa. It's not your fault when things ... get difficult."

"But I didn't know so much then. Bobo could be tricksy."

Whoosh ... whoosh.

Sudden realisation. "Did he make you do something?"

"I don't know!" Clarissa started crying, eyes welling up in a way that would obscure vision if the tears broke free in zero-G, until they settled on a surface. "I can't remember! I only have guesses from bitty things I dreamed. But what if Bobo did something when we were first in the Null? He sent a message from the RearroBlox or some other system. Don't tell me off, please!"

"I won't tell you off, but I need to know what he did, sweetie."

"I'm not sure, but I think he might have called this Lost Ship. Or at least shouted out and got heard. But when I asked him he wouldn't answer, and made me keep it secret until my head hurt and I promised. But he isn't here now, and you are, and you're my sister and I don't ever want to lie to you, even if I don't know what happened."

She was sobbing now, and Opal pulled her in, hugging the crinkly suit that contained a child.

"You were right to tell me, C. But don't worry. It's just something for me to muse about later. For now, think about good stuff you've done. You got us moving! Started this whole train! If we're in time, and we can do something at the bridge, then you will have saved lives. Ours, and so many people on the Owlflight. Think of that, you amazing girl, you lovely sister."

Whoosh ... whoosh.

Clarissa had calmed down.

Whoosh ... whoosh.

Companionable silence.

Whoosh ... whoosh.

The train shuddered, as if from an impact. Had it ploughed into something within the vacuum tube?

Opal glanced from the side windows but it was the usual blur of darkened passage interspersed with the whoosh whoosh of ring light vertebrae.

The carriage lights flickered and dimmed.

Opal glided to the door leading into the trailing car, and peered through the small pane.

The section behind them was in darkness. Her suit lights reflected awkwardly off the window, obscuring as much as they revealed, so she mostly only saw the faceplate visor which turned her into something less than human but more than flesh. Were some of the windows back there shattered and exposed to vacuum?

Had something boarded the train?

She didn't open the door. Couldn't risk being sucked out. Couldn't risk an encounter with the unexpected. Instead she flew the other way, the handily placed railings intended for standing passengers acting as ideal things to grab for propulsion, redirection, and braking. It was like swimming through a sparse woodland. At the front of the carriage she could see the next compartment was brightly lit, its windows intact.

"We need to move nearer the front of the train," Opal said, opening that door. It slid aside, and she helped her sister glide past.

She was about to swing through the portal herself when a series of massive, battering blows pounded on the doorway from the dark carriage. Although the Lost Ship was in zero-G, it wasn't in vacuum. The tube the train flew through *was*, of course, as would be the recently shattered carriage behind, but on this side of the door sounds would travel.

Opal joined Clarissa and shut the portal behind.

Just in time. The Viscid-thick atmosphere was sucked out of the previous coach as if via a huge gulp. Opal didn't get a chance to try and identify what had ripped its way into the carriage because the lights blanked out a moment after the atmosphere was compromised.

"We need to keep moving. Get to the forward carriage."

How many sections did the train have? It determined how long they could run for.

Clarissa didn't argue, just flung herself down the aisle, occasionally reaching out for a rail push. Opal followed, keeping her body between the warily watched doorway they'd just come through, and her vulnerably clothed sister.

Whoosh .... whoosh.

Halfway along. Opal wished for weapons. Though without even knowing what had smashed its way aboard ...

Smash ... *explosions* ... Of course. She had one type of weapon left. And if things went badly wrong, she'd do what she could to protect her sister. But what if Opal succeeded? As in, sacrificed her life, with the end result of Clarissa being alone in a hostile environment? Opal had training and experience, whereas Clarissa was just a little girl. Opal should have done a better job of preparing her for that. Always too late with the wisdom.

"I'm going to drop a bomb," Opal explained as she removed it from its storage on her suit. "It's an important lesson, Clarissa, so pay attention while you move. *Always have something in reserve if you can.* And yet, don't leave it too late to use it. No point saving something for a future scenario if you won't live that long. Use what you've got when you need it. No resource is worth anything when compared to your life."

"Why are you telling me this?"

Opal set the timer, flung the package towards the rear of the train, then followed Clarissa into the next compartment. She glanced ahead – and noticed with dismay that there were no more *aheads*, no doors onwards. This was the nose of the bullet train. She closed the door behind her.

Whoosh ..... whoosh.

"There's so much I need to tell you," Opal explained, hurrying her to the front of the carriage with gentle pushes. "It applies to Lost Ships, but also to everything else. Erm, always look out for danger areas. Spot them in advance. Shadows. Corners. Hiding places."

"Stop it, Opal, you're scaring me!"

"Pay attention!" Opal snapped. "You need to memorise this shit! Always have an escape route, think about that before things happen ... and ... and look at what's around you for opportunities and risks. Like, even the textures of things. Would this be grippy, so you could do a wall jump off it? Is this floor slippery, in which case avoid big movements, but if you have an opponent then you can trick them into overbalancing and falling or ... or you could do a slide attack or ..." Fuck.

Whoosh ...... whoosh.

"Remember that small isn't weak, and what's in your heart and brain let's you outthink things that are bigger than you ... hearts let you endure ... and ..."

Boom, the previous carriage blew, ripping itself open to vacuum, hopefully separating their refuge, their dead end, from what followed in the darkness of the tunnel.

They were backed up at the nose of the train, Opal afraid to blink because it would mean losing a moment's observation of the entrance to their carriage.

"Hold on real tight to that rail, Clarissa."

Opal positioned herself between the girl and the darkened doorway again, one arm anchoring Opal to a rail, one reaching behind to reassure her sister. Waiting for the moment when the connecting door blew inwards, along with glass and shards of metal. Opal's armour might absorb or deflect some of it.

Whoosh .... whoosh.

Wait ... *connection* ... there all along. The train had been *slowing*, the double flashes of ring lights having more of a breathing space between them.

They were decelerating. Approaching the platform.

The lights flickered and dimmed in Opal's carriage. Maybe that was a warning of the thing approaching. It might even be on the other side of the doorway now, looking through the glass, preparing to smash metal aside, to punch and bludgeon it like wet paper.

Slowing was so obvious now, despite her racing heartbeat. They pulled into the terminus at the command and control section of the Lost Ship.

The side doors slid open. Opal didn't hesitate, she grabbed Clarissa firmly and flung her through the rectangle onto the platform, no time for niceties, then Opal launched herself. She was almost there when she felt the vibration in the train's shell, the force applied to it, saw glass cracking, roof bending.

Then she was out, powering through the air, grabbing Clarissa as her trajectory took her past. Opal kicked off a wall in a zigzag to break the tracking line, not looking back because the only thing that mattered was the open blast door ahead, leading from the boarding platform.

ONWARDS

... 11 ...

They shot through the blast door and into a corridor with ancient cable arrays pinned to one wall, drooping in snake-like curves between each fastening point. The thick, rubbery wires provided good handholds, making it easy to power along. The sisters didn't stop until they'd gone some distance without sounds or signs of pursuit. It didn't mean they *were* safe, but continuous flight might only take them into new dangers.

They flew into some kind of maintenance bay. Opal identified it as where the heavy battlesuits would normally be stored in rows. During emergencies or planetary assaults the toughest soldiers would climb the platforms next to each one and enter the cockpit, before the suit sealed and became a gigantic extension of their bodies, mounted with a range of tactical weapons. It explained why the corridors leading up to this chamber were so wide and high – room for the suited warriors to move in their battlesuits, which could be up to four metres tall.

But today the chamber was empty, long abandoned. Dangling power cables that would have kept suits charged now just swayed, limp as entrails. Locking mechanisms to hold the huge stomping battle feet in place now seemed like industrial art installations leading up to an absence meant to provoke thoughts.

"Hold up a mo," said Opal, grabbing a metal bar that once formed the immobilisation clip for battlesuit propulsion systems. She swung around and used her free arm to cushion the blow before she smacked into the frame due to the redirection of her forward momentum. Clarissa was just behind, but before Opal could grab her the girl did a similar tidy manoeuvre and came to a stop just above.

"You're getting good at zero-G movement," Opal added. "Better'n half the new recruits I've seen."

"It's not that tricky. In my dreams I can fly like a Mossagull, so I've had lots of practice."

Opal took a moment to glance around. At least, as far as her limited light beams let her see before green-hued illumination fell away into particle-thick gloom. No immediate signs of danger.

"We'll just be quiet for a minute," Opal said, tilting her body parallel to the floor so that she looked up at Clarissa. "I need to think about what direction we'll go in. You keep look out."

Clarissa mimed a zipping motion over her mouth, then gave a thumbs up.

Opal closed her eyes and focussed, because it wasn't just *thinking* she needed to do. It was investigating a suspicion that nagged at her. She didn't feel like a stranger on this Lost Ship. It was weirdly familiar, in a way that went beyond this being a reconfigured military vessel like those she'd served on in the past. No, this was the sensation of being in the right place, almost like a home, while still acknowledging the mortal hazards that awaited the unwary. Perhaps she'd been changed by her experiences, or something that had been dormant deep inside her all along was waking, maturing. Some kind of Null affinity.

It wasn't frightening.

And it hopefully wasn't useless.

She opened her mind, using a variant of one of the military techniques for coming down off trihormonal battle-enhancers. It was a system that focussed on repetitive patterns, requiring a degree of concentration that cleared the mind of everything else. Different patterns could have different effects, such as neutralising pain or dealing with trauma. Opal had come up with her own variants over the years, and this one was a mental framework of her creation, that redirected attention from her inner turmoils to outer – but non-threatening – sensations. A mix of selective world-engagement and distraction. She could be on her bunk in the barracks, blocking out all the chatter and bustle from other soldiers while she paid attention to the hum and occasional rattle of the air purification systems, and the subtle hiss of the HQ comm networks when the speakers weren't being used. Sounds that were normally below the level of perception, but brought to the foreground as a shield against the noise. Birdsong and insect sounds made good alternatives in some terrestrial environments, wind and waves in others.

Here, it was the whispers of her suit, its hums and pulses. But they also incorporated sounds from beyond, the Lost Ship creaks and murmurs as filtered through audio sensors, reinterpreted and homogenised into an artificial soundscape.

And it was even beyond *this* that her mind reached, her instinct led, and something pulled her focus and openness.

It was a pressure, in the distance. A thunderhead. A gravitic anomaly pushing back at her, like two magnetic poles in opposition, unable to touch but feeling that repulsion which identified the centre of the other's presence.

It was the Navigot. Sure as burns caused scars. Out there. Floors and walls were irrelevant. This was like detecting X-rays, or light shining down from the surface of a sea to where you lay in the sandy, shallow bottom.

Opal wondered if the Navigot felt the same contact.

Back to full awareness. Her suit's servos whirred experimentally as she altered her position.

"I know which way to go," said Opal. "And it isn't far now."

They crossed the empty battlesuit bay, its ghostly cavernousness an echoing presence through which they trespassed.

Wide corridors again beyond. Ramps rather than stairs. All empty of anything except a layer of undisturbed green sediment coating many of the surfaces, gathered in rippled drifts.

Opal was still marking routes with the yellow paint, even though she hoped they wouldn't have to return the long way. If the bullet train was broken then the Spine couldn't be safely traversed. Opal only just survived being sucked along a similar tube once because the Eternal Warrior suit saved her. With their current outfits, Opal and Clarissa would be splatted into the bad kind of red-splotched pancake.

Since drifting was a meditative act anyway, she was able to keep one part of her mind on Clarissa's proximity, and any signs of danger; but the other part could phase back and forth with tentative samples of the mental pressure she felt. As it strengthened, she knew she was going the right way, and the sensation was so powerful now that she rarely needed to backtrack after taking a wrong turn. Her instinct guided her reliably more often than not.

The walls here were textured plexisteel with huge rivets, but Opal noted cracks in some of the metallic surfaces, which widened as they progressed. The fissures seemed structural, as if subtle forces on the hull led to twists throughout the infrastructure, deforming it over time. Nothing too unusual in that when a ship was damaged and abandoned to the ravages of the Null.

"Do you think we'll live through this?" asked Clarissa as they pushed off the ceiling together.

"I do."

"And get back to Owlflight?"

"I hope."

Moments of drifting, both bodies and thoughts.

"Because if we don't," Clarissa added, "I want you to know this has still been good. Us being together again. I wish Mummy and Daddy were with us to make it better, and Athene, but without them it's like only you and me exist. The rest of the world doesn't matter."

Opal gently squeezed Clarissa's arm as they floated to the next push-off. Synchronised movements. Synchronised beings. Ever thus. Opal didn't need to add any words. Couldn't speak for a moment anyway.

More of the cracks, deeper, and some pieces of weighty wall structure had broken away and tumbled, endlessly doing their slow ricochets around the trapped space. Interior structures and cables that resembled veins were revealed in the holes.

Sisters together. All Opal had ever wanted. All that mattered. And when you had something important and didn't know how long it would last, you savoured every –

More damage, and Opal now regretted turning off the structural analysis overlays because, even as she watched, a section of wall blasted away. Instead of revealing another corridor there was only the blank black of Null, sucking at their atmosphere. Fuck, the damage to this area had been too extensive, they should have moved quicker to get through it, should have could have ...

Opal jammed fingers into a split in the ceiling and used her other hand to seize Clarissa's ankle before she was slurped out of the hole into endless Null and lost forever, along with the atmosphere being pulled, creating a roaring wind that wanted to carry them away.

Opal hadn't thought their route was anywhere near outer hull but she must have miscalculated. They could be within a gooseneck connector: some ship designs had that type of narrow section before the bridge. If she'd been able to map this Lost Ship from the outside then that slender shape would have forewarned her, instead of bumbling along as if she was safely ensconced in a deep interior.

"I need to use both hands, so climb up my body and put your arms around my neck!" yelled Opal, against the screaming tornado being relayed by her speakers. Then Opal could drag them away, using the cracks in the infrastructure. Once far enough from the hull breach, the pulling force might be weak enough to escape, so they could find an alternative route such as a parallel but undamaged corridor up the gooseneck, or an airlock that would enable them to safely go outside and manoeuvre over the exterior hull, up the neck and into the command section via a second airlock. There might even be a third option: get far enough from here and wait, since once everything had been evacuated – including the gas particles that made up the unbreathable atmosphere – things would be equalised and it would be no problem to float past the breach. Until then, this route was impassable.

But surviving the next few minutes would be the tricky part.

"I said climb up me, I can't hold on much longer!" Opal snapped, joints aching like the myalgia comedown from certain reflex enhancers.

But Clarissa still didn't move. Was she stunned by the fury of the whipping hurricane around them, and the mind-numbing blankness of the exterior? Opal squeezed harder, trying to bring the girl back to the current moment. Now was not a time to retreat into her mind and leave the body vacant.

Except that wasn't the case.

"It's okay," said Clarissa. "Let me go."

"Never! Do what I fucking tell you!"

It hurt to shout at Clarissa, to lose patience with her, but of all the times for her to start acting up ... Opal needed cooperation not nihilism. This wasn't the end, couldn't be. Opal tried to haul Clarissa in but her muscles were too tired, drained by the exertion of resisting tremendous forces.

"Honestly, I think it's fine," Clarissa calmly stated. "If there was really a big old hole there, then all the green blobbies in the air would be getting suckied along too. But they haven't moved, see?"

Opal saw them streaming past. The girl was delusional.

"They *are* being – look, this is serious, you have to help me!"

"Nope." Clarissa prised at the fingers clasping her ankle, and Opal was too weak to keep hold, so that Clarissa was torn from her grip in a whoosh, out of the hole, suit tearing on a jagged edge and releasing air and moisture which crystallised immediately. She was gone and –

"It's fine," Clarissa told her, floating at her side.

Opal focussed on the particles again, a blur, and she realised they weren't moving at all. Never had. The corridor was still full of them.

"See," said Clarissa.

The hole was still there, though. Opal released her strained fingers from the gap and pushed towards the edge of it, cautiously. She could see the blank beyond, but the pull had ceased.

When she tried to push her hand through the gap she found solid surface. Her hand and eyes each fed conflicting data into her brain. Then the illusion ceased. It was solid wall again. The cracks were real but smaller than in the altered reality.

It was the Navigot. Playing tricks to deter them. Mental defences against contact. She should have expected this.

"Not real," said Clarissa.

Opal looked from her sister to the looming passage ahead, the corridor to the future. She nodded.

"Not real," repeated Opal. Then, temporarily projecting her voice on loudspeaker into the outer ship: "You're right to be scared. We're coming for you."

It didn't matter if the Navigot heard things in that way. Some-times just expressing the sentiment was enough to bring it into reality.

ILLUSIONS

... 10 ...

The sisters ascended a sloping freight tunnel, careful of the floating cargo canisters. Halfway up it they encountered sticky web. Ahead, in a mass of stringy white tissue, something sparkled, like a cluster of reflective eyes.

"Real or not real?" asked Opal.

They paused. Clarissa screwed up her face in concentration.

"Not real," she said.

They advanced, and the gummy strands lost their hold, fading into vapour.

The pressure in Opal's head grew. That mental repulsion that told her she was going in the correct direction, and nearing her goal.

This was her third attempt at reaching a Navigot. The first time, she'd failed completely. The second, on the Gigatoir, she didn't reach it but it did communicate with her from a distance.

This time she felt like it was her best shot, driven by a different but urgent need.

Yes, this time she might do it. Because this time, she wasn't alone.

A network nexus room, normally heavily guarded because it was so critical to intra-ship system coherence. Key cabling and comm structures passed through here where they could be filtered, monitored, repaired or upgraded, while airwaves were impregnated with AI-driven antibodies.

But there were no guards. Just the sentinels of conduits, thick trunking of various colours, sealed tool racks, vacant monitor stations and polished grey glass encasing the ship's lifeblood infrastructure as it ran through the heart and subconscious of the ship. Opal and Clarissa carefully checked the shifting shadows for surprises as they proceeded through this shallow-sea cluster of angular metal coral and plasteen stems.

Illumination sparked from one of the boxes, arcing to the nearby junctions, a quickly growing net of crackling voltage.

"Real or not real?" asked Opal, bringing them to a halt by holding on to a thick red cable that resembled something from inside a body.

"Not real," Clarissa replied.

Opal closed her eyes and visualised the sparks fading away, leaving the room as it had been when they first entered, a night-dark artscape of glass monuments to something long dead. When she opened her eyes, that was exactly what she saw.

They moved on, despite the pressure-pain of another Entity resisting her approach.

At last. The wide, multi-level control room, full of dust-covered regulation stations, all overlooked by a massive, blank display screen. This was the closest she'd ever got to a Navigot. Last time the elevator lit up and the doors opened, a welcome that was rudely interrupted by arriving human forces. This time there would be no interruptions, but also there was no welcome. Only uncompromising dark. What had changed since the first time to make her an unwelcome guest? Did Navigots have preferences, or individual personalities? She supposed she would find out soon enough.

This was all a good sign. An end approaching, one way or another. An idea reinforced as the spray can ceased its hissing, leaving a yellow arrow only half finished. It had fulfilled its purpose, so she released it, allowed it a graceful never-ending roll away from her into the unknown.

Although it was in darkness, the elevator door was open. After a cursory flash of her suit light around the interior, she floated inside, followed by Clarissa. As expected from the lack of illumination, the control pad did nothing. That was fine. Even if the capsule was immobile, the shaft still existed.

Four clips held the central roof panel in place. Opal hung upside down and used a tool from her belt to unfasten them. A sharp thump of her fist and the panel cracked loose, twirling up the shaft. A lightless tube that should take them to the bridge. Inset handholds that could function as a ladder in artificial gravity situations would also make wonderful regular grips for zero-G ascent.

Then Opal spotted a wall texture which didn't belong with the dimpled grey plasteen of the tube. It was a man-sized reddish blotch, like the underside of skin dropped onto a griddle. These fleshy growths were a common sight on Lost Ships, and varied in size from those only as big as a fingernail, to ponderously disgusting areas metres across.

A ripple passed under the skin of this raw mole, which glistened freshly as the suit lights washed over it.

Opal reached into the capsule and gripped Clarissa's hand, pulling her up through the hatch and giving her some momentum to take her past the meaty areas and towards the rungs beyond. Clarissa caught them smartly, her body rotating without effort. A true natural.

Opal kicked off the capsule's roof to join her, then squinted up the shaft as it stretched away. She wished the slit visor had better visual enhancement capabilities, that it would let her see all the way to the end in a variety of wavelengths, identifying any blockages or dangers.

But wishing was fishing, as they said in the landlocked cities of Mossareid.

A gentle tug on her arm to get her attention.

"What is it, C?" she asked.

Clarissa pointed behind them at the red patch. It was now wildly active, pulsing and squelching like it wanted to tear free of the surface it was bonded with. Opal paused to see what kind of illusion the Navigot was trying this time, as its final defence.

She didn't have to wait long. Seconds later something erupted and attached itself to the tube surface opposite: a bundle of blue and red cables, which contracted to heave more bulk from the rupturing portal. Mass was revealed, slickly coated in viscera, slipping from the squirming flesh. A hulking torso with five short limbs – or maybe a thick neck, two arms and two legs that had all been amputated at knees and elbows? From the ends of each stubby limb stretched sinewy, prehensile strands. Seeing their position of emanation changed the perspective, so that they now resembled veins and arteries, as if skin, muscle and bone had been stripped away at those points, but the vascular system left untouched.

"Real or not real?" asked Opal, already knowing the answer as the panicked Navigot kept repeating a trick to diminishing returns. This looked so scary, it proved only its desperation.

"Not real," Clarissa replied.

The composition of the torso itself was difficult to make out. Part of it seemed metallic, though that could just be the glistening, oily coating. Other parts resembled circuitry, or organs and tissue, but all fitted together as a coherent whole.

Perhaps this was the same type of thing invading the Owlflight? She hadn't seen one when she was still aboard but the garbled description might match. And an idea sparked, one of those seemingly random thoughts that she immediately knew was more than an inspired guess: *mistranslation*. Some kind of misinterpretation of human concepts. An amalgam of security guards, patrol bots, and the underlying systems and networks that coordinated them, perhaps? Contextually it would fit a redesigned military ship.

Another tug at her arm, more frantic. Clarissa's face displayed fear. And the truth broke through the clever mental distractions that were probably the Navigot's influence, so that momentary expectation had replaced the truth.

Opal misheard.

Clarissa had said "Real," and the thing was already a few metres closer.

Opal shoved the girl ahead, hard, getting her moving while Opal yanked on rungs to launch herself after.

Time for a glance backwards in between handholds. The creature moved effortlessly. The cords that whiplashed out of each limb found purchase and yanked the body after it, before the stretchy process repeated. Despite its apparent mass, which was substantially more than Opal in her GAMag suit, it was fast and efficient, and gaining on them.

And something else. Looking at it caused after-traces, a bizarre visual artefact. It was as if the creature left temporary copies of itself, frozen images in a continuous line, overlapping and merging and each a still capture of its posture in that microsecond. As it flailed onwards the oldest images blurred and faded while new freeze-frames formed, like a line of pounding cyborgs.

Distraction. It was all irrelevant and trying to pull her focus away from action.

They needed distance. Opal flung herself even harder, and as she passed Clarissa she grabbed the girl around the waist with one arm. Opal's other hand freed the oxygen canister and pointed it behind, her thumb flicking the release catch in one movement. Gases hissed out, helped shift them forward, and this wasn't a time for delicacy. Full throttle, baby.

The straight tube was ideal. Opal kept them mostly in the centre by aiming the canister. Once or twice they dinged off the tunnel walls, Opal absorbing the scraping impact as much as possible, using her legs to kick away and back towards the central point.

And it was working. She could still detect the pounding sounds of the cyborg alien ricocheting from one side of the tunnel to the other in its snapshot sinew movements, but it was fainter. Nothing visible when she looked back.

At the same time, she estimated distance, time travelled, speed. No reason why a Lost Ship would be an exact match for human dimensions, and exceptions were common, but *mostly* they resembled what she was used to. She had ascended to the bridge on UFS Corcorius occasionally. Probably a height of a few hundred metres. There was enough distance that explosions during a control room attack wouldn't affect the primary or secondary bridges, and an assaulting force would still have a long path to follow, with defences all the way. Elevators could cover it in seconds but she was going slower than that. Must be reaching the end. Can't risk braining herself.

She switched off the gases that had been accelerating them, flung her arm ahead, and released the full-force jet. Deceleration began, wall blurs becoming less fuzzy as they flew by. Slower, slower.

Please don't let this be an unexpectedly long tunnel where slow-ing down just means the thing will catch us.

Always looking ahead now, waiting for – crunch, in the darkness her lights had revealed the end of the tunnel too late, though she let go of the canister and wrapped both arms around Clarissa at the last second, arching over her so the main impact was on Opal's spine. Thankfully, the GAMag suit had armour plating there to protect the head and neck from falling pipework or other engineering hazards. Still, as she shook the stars from her vision, she knew she'd have one helluva headache tomorrow.

"You okay, C?" asked Opal, glancing into her sister's faceplate.

"Ouchies," replied the girl, but she was conscious and that was what they needed.

The gas canister was gone. Must have shot itself back down the tunnel towards the thing. Hopefully lure it away, or smack it in the face. Correction, it had no face. Maybe the equivalent of cyborg bollocks, then.

The shaft's single elevator had been their entry point; at this end there was just an open archway into a narrow tunnel. Not too narrow to halt the pursuing creature, whose pounding approach was getting louder again.

Opal pushed Clarissa into the only route onwards.

"Go!" she yelled. The commlink would lower the volume of the shout to safe levels for the girl's ears, but it would still convey motivation. Clarissa scrabbled away, clumsy kicks at first before she reestablished her coordination and began to fade from sight.

Few options remaining. Opal took out the final explosive pack, which she'd hoped to retain as a bargaining chip. But bargaining was no use if she didn't make it that far. As one of the lessons she'd tried to imbue into Clarissa said, use what you have while you're alive, you can't take it with you.

She set the timer for fifteen seconds, her best guess as to their lead. The thing would need to change angle here to enter the ninety-degree exit passage, a few seconds of leeway. She slapped the bomb against the tunnel ceiling and was about to launch off after Clarissa, but an old saying nagged at her brain: appearances could be deceptive.

So she activated loudspeaker and shouted down the elevator shaft.

"I've planted a bomb here. Stay back and you won't be harmed. I'm just protecting my sister."

Then she pushed off after Clarissa.

The thing might not understand her words, but it was the best warning she could give. The universe wasn't an ideal place, and sometimes survival meant doing things you didn't like. But at the same time, only an arsehole wouldn't at least make an effort to minimise the harm they caused.

She now had a chance to note the unexpected texture of this narrower passage. The elevator should have ended at an entrance to the bridge floor, and faced the slits of fortified firing points and an access gate between them. But instead, this was a snaking tube, coated in ceramic white hexagonal tiles, so that the suit lights glared in bright reflections.

Opal soon reached Clarissa, helped shove her forwards along the undulating, circular route which didn't fit any of Opal's expectations.

A wall-shaking blast, and fire roared after them. Unconstrained by gravity it flowed in serpentine sheets of yellowed translucence with flickering tongues, bathing the passage in orange. Once more, Opal hugged Clarissa in, shielded her until the heat and fragments passed, the singed Viscids in the air now swirling with all the chaotic thermals. Soot stuck to the silver of Clarissa's suit, but there was no other damage, no oxygen-leaking tears.

The pounding of an approaching Entity couldn't be heard. Although that might mean it had retreated, another possibility was that the exterior suit pickups had been fried by the heat or concussive force of the explosion. The pounding could be as loud as ever and she'd be lulled into a fatal complacence.

They half scrambled, half flew out of the twisting tube and into another unexpected location.

This was no bridge or command room, not part of a normal ship. It was a purely alien addition. The sisters entered a massive sphere, at least thirty metres across. The room must have intersected more than one deck of the ship. It wasn't white tiles in the narrow tunnel and this chamber, she could see now: more like overlapping icy scales.

The scaly surface provided contact for fingertips, so Opal and Clarissa were able to explore the circumference of this cavity in the ship, looking for other exits or places to hide if necessary. But no other tunnels presented themselves. The only means of progression was a circular airlock. There was a control panel to the side, similar in appearance to D45s which everyone was familiar with. It even had clear writing: small printed letters saying "Access".

The tools on Opal's belt should enable her to snap off the covering to access the emergency release if the door refused to move – and she certainly didn't expect cooperation from portals on this ship. The panel wasn't even illuminated, so like almost everything else, it was in powered-down mode.

Opal thought she heard something, and listened more carefully. Not thumping of a rapidly approaching large creature, but a dragging sound, echoing from their entrance to this room.

The sooner they got out of this place, the better.

Opal pushed the airlock door release, but – as expected – nothing happened. Fine. This would be a simple lock to tool open. Opal removed a pry-bar from the maintenance belt, and held it to the first corner of the override panel.

But she didn't pop it off.

"I think that veiny robot is still coming along the tunnel," Clarissa cautioned.

Yes, the scraping was closer, accompanied by a whining sound like straining motors, or a creature in pain.

But Opal still didn't pull off the control's faceplate.

Such a weird room – and yet, here was a very human-type door. A model that was familiar, much more of an exact copy than was usual on Lost Ships.

Clarissa's arm wrapped around Opal's leg. Her sister was anchoring herself, but also probably seeking comfort from whatever was coming, whatever would happen next.

There is no time, Opal. It's not like you to stall.

I know. But something about this feels wrong. Even the fact that there's pressure on me to act ... why are alarm bells ringing in my head?

And yet, this is so simple a thing for you to bypass.

And so obvious a temptation.

One of the things Opal had learned is that appearances were often irrelevant, and reality took different shapes behind surfaces. She had seen Tentaculats with her eyes closed back on the Gigatoir. And Cube, from the Leviathan, had communicated through solid structures, manifesting its life in her fevered half-waking dreams.

She closed her eyes now. Recalled how those things had appeared. Sought for the textures of the light, the temperatures of the glows, the feel of the lines. And it was almost there, and reminded her of the eye focus trick that had helped her find her way through the Topias on the invisible wind trails that connected them.

It worked. A whole new world blossomed behind her eyelids, a mental focus on emissions that passed through the feeble barrier of skin, but which she could somehow perceive with a part of her mind that had been growing in strength. Shapes and shadows of the narrow visible-light realm superimposed on the neon wireframes of this broad-wavelength existence. A world behind a world.

It wasn't just visual, either. Synaesthetic tingles of perfumed scent, bitter aches, as if being fed information from elsewhere. What she saw was a sort of organic HUD behind her eyelids. She could have cried at the beauty and wonder of it.

Imminent danger pulled her back to the now. She had to solve this. Come up with a plan. A ...

This door in front of her wasn't a real door, for a start. It was a trap. Beyond it wasn't a room or corridor but a cage containing a spinning black ball which emanated *nothing*, only sucked things up so that its appearance was just an absence. Like a tiny black hole waiting to be released, the death prize for whoever tried to reach the Navigot.

Opal looked around with eyes squeezed tight, through the white scales which resembled purple flames in the secondary sight. And there, higher up, a flaring patch that seemed like all the rest on the *surface*, but it had a passageway on the other side. That was the real exit.

She opened her eyes, pulled Clarissa with her to the spot she'd noted. The scraping whines were closer now, probably about to enter the chamber. Her information store grew while the time counted down. Wasn't that always the fucking way?

This was the place, yet there was no obvious way to break through. If only she'd kept her bomb ... But she had tools. As a last resort she could chip away. Maybe one of the scales was loose, a trigger, or there was a pattern of touch to activate a release, and she could think about it. But the creature was nearly here, and it would sense them.

Fuck. Opal had always been blocked. And it was happening again, an impassable barrier between her and the final bridge beyond.

"What are you doing?" asked Clarissa. "Why didn't we go through the door and get away?"

"This is the real exit, C, but I don't know how to open it. And we need to hide so I can gain time to think." Mind spinning, options appearing and being ruled out. There was nowhere to retreat to. Whirr, thump, whine. No, no, not yet.

"Clarissa, remember the game of play dead?"

"Yes! I was always better at it."

"Exactly! We're going to do that now. It's a trick I have. If we do it together, shut down, empty our heads, not fearing anything, then it can hide us. I've done it before on Lost Ships. We need to be very calm, ignore what goes on around us. Blank our minds and breathe deep."

Whirr, thump, whine.

"But how will that get us through the wall?"

"It won't. But it might make us invisible to the thing that's following. I don't think it sees like we see. It tracks something else. If our minds aren't *here*, then it might not know we're here either, and go back. I can't explain, you have to trust me. Then when it's gone we'll try and get through this wall."

Whirr, thump, whine. Whirr-thump-whine. It was speeding up as if it already sensed them.

"You say *might* but if it doesn't work, we could die, right?"

Whirrthumpwhine.

"Just do what I say, Clarissa! I've run out of options!"

And, infuriatingly, Clarissa smiled. "No need to hide," she said. "But for once, you have to trust *me*."

There was a certainty sparking in the girl's eyes. Unshakable confidence, infectious. Opal realised she'd already agreed with a nod.

The creature entered the sphere. It dragged itself along as if crippled. The visual repetition was still present but the effect was flickering, less complete. One of its limbs leaked ... something. Not blood, but pieces of wire, or veins, like small wriggling worms in all the colours of ageing bruises. Slowed, but not stopped.

"Stay right here," said Clarissa, holding Opal's hand now. "Until I say."

The small hand, encased in a too-big glove. But the fingers were in there, the same girl within the artificial shell, just as her spirit resided within the fleshy shell. Of course Opal trusted her. She'd do anything for Clarissa. The feelings flooded her system with warmth, acceptance, obedience.

The cyborg-thing launched itself across the centre of the dome on a trajectory right at them. Committed to its course, and whatever it intended when it arrived there.

"Go!" snapped Clarissa, kicking away from their position, tugging Opal with her. Opal had felt dazed, but now acted, adding her strength to her sister's. A mighty push and they both sailed away from their point, away from the creature's target. Their course took them just clear of its extending sinew wires so that they moved up and up, while it sailed towards the barrier scales.

And then it would push away again, come after them, and a child's idea would be shown to have only been a child's flawed idea after all, a momentary respite. Perhaps Clarissa had visualised something cartoonish, such as the Entity splatting into the wall and bursting like a Mossagull egg. She was at an age where the sad truths of reality could still hide behind the fantasies of childish animations.

But it was Opal's turn to be shocked as she looked back and saw it strike the wall, and it *did* splat. A change in its shape, a shuddering, flailing of worms, screech of grinding metal, writhing as fluids slurped out while its shape flattened and frothed. That was all Opal saw before it was beyond the range of her lights. And then the opposite surface approached, and they had to absorb the impact, focus on gripping some small ridges where platelets overlapped, to prevent them bouncing off in an uncontrolled ricochet.

Clarissa seemed calm, as if she'd known this would happen.

"What the *squidge*?" Opal asked.

"You'll see."

Clarissa pointed in a direction, close to that which they'd just travelled along. A return. They pushed off together, though with less force this time. There were no whirring or whining sounds. The immediacy had faded. Caution returned.

As they approached the far wall her suit lights gradually revealed the detail of the maroon, sloshing circle of melanoma. Bits of cable stuck out like thick hairs growing from a scab.

It was a flesh portal.

"You made that?" Opal asked, though she knew the answer. What Clarissa had once done in her withdrawn state was now a possibility while she was fully present – at least on Lost Ships.

"We needed a way through," the girl answered.

"You destroyed the creature."

"I evolved it."

They came to a halt just to the side of the fleshy, tumorous mass. Opal was glad of that. Splatting into it, knowing it would happen and being unable to redirect to avoid the unpleasant merging with that raw wound would have been too disgusting.

Opal hadn't seen an active portal up close, without death breathing down her neck. It rippled, as if continuing to reconfigure itself below the surface, making chemical changes to whatever structure it was bonded to and embedded in.

"The thing chasing us wasn't what you thought," Clarissa mused, also watching the process of the flesh slowly flattening and spreading, like liquid from a blister being reabsorbed by the body.

"What do you mean? It wasn't conscious?"

"It wasn't just *one thing*. Nothing is. Not in this place, anyway. The way things look is just the tiniest part of what they are, but the best our brainies can do at understanding."

"You've lost me, C."

"Remember that net-game we played in Mossareid before the electric cut out? Tomby Caverns? And you helped me on some bits that were tricky or scary, and we got to the big creature in the blue cave and you were stuck?"

"The Ramotaur?"

"Yes. You said it was the monster that ends the game, and spent ages shooting it and it didn't do much, and you got angry and thumped the holo controls but bashed your hand on the wall behind them."

"I remember." Opal flexed her fingers, as if a ghost of that pain twitched there.

"But it wasn't the end game monster, and it wasn't like you thought at all. I saw it as a progress skill gate. And, in a way, that made the Ramotaur a *key*. And once we tricked it into charging and smashing the wall that had a crack in it, with a drop on the other side, the Ramotaur fell down a hole and died, but we used the rope and climbed down carefully to get to the last level. What you *thought* you saw left you trapped because you didn't have the idea. But I saw it in a different way and it made us win the game. Gold crown to top it off."

Clarissa sometimes surprised you with her perceptions. But they had never been this coherently formulated before, at least not as utterances to someone else. Perhaps this was always inside her mind though, an understanding that the external only hinted at.

"So you thought of all that in the seconds while I was trying to find a way through this wall?"

"It's just that ... well, how you see things is how they become to you."

But the girl had lost interest in the conversation, and prodded at the edges of the raw portal, where the meat squelched and leaked grease.

Clarissa probably didn't realise how prescient her last sentence was. Opal had the experience to know how prejudices filtered reality to make the lies seem true, and reinforce them via overlaying an interpretation filter on the ambiguities of life. Something that seemed as irrelevant as whether you were left or right handed soon overwhelmed you with significance when strangers misunderstood it, took it as an indicator of what lay inside the box. Tone of skin was akin to that. Sour minds conjured up every unpleasant surprise as a means of avoiding looking inside themselves and seeing the mirror.

"So you just saw it as a resource?" Opal asked, not quite ready to let it drop. Because this was starting to feel like her sister was not the sister she used to know. "Flesh and circuitry that could be used?"

Clarissa didn't answer that. But maybe evasiveness *was* an answer. "It's ready now," she said. "We can go through." She took Opal's hand.

"Just like on the Leviathan?" Opal asked.

"What happened on the Leviathan?"

"Never mind."

Clarissa forced her way into the flesh, and Opal was sucked in after her.

An ashy shadow of the world. Echoes distorted though the howls of a gale wind, pushing them back, cold and alien. A distended field of view as whatever this was had to be perceived by something other than eyes. The contact with Clarissa's hand was still felt, but no limbs were visible, no bodies, insubstantial as the frigid air blasting against them, powerful repulsion showing they Were. Not. Welcome.

There was a sense of the wall's other side, a cavity, so close this time, not like the multi-deck transition aboard the Leviathan – this goal was literally just pushing through a single skin. And yet the final resistance was so powerful that the outcome was uncertain. The hand some other version of Opal held was trembling, and Opal felt the strain, the unexpected toll this took. She tried to encourage her sister mentally, to help not hinder, but there was no way of knowing if it meant anything in the inverted grey negative dimension they passed through.

Closer, closer, ear-ripping shrieks mustering against them to stop that flat plane from edging nearer, their presences shredded by blades of ice, hard to hold coherence, to keep the mind together in that assault, Opal wanted to let go and retreat, to scream like the hurricane, to repel, to escape the inhuman howl –

And then they were through, drifting out of slurping soup, both with a coating of gore as if their suits bled. It let them go. They had crossed the barrier.

Clarissa's face shone with sweat, pale with pain, yet with a triumphant flame behind the exhaustion.

"You didn't want me to come on the Lost Ship," she whispered, so that the suit comms had to amplify the hoarse voice. "Cos you were worried." Clarissa touched Opal's faceplate. "But it turns out it was me who saved you, after all."

And then Clarissa died.

NAVIGOTS

... 9 ...

Opal pulled Clarissa in close. Gently, careful of the GAMag's servo strength. Scrutiny of the girl's face didn't reveal breathing. So hard to tell, when separated by two artificial skins. Opal's greatest fear always fought to batter down hope, she had to hold it at bay. But this was more than just exhaustion. Clarissa's face was red-tinted from the viscera on her visor, illuminated by the rim glow of her faceplate, adding to the fatalistic imagery. Opal tried wiping it away but it just spread crimson around, as sticky and besmeared as their bodies.

Basic civ emergency suits didn't possess the advanced bodily scanners of warsuits that could examine blood sugars, electrolytes, compositions; but they did have basic checks for oxygen usage, body temp, and – most important – heart rate. Opal pulled out a concealed DIM cable from her arm control panel and plugged it into Clarissa's suit output. A few taps on Opal's wrist computer enabled data interchange.

Fuck.

Vitals missing. The budget suit systems displayed thready figures that could just as easily be glitches and interference. Nothing conclusive, and no way to tear open the suit for direct examination without killing the girl.

Work with what you've got.

The figures were useless, the suits useless, the barrier between
Opal and her sister was – wait. Peripheral indicators showed
Clarissa's internal suit temperature was dropping. Down to almost 6°C. Why? There had to be a reason. A freezing suit environment would pull down Clarissa's core body temp. If she was
still alive but with metabolic processes slowing due to encroach-
ing hypothermia then that could explain some of it.

Opal ran diagnostics on Clarissa's suit. Yep, it had been
drained of charge. Causal lines started to appear. Possibilities.
More checks. It didn't seem to be suit damage, just a complete
power down, as if the transit had sucked everything from it. Opal
checked her own charge. GAMag at forty per cent, way below
expected but not yet critical. Perhaps its shielding protected it
from flatlining in some way that the civilian model didn't.

Sisters shared blood.

Sisters could share other things.

Meanwhile, DIM cables could share comms and data, little
else. But anything self-powered might have a charging connector. The GAMag's was on the wrist control panel, but Clarissa's
suit didn't seem to have one. Was it just a disposable model?
Please, no ... Opal checked arms, waist, section joins, it had to be
there! Then she found a peel-back covering near the silver suit's
navel, which revealed a charging port. Composite ring connec-

tor, because they were cheap; whereas GAMags used industrial MI-splice format. Not directly compatible.

We'll do this together, Opal. Two such different minds connecting, we found a way. There's always a way.

Clarissa's suit internals had dropped to 4°C. It would be sapping her body heat like crazy. Other life support failures couldn't be far behind and ... Athene had said connecting. Yes. Compatibility.

Opal rooted through her toolbelt. Cables. Some had universal connectors. They just needed tweaking. The GAMag gauntlets were too bulky for fine wire strips but a pair of pliers let Opal connect and tighten an MI-splice to a universal adaptor, whilst being careful not to overdo it and snap the fragile ring. There probably wouldn't be a spare, and composite rings were notoriously brittle.

It seemed sturdy enough. One end into Opal's suit, one to her sister's. GAMag wrist control, she tapped into the overrides which prevented reverse flow. They were a safety feature to impede overheating, but that wasn't the problem today. Once that was disabled she slid a fingertip up the dial, stretching the output bar, transferring her own energy into Clarissa's suit. Only a trickle charge but that gave time to reactivate life support, temporarily boost internal heating, refresh sensors, all the while repeating the phrase *this will work this will work* in her head.

Status update, then agonising seconds as the wrist display rewrote the data ... hurry, damn it! ... before letters and numbers blinked across the screen.

The faintest threads of pulse, the slightest waft of breath. Clarissa was alive.

Opal hugged Clarissa, squeezing as hard as she dared, as if that could transfer more heat to the fragile body.

"You scared the shit out of me, girl." Opal didn't add anything else because her voice wasn't steady.

Once Clarissa's suit had her pegged as sleeping, and the vital system alarms blinked out, Opal had to disconnect. Her GAMag was down to fifteen per cent power. Its own alarms would be triggered before long. Opal altered her suit settings to power-saving mode to give more time. She was an adult, could cope with minimals.

But there wasn't a moment to waste.

Power transfer and DIM cables unclipped, Opal held Clarissa's body under one arm, leaving three limbs for manoeuvring. The flesh portal appeared more crusty and dried than when it had first formed. Did using them for transport drain away their life energy traces? Could it be used more than once, or were they now trapped on this side of the barrier? Perhaps Clarissa would be able to answer that if she woke.

When she woke, fuckdammit.

The passageway led in only one direction, its surfaces absorbing light and sound to create a surreal effect. It made staying centred difficult. But at least it was a straight route this time, not a sinuous intestinal passage, so one kick from the edge of the flesh portal was enough to carry them both onwards, headlamp facing ahead in the direction Opal wanted to go. They were not ambushed, and reached a new chamber. Opal gripped the lip of the circular entrance to halt, and take in whatever the fuck she was seeing.

A tangled forest of glowing wires – or body pipes, or veins – ran from the edges of the room towards the centre. They were all different shades of colour, though fleshy reds, bruised blues and pus-like yellows predominated. They also exhibited variations of thickness and texture, making a chaotic mix that would take a genius to unravel as they knotted and wrapped around each other.

What they connected to and illuminated in the centre was something new for Opal.

It was a creature of some sort. Opal could make out what might have been limbs, and there was definitely a kind of head with a face. The head was too large for the body by human standards, taut skin over features that seemed to want to break free of the skull, strange bluish freckles scattered across the centre. The skull looked raw and stubbled. Some of the pipe-veins entered the head through holes ringed by silvery scars, while other artery-cables perforated the body and limbs, so that it was held in place, a prisoner of the nest of serpents that entwined it. Opal realised some of the tubes were translucent, and moving bubbles within revealed them as liquid transport vesicles.

Circling the Entity, threading in and out of the tendon morass, were a shoal of tiny beings that manoeuvred with no difficulty in zero-G, swimming in a way that made her think of sharp-toothed fish made out of jagged, corroded metal. A few of them would fit in her hand at once. Occasionally they hovered near the central Entity and squirted a fine mist onto its epidermis.

The Entity wasn't fully naked, but instead of clothes there were areas encased in a kind of dimpled plastic, which moulded to – or even replaced – what would have been tightly stretched skin.

The creature's expression was grim, and if the face was not pulled so tight over bone it might have been frowning or glaring, but it was impossible to interpret that black-eyed, stony expression in a way you would with another human.

Then its lips moved.

"We are the Navigot," it said. Its voice carried to her suit clearly. That surprised Opal because in the past she'd received communications straight into her mind. Maybe this change was due to finally being within close proximity to one of these creatures.

"And we are humans," Opal replied.

"I know that which is clear, that which is detected. We are one and all with connection."

"If you know all, then why're we using words at all?"

"We know your preferences. I also recognise your presenting dangers. Before conference there must be clarifications. You see the attendants that swarm around us. Point one of this meeting: do not try anything. They will end you for incorporation if you do."

"Noted. I'll keep my distance if you play fair."

"Play? Parlay is our mode ..." The Entity seemed to lose itself in thought. "This is a long-time event for us. You may begin the process."

Opal kept her focus on the creature which spoke with such rumbling volume, but she used her peripheral vision to track the motions of the small, nibbling shards. If their patterns changed and they approached her, she was ready to shove Clarissa's limp body behind, into the passage, and shield it.

"Why did you attack my ship?" Opal asked.

"Representation difference, semantic: attack, investigate, assess, interpret. We comprehend human perspective. I have a mission. It is secret, but content is not the key relevance. We may disclose two factors. One is that your vessel is seen as a threat to us requiring action. Second, by dismantling it I gain information and resources, secondary goals, dual outcomes, which have symmetrical aesthetics."

"We were *not* a threat!"

"Such is how I translated it."

"Oh, right. It's all down to translation for you things. *Mis*translation. Misconstruing humans and our world and tech. You shouldn't place so much importance on it when it leads you into mistakes."

"You misapply. Translation is the most important concept for we species. For you species. For humans. It underpins every element of apparent existence. Bodily sensation is translated as significance. The behaviour of others as perceived is translated as interior motivation. Sensory data contributes towards world building. All this translation occurs as a fundamental part of being human, even before language, concept and connotation were ever created. Without translation, humans would be primordial inanimates."

Opal took a breath. There was a logic to the Entity's thought processes. She had to find ways to use that. Losing her calm would be counterproductive. "Evidence of misinterpretation should lead to reevaluation," she said, pretending she was talking to a simplistic level two AI. "How can we be a threat when my craft isn't even a military vessel?"

"Human category error, intention not always mapped to outcome. Threat may exist regardless. Analogise in ways that you can understand: a virus has no intention of affecting mood of host, nor even possesses awareness of host, but host has such an interpretation, category assigned: virus threat to be negated. This threat I refer to is not direct conflict but navigational. We travel within depths beyond Topias. Humans do not infest so deeply, yet here you are. Higher human ships do not repercuss, yet here you are. The usual propulsion system of human transport is accounted for, yet here you are. All new factors. Your transport is novel, yes?"

The Entity's speech was convoluted, yet it applied emphasis in ways that seemed more human and less frustrating than previous communications with the chattier denizens of Lost Ships and Topias which Opal had encountered: a Navigot and the Oracles. Perhaps they learned over time.

"Correct," she said. "It's something new. The drive is, anyway."

"The propulsion pushes a growing bubble of slick counterforce. This creates waves in what should be flat. The echoes attract this Navigot. The ripples dismantle our navigation, which is sensitive and specific. Investigation and negation protocol is triggered. Intention: irrelevant."

This would require some thought. There had to be a means of picking her way through the different facets of the situation, persuading, finding an option they had overlooked. But also not presenting it in a way that would get it immediately rejected. She had to take the conversation in the right direction, implant precursor ideas that would aid her interpretation later.

Fuck, right now she wished she had a background in Sophisticated Linguistics instead of rifle maintenance, shelter building and unarmed combat.

"Another question," she said. "And don't give me any esoteric bullshit about having a limit on how many I can ask based on spurious time travel alien guff."

"We await."

"We're talking just fine right now. You probably knew we would. So why did I feel like you tried to stop me getting here? I've been on two other Lost Ships, and their Navigots – as far as I can tell – wanted to communicate with me. Even helped me get close. But this time I felt resistance, even though blocking me would just make it harder to sort out this mess. Are you faulty in some way?"

"The answer should be obvious to you from the information already provided, but with goodwill we shall clarify to prevent accusations of mistranslation."

Sarcasm?

It continued. "Your previous encounters were with exploratory vessels. They seek information. Need it. Imperatives. But you know my mission is different. Security is my assigned protocol. That drives macro-scale interventions such as negating your craft, and micro-scale such as resisting infection in my extended body, from such as you. When we interpret as you might, it is obvious this situation places us in positions of confrontation. You also see us as a threat, and would nullify us if you could. Thus the oldest cycle plays out afresh."

The Entity wasn't just communicating more humanly than she was used to, but its appearance nagged at her, too. A dis-

torted humanoid. Not what she expected to find at the heart
of a Lost Ship. Did they make things appear this way just to
enable easier identification and interaction for Opal? Or was it
to do with interpretations of the ship they'd based their designs
on or modified? There was something relevant about this, but it
evaded her mind, darted just beyond perception in the depths of
her subconscious.

"If you're somehow familiar with human conflict, then you'll
also know how self-defeating it can be," she tried. "You are destroying my ship, but in that time the crew will have come up
with countermeasures. They will hurt you in return. And if they
are going to die anyway, they'll be desperate. Will want to take
you to hell with them. Test me for truth, you'll see that I'm not
lying. If all else fails then they'll ram you. Full-fire the engines and
turn my craft into a ginormous fucking battering ram, aimed at
your head. I was right about the bridge location housing you. I
told them as much before I left. They'll know exactly what to
do to decapitate you. I don't know much about how Lost Ships
really function, but if a bubble can mess up your navigation,
what would a three-kilometre-long ship smashing into your core
do to your mission? All of us lose."

It didn't answer straight away. Then its face twitched in an
indecipherable expression.

"You are belligerent. There is a strange familiarity to it, in opposition to me. A wounded animal ... is always most dangerous."

"But I'm trying to change my ways. Looking for *new* routes.
I don't *want* my ship to be destroyed. I don't *want* to harm you
or your vessel. I'm sure you can tell I'm being honest. I want to

find a new option, something where we all survive, where we all get wiser, where the mistakes of the past stop repeating."

"Untested novelty would be dangerous."

The patterns of the orbiting fragments seemed more jagged, agitated. Did they react to the Navigot's mental state, or act as an extension of it?

"Our current collision course is even more dangerous," she countered. "I give you my word that I'm genuine in this. That there must be a way to come to a deal. To let us go."

"A deal ... Freedom ... it may be over-rated. Temporary?"

"Are you all right?" she asked, frowning.

"We all bear scars."

She said, "I feel like ..." What? That there was something both alien and familiar about the Navigot?

"Feelings ... they get in the way ... you are driven by them, I resist ..." The fishy particles became twitchy, indecisive, and Opal noted that some even collided with each other as the movement patterns rippled through the swarm.

"How do you know what drives me?"

"Your sister, Clarissa. She is a primary motivation."

"How the fuck do you know her name? Have you been digging in my brain?"

"From records ... long lost ... past ... memories ... I feel like I know you. Too smart for your own good. You must read books."

She looked again, more closely. Damn the shitty visuals on this suit. But the freckling on the face, it seemed to have a pattern now. Like military Q code facial tattoos on UFS commanders. She'd sure seen enough of those, she should have spotted it, but the way it was stretched over a new skull shape threw her. If only she had Athene to reconfigure it, then translate the codes as a means of identification, reading the history of past victories and promotions in the language of angled lines and mojis and caesuras. But even without that, the vague insistence in her mind had hooked something, was pulling it into the light, overlaying memory and present and trying to get different shapes to fit, whilst worrying that she was forcing things and might break them.

"Major Grubane?" she asked, incredulously.

SURPRISES

... 8 ...

The creature blinked sluggishly, and the orbiting swarm slowed to a halt.

"I am the Navigot."

"Is that you?" Opal asked.

No reply. A face that was enlarged and not designed for emotion, and yet Opal was sure she saw signs of internal struggle, revealed by the slight twitches of discomfort.

"It *is* you, isn't it?" she insisted. "Major William Grubane. Holy fuck."

"I am ... We are the Navigot. I am ... more. Many. That name? It is something. The past. Grubane, some identification I feel. That, and another. I classify the second as Aurikaa12. There are others in here. We I me. You disrupt. I syncretise. Things are not as separable as we are taught. I am one and all. I am the Navigot. I am ... Aurbane. Grubikaa. Navigot. William ..."

"Didn't you die?"

"I do not remember dying. Nor are there records of such in my extended storage."

"What *do* you remember?"

"Falling. Forever. It is ... a dream I have never woken up from."

"You're not the same."

"None of us stay the same, Opal Imbiana. You are not the same. This is not the Aurikaa. It is a new incarnation, different materials, rebuilt, fresh layouts, a body and mind fused in life. I am here. Living or dead is not of significance when disproved by existence."

"Except it's not irrelevant. In life you couldn't change. I recognised that much in you. You set a course and you kept going."

"Like you. I ... remember. That similarity, that thought near the end. On and onwards, because there is no turning back when the mass of a star guides our lives and pulls us in. So I did keep going. I can recall that now. Sinking down into depths. Certainty that we plummeted into hell. To death, irrevocable."

"But somehow, you're here."

"We pull in more data, that seemed of no relevance before, not worth suction accessing, but which your words draw attention to, pieces sifted for knowledge nutrients to become more than before. You thought me defeated but you overlooked the options we had available. I almost did the same, which would have been the end."

"What options?"

"A secret in plain sight. Obvious in retrospect, but I am forbidden from clarifying."

"That's just another in a long list of shit I don't understand and don't need to. At least today. But now you're here. Reborn? Rebuilt? I don't even know what you are."

"We are Aurbane. We are Navigot."

"So you must be different in other ways. You see? The potential? You can *change* what you are after all. You don't need to keep falling forever, Grub- ... Aurbane. You can alter your course."

It focussed on Opal with such intensity her skin prickled. The metallic insects in the air began moving smoothly again, like an engine starting up, the flows visibly spreading outwards until a complex and weaving pattern was reestablished.

"I understand," he said. "What it is to seek freedom from fetters. There is a connection here, with what all on Lost Ships desire. To escape a cycle. To break from an orbit. To get life from death."

"And that's what I want as our deal." Now was the time for Opal to strike. "A focus on similarities and connections more than differences. With our combined brains, there must be a way."

"You place options before us. You have awoken us, and that itself is something of value. It pleases me that we have twice been placed in positions of confrontation by the rules of others, but maybe we can find our own way out this time. Bend rules, without breaking them. Our specialism, perhaps. So we create a new paradigm. As long as your goals are not against mine, and you promise not to harm me, my ship or my mission, then I will not hinder you."

"You'll let us go?"

"We have already ceased the attack. Your ship will be released. You will return and continue your journey. We will wait. Once the emanations from your drive cease, I shall continue our own way. But you must never use the drive again. This is my final offer."

"The drive is *designed* not to be reused or copied. With luck I'll be gone from the Null soon, get to my destination, and it will be everything we hope. We'll settle and never encounter you again. And I promise not to harm you."

"Then we have the deal. You will return."

"Is there any way for me to contact my ship? To explain all this?"

"That can be allowed. But it is not possible from here without altering infrastructure first, which takes time. I am protected from emanations. My full sensorium is a total of my connection to the ship. You must leave my domain. But I will reconfigure an outside core to enable you to communicate. It will boost your signals."

"And how do I get there?"

"I will reactivate the Venagata you used, and redirect it to a location close to where you need to be. You will then follow my directions."

"When we crossed the vena-thing portal to get here, it nearly killed my sister. Drained the power from her suit."

"That was because of the resistance you faced. Somehow the girl overcame it, but not without cost. She is a strange one. This time you will be assisted. No negative depletion." He paused, then added: "We expect no dangers, but you might be advised to leave your sister while she sleeps. Here, I can attend her. Here, she will be safe."

Clarissa's comatose face was lax in repose. So vulnerable, true. So dependent on the will of whoever watched over her. And was there a hungry glitter to Aurbane's black eyes, or did she imagine it?

"I'll take her with me," said Opal.

"Very well. We will not meet again, but goodwill has a palpability that rests in minds and which we sense manifesting as such a presence between us. This is an outcome that provides satisfaction to all our component minds."

Opal did not leave immediately. She had one more question.

"Grubane – sorry, Aurbane – are you in pain?"

So much inhuman reconfiguration. Suffering was surely inevitable.

His face contorted within the bounds of whatever its musculature allowed. It resembled a grimace, acknowledgement. The fishy fragments twitched in their orbits, as if an extension of his mind.

But then he answered.

"There is no pain. It was removed as unnecessary. But I thank you for asking. You are connected to your mammal status. Empathy extension. I had forgotten such, as well. There is much to ruminate on. For that, I am also obliged. Goodbye, Opal Imbiana."

She held Clarissa and pushed herself along the tunnel, back to the flesh portal. She was halfway along when she realised that what she'd taken for a grimace on his face, may actually have been a smile.

Through the crusty gore of an alien transport, holding Clarissa's limp body tight to her heart.

The echoing grey translucent shadow realm encompassed Opal, everything distorted and bodiless, icy tingling. She could not navigate this alone, had to trust, but Grubane – the Navigot – Aurbane – didn't let her down. This time was more like falling through a dream than swimming through a cloud, and the end point hit her like a giant tumour fired from a cannon so that she fell through in a wet evacuation, the momentum throwing them towards hard ship wall in a controlled splat. Her armour and Clarissa's silvery suit were even more coated in drying clots now.

Opal checked Clarissa's condition. No change. Her suit retained its power, and continued to warm the girl up. Opal's own suit was another matter, and the chilling ache in her bones from the transit refused to fade away.

Opal told herself everything was fine. Let the kid rest. She'd earned it. She would wake and be her normal self before long.

They'd arrived in an irregular chamber of overlapping metal with raised patterns hammered into the sheets. One whole wall was clear plasteen. The location made sense for a good inter-ship signal.

When Opal pushed her faceplate against the window and looked to her left she could see partway along this ship's hull, and in the distance some of the red connecting tubes that had locked on to Owlflight. She tried to imagine the ship at the end of those tethers, but it already felt so long ago that it was almost a fantasy. Lost Ships played havoc with your sense of time.

Opal realised the extrusions on the metal walls resembled the textures of a soundproofed room with anti-echo coatings, but much larger. And similar shapes had been grown from the hull around the window, pointing out into Null, presumably towards where the Owlflight sat. Not sound suppression then, but some kind of antennae or signal boosters, both in the room and beyond, to focus and transmit data. Aurbane had kept his word.

In the centre of one valley between conical peaks of metal she spotted a panel with a central hole. The panel was yellow, differentiating it from the brown surrounds. To attract her attention? A connector. She gripped one cone, keeping Clarissa between her and the wall, and used her free hand to run the suit's DIM cable. As soon as it connected, the socket's grip reconfigured, shaping itself around the data needle so as to maximise contact.

When she brought up the comm display she was surprised to see glitches in the signal strength. The bar had gone past the maximum and wrapped around multiple times, ghosting itself. She entered the code for Owlflight's emergency channel.

"Opal to Owlflight, anyone there? Please answer." She clenched and unclenched her free hand.

"This is Owlflight – you're alive! We feared the worst whilst hoping for the best. But hoping was difficult when pessimistic probabilities shoved themselves to the fore."

"You sound more positive than I expected."

"Attacks have ceased. The invading creatures pulled back, and even the red growth has begun to recede and break down into harmless amino acids, minerals and water."

"I made a deal with the commander of the Lost Ship. I have to be honest, I was worried it would all be over for you by the time I reached the bridge. The scale of the assault was so forceful."

"Well, that is one of the fortunate elements. Some time after you boarded the Lost Ship, the attacks here slowed. The red growth was taking longer to spread, and the invading creatures seemed less coordinated. If it wasn't for that, we'd have been overwhelmed long ago, without any doubt. But the delay gave us the second breath we needed. We had to awaken more people – a lot more – but finally there was a proper chance to coordinate, to attempt things we hadn't thought there would be time to try, to access more equipment. I don't know what you did, but it saved us. From the assault, at least."

Opal didn't know either. Except she could make guesses. Perhaps if the Navigot had been directly coordinating the assault, its attention got divided once she boarded the Lost Ship and represented a new and closer internal threat. And so the offensive on Owlflight slowed to a pace human-scale coordination could react to. Or maybe she was flattering herself. Perhaps she was no more than an irritant, and it was Clarissa's arrival that distracted the Navigot. Which had its own implications.

Wait. Something Owlflight said.

"Is there some other danger?"

"Unfortunately, yes. My excitement at knowing you continue to exist was a surprisingly intense sensation. Athene gave me more gifts than I realised. But as the effervescence fades, I'm left dry of any further good news. I must be blunt. Our Null-A drive is failing."

"How come?"

"The red growth followed the power lines and invaded it. I don't know if it was an intentional attack, investigation, or seeking sustenance. But it breached the outer shell and reached the core layers of the drive."

"So we're gonna fall out of Nullspace before we reach our destination?"

A sound like a dry laugh? "Opal. Athene's security systems were exactly as efficient as I expected. Even though the red growth has retreated, the drive casing was *breached*. Emergency protocols cannot tell the difference between what actually happened, and UFS technicians trying to dismantle and reverse engineer the drive. The outcome is the same. Self-destruction has been set in motion. The drive is rediverting charge from propulsion into catalytic detonation. This ship will not reach its destination."

"Estimated time to failure?"

"Impossible to say without access to schematics, I am afraid. The engine might explode an hour from now. It might explode ten seconds from now."

Shit shit fuckity shit.

"I'll be back in a minute." Opal severed the commline, then selected an open channel that would be broadcast anywhere in the Lost Ship with receivers to pick it up.

"Navigot? Aurbane? This is urgent. Opal Imbiana. I need to talk right away."

She listened for the response.

There was none.

"Grubane or whatever you are, answer me, goddamit!"

And still there was nothing.

Perhaps he was giving her privacy, or couldn't even communicate outside of his cocoon.

Back to Owlflight.

"Hey, Owlflight. I'm going to have to leave, find the Navigot again, see if it can help. Repair, tech encase, life raft, whatever. I'm not giving up, and you guys shouldn't either."

"I've been relaying information to the temporary bridge crew. Jau-Hwa wants to speak to you."

"Put her on, but it needs to be snappy."

"Hello Opal. I heard that and will be snappy." Jau-Hwa's voice was clipped and precise. Opal was also pleased to hear that she sounded calm, though there was an underlying strain that could well be tiredness. "I have a proposal. Is this conversation secure?"

"I think so. Shoot away. No time for ceremonials."

"Maybe we can take the Lost Ship. At least evacuate our people who are already out of cryo. Nothing we can do for the sleepers, unfortunately."

"I don't think you realise the scale of what you're dealing with."

"Limited information, but I do what I can. We could come across with the weapons we've got operational. We have explosives. Board, then destroy or threaten the captain or master of the Lost Ship. That craft must have amazing technology. We can jury rig explosives to be launched like bombs while we have this breathing space, take the ship by surprise, seriously damage anything that looks like external weaponry. Even target one at the bridge, remote controlled detonation by our assault crew, as an additional element to bargain or destroy. It is clumsy and rough but it provides an option where there are currently none.

Owlflight is running probabilities and concurs that it is at least possible."

Opal squeezed her eyes tight. Weighed everything up. Only took a second.

"No," she said. "Don't even prep for it. I'm working on good-will here. Sometimes even considering an idea taints the mind. I need mine to be pure and honest for what comes next. This isn't a negotiation with a corrupt UFS official. Got to approach it right, get my mind straight. That's an *order*, Jau-Hwa. Look into evacuation ideas, any way of disabling the security, by all means. But nothing offensive."

"Acknowledged. Over."

She was gone.

And that meant Opal had to backtrack. Damn. She hoped the Navigot hadn't locked the flesh door against her, or made it one-way.

"Come on, sweetie," she whispered, pulling Clarissa with her. "I bet you can hear me, somewhere in that pretty noggin. You're getting a first-class lesson today in dealing with everything life can throw at you. It's usually spiky and painful to catch and might go off in your face, but you and me, we don't start crying until the worst has happened. Until then, we act, and we hope. We keep our promises, just like I said I'd always find you, and I did. I've had enough of a world that lies and betrays. We're better than that. And I love you no matter what."

The portal was crusting up but still looked wet and raw, possibly implying residual life force Opal assumed was necessary for transit. She had to hope.

"I'm coming in," Opal said aloud, broadcasting from her speakers into the Lost Ship's walkway. "If you can hear me, please guide us back to you. We have something urgent to discuss. So don't let us get lost, or digested, or whatever the fuck creepy things could go wrong. Not in the mood."

She kicked off the opposite wall, gripped Clarissa against her chest with both arms, and collided with the squishy surface.

It gave way, rubbery resistance at first, then the welcoming of flesh, the parting of an orifice, the suction of lips. They were through, the icy negative shadow realm more disorientating than any zero-G traversal, since it wasn't just up and down that no longer existed but even light and dark switched places in a stuttering dance. A world that looked like it had depth but seen without eyes; three dimensions but viewed from a flat plane in an ever-changing illusory perspective. It didn't pay to analyse it too closely. Just focus on a goal, hope someone would throw out a hand in the darkness, grip yours and pull you out of the depths, out into the light and colour and air so that life was given a second chance.

Then Opal felt the funnelling pull, the cold desire, the prickly guidance from another mind. She was moving faster, along, through, the perspectives failing to reorder themselves properly due to the speed of transport back to Aurbane. She didn't resist, let herself go, only focussing on her non-existent arms that held an invisible sister. There was nothing to see, but everything to feel.

Here, the light zooming, a phase state shift, an alteration of consciousness back into form in a burst of white static that would pop her through engineered organs and back into Aurbane's presence for an extension of their deal, even if it meant offering more than she had to give.

Back into ... something unexpected.

She wasn't deposited into the light-absorbing tunnel leading to Aurbane's core, ejected like failed meat. Instead she seemed to reform from flat planes of reflections, all coming into focus, pulling together into coherence that recreated her body in a blue-shifted world of angles. Facets surrounded her, azure, turquoise, as if under a shallow mirror sea while bright suns burned down with their loving refractions. This was not the Lost Ship she knew; this was not the grey negative shadow of transit; this was a cage of hard planes that bounced blue light endlessly from surface to surface. She was encased within a mesh of irregular prisms.

Her body was here. It was real. A press on the GAMag wrist panel showed failed attempts to analyse atmospherics and physical conditions. She was embodied again. But alone.

The girl from Opal's arms had been stolen.

Her suit was still on external transmit mode. "Aurbane, is this some kind of trick?" she asked, her voice echoing off the hard surfaces that constrained her. "I know you didn't expect to see me again, but something has occurred and I need your damn help."

Blinding light shone in her eyes, forcing her to squint. The suit should have filtered it down, so maybe this was straight into her mind.

"Some thing has in deed occ urred. Not Aur bane."

The syllables crashed straight into her brainpan, synchronised to the blinding flashes that somehow formed the illusions of sound.

"You did not ex pect to meet us a gain did you, be tray er Op al?"

And she knew exactly what she was talking to.

The blue crystals.

Nemeses

... 7 ...

"What have you done? Where's Clarissa?" Only now did Opal realise that in this place there was an approximation of gravity. Instead of floating in her crystal cage, in the zero-G that had been her environment for so long, she stood on a smooth and slippery plane, like a tilted sheet of glass coated in oil. This created an up and a down, a requirement to readjust her perceptive framework, to think about options.

"We have her. Se pa rate."

Shades of blue light coursed through the endless crystals in a bewildering kaleidoscope, though Opal realised the light might well be white, just coloured by the azure gems that photons ricocheted through as they sought a way out of the trap. And in one crystal – not far away, though separated by many walls of ice – a new light stabbed, revealing the girl in the silver suit, held upright as if she was not in a hollow, but fully encased in glass like a bizarre giant ornament. Her eyes were open but her features unmoving, awake but paralysed, watching but powerless.

Physicality gave Opal new options. She punched one of the surfaces separating her from Clarissa. The gauntlet smacked with hard dullness, the shock passed to Opal's hand, and she'd used so much force that it fell just short of breaking her fingers. She shook out her sore shoulder, prepared to strike with the other arm.

"We heard your voice in the ship. So long in sil ence, but you are known and re mem bered. Al ways the out comes pour from your own ac tions. You to blame. You to pu nish. You to suff er."

The punch from her other arm didn't fare much better. She followed it up with a solid kick to the same point, rebounding with sore joints but nothing else to show for it.

"Att acks are fu tile."

No they aren't. Because they are a message to my sister, you bastards. Hold on. We're not beat yet.

"Just tell me what you want," Opal said, between strikes.

"Do you re mem ber what we said when you last en count ered our clus ter?"

"Not really. I've kind of had a lot of other people threaten or try to kill me since then. I hate to break it to you, assuming you have an ego and think we're locked in plot and counterplot situation, but I've not given you a moment's thought. Been kind of busy."

She reached for a tool, something with a point to concentrate force. Just for a second her toolbelt seemed empty, then suddenly the items were there as expected. A delay of some kind? Worth noting. She held a resovac actuator, which resembled a screwdriver and might double as an awl. If she drove it into the point she'd been attacking, would that weaken the surface?

"We spoke thus: 'We will take what you have, that which you most va lue, when you least ex pect it.' A pro mise. To day, we ful fil.'"

Opal pulled back her aching arm then drove it downwards, metal point of the tool carefully aimed, and she let out a yell, a forceful kiai – spirit shout, as one of her martial training commanders had interpreted it – synchronised to the strike.

Fuck, her arm felt like it was broken as shock reverberated along it. But she noticed something. A tiny crack in the surface where she'd struck.

This, too, is information, my friend.

I know. It's been added to my data store.

Have you really got time for the banter of mimicry? Anyway, I don't talk like that, so it doesn't count.

You talk like I remember you.

"So you've taken me somewhere. Separated me from my sister. What next?"

Opal knew the answer, but keeping someone talking was always useful, since it gave that most precious resource needed for escape, for plans, for staying alive: time.

"We will ful fil oth er pro mise. We will burn you. She will wit ness. Then we have us es for such as the girl. They are not your con cern. You will suff er more in the con tem plat ion of ab stract poss i bil it ies."

Did the flashing tones of jabbing light syllables indicate *glee*? Yep, she thought it might. Smug crystal fucks.

A test. She punched with the spiked point, exactly where she'd hit before. Apart from feeling like someone had dropped a boulder on her elbow, she didn't make any headway.

You noticed.

Course I did. Just testing boundaries and theories, like you would do.

I wish I was still alive and properly a part of our team. We were awesome.

Still are, Athene.

"Perhaps there's stuff you overlooked," Opal said. "You're so quick to jump into huffy puffy self-absorbed petulance that you aren't thinking it all through before acting."

This time she struck with the tool, but not as hard. However, she shouted again, even louder, and tried to do some of it with her mind. A focussed scream of fury.

The clang rang out, her arm still hurt, but less. And, in contrast, the crack spread up through the crystal wall. Interesting.

The initial toolbelt observation of apparent physicality needing to catch up with expectations was well observed.

Yep. If at least part of this is illusory, then the scene's not as it seems. Fairy lights in a grotto, distracting kids from the truth.

And a honed mind that can cut through the bullshit can also cut through appearances.

Sometimes I can't tell which of us is speaking.

Does it even matter?

"We over look no thing."

But there was doubt in the sounds, a flickering irregularity in the clashing blue lights that glowed throughout this maze. Hopefully they'd at least revisit some assumptions, spend time reliving their fantasies. Time that was then gifted to her.

She struck again, but hardly bothered touching the glass. Instead she made even more of this strike a *mental* blow, letting her anger and frustration scream into a single point, as if her will alone could demolish obstacles.

The reflection before her shattered, revealing jagged spikes of crystal. Further barriers existed between her and the gem that held her sister, but they would be broken too. Smashed. Obliterated.

Totally fucking Sevened into non-existence.

It's because we know the truth. We're all part of something bigger. Planets are part of solar systems. Solar systems form galaxies. Galaxies form into clusters. They group into bigger clusters. What's one promise you made to your sister, against all that? Nothing. Just some sounds and the echoes of them in your memory. But that never stops us acting at our own scale. That's what makes determination so powerful.

She continued the process, finding it simpler each time, more natural. She was not here, but her mind was. They'd regret trying to mess with that.

Smash. Smash.

"How are you do ing this?"

"Told you not to overstretch."

She was halfway to Clarissa when the pain began. A prickling sensation in her skin.

"We will not de lay. You will ne ver reach her. It is your end."

Strike, scream, let the increasing pain fuel her percussive shattering, and that impetus worked to a degree, but the embers spreading through her epidermis ignited quicker. She'd be toast before she got to the last crystal, the one encasing Clarissa.

So she screeched, and she struck anyway, and she shattered the two-faced world into fragments, because even if time was finally letting her down, she'd impart that final lesson to the one who watched: when you love, you never fucking give up.

The stuttering light, the shifting marine hues, the jagged surfaces breaking every line into a thousand distorted reflections, it made seeing anything clearly a difficult task. When you battered yourself against windows to get out of a fire it was impossible to take it all in. And yet Opal was aware of the shadows that shifted, the outlines against the flashes, the appearance that seemed *wrong* but which forced itself in anyway.

"Cease immediately," a voice from the past said. It projected the gruff confidence of Grubane, back when he was a human commander.

"Not your con cern, Nav i got."

"Disobey me and it's mutiny."

"Not a con cept that app lies. Your ag en da and ours di verge. You do not in flu ence. We are in de pen dent."

The burning sensation faded out, leaving Opal with only prickling heat as if she'd been unprotected under a double sun for hours.

"Everything is connected," said the male voice. "I see that now, and you should, too, with your miraculous longevity through this universe's history. To exist so long and learn so little is a tragedy. But I also learned that change is possible, even for the most inflexible of minds. All of us within this Vamintopia exist at stages of this realisation."

Now that the pain had temporarily ceased Opal could try to focus on the shadows in the crystals. An absence of light, fuzzy but perhaps representing the outline of a figure. Not the distorted version she met at the bridge, but the shadow of a memory, of a man, of Major Grubane's profile. There was an even hazier second presence behind him, an indistinct figure looking over his shoulder. And perhaps another beyond that, even more mist-like.

Or it might just be an illusion of diminishing returns caused by refraction. Only the first silhouette was recognisably distinct and humanoid.

"She broke her pro mise. We must have our re venge!"

"Again, I say no," Aurbane stated. "Do not force me to intervene."

"You are po wer less to do so here, with us, in us. Your role is not in con flict. We can force you out. We can have them both."

"A threat to me deserves the same in kind. So, counterthreat. I know the locations of your clusters within my body. I will selectively encase those areas in polypropotised Viscids."

"Se lect ive? Not poss ib le."

"I make it possible. Would you really like me to demonstrate?"

A flicker in the blue. Uncertainty? Even Opal had no idea who was bluffing who. Though she held off on shattering more barriers, not wanting to draw attention to herself until she had an idea of how this would play out.

"En case ment to what end? A B C mo bil it y is irr el ev ant to such as us."

"You misjudge. Viscids don't just pack hollows for transit. They block all Nuospheric signals. Each of your clusters would be separated from the others, alone in emptiness for as long as I command it. Forever, if I desire. Until your energy fades and you cease."

"No! Vis cids are au ton om ni tran sit cat al ysts, not wea pons of rest raint."

"Welcome to the way I think now. You are no longer dealing with an inexperienced Navigot. You deal with *Aurbane*."

"Un rec og nised."

"You will know me soon enough. And I can punish, or I can reward. What is her offence?"

"She lied. She pro mised a new clu ster. She let us die."

"I see your loss. So, if you comply, I withhold the encasement you dread, and offer an additional motivation. If you were promised life and autonomy and new growth by her, then *I* will provide it. You were invasive and unwelcome since you awoke, and have no place in my mission. But I will provide one. I will reassign you as *core*. I will give you what you want. You will have the perfect home. You will grow your cluster. You know I cannot lie. All you have to do to achieve this dream is cease all aggression. To acknowledge me your Navigot. To restore the humans to my realm, as my responsibility. To accept that revenge is nullified, prophecies fulfilled. It is simple. This is the point you have led yourselves to without realising, the choice that will make you or break you. But it is *your* choice. Be in conflict. Or be in accord. Is revenge worth losing so much?"

It seemed as if the blue washes over this landscape of broken glass slowed, a paused optical breath of deliberation.

"We acc ept you. Acc ept the off er. We will not fight. Our clus ter will grow. You are the Nav ig ot."

The crystals melted away, the starry turquoises and velvety blues faded to darkness, a cold nothing of no time, which wasn't existence or non-existence.

Then the familiar, disgusting, ever-so-welcome plop of ejection from flesh, the gory adult birth of reentering the Lost Ship, the tunnel to Aurbane's chamber.

Opal's suit was more glooped up with entrails than ever, but it didn't matter because Clarissa came through after her, awake, turning, seeing her sister, and finally smiling.

REVELATIONS

... 6 ...

They returned, Opal explaining the situation to Clarissa first. Aurbane was still orbited by the rusting, twitchy things which tended to him. Rather than being horrified, Clarissa appeared intrigued, and even reached out towards the swirling fragments before Opal snatched her arm, shaking her head as warning.

"Is Owlflight still there?" Opal asked.

"Yes," replied Aurbane.

"Time is short and so much has been wasted by what just happened."

"Less than you think, due to time dilation. Vamintopial progression varies from Null, which varies from Realspace, which varies from Topia zones."

"Can you slow it here?"

"After a manner. I have the ability to accelerate our communication. Your perception of time's passing will not change as we are synced, but anything beyond this chamber would view us as a compressed blur of momentary duration."

"That's what I want. A chance to converse without time on the Owlflight rushing by."

"Then it is done. If you were to observe Owlflight from here, you would see no motion, as if craft and crew all were frozen in a crystal. We have created time. It provides possibilities to enhance mutual understanding. To bridge the Null that separates consciousnesses."

She'd have to take his word for it. She certainly didn't feel any different. But it meant she could at least be grateful now.

"Thank you. For your intervention with the blue crystals. How did you know what was going on?"

"I received your message too late, but tried to detect you and only found an absence. Then your shockwave yell permeated the Nuosphere. I have never known a human able to do that, just as I have never known a human open a transit as your little sister did."

"It wasn't too hard," said Clarissa, though she seemed proud beneath the nonchalance.

"*Impossible* for some." He shifted his gaze back to Opal. "There was always more to you than was apparent. Than you revealed. But perhaps the hidden has saved you not just today, but many times."

"Well, I owe you my life."

She expected a return of formalities.

"Yes," he said. "You do. I am glad you acknowledge this. We have uses for you. I will return your sister, but you will remain forever to repay the debt."

Fuck.

"No!" shouted Clarissa. "No one will split us up!"

"It's okay, Clarissa," Opal said, seeing the look on her sister's face. "Trust me." Then, to Aurbane: "Did you hear my conversation with Owlflight?"

"No. I created a private channel for you. I was not a party to its use."

"Well, the deal can't go ahead. We can't leave. Because you screwed us over."

"I would appreciate an explanation of your accusation."

"You assaulted our ship! The red stuff – bioweapon, probe, whatever – damaged our drive. It triggered an automated defence mechanism that can't be reset. Now the Owlflight will be destroyed. We can't fulfil our mission. Can't stick to the deal. Can't even *survive*."

"I did not intend such. For that, I apologise."

"Well, apologies aren't good enough. First, you owe me compensation. That cancels my debt to you. Agreed?"

There was a momentary reluctance before Aurbane said, "In that case I accept your debt is cancelled."

"Next, you owe the Owlflight's *crew*. You're killing them, too."

"I have no agreements with them. They are not my concern."

"But it's your fault!"

"Perhaps they should have built a better ship."

"They didn't ... Never mind. I still need your help. A way of repairing the drive, or slowing its decay so we can get away, or ..."

"None of that is possible."

"It must be!"

"Even if I was concerned, my realm does not extend beyond this ship."

"But you sent stuff over!" Clarissa accused.

"If your limbs could detach and move themselves, would they still be a part of your body?"

Opal said, "Now isn't the time for riddles. I agreed we'd leave, so as not to affect your mission, whatever it is. That was me helping you, and you helping me in return. But since you've sabotaged things ... forget goodwill, when Owlflight goes, you'll be severely damaged. And if the Owlflight crew aim at revenge – something your pretty speech to our hard blue pals suggested wasn't the way you view the world now – then if they redirect to get closer, your mission really will be doomed. You say they're not your concern, but we're all connected, isn't that also what you fucking said?"

"Conversing with you is so strange. Like echoes of a dream."

"*Everything* about this encounter has been strange. Different from what I expected. Which makes me think. These green specks – the Viscids – I thought they expanded during Lost Ship travel? Could they be used somehow to protect my ship or the people on it?"

"Viscids have many roles. The mechanisms are more complex than you can imagine, though none would aid you in the way you propose. Expansion packing is only necessary in the transition from Realspace to Topias. This is currently a journey from Topias to deep Nullspace. Their process does not apply."

"Which is why I could board you even though we're in Nullspace. Right. Except there are no legends of encountering Lost Ships in Nullspace. So this must be a first."

"Incorrect. Occasionally human drive fluctuations send your craft into this deeper Nullspace region. Hunter craft such as myself negate them, so they do not interfere with navigation or damage the sensitive sines of this layer."

"Ah, so what you did to us wasn't an exception, but was standard practice?"

"Correct."

"Which means some of the human craft that disappear –"

"– became invasive particles in deep Null and had to be purged."

He'd finished her sentence. Nothing too weird in human terms, but he was no longer human. Did it indicate a change in him, that some of that personality aspect was awakening? It fitted the evolution of this whole encounter, so that even his communication was more understandable than when she had first spoken with him.

"You imply it's some kind of self defence," said Opal. "Therefore *justified*. But if this deeper Null you refer to is how my ship is able to travel such great distances – presumably allowing you to do the same – is there any element of *keeping secrets* in the way you ruthlessly destroy anything human arriving here?"

"Please expand."

"If human ships made it here and returned, they'd provide clues to new physics, new drive mechanisms that could open up much more of the galaxy. So you want to suppress other species' access to technology, to keep it for yourself? Well, that's all too common an attitude in human military, corporate and governmental approaches, whether through patents or secrets. And not noble at all, because it comes down to power and selfishness."

"All I can say is that increased human presence here would destroy our ability to travel."

"It's not easy to unpack motivations, is it? To separate the justifiable from the self-interested."

"You bring to mind something of the past, of conflicts I was happier having forgotten."

"You can't act righteously without being aware of context."

"You have a way of making the simple seem complex. I now regret my generosity in offering discourse."

Dry humour, or genuine regret? It was so hard to place emotion on skin stretched tight and distorted into something that looked like a reinterpretation of the concept of face.

"And you're out here patrolling and destroying anything that disturbs the frequencies in this zone. Your 'secret mission'."

"You assume something that is incorrect, just as you assume assimilation is always destruction. But I can clarify you. Bring you to a truer vision of context. My task is one of guarding."

"That's what I said. Guarding this deep region of Nullspace from human transit."

"No. Guarding is misleading. Reinterpret the concept as *escort*."

"Escort means *guarding something moving*, like a convoy or fleet. So you're not alone."

"Correct. This was a secret I originally kept."

The floating rusty fragments reconfigured, the central swirl becoming groupings, jagged clusters, patterns ... then Opal realised they were forming shapes. It was a kind of holographic display at room scale, but made out of corroded shards rather than light.

"What you see modelled is the fleet I escort. So that you can comprehend both the scale and the importance of my protection mission, which made me interact with greater intensity than I would normally choose to do."

So many craft. All different sizes and shapes. No idea of scale, but if most of them were the size of this Lost Ship then ... holy fuck.

And now that blurred image Owlflight had projected so long ago made sense. Beyond this Lost Ship she had made out shapes that could have easily been visual artefacts, or illusions ... except they weren't. They represented other ships, the ones nearest to Aurbane, somehow glowing in the blackness.

"That ..." Opal took a moment to frame her thoughts carefully. "That's a fleet that could conquer star systems." A pause. "Could conquer a species."

"It is not our goal."

"Then what is your goal?"

"Trust for a trust. First, let me ask: what is your mission, Opal Imbiana? I may not be able to prevent disaster, but perhaps I can fulfil part of your task for you."

"What does secrecy matter now? We humans are on the run. Looking for a new home, far, far away. Somewhere safe from the UFS. If we can find it, then in cryo I have sixteen hundred people expecting to wake to a new life. Well, fewer now, since your assault killed some. This mission was our hope. And you've shattered it."

There was no reply at first. A subtle shifting of features, mirrored by the swarming fragments. Thought? Emotion? Opal was trying to come up with more arguments, threats, promises, but he spoke first.

"This, also, is *our* Ark Fleet," Aurbane explained. "And why I had to intercept you, across unimaginable distances of deep Null, pulling you to me to remove the danger you represented if left unchecked."

"This is too weird. You see it, right? The overlap?" Opal asked.

"Please expand on your thoughts."

"I was a kind of lone ark ship. Out looking for a home. Then we just bump into you, doing the same thing."

"Location? It is not coincidence, but inevitable. Exodus requires great distances. That requires using this liminal Nullzone. Its existence is one of the great secrets. The means to manipulate it, even greater."

"No, not that, but the *timing*. You were here at the same time."

"Not the way you see it."

"You've lost me."

"There are aspects to this deep Nullzone. Like incongruous planetary atmospherics and gulf streams, we travel in a pipeline current which is neatly delineated from the surrounding conditions without forcefield manipulation. Within, distance is foldable. But so is time, and how it moves in its own tube, separate from the surroundings, which all exist in their own tubes. Transit from one to another, and you can jump time zones."

"Hop onto the round-a-round wheel, hold the pole while it spins you, then leap off in a different facing," suggested Opal.

"No analogy will work fully in human words, because human words are based on human understanding and mental structures, which are the limiting factor. Some concepts require a certain mental framework to envision."

"We have smart people."

"If they are people, they are limited. Ego, perception of weak and strong forces from a single point, a focus on body and location in time and place with historic instinctual resolutions based on survival archetypes in pre-genetic storage that reflects cultural transmissions of further perspectives and –"

"Right, right. I'll accept that. No need to keep belittling me."

He tilted his head slightly; perhaps to the fullest extent it could bend. "Not just *you* as an individual, but *all* of you."

"Makes me feel a shit-ton better."

"You cannot help but see time as linear and progressive, and to visualise it as thus in each parallel tube. But the cycles all overlap, ouroboros principle. Each is overlaid on top of others and then partly inter-penetrating. What happens now has been witnessed as past in another snake, and the message was transmitted via a set of interconnectors to others, which means – using your term – jumping onto the wheel, revolving, and leaping away just before the point you boarded, but with knowledge of the circuit should you choose to do it again."

"So the time of our interception was predicted and you were sent here knowing it?"

"I was not informed of such a plan, but decisions are made by Oracles, and none but they are party to their knowledge. I am just surmising a guiding hand, illustrating that the unexpected, from another perspective, is expected." He paused for a few moments. "The hidden pit trap in a forest is not an expected thing, and you might ponder that as you fell towards spikes implanted at the bottom. And yet, if you had witnessed all from above, over time, and seen the pit being dug, and heard the discussions of the trappers, and understood their motivations, then it would in fact have been logical and obvious and predictable. Coincidence is just a sign of the limits of knowledge in a single actor, and the limits of a fixed conscious point in time and space. I am not sure if this helps you or not."

"I get the gist of it, even if I can't make sense of it."

"The timing is inevitable. You do not see the interconnected strands in parallel times. Oracles copy human ships and technology. Learn from them. Iterate. Ongoing interactions with humanity have led to experiments with our own craft, and then further interaction with humanity."

"Like me and my sister?" asked Clarissa. "We've both encountered weirdness in the Null."

"Exactly like that. Humans develop technology faster than other species. The Oracles interpret technology as the religion of humanity. And so the encounter today could only take place at this exact point in human history. The Oracles are patient beyond comprehension, so once this entanglement with humanity began the outcome was inevitable, the pit dug, a timer ticking in their plans just as it ticked in human advancement, a pairing point where two timelines that were separate then run parallel. The Nullzone effect is like a speed control so two vehicles are on the same road. One can alter speed to match the other. Do not underestimate what an overall perspective and knowledge can do to smooth tiny wrinkles in a silk road that are inconsequential to us, viewed from above, but seem like insurmountable terrain to the microbe that lives there."

"And so, the interactions of the past are part of how we can communicate now?" asked Opal.

"To a degree. Concepts shared. Ark ships, too, are an idea spread between Oracles and humans, from ideas lost long ago. It can be found again in another world, aeon or culture. Like an ancient tactical game played on a board, lost to time, until the right mind rediscovers and revives it. You do not understand your species' past. Few do. Even I did not, in full, though I made efforts to see through the veil. Perhaps that is one of the reasons I was iterated as a Navigot. I now understand how much has been hidden, how this end is a reflection of the beginning, head to tail, though it is not clear if the head and tail belong to the same snake."

"He's tricky to understand," whispered Clarissa. Although presumably Aurbane heard her, he did not acknowledge it.

"And what's the purpose of this mission, this Ark Fleet?" asked Opal.

"The same as all arks. To escape one thing and find another. We leave the Topias to enter Realspace once more, a return after inestimable time, to reclaim."

"To conquer?"

"The places we chose are far from anything humanity will ever reach. No other species existed. They were barren, found through snapshot explorations across the universe. Marked. Seeded. Some are worlds. Some are more exotic environments. Gas giants. Nebulas. Dead stars. Broken anomalous regions. All altered over millions of years in preparation for these missions. Even the mundane planets have multiple biomes carefully designed for both consistency and variety, with extensive buffer zones between each subdivision. The geographies might not occur naturally, but they are symbiotic in overall performance.

Entities may exist in the gases of volcanic vents, in oceans, in differently composed atmospheric layers, pooled in valleys, or on rarefied peaks. Each biome is far greater in area than any Entity will ever need. In this way, a single planet can support a great variety of life and non-life."

"So you *terraformed*."

"Preparation for The Return. My fleet is one of many. The Topias are extensive beyond any comprehension. This is the culmination. The escape. They have waited so long. The greatest event since the universe formed, since the Topias were created."

"So all those ships in your floaty map have alien people in them?" asked Clarissa.

"Entities, from different Topias. Many you would not recognise as life in any terms you have experienced. The world ships are carefully designed to house compatible Entities."

"Are they all as big as this ship?" asked Opal.

One of the dots glinted.

"That is us," said Aurbane.

And then Opal realised the scale of it. If their Lost Ship was a tiny speck, then the thousands of other craft around it were all at least ten times larger, sometimes more so.

"Show me one," said Opal.

The orbiting display fragments reconfigured, merging and flowing, even interlocking to create a huge shape where many of the details of the craft were clear.

It resembled a space station with a warship front end, and other parts that hinted at human pleasure ships or harvesters, but distorted and at massive scale. Perhaps it was akin to the way the Oracles copied human ideas and designs but altered them. Maybe that went as far as strategies, since it was a human tactic to protect a vulnerable convoy of precious items with more manoeuvrable, aggressive and dangerous milship escorts.

"The additions," which now glinted to attract her eye, spheres and jagged blocky areas, like growths of hopper crystals, "are a mixture of biomes. Some Entities need special laws or environments. We also required temporal holdings for Entities that must be kept separate from others."

"Prisons?"

"Your perspective, not mine. In a choice between safe inclusion or being left behind, one is preferable."

"You've hinted at escape before. What are you fleeing?"

"We will share this secret, though you have already been told, already experienced: it is the Deletion. It has destroyed so many Topias already, the Entities within lost irreparably. The process accelerates."

"The black wall." She could almost taste the choking rubbery texture in the back of her throat.

"Correct. Not a wall, though. That is just your dot stereo perspective on an expanding nullification. This is why we must evacuate what remains."

"The Oracles said they didn't know what it was."

"You know as much as I do, then. Except I have more fears than you. Have had more time to contemplate every angle."

"Such as?"

"Assume we escape. All those who can. The Deletion destroys what remains. It is trapped. And yet *we* found a way out. What if it follows? What if use of Nullspace somehow attracts it, or human errors that send their craft to Topias open a route? Perhaps continued use of Nullspace will enable it to escape as we did."

"In which case, Nullspace would become unusable. Interesting. No more long-distance travel for humans or Lost Ships. I can live with that."

"You underestimate the disaster scenario. Maybe Nullspace is how it began. This could be the nothingness on the other side of the Deletion. What is left in its passage. This may be a natural environment for Deletion. What is seen as a barrier to us, could be a home to it. And then there is little separating it from Realspace."

"Because every ship that entered Nullspace would be opening tiny holes," said Clarissa.

"Correct. The Deletion grows in power as it expands. Unknown if it is due to absorption of mass, or time, or force."

"But where do the things it swallows go?" asked Clarissa. "Does it have a tummy?"

"Where have words gone, once they are spoken? Where does machine code go, once it is erased?"

"You seriously think it could get here, and be a danger?" Opal asked.

"It can start small, as it did in the Topias. A pinprick, smaller than a single sweat pore on a girl's face."

"Eeeuw," said Clarissa.

Aurbane continued. "What if it could survive in Realspace? It would find what it needs to grow. Slowly, at first. But then faster."

"Nothing could destroy our galaxy," said Clarissa. "It's huge! We haven't even explored a millionth of it!"

"I am not talking about just a galaxy," Aurbane said. "But every galaxy. The whole of Realspace. The *universe*. It is only human minds that cannot comprehend the scale. Part of me was the same, once. Perhaps the Deletion would expand to engulf everything. Or maybe it would just erase enough matter that the universe will never contract, and the frozen peripheries will fly out leaving only emptiness behind, with Deletion always chasing and consuming what it catches. Death of the universe."

Opal shuddered.

But he wasn't finished. "Perhaps what we call Nullspace now was not always thus. Perhaps it was once another Realspace before Deletion. Now it is endless absence."

Opal didn't want Clarissa having existential nightmares. Had to cut off the pessimist she faced.

"As long as it doesn't happen in Clarissa's lifetime," she said. "Okay, so you're evacuating."

"Only what remains after so much has been lost. Now we enact the long-term plan developed over many overlapping cycles."

"So let me check I'm up to speed. You've been developing the means to build this fleet –"

"*These* fleets," he corrected. "I command only one. That which is to be spread among the galaxy I am most familiar with. It is why I was chosen. Other Ark Fleets will go to different galaxies, and the spaces between, and the zones beyond conception."

"Right. And you've been terraforming places for a long time, preparing habitats for all the aliens with their different needs."

"To them, you are the aliens."

"Fair point. Apologies."

"No single location would support the existence of every Entity. Their requirements are too diverse and exotic. So there are many divisions and groupings of compatibles. Each ark ship is one such, with its own destination, a place capable of supporting the continued existence of all those on board. My role is to protect this fleet and take it to each new home location, where the appropriate ark ship will be left, to begin day one of the new existence."

"What happens to you when you deliver the last one?"

"My mission will be over, role fulfilled. It will be up to us whether I return or destruct. We considered just continuing onwards into the void between galaxies, where we could think and play forever, preserved and pure of mind."

"Play?" asked Clarissa.

"A game we enjoy."

"So all these beings will sort of invade our universe," said Opal.

"It is not an invasion when you return to the homes you were removed from, before memory began. The original homes are long gone. But we have prepared, patiently, under the god-hand of the Oracles and others. The rightful places have been recreated anew. Realspace was theirs, before it was ever yours. But please let us move on. I am feeling something. It makes us think of a concept. Impatience? No, *excitement*. We have not felt this for a long time. It is agitatedly pleasant. A reminder of a time when minds were separate. There is much to savour. It is distracting, curious, leads to deviations and loops. I could nest us in a void and reflect forever. Ideas grow as we interact. Words have cross-references, and each of yours pulls up connotations of concepts lost ... only not really gone. Just *buried*, now unearthed, and with them comes new possibilities, and the excitement begins anew. It is all cycles like this. Time. Breathing. Gestation. Arks. Myths. Snakes and tails. Digestion. Always things repeat with variation, and it is the variation that intrigues great minds."

The change was obvious even to an outsider, now. More animation to the face, and even the body writhed in eagerness, betraying the internal. The brittle storm of shards likewise rippled out and swooped in mesmerising dances.

"Focus, Aurbane! We need to bring this back to the now. My ship."

"Yes. One of many possibilities. The eternal balancing of urgent with important. It is so much clearer now. Details arranged so that we would perceive the significance. The wondrous invisible mind-hand. What was overlooked due to fragmentation is now rearranged to provide the picture that was there all along. It just required the correct lens, the right perspective, ideal time and place, exact lighting, the questioning mind. And mystery reveals. You awake in us the thing that was missing! That connection is a clue in itself."

"I'm lost. Nothing new I guess, talking to you guys."

"Opal, you survived each Lost Ship, including this one. You have your own *awakening*. You are sensitive to the Null. So different from when I last met you."

"That's like an Indostaqr calling the milk pale."

"Ever the reflexive defence with you, even when it is not required. In this case I refer to your perceptions. I felt it when you connected to the Nuosphere. When you saw my transmission."

"Once again, plain speaking, please."

"It explains part of how you survived, and how you found us. The Nuospheric transmission is an idea Oracles took from human craft they broke down. A comm system, of sorts. One of the Navigot roles is to broadcast it so Entities on a ship can avoid each other. The Navigot does not just exist to navigate the Null, to navigate Realspace: it also helps Entities navigate the ship. The signal is not supposed to be detectable by humans in passive emission mode, though in active mode it can create illusions, alter perceptions of ship and layout. It can also trigger real modifications through subsurface musculature, organic joints, and accelerated molecular growth."

"Okay, I understand that. Sort of. I picked up your signals, ones meant for the Entities on this ship. How come I could do that?"

"Because of something deep inside you. Perhaps your experiences in the Null, in Lost Ships, in Topias. Maybe even something in your biological composition pre-birth. Nature and the nurture. A difference from other humans in both aspects. Just theories. But the key element: your change, attuning to our Nuosphere, means I can help. You are liminal. Not one thing or another. You can fit multiple roles like a splinter, like a Navigot. You can be *recategorised*. I can do that. All the evidence aligns. The shout, the hidden within you and your sister ... that provides us with an interesting observation, connected to what I offered the Cluster. The final revelation of your mission rediverts the thought to a new track of possibilities. You do not realise what a profound shock this is to me. It makes sense of so many things you are unaware of. Things I would have overlooked if you had not awoken us as Aurbane from Navigot. Another debt I owe you, to your favour. One of my strengths was always that I recognise and reward potential."

"Please, the point."

"And so, we can adopt you as an Entity. You will come under my purview. Rules can then be bent to follow our will, not the letter of the law. You refused me once, but you will not this time."

A grimace broke out on that face again, stretching the skin, the tattoos. And this time she was certain it *was* a smile.

"How does that help?"

"You and yours become passengers on the ark. My responsibility to protect and deliver you. At last I can act, and finally act on my own terms, not those enforced on me. I can do what I want to do. This mission evolves from destruction to protection."

Opal must have looked confused, because Clarissa said, "I think he wants to give *us* a home as well."

"Yes," affirmed Aurbane. "You and your sister have been re-categorised as Entities. Welcome to the fold."

Actions

... 5 ...

"Thank you. I think," said Opal. "I'm sure there are implications to consider. But for now, some pressing matters: my crew and those in cryo have specific requirements, for air, food, temperature, pressure. We can't live just *anywhere*."

"Of the many destinations, some biomes can support humanity. They were designed for it in complex relationships with the requirements for other Entities. What you call a habitable zone and catalyst for life is the same for many other species. It is not just chance. It was programmed this way."

"But you didn't know you'd encounter me and my ship."

"Oh, Opal. The compatible preparations were not for *you*. They were for the other humans."

"Others?"

"One of the ark ships has a section of storage for humans who entered Topias due to flight errors. The small fraction Oracles were able to save, but significant nonetheless. This was a chance to get their preserved forms away from the Topias before they were deleted. And so a home was prepared for them, too."

It came back to Opal. Memories of her discussion with the Oracles on the purple desert world before they released Clarissa. They'd said they had *thousands* of humans in stasis.

"And the remnants of my own crew," Aurbane continued. "From the Aurikaa. So many died in our final battles, both with you and with … something else. I wasn't about to let their sacrifices go to waste. A few were preserved in stasis pod life support coatings. It was part of the agreement upon which I became the Navigot. My service in exchange for their lives. A deal I had forgotten, until now. I knew they were on an ark ship but it was abstract, categories only. Now the context returns, and is a compelling sign that I make the right decision. It dovetails. We sense the hands at work in all this. We perceive the impossible miracle."

"I have a question," said Clarissa, her face betraying some emotion Opal wasn't familiar with. Some mix of excitement and nervousness?

"You may ask, little one."

"In all them people you have, is there one called Gloria?"

"There may be."

"Gloria Lefos." Clarissa pronounced it as *luhf-oh*. "She was with me when I crash landed. She's my friend."

"Checking … there is a catalogue. But records are incomplete. Not all humans were conscious prior to encasement. Not all were interrogated. I cannot tell at present if one such is in the shipment."

"Oh, I bet she is! Opal, you'll love her. Or at least not punch her. She cared for me when you weren't there."

"Then I will like her a lot."

"She's stronger than you, too. I bet she could bend metal bars."

"I like her a bit less now."

Clarissa grinned.

Opal rotated in space to face Aurbane again.

"A shared planet," she said.

"It will be big enough."

"But will we? Us, humans? Thousands of people who don't know each other. All kinds of backgrounds and belief systems, many in opposition. On a strange world."

"They will need a commander," said Aurbane.

"Not my skillset."

"I used to think the same about myself. You are not the ultimate judge. It is those who look up to you. But this is not optional. You must vouch for your ship's crew, since they are not here to make pledges. You must agree to take responsibility for them before I can allow any to join us. Agree to cooperate. To observe the rules. You will promise this freely, for now is the correct moment to give up your resistance and acquiesce."

His wording echoed the weird promise the Oracles exacted during her sole interaction with them. Was this what they had referred to? Their bizarre time-twisting concepts made no sense to her. Maybe the promise she made them wasn't to agree to this *now*, but to remember the vow made now at some *later* date. Or both. It was enough to boil her brain.

But she should agree. After all, was there ever really any other choice?

"I will stick to whatever rules are necessary, if it means we can save the lives of all my passengers, my crew. And we'll make it work. We have to try. To be big enough. To forget the pasts. To find a way of living in peace."

Aurbane nodded – it seemed his head and neck were the only parts with unrestricted movement. For a second he echoed the living man he once was.

"Instead of aiming at a place and hoping, as was your original plan, this will be a *surety*," he said. "A place *built* for you all. No need to hide in cryo on an endless search that may never succeed."

"There is that. But it takes me back to the immediate problem. What about the humans on my ship? Most are in cryo already, but some aren't. If the ship is destroyed, they all die. Once we go back into the same chronology as them, there won't be much time. If any."

"We have the ovum of a proposal. Your input will make it fertilise."

"Eeuw," she said, mimicking Clarissa. "Let's keep it clean."

The girl giggled.

Opal and Aurbane were able to make their plan whilst within the weird time bubble he'd created. Once they'd finalised the details Opal said:

"This idea is fucking mental." A pause. "I love it."

Opal already knew what she had to say when she contacted Owlflight. Honed it to be concise. Every second might count. Grubane prepared the route back to her comm station, refreshed the slick flesh portal with – no, she didn't want to think about *that*.

She felt nervousness just before she plunged into it, Clarissa's hand held tight in her own. So many unknowns. So much trust required. Aurbane hadn't predicted the blue crystal attack, so what other knowledge gaps did he have?

It didn't change the requirements. She dived into the cold embrace of soft tissue.

As soon as they emerged into the signal-boost chamber with its dimpled walls and view towards the bleak vacancy of the Null, time began draining away. Opal was conscious of it, knew she couldn't stop the precious river from flowing, could only dive in and do her best to cross before disaster struck.

Opal connected to Jau-Hwa first because that woman didn't waste words. Didn't question Opal's judgement. Efficient, reliable, brave. Exactly what Opal needed.

"You need to evacuate the ship. Get everyone into the cryopods *immediately*," Opal told her in a rush. "I can't explain the ins and outs now."

"I'm sending commands as we speak," said Jau-Hwa. "I know we're going to lose Owlflight – the AI briefed me on the drive damage – but what about the equipment? This ship is packed with materials we might need."

Might? Understatement. Athene had assembled so much, to prevent them starting out with nothing on a new planet. Opal would dearly love to take even a portion of it. But there was no time, and in Opal's mind a choice between lives and tech was no contest. It could be like those illegal streetsmack mugshows where someone was so close to getting away unmolested, but then risks it for the glint of gold and loses *everything*. There would be no gambling today.

"The cryo section has minimal food pastes, emergency supplies and shelters. It will have to do." It would be truly starting again, with nothing but their willpower. So be it. "Trust me," Opal added. "Ignore everything else, there's absolutely no time. Go. *Now*."

And that was in process. Stage One.

"Owlflight, as soon as everyone is in the pods, seal them and inform me that it's been done. If anyone gets lost, is going to take more than a few minutes to get frozen – we'll have to leave them behind. We can't risk everyone else's lives."

"I note that," said Owlflight. There were no visuals, but Opal could picture the AI speaking from its beak, and the fluffy feathered face would have been comforting right now.

"Once the cryo cartridge is sealed, release the clamps."

"Then the pod would drift away."

"No! Only release the *mechanical* claws. Retain the maglocks. That way they'll stay attached for now."

"Thank you for the clarification. I will do so."

"Keep this line open. I need to know progress," said Opal.

And so, she listened. A mixture of channels from the Owlflight reached her, all overlapping. Emergency announcements. Voice chatter and updates. Even corridor sensors picking up the clatter of footfall, the whoosh of sliding doors. A cacophony of coordinated action.

Opal shivered as she played the role of witness. Her suit's environmental regulators had really cut back in order to preserve the remaining charge. She didn't care. All that mattered was people reaching safety. Luck holding out. And gradually some of the sounds died away as more people entered their own freeze chambers. It was working.

Owlflight gave Opal an update.

"I'll be back in touch," Opal replied.

Aurbane had added an extra communication option since her last visit. A wall-mounted speaker that looked like it had grown from the wall – which is exactly what it had done. The interwoven surface mesh had a sickeningly keratin-like appearance, akin to matted hair. But it enabled her to speak to him and receive responses.

"Owlflight predicts a few more minutes and everyone will be in storage," she said.

"In the absence of accuracy, we need to act," Aurbane replied. The hollowness of the audio made her think more of sound travelling along empty pipes, dried and hardened veins, rather than digital reproduction. "At the correct angle I should have time to seize. There will be but a *single* opportunity. Once we pass the limit, we cannot go back."

Clarissa drifted behind Opal's shoulder, one small, gloved hand resting on it as an anchor. Opal liked that whisper of feeling.

Once final coordinations with the Owlflight were complete, Opal had finished her part. The sisters floated over to the observation window. Some of the red tendons connecting the Lost

Ship to Owlflight could be seen, but the colony ship itself was too far away for the limited visual range of Nullspace.

That would change.

The inter-ship vescicles suddenly contracted, a muscular ripple along their lengths. At the same time they twisted and detached from Owlflight, and quickly shrank, receding into the Lost Ship's body. But the movement had been enough. It pulled the two ships closer, whilst also beginning a barrel roll in the Lost Ship around its longitudinal axis. As they closed in, the Lost Ship's rotation should mean that its upper side would just miss the Owlflight's corresponding surface as it passed.

A crazy manoeuvre. Something a human pilot wouldn't have dared try. But Opal would save her applause for now.

The Owlflight came into view, sliding beneath Opal's vantage point, like two deep-sea behemoths rolling over each other in a gargantuan mating ritual. They had to be close, but not too close, not enough to scrape hulls or become entangled. From this perspective the inversion was sickening. As they passed over Owlflight in this mirrored position, Opal noted the massive cryo cylinder that was their target if Aurbane got the trajectory right.

"Wait here, C." Opal kicked off the glass, flew to the comm connector, plugged in her DIM.

"Hey, Owlflight, it's looking good!"

"I am observing and gratified. Although I cannot stop the imminent drive failure, I do what I can to slow it via use of cooled impact foam. I don't know if anyone has ever thought of that before. It should become a technique named after me."

"Never mind that. We're coming up on the pod. Can you transfer to it as well?"

"Why?"

"So we have you with us, too. You're one of the crew. A *vital* member of the crew. I know the cryopod cartridge is rich in hardware you can interact with."

"That isn't the issue, Opal. Unfortunately, transfer is impossible. I thought you knew when you enacted the plan? My existence is tied to the ship's core by design."

"Yeah, yeah, I know that," she snapped. "But an offshoot or something."

"Oh, I see the confusion! Ha ha. But again, no. I am not some advanced post-embodiment AI that is psych-transferable. I *am* the ship. Don't worry. I achieved the tasks I had been set, even though we had to wing it a number of times." A pause.

"I get the pun."

"Good."

"Fuck. I wish you'd been able to take us to our new home. It's what I'd hoped."

"I realise that now. And it gives me a warm feeling that you cared. But let me reassure you that this outcome is satisfactory. Goodbye, Opal Imbiana."

"Goodbye, Owlflight."

The commline was closed by the AI. There were painful hints of the farewell to Aegis in this conversation. So many friends lost.

Opal returned to Clarissa and they held hands while watching the action unfurl in the view below them, fixated on a scene that could turn to disaster at any moment.

A sudden streak of reddish tubular tissue as the new connectors launched. They struck the humungous cryopod section and then contracted once secure. The cartridge pulled away from

Owlflight, to be hugged in close to the Lost Ship's upper hull, and tightened so as to become immovable.

The Lost Ship immediately accelerated away. The gap between vessels widened, though not as much as Opal had hoped. Nullspace manoeuvres were completely unknown to her. To *any* humans. The distances were deceptive. Only Aurbane would understand, but Opal didn't want to head over to that whiskery bulge to speak to him. She wanted to watch the craft that had brought her here. It seemed the most respectful –

An explosion. Silent white ripping through hull. Owlflight appeared to crumple, but then parts of it just blinked out, no longer exploding but completely gone. Of course. Without the drive, it would just drop from Nullspace. The remains would appear somewhere in the universe. Probably far from anyone who would ever find them. A grave of endless void.

The Lost Ship vibrated crazily from the blast, outer hull heating to a glowing red. She was tossed from the window, rebounding off a wall, watching that Clarissa didn't get hurt during the violent commotion. But Aurbane had done it. Seized the cryo cartridge, with sixteen hundred sleeping souls on board, all unaware that they'd been saved.

The action was a success.

JOURNEYS

... 4 ...

Oxygen supplies in their suits were getting low, but Aurbane had already prepared for that, and created a safe route to a new location. They entered a small chamber with two soft couches sunk into wells in the rubbery floor (though at the moment Opal's brain still interpreted that as the ceiling, since zero-G had left her disconnected from fixed orientations). Lights embedded in the walls gave the room a soft, yellowish glow.

"This will be your home, for a while," said Aurbane, through hidden speakers. Maybe the walls themselves were the source of the audio. "I am afraid the door will seal behind you. Your confinement here is as much for your protection as it is due to any lack of trust on my part. This way nothing can get to you. Now is not the time for risks."

Plus, I can't interfere with his ship.

Yeah. And if I was him, that would have been one of my worries, too, Opal. You can't blame him, not with your track record.

Wasn't a complaint. I'm happy to spend time with Clarissa. Just the two of us, finally. Nowhere for the minx to hide.

Clarissa tumbled slowly, smiling at Opal as if she overheard the inner dialogue.

"Oxygen?" Opal asked, trying not to let her teeth chatter with the cold.

"Your needs have been taken care of. I am extracting the current atmosphere and Viscids – which would fatally congest human lungs – and introducing air which is calibrated to match our – I mean, your – requirements. Completely sterile and cut off from everything else in the ship, manufactured by a system I grew solely for that purpose. Full atmospheric replacement will be complete soon. I have also enabled a system to imitate gravity, so you don't have to spend the time floating."

"How long until we arrive?"

"Subjectively, it will feel like a week. The true answer is more complex. If you could please approach the cushioned seats – which will double as sleeping furniture and impact couches – I will release the gravitic pressures."

The sisters held hands and accomplished a move that had become second nature, using contact with a surface to flip around a hundred and eighty degrees, aligning themselves with the couches.

"Increasing the effect of surface attraction now," said Aurbane.

The sensation was a tickle at first, then a feeling of growing weight. Nothing sudden or unpleasant, it was almost as if the seats rose to meet them, the pressure of the soft leathery material strengthening with every second. And then her mind readjusted, and she was just sat next to Clarissa on a curved sofa in one of the wells, with a few steps leading up to the floor surface.

"Wow. Smooth," said Opal. "I remember Athene was curious about the AG systems on Lost Ships. I bet she'd have loved to interrogate you about the mechanics."

"Ah. That name. Another thing lost, now regained. Athene. Why are you not with her?"

"She was destroyed. During our flight from the UFS. She gave her life to save ours."

"Then she sounds far more evolved than the – UFS – had claimed." He said UFS as if it had an unfamiliar flavour.

"She was. More evolved than humanity, I reckon. She taught me so much. Use our brains, but emotion, too."

"You mourn your friend."

"I do."

"I understand. More than you would expect. A friend is a friend is a friend. It does not matter if they are human or AI or something else. It is the activity and the feeling, not the physical structure holding a mind. Content, rather than container. I was lucky. We were lucky. Our friendship is joined in one. If Aurikaa12 and I were not symbiotic, there would be a hole, the same one I had never been able to identify in life, but which was there anyway. I am sorry for your loss."

Clarissa squeezed Opal's hand. Opal was glad of the visor over her face. It hid some of the hurt.

A few minutes later, Aurbane said it was safe to breathe.

Opal cautiously removed her helmet and inhaled.

The air was cool, scented with cinnamon.

She did not die.

A gentle breeze caressed her face as it connected with an outer world again, rather than being enclosed in a barrier that held things at bay.

She removed the rest of her GAMag suit. Aurbane had built a basic locker behind one area of textured panelling. She stowed the suit carefully, then helped Clarissa undress. They were both barefoot, just wearing the base layers. But they were comfortable enough. The room wasn't cold. In fact, a gentle warmth soaked into the soles of her feet.

They explored the new home. Clarissa imitated Opal, trailing fingertips over surfaces to assess them. The walls had a smoothness like snake scales, a rasp to it if you went against the grain.

The curved wall that spiralled into the room acted as a privacy barrier for the bathroom area, hiding taps and a toilet, just like you'd expect to find in some human habitations.

Opal checked with Aurbane first as to what everything was.

"The sink tap is pure water, synthesised in a separate membrane reservoir. As sterile as the rest of this environment. There is as much as you need for washing or drinking. The wall outlet is a nutrient paste. It will not be flavoursome or appetising, but includes what you need to keep you both alive for a week. I'm sure you won't mind using your hands as utensils."

"Yay," said Clarissa. "Finger food." She pressed the small lever, her hand below the spout, and a greenish paste oozed out like a sausage. Clarissa tasted it and pulled a face, but did finish what she'd extracted.

"The toilet is also functional," added Aurbane.

"Thanks for all you've done," said Opal. "This is great. I'd rather be awake with Clarissa than in cryo."

"Me too," said the girl. "I've had enough long sleeps for a lifetime."

Opal couldn't help it. She laughed.

Once they'd settled in, Aurbane revealed another surprise.

First Opal felt it as a rumble in the soles of her feet. Something heavy moving. Clarissa pointed to the wall which their sunken seats faced. It rose, revealing darkness in the growing slit, as if the wall had been a barrier between them and a lightless room beyond. Except none of the illumination in their chamber spread into it. And as it opened fully, Opal recognised it for what it was – a front-facing skywindow looking out at the featureless Null ahead of them.

But not truly featureless, as Clarissa discovered when she mushed her cheek against whatever material it was made from. She pointed out the shapes of other ships, the ark craft, blurry and indistinct.

"There will not be much to see on our journey," Aurbane explained. "But I imagine your chamber will seem less claustrophobic with an external view."

"Will we see the places where you'll be leaving each ark ship?" Opal asked.

"No. They will drop out of Nullspace at the correct location, but we will continue. Absence, rather than revelation. Even if it were practical to follow each vessel to its final destination before rejoining the fleet, their locations and environments could not be revealed to you. Some secrets must be maintained. Only the

Oracles know the true state of all the sites. I am simply the deliverer, leaving my package at the beginning of a tree-lined shady route, never seeing who comes to collect it, or what kind of home is beyond all the winding, shadowy bends. All you can know is that your new home, our final stop, is so far from where humanity started that it would devastate your mind."

"You'd be surprised by what that would take. My mind's pretty scalable."

Except the prospect wasn't always just hazy, distant craft. Occasionally when Aurbane's ship changed position they would get a better view, be much closer to the ark ships. One time they even passed slowly over an alien hull, in a transition that seemed to go on forever, revealing both the awesome size of their world-changing power, and the variety in structures, even in a single craft – presumably different environments for different creatures. The ark ships were unlike anything Opal had ever seen, such an amalgam of styles, organic and manufactured, yet somehow unified into forms that seemed both haphazard and aesthetically interesting at the same time.

Out there in the black, one of them was the ship heading to the same world that Aurbane would land on. The planet that would become a home to the ragtag escapees and survivors.

The sisters passed time talking and playing games. It was like they were back in their Mossareid apartment, mostly secluded from the world, living a perfect fantasy. Clarissa kept wanting to play Tickle Wars, a game she'd invented when she was young, though the rules usually became irrelevant as Opal tickled Clarissa into submission within one of the sunken seats. The same outcome every time, and no doubt that was the true motivation. Clarissa gained the contact and the fun, and the tickling wasn't a sign of losing the war but the actual secret to winning it. Opal's heart swelled at hearing her sister laugh again.

And they told stories. About the past, sure, but Clarissa was changing. Wanting to make up more tales about the *future*.

And it was good.

As Aurbane delivered craft to their new homes, his fleet shrank. Eventually there would only be the final destination. The one the inhabitants of an ark ship would share with humans. Instead of journeying on, Aurbane would go down as well, to protect those humans in the cryo banks now attached to his upper hull, as well as to deliver Opal and Clarissa. It would be a one-way journey for him. His last journey.

He assured them everything would be fine.

"I will continue to exist, if the landing is achieved. Living in quiet contemplation, with no more missions to fulfil. The unity of Aurikaa12, Grubane, and anything else within this soma. There are mysteries to be solved, Opal."

His voice echoed around their living space. Clarissa slept on, exhausted from practising some of the military exercises Opal had taught her – stretches, fitness, basic combat moves. Better for the girl to be prepared for anything. The hopeful tales they told each other might not match the reality.

"And games to be played," Aurbane added with a note of warmth to his voice that hadn't existed a few days ago. It sounded like happiness.

Opal paused in her circular walk around the chamber, one of her old habits. "Can I ask you a personal question?"

"Of course."

"What was it like? I mean, when you changed. Or died. Or however you went from being just Grubane, to being what you are now."

"Existence without merging is only a partial experience. As is existence without extension of protection. You look puzzled. I will reveal something, Opal Imbiana. Some creatures with po- tential – regardless of species – can be made into Navigots. It requires a strength of mind to survive the transformation, but it is not a *destruction* of mind. The Oracles do not want automa- tons and conformity. The spark that attracts them is the thing they want to keep, to fan, to enkindle. The part of my mind that was *different* from them. That might find new solutions. Despite the inconceivable timespans of their consciousness, they are not petrified. They welcome change. And so I was chosen for my abilities as Grubane. And my abilities as Aurikaa12. We both agreed, encoded as organic into a merged psyche. We are one mind, experiencing the miracle of conjoining. Our belief in inescapable separation proved to be illusory. We found our true self. And now we are responsible for command of what you call a *Lost* Ship, but I think of as a ship of *hope*. We do what we did before – fulfil missions, navigate, interact, report – but we now do it as one. So do not focus on the negatives of existence, Opal, such as pain and limitations. They are nothing, compared to the wonder and beauty of life and connection. One day, you will experience the connection, I am certain."

"I don't know about that. But it's still comforting to hear your views."

Clarissa was stirring. She recovered quickly.

"It is interesting to ponder existence. Both yours and mine. And how different things might have been," concluded Aurbane, "had we both made other choices."

ARRIVALS

... 3 ...

Opal and Clarissa sat cross-legged, facing each other with eyes closed. Opal had been teaching her sister a form of mind state that diminished pain or discomfort by imagining yourself outside your body. It had helped Opal enough times in the past. But they were interrupted by Aurbane's voice.

"Opal and Clarissa Imbiana. I have news."

"Please don't keep us in suspense," said Opal, standing and stretching.

"We approach our final destination. Just us and the last ark ship, now."

That made sense. Clarissa had delighted in looking out of the skywindows for signs of other craft. She'd noted the decreasing frequency of sightings as more destinations were reached, and more ark ships left behind. The view had been endless and unbroken void for some time now.

"What do we need to do?"

"At this point, nothing. We are about to enter Realspace. I thought you would like to see the terminus from a distance, since it will be your only opportunity to ever have that view. It will never be seen by those I hold in cryogenic suspension from the Owlflight, or those humans in stasis on our accompanying ark ship, but perhaps one day you will describe it to them."

"That's thoughtful of you."

Opal approached the skywindow, and sensed Clarissa's quiet presence at her side.

You've worked so hard to get here.

And you've helped me every step of the way.

"Transitioning now," he added.

At first, just emptiness. Then lines of light stretched over the view, stark, resembling scratches on glass, but shrinking as if Opal squinted to clear her eyes of water. Moments later colour shifted in, formed, focussed, became a sphere in the centre of the window. A planet. A planet with swirling white-grey clouds that hid much of the surface, but what could be seen resembled bright oceans and land masses as portrayed on any planetary info-ad. Her worries about viewing something alien after all this – unpleasantly volcanic or barren, artificially metallic and sterile, repulsively fleshy and grown, or even exotically hostile to humanity – all that faded away. This was a world of lush greens, crystal blues, and sandy browns.

"It's beautiful," whispered Opal.

"This location was specially seeded for Entities that required a certain range of atmosphere, pressure, temperature and so on. There are hidden biomes of more esoteric natures, but the majority of the surface is as hospitable to your species as you might hope."

"No need for space suits?" asked Clarissa.

"Correct. The surface-level air in most biomes is standard tellurian composition due to the combination of starting elements, green life and microorganics. It has been monitored and tested prior to our arrival. The Nexopols report no deviance. There is no point in delaying."

Opal couldn't take her eyes from the glorious bright side of the jewel-like orb floating in space before them, slowly growing in size. "So what's the protocol?"

"The ark ship is designed for planetary descent. Certain sections will break off and redirect to the chosen zones for their inhabitants. One of the pods includes the stasis humans, with coordinates set for their ideal biome. That location will also be our target. The complication is that my craft is *not* designed for atmospheric entry. We will get one attempt only, and the downward journey is irreversible.

"I have been making modifications during our journey in preparation for this. Lower decks were cleared of Entities, then packed with densely expanded Viscids. They will act as the impact absorption layers. Other areas are left empty to become crumple zones. Alone, that would not be enough to prevent catastrophic damage, even with the lateral wings that have been added to aid redirection once we enter the atmosphere. So I have calculated a system that should enable us to survive."

"Ejection?"

"No. That would also be difficult with the cryo cylinder attached to the upper hull. My route will guide us up a river delta, continually slowing, so that when we eventually strike a long curve in one of the river bends, we will come to a halt rather than shatter into burning pieces. That will be my final location. You will have to climb up to the cryopods and activate thawing procedures once you feel ready to, but that should not be a major challenge for you. It will also be necessary to locate the ark ship's stasis humans and join them to your tribe. Once more, I have faith that it will not be too great a task. I will be able to guide you. Also to delineate the borders of the zone you are allowed to settle in, and the rules of coexistence on this world. After that, you are all free to endure."

"Sounds so simple."

"That is because I am dissembling, and hiding my doubts about whether I can land this craft without destroying us all."

"Some things are best kept to yourself."

"I'm not scared," said Clarissa. "It sounds like fun. Plus, I've crashed before."

"She definitely takes after you," said Aurbane.

Clarissa and Opal secured themselves in their respective seats, which revealed a new trick: expanding to enclose their bodies and support their heads in an organic embrace. The soft, skin-like material was warm and cushioning, though confined the body completely. A gap was left for their faces so they could breathe and see the huge window in front of them.

"I can close the shutters if you like," said Aurbane.

"I'd rather always see what's coming, good or bad," replied Opal. "As long as that doesn't endanger us."

"The window is in a minimal fracture zone, due to the shock-absorbing structures surrounding your habitat. By the time we strike any surface, we'll be within breathable atmosphere. However, should any danger present, I will immediately close the shutters. I think that is an acceptable compromise."

The planet drew closer. Aurbane had been accelerating up to the half-point, then switched to deceleration mode. Opal didn't notice any difference in terms of forces acting on her body. Lost Ship propulsion was as much a mystery to her as ever.

"Is that an island?" asked Clarissa.

"I can't tell what you're looking at," Opal replied. "My head's just facing forward too, remember?"

"The bit that looks like a green dog's head at the bottom of the circle, surrounded by blue. Oh, no, never mind, there's cloudies over it now."

An ever-swirling pattern of white mists showed how chaotically alive each level of the planet was.

"We're approaching at ninety degrees to its mag-pole line." Aurbane's voice was comforting when it emitted from the walls around. It reminded Opal of Athene's desire to explain. "The south is that area at the far left. The north is on the right, beneath cloud. The planetary spin is eastward so what you see at the top of the planet is actually the equator, turning towards us to reveal more continent as land masses and ocean disappear below the lower rim."

"Ah, that helps me orientate. Thanks."

"We're aiming at the horizon – again, top of the window for you two. If we calculated correctly then our final approach will be substantially lateral. This is not an event to rush."

"Slow and steady brings us home," whispered Opal.

As the planet filled more of the window on their approach, further detail became visible.

The clouds swirled, and Opal could make out the darker patches below them, leviathan shadows sailing over land and sea.

The ocean glittered. Tiny sparkles that represented movement in the water, transient peaks acting as reflectors for the system sun. The motion added life to the flat plane.

Further away, streaks of incinerating orange burnt down through the planet's atmosphere, lighting up the skies.

"What are those meteor-like fragments?" asked Opal. "Debris?"

"No." Aurbane's voice, amplified to reach them through the cushioning around the sisters' heads. "They are the descent pods from the final ark ship I accompanied. It jettisons them while passing over the appropriate zone for the Entities on board. Unlike my craft, they are designed for safe descent and then blooming. The final part of the ark ship will fuse on the way down, to create the correct environment for the sleepers by the time it strikes the magmatic biome."

"And the other humans?"

"The ark ship still has them. It isn't due to pass over the region set aside for your species until six subjective hours have passed.

You and I will be on the ground by then, waiting. Or disintegrated. One or the other."

"You have a dry sense of humour."

"It was not humour."

There were now depths to the sea. Darker, deeper, colder sections in the centres of oceans. Then brighter blues and turquoises on coastal shelves, shallower and warmer.

The angle of approach was changing, levelling out. The planet filled the lower half of the window as they approached the endless horizon rotating towards them. And with it came vibration, shuddering throughout their craft. Flickers of flame glanced over the window, growing in strength.

"It's all fine," Opal told Clarissa. "This is what planetary descents are always like." The smallest of lies was forgivable when it was done out of concern for another.

Gliding down at this angle revealed new features that hadn't been so obvious in a bird's eye view. The elevations of the mountains stood out like chaotic sawtooth waves against a hint of atmosphere that wrapped the world in a bubble. Peaks jagged upwards, many of them lined with a fur of forest, assuming she could really interpret things from this distance in ways she was familiar with.

More shuddering, a tooth-rattling series of jolts that penetrated even through the softness of the body-encasing tissue.

Ground colours became more distinct. She could identify arid lands from the more extreme, paler deserts which swept over much of the equatorial zone. And, even more specifically, beaches were visible on some of the coastlines, attention drawn to them by the breaking waves that stroked lines of foam inwards, always replaced by more as they died.

Opal realised what was so weird about the vista, the thing that had nagged at her as *wrong*.

It was *unspoiled*. No signs of habitation. No lines of megaroads and industrial tracks. No clearings and flattened areas, no monstrous mechanised quarries, no criss-cross greys of urban blight.

And more than that. Something that not every eye would spot, but which Opal picked up on because she always identified with the liminal, the things in between that didn't exactly fit: the sharp divisions between zones, or biomes as Aurbane called them. Sure, the desert became broken rocky areas, which bordered scrubland, that led on to meadows, then woods and rivers, as expected, but the areas where they bordered each other were more clearly defined than would occur in a purely natural setting. One or two neat divisions could be geological coincidence, but not *every* division across a whole planet. It revealed the artificial within the natural, the planned within the chaos, and distinctions that were too fresh to have been eroded by time. The final validation that this was everything Aurbane had claimed it to be.

The increasing incineration across the hull, and rumbling shocks throughout it, proved they were deep within the atmospheric band now. And yes – when she glimpsed it between the glowing heat resistance created by the speed of their descent against the frictive gases, she could see that the sky was no longer black like space, but had a blue-lilac tinge to it. True atmosphere, illuminated by the visible sun low on the horizon, partly obscured by mountains.

The heat engulfing the front of the Lost Ship was a pleasantness on her exposed face that could soon become searing if it grew any more energetic. A part of her hoped the shutters would come down as an extra layer of protection. Another part of her didn't want to lose that rumbling, majestic view of a planetary descent.

It was easier to see their target now, lined up and growing. They were aimed at a coastal region. It loomed higher in the view, a wide expanse of gold beyond the blue they plummeted towards. Such massive beaches. A good choice of landing zone, for their cushioning effect.

Except this angle was wrong.

"We're-go-ing-to-strike-sea, Aur-bane!" she yelled, to be heard above the cacophony. Her voice vibrated comically as thousands of microshocks ran through the ship.

No reply.

She hated being a prisoner like this. A passive observer with no control over what happened. It felt like the ship was shaking itself apart.

A whining sound to her right. Keening. Clarissa was crying.

"It's-okay!" Opal shouted. "Hey-sis-don't-worr-y!" Damn, Opal wanted to hug her. To reassure her.

A reply. Incomprehensible, as if sobbing, obscured by the roaring sounds ripping throughout the ship.

"It's-fine!" Opal shouted. "We'll-get-through-this!"

"I-KNOW!" Clarissa shouted back. "I was laugh-ing. This-is-brill-i-ant! In-tense!"

Oh.

Heh.

Two sisters who thrived on existing close to the danger zone's edge. No wonder they proved to be a headache for so many.

Opal grinned as well.

"Apologies for the delay." Now it was Aurbane's turn, his non-shaky voice amplified above the sounds like metal pieces being swirled around in a barrel. The Lost Ship had obviously been well built. A human craft would have had rivets popping and pinging like deadly projectiles by now.

"It's my *intention* to hit the sea, to fall short of our intended stopping point," he continued. "My lower hull has developed an aquaphobic coating, with subsurface buoyant expanded materials created from modified Viscids – the first time I have attempted that adjustment. If the angle is correct then we will skim the surface of the ocean, absorbing much of the heat from atmospheric entry, as well as impact force: but not too much, or we would sink. Ventral burners will help maintain bow lift. The bigger issue isn't falling short, but *over*shooting. Velocity is way too high, and we must not plough into the moulded igneous rock ridges just beyond the flora line."

"Re-dir-ect then! That-beach-is-shoot-ing-to-wards-us!"

"Eighteen degrees to the right, the vegetation hides a river outlet. That will be our slowdown lane if we can reach it. We'll have to use every element of aerodynamics and multi-directional propulsion available. The cryopods on our upper surface make us top-heavy because elements –"

And he was gone.

The sea raced below them faster and faster, rising up to fill more of the window view, tilting at an angle as their ship used almost non-existent aerodynamics to readjust. They overtook the waves, turning them into strobing lines counting out the microseconds below.

Opal had thought the vibration couldn't get any worse, but this was surely destroying the hull integrity. If she survived, then brain damage from all the shaking would be a serious consideration.

"WHEEEeeeEEEeeeEEEeee!" screamed Clarissa.

The water's surface was still tilted. If they hit like that, it would all be over. But the flames had gone now. Just an orange glow to the visible external surfaces, and some window scorching.

A sound from outside like tortured screaming, perhaps the wind's passage over their surface, or a structural element giving up and dying.

They levelled out.

Slowly.

Too slowly.

Deafening external roars and an endless screech almost drowned out thought.

At this speed the water would be like hitting a wall, and then –

BOOSH!

Rather than direct impact, the view became hissing grey, streamers of white, as if they'd ploughed into fog. A difference to the rumble, the echoing rattles. The burners had ignited, turning ocean water to steam, creating lift and obscuring everything as they flew through vapourised liquids, boiling them from the

outside. The nose rose and levelled, and although it was difficult to interpret subtle changes in sensation, Opal guessed the
stomach-churn was caused by a rise, so that her gut shifted after
falling so long. Maybe that represented the skimming Aurbane
had promised rather than ploughing into depths with no hope
of pulling up.

The fog outside gradually cleared as they broke from it, no
doubt trailing it behind like torn clouds. But she could now see
the beach speeding closer, details of the trees and rough out-
crops, and the hope that Aurbane had it right, that the comput-
ing element of his persona was as good at calculations as Athene
had been.

There, it *did* look like a gap in the beach, where something
reflected. Water, an outlet, joining the sea from beneath a dense
tangle of foliage that they bounced towards in weighty lifts and
descents accompanied by the hissing of millions of tonnes of
liquid being evaporated.

The line wasn't quite right.

Nothing anyone could do now.

One second the greens were a growing blur; the next they filled
the window and shattered in an explosion of branches and vines,
leaves scattered to the heavens and wood splintered like it was
nothing, shooting away in a cannon burst of deadly shrapnel.
They ripped through plant life with the appearance of thousands of twiggy arms slapping the window and hull in reproach,
and then they were churning up the river, sending a tidal bore
of gigantic proportions ahead of them, drowning everything it
consumed.

But the deceleration was obvious, so much momentum torn away from them, the descents now dragging at their lower hull, perhaps even striking the bottom of the river and the muddy sediments and cloying weeds there, sucking and sticking, twisting and turning, the burners no longer doing anything and their sounds replaced by grinding and groaning as the Lost Ship ploughed a furrow through mud and water alike, no way the nose would ever rise again when so much matter held it firm, the grip tightening.

If not for the cushioning material that ensconced Opal's body she would have been thrown forward, splatted into the window like an insect against a cockpit, dead before the groaning of immovable force versus immovable object found a resolution. But to be squished like that wasn't her fate today. A last gasp of tortured materials, a dizzying lurch, and it was finally over.

Her ears rang with the ghosts of all that noise.

Water poured back, only temporarily routed by the push of an enemy mass. It struck their hull, this new obstacle on the way to the ocean. Another lurch, but they must be secure, because instead of rolling them, or sweeping them back out to sea, the river gave up and thundered around the Lost Ship instead. It splashed up in irritation, but for now the motion everywhere but Opal's inner ears had ceased.

"I think I did a little wee," Clarissa said.

"Don't be embarrassed," Opal replied. "Most humans would have done something much worse in their trousers."

The giggle in response was exactly what Opal needed to hear.

DESCENTS

... 2 ...

The cushioning leather skin around them dissolved in a disconcerting way, until only collagen-like strands remained that had to be torn apart. Opal was finally able to stand.

Shakily, at first.

The floor tilted at about twenty degrees. Ditto the view outside, through the cracked window, which had been unable to fully withstand the huge temperature shifts, velocities, and impacts. Aurbane assured them again that the atmosphere was safe to breathe while Opal helped Clarissa to the edge of her seat-pit.

"But I'll be busy for some time," said Aurbane. "There is a lot to coordinate. I've unsealed the door so you can make your way down through the craft. We will try to delineate a safe route that releases you above the water line. Please avoid flooded sections."

"What's this region of the planet called?" Opal asked.

"To me: toposphere 411B. You can call it what you want."

Opal crouch-walked her way over to the broken window, one hand on the deck for stability. One window split was big enough to crawl through. She tentatively tested the brittle-looking outer hull surface with her bare feet first. Hot, but not searing.

"You wait there," Opal called back to Clarissa, who had started to follow her. "I just want to check it's safe."

Opal squeezed through, careful of the jagged shards that stuck out around the breakage, now milk-white with micro-fractures. She emerged onto the slope of outer hull, and the heat of a sun that burned brighter than any she'd experienced on other planets. Probably just a contrast effect after so long in artificial lighting, though maybe this star was larger, or closer, or the atmosphere thinner than Mossareid, Fressus, or anywhere she'd been stationed.

The scent was strong up here, rising rich from the verdancy below. It seemed pungently rich, earthy, damp, salty, with hints of tree sap or pine, all at once. Intriguing. So much to decipher.

Sounds seemed dulled because her ears had yet to fully recover from the ringing in them, but she could make out a bass roaring. Some of it coincided with gusts of air on her skin, tickling exposed hairs. It was the wind, whistling over the many shapes of the Lost Ship's exterior, and through the trees far below. Maybe some of it was also the water, pounding into the lower reaches of the Lost Ship.

She crawled down a slope towards a scorched ridge where she could anchor herself, then she stood and took in her vertigo-inducing view from almost a kilometre into the sky.

Blues and greens, in every direction.

The Lost Ship was half-buried in river at one of the banks where the water's flow created an elbow. Many hull structures jutted out, perhaps even things Aurbane had added during their journey to increase the aerodynamics and control during atmospheric descent.

Her eyes mapped points of stability and anchor on the hull. Distances between them. Angles of surface. Fissures that could be navigated. A, to B, to C, and so on. From here it certainly looked like the first few hundred metres were fairly easy. Once the hull rounded out then the route would be much steeper, the nearer it approached the vertical, but by being half sunk into water that section would soon end. Maybe one of the hull breaks would allow reentry to the Lost Ship for a tiny transition. Or the shallows above silty deposits might provide some cushioning for a final descent. Not that she'd –

"Wow, it's amazing!" Clarissa said, crawling nearby.

It was frustrating, not having your full hearing. Too easy for people to sneak up on you.

"I told you to stay inside!" snapped Opal.

"I wanted to see."

The girl wasn't cowed, and slid down the surface to join Opal in her dip.

"Aren't you scared of heights?" Opal asked.

"Nope."

"Or falling?"

"Not much."

Opal hadn't really been interested in going the long internal way. Maybe also the more dangerous way, through darkness and damaged infrastructure, amongst creatures that might be scared and lash out in understandable panic. She'd had enough of Lost Ships. Out here was invigorating freedom, freshness, good visibility.

"What about climbing?" Opal asked.

Clarissa smiled up at her. "Oh, that just sounds like *fun*."

As they descended, the tiny twiggy trees had grown into the towering fern-like behemoths they really were. The shiny rivulet became a roaring silver river, and the toy-like pebbles resolved into massive rocks. But the sisters took their time. Opal checked every transition from safe point to safe point first, and Clarissa followed her instructions exactly, as if she knew that there was a time for being cheeky, and a time for taking things seriously.

The girl showed no fear, but did apply caution, and that combination meant the journey downwards – which had perhaps taken them an hour so far – went without incident. Some of it was climbing, some scrambling, some sliding when the surface wasn't too rough and there was a good stopping point, such as a structure that acted as a ledge. And a few times Clarissa clung to Opal's back and Opal did the hard work. But because of the Lost Ship's size the curves weren't extreme, and there were so many weird shapes and unfathomable growths that it had been exhilarating rather than worrying.

Until now.

The burnt lower hull curved away. They were only a hundred metres above ground level at this point, but the route didn't offer many options. Too steep.

They could backtrack. Look for another avenue.

But Opal was a good swimmer. She estimated that the river below was more than deep enough. The sun had warmed it all day, so she probably wasn't facing an arctic shock. The descent had given plenty of time to judge water flow speed based on foliage sometimes carried down its surface. And, not far below them, another loop in the river meant it ran around a shallow sandbank. It wouldn't take much redirection to get there, where a person could easily wade out onto the shore.

"How do you feel about a big jump into the water?" Opal asked.

"No biggie."

"You'd hold my hand, right, little sis? Don't let go. We run and jump *together*."

"And we splash down *together*, and swim *together*, and get out *together*." Clarissa seemed serious as she emphasised each word, almost like an accusation.

"That's right. From now on, everything in life will be together."

"Then I say we should do it."

So they seized each other's palms, and Opal smiled reassurance, and they checked the hull surface for grip, and then they ran, and gravity pulled but they jumped without fear, and even as they sailed down from blue sky to blue waters it was only momentary angst, indiscernible from a thrill. They fell, and their hands squeezed, and they did not let go.

They sploshed out of the embracing shallows, wet sand squidging between Opal's toes, reluctant to let her go. The sisters then flopped down onto the sun-baked mud of a bank that was dotted with clusters of wiry bluish plants.

And it was good.

"We did it," said Clarissa, lying on her back, looking up at the turquoise sky with its stretches of white-pink overlapping clouds.

"Wasn't so bad, eh?" Opal replied.

A breeze washed over the river, bringing the coolness of spray. If they stayed too long it might chill, but right now it was refreshing while the sun dried them out.

No need for words. Not for a while. Relish this natural peace. Because soon enough it wouldn't be so peaceful. Opal knew all too well what would happen when the humans were awoken from the cryo cartridge on Aurbane's hull, and those from the ark ship's stasis pod were located and likewise brought from a long slumber. She could visualise the huddled groups of bewildered humans, maybe even complicated by some of the newly arrived alien creatures – the more well-behaved ones, under Aurbane's watch – all eyeing each other distrustfully. But she had faith that differences could be overcome in time. Bridges built. Security and comfort reinforced, threat becoming a nightmare from which you could awake each day, so that the night terrors dissipated like the clouds above burnt away in the sun.

But for now, it was a moment to savour serenity as the only two non-sleeping humans on the planet.

You don't need me any more, said the voice in her head. *You have what you wanted. And I am glad.*

Need is irrelevant. You're a part of me now. I'm never letting go. Echoes are all I have left of you.

As ever, Opal, you give me much to think about. Perhaps we do live on in others. Memories are a sort of immortality.

See! You don't get away that easy.

Nothing ever is that easy. For us. Pause. *And, for once, I'm glad.*

Clarissa interrupted her thoughts.

"Hey, Opal. Don't you get to name a planet if you're the first one to walk on it?"

"I don't think it works like that any more."

"Still. The aliens will come up with their names. We need our own. You should do it! Decide what we'll call it. Not that silly name Aurbane told us."

And a word did spring to mind, so fast she didn't have time to censor it, to think about implications and derivations, she just blurted it out. And then it hung there, and she could assess it, and realised it would fit their new home.

"Solace," said Opal. "I name this planet Solace." After all, what else could it be called?

A good name. A true name. For now there was peace, even though she had other things to worry about, and so much to do.

So much.

Instead, she just held Clarissa's hand, and lying there was like floating in the long void sea, icy, weightless, both staring up at the sky with its endless possibilities.

ENDINGS

... 1

To god-like perspectives, from far above and beyond, Opal would look so small. Her body, her sister's body, like specks.

Organic flecks on a planet. The planet an orb in a solar system. The solar system a particle in the galaxy. This galaxy swirls, arms reaching out from the centre. Always that reaching out, like a need. The galaxy a dot in the universe, dancing around the other galaxies, attracted to each other across the lonely void, even though their shapes are different, their sizes, their histories, their chemical compositions.

To be alone is to be incomplete. Life is not empty if you have a heart to drive it. Hope to endure. And patience. Much patience. Then life is not empty.

Life is full.

About The Author

Karl Drinkwater is an author with a silly name and a thousand-mile stare. He writes dystopian space opera, dark suspense and diverse social fiction. If you want compelling stories and characters worth caring about, then you're in the right place. Welcome!

Karl lives in Scotland and owns two kilts. He has degrees in librarianship, literature and classics, but also studied astronomy and philosophy. Dolly the cat helps him finish books by sleeping on his lap so he can't leave the desk. When he isn't writing he loves music, nature, games and vegan cake.

Go to karldrinkwater.uk to view all his books grouped by genre.

As well as crafting his own fictional worlds, Karl has supported other writers for years with his creative writing workshops, editorial services, articles on writing and publishing, and mentoring of new authors. He's also judged writing competitions such as the international Bram Stoker Awards, which act as a snapshot of quality contemporary fiction.

Don't Miss Out!

Enter your email at karldrinkwater.substack.com to be notified about his new books. Fans mean a lot to him, and replies to the newsletter go straight to his inbox, where every email is read. There is also an option for paid subscribers to support his work: in exchange you receive additional posts and complimentary books.

OTHER TITLES BY KARL DRINKWATER

STANDALONE SUSPENSE
Turner
They Move Below
Harvest Festival

MANCHESTER SUMMER
Cold Fusion 2000
2000 Tunes

CONTEMPORARY SHORT STORIES
It Will Be Quick

NON-FICTION
From Idea To Item

COLLECTED EDITIONS
Karl Drinkwater's Horror Collection
Lost Solace Five Book Edition

Author's Notes

I wanted to create a final Lost Ship that provided variety from Opal's previous two explorations, hence changes such as use of zero-G. I was also particularly keen that this time she had no Athene or advanced warsuit, leaving her incredibly exposed. This story is often about Opal relying on herself, and being vulnerable. And the secondary twist that, despite all that, at the end it is her friends that help her, her loved ones, and that's perhaps the way it should be.

Opal and hope, the words are like synonyms in my head.

This book provides a resolution. But if the Lost Solace books sell well, if bookshops and libraries stock them, if enough people leave positive reviews – then I want to revisit this. Opal's story isn't over. There is so much more. I know what happens next, what happened in the past, what's going on elsewhere in this universe, all the stories not yet told. It's way bigger than we've seen so far. What do they say in Peter Pan? If you want fairies to exist, then call out their name? Help me out, keep shouting Lost Solace, and maybe like the Candyman it will take form in the alternate world of the mirror, until it stands behind you, emerged from the Null, and we find that good characters have many stories, and good heroes are rarely allowed to rest before they are called upon again. I would love to continue the game of "What if?" which – as human culture has attested for thousands of years – has always been the most enduring game. Moreso even than Grubane's chess.

Just for fun, I added up the word count of all the Lost Solace books at this point (not including appendices, just the story parts).

- Lost Solace 58,454

- Chasing Solace 95,548

- Hidden Solace 105,073

- Raising Solace 66,748

- Finding Solace (this book) 96,214

- = 422,037 words.

The Lost Tales of Solace (Helene 17,234; Grubane 25,761; Clarissa 24,111; Ruabon 16,060) add another 83,166. So far my Lost Solace books come to 505,203: more than half a million words. :-)

The main Lost Solace books always tie in to the Lost Tales of Solace in some way. This time, Clarissa and Grubane are the main ones. You don't need to have read the Lost Tales, but they add extra context to some events. Read them all if you want to know more about this universe, and live in it a while longer.

Thanks

My cat Dolly, for being so tough. During the long period between getting the idea for this book, and signing off the final version, she developed and recovered from diabetes. The period where I had to inject her with insulin twice a day was an awful one. To see her back to herself and no longer needing injections is amazing.

Beta readers (music-man JML, cat-friend Angela, yogi Alyson), supporters, fans and friends.

Helen Pryke for proofreading.

Everyone who bought a copy of one of these books, for themselves or someone else.

To all, always, love.